About the Authors

A *New York Times* bestselling author, **Christine Rimmer** has written over ninety contemporary romances for Mills & Boon. Christine has won the Romantic Times BOOKreviews Reviewers Choice Award and has been nominated six times for the RITA™ Award. She lives in Oregon with her family. Visit Christine at http://www.christinerimmer.com

Barbara Hannay lives in North Queensland where she and her writer husband have raised four children. Barbara loves life in the north where the dangers of cyclones, crocodiles and sea stingers are offset by a relaxed lifestyle, glorious winters, World Heritage rainforests and the Great Barrier Reef. Besides writing, Barbara enjoys reading, gardening and planning extensions to accommodate her friends and her extended family.

Christy Jeffries graduated from the University of California, Irvine and received her Juris Doctor from California Western School of Law. But drafting court documents and working in law enforcement was merely an apprenticeship for her current career in the relentless field of mummyhood and romance writing. She lives in Southern California with her patient husband, two energetic sons, and one sassy grand-mother. Follow her on Facebook or visit her website at www.christyjeffries.com

Twins

Twins: Double the Love

CHRISTINE RIMMER

BARBARA HANNAY

CHRISTY JEFFRIES

MIX
Paper from
responsible sources
FSC
FSC C001434

This book is produced from independently certified FSC™ paper to ensure responsible forest management.

For more information visit: www.harpercollins.co.uk/green

Printed and bound in Spain
by CPI, Barcelona

MILLS & BOON

First Published in Great Britain 2020
By Mills & Boon, an imprint of HarperCollins*Publishers*
1 London Bridge Street, London, SE1 9GF

TWINS: DOUBLE THE LOVE © 2020 Harlequin Books S.A.

The Nanny's Double Trouble © 2018 Christine Rimmer
Executive: Expecting Tiny Twins © 2010 Harlequin Books S.A.
The Matchmaking Twins © 2016 Christy Jeffries

Special thanks and acknowledgement are given to Barbara Hannay for her contribution to *The Brides of Bella Rosa* series.

ISBN: 978-0-263-29880-2

THE NANNY'S
DOUBLE TROUBLE

CHRISTINE RIMMER

For Marie Campbell,
friend and fellow-booklover,
whose totally adorable basset hounds,
Fancy, Luke, Beau, Moses,
Rachel, Clementine, and Sampson,
are the inspiration for Daniel Bravo's basset,
sweet Maisey Fae.

Chapter One

When Keely Ostergard entered the upstairs playroom, she found Daniel Bravo lying on the floor. His eighteen-month-old daughter, Frannie, sat beside him, rhythmically tapping his broad chest with a giant plastic spoon.

"Boom, Da-Da," Frannie said. "Boom, boom, boom."

Meanwhile, Jake, Frannie's twin, stood at Daniel's head on plump toddler legs, little hands over his eyes in a beginner's attempt at peekaboo.

Watching them, Keely couldn't help thinking that for a man who'd never wanted children of his own, Daniel sure was a dream with them. The guy rarely smiled, yet he lavished his kids with attention and affection.

"Boo!" cried Jake, followed by a delighted toddler belly laugh that had him toppling head over heels toward his father's face. Daniel caught him easily and started to tickle him, bringing more happy chortling from Jake.

Frannie spotted Keely first. "Keewee!" She dropped her spoon, lurched to her feet and toddled across the floor with her little arms wide.

Keely scooped her up. She smelled so sweet, like vanilla and apples. "How's my girl?"

Frannie's reply was almost in English. "I goo."

Daniel sat up, Jake still in his arms. "Keely." He looked a little worried at the sight of her. She came by often to see the kids, but she'd always called first. Not this time. He asked, "Everything okay?"

"Absolutely." She kissed Frannie's plump cheek. "Sorry, I know I should have called." But if she'd called and said she would like to speak with him, he would have asked what was going on, and she didn't want to get into that until they were face-to-face. He could too easily blow her off over the phone.

Grace, Daniel's youngest sister, who had answered the door at Keely's knock, entered the playroom right then. "Keely needs to talk to you, Daniel."

"Sure—down you go, big fella." He set the giggling Jake on his feet.

"Come on, you two." Grace took Frannie from Keely and held out her hand for Jake. "Bath time." She set off, carrying Frannie and pulling Jake along, on her way to the big bathroom down the hall.

Daniel stood still in the middle of the floor, watching her. "How 'bout a drink?"

"Sounds good."

Downstairs in the kitchen, he poured them each two fingers of very old scotch, neat. Keely wasn't much of a drinker, and scotch wasn't her favorite. But she had an offer to make, and she wanted him to say yes to it. Sharing a drink first might loosen him up a little.

She raised her glass and took a small sip. It burned going down, and she tried not to shudder. "Strong stuff."

He looked at her sideways and grumbled, "Why didn't you just say you hate scotch?"

"No. Really. It's very good."

He stared at her doubtfully for a couple of awkward seconds and then, with a shrug, he looked out the window. It was after seven on a cool Friday night in March, and already dark out. Beyond the glass, garden lights glowed golden through the thickening fog. Behind her, somewhere far out in the bay, down the tree-covered hill from the front of the house, a foghorn sounded.

Keely rested her hand on the cool, smooth soapstone counter. It was a beautiful kitchen. Her cousin, Lillie, had redone it with meticulous, loving care. It had lustrous heated wood floors in a herringbone pattern, a giant farm-style sink, twinkly glass backsplashes and chef-grade appliances.

Lillie.

Keely's throat got tight just thinking of her. She'd died eighteen months ago, leaving behind two adorable newborn babies—and one very grim husband. For the last fifteen years or so, Daniel had hardly been what Keely would call a happy guy anyway, but since they lost Lillie, the man rarely cracked a smile.

She took another sip and inched up on the reason she'd stopped by. "So then, what will you do for childcare now?"

He shifted his gaze back to her. "What *can* I do? Guess I'll try the nanny service again."

Keely almost laughed, though it wasn't all that funny. "Will you ask for the one with the alcohol problem or the one who gets sick all the time? Or maybe the one who's in love with you?" Daniel was a Viking of a man, big and buff and really good-looking in his too-serious, borderline-broody way. It wasn't the least surprising that one of the endless string of nannies and babysitters had decided she was meant to become a second mother to his children and show him how to heal his wounded heart.

He pinched the bridge of his manly nose as though he might be getting a headache. "Something will come up." His eyes—of a rather eerie pale blue—had circles under them. Clearly, he hadn't been sleeping well lately.

Keely felt kind of guilty for teasing him. Okay, she harbored some animosity toward him for what had gone down between him and her cousin in the last months of Lillie's life. But that was private stuff, husband-and-wife stuff, stuff Lillie had shared with Keely in strictest confidence.

Daniel wasn't a bad guy. He'd just had to shoulder too much, too soon. On the plus side, he was a man you could count on—and pretty much everyone did. Keely needed to remember his good qualities whenever she felt tempted to blame him for making Lillie unhappy.

He was doing the best he could, and he did have a real problem. President and CEO of Valentine Logging, Daniel worked long hours. He needed reliable childcare for the twins. Yet the nannies came and went. And Daniel's mother-in-law, Keely's aunt Gretchen, had always been his nanny of last resort, stepping up to take care of the kids every time another caregiver bit the dust.

Then two days ago Gretchen tripped and fell—over Jake. The little boy was fine, but Gretchen had four broken bones in her right foot. At seventy and now on crutches, Keely's aunt was no longer in any condition to be chasing after little ones. Daniel needed another nanny, and he needed one now.

And that was where Keely came in.

She knocked back the rest of her scotch. It seared a bracing path down her throat as she plunked her glass on the counter. "Okay, so here's the thing…"

Daniel gazed at her almost prayerfully. "Tell me you know a real-life Mary Poppins. Someone with excellent references who can't wait to move in here and take care of my kids."

"'Can't wait' might be a little strong, and Mary Poppins I'm not. But as for references, your mother-in-law will vouch for me. In fact, Aunt Gretchen has asked me to take over with the kids for a while, and I've said yes."

Daniel's mouth went slack. "You? You're kidding."

Should she be insulted? She answered tartly, "I am completely serious. The kids know me, I love them dearly and I'm happy to step in."

He pinned her with that too-pale stare. "It's just not right."

"Of course it's right. Lillie was my sister in all the ways that matter. Jake and Frannie need me right now. I know you and I aren't best friends, but you've got to have someone you can depend on. That would be me."

"You make it sound like I've got something against you, Keely. I don't."

She didn't believe him. But how he felt about her wasn't the point. Jake and Frannie were what mattered. Yes, he could probably hire yet another nanny from the service he used. But the kids deserved consistency and someone who loved them.

"Great." She plastered on a giant smile. "Daniel, It's

going to be fine, I promise you. Better me than yet another stranger."

His brow wrinkled to match the turned-down corners of his mouth. "You're busy. You've got that gallery to run and those quilt things you make."

Quilt things? Seriously?

Keely was a successful fabric artist as well as the proud owner of her own gallery, Sand & Sea, down in the historic district of their small Oregon town of Valentine Bay. And whatever Daniel chose to call textile arts, he did have a point. Taking care of Jake and Frannie on top of everything else she had going on would be a challenge.

She would manage, though. Gretchen had asked her to help. No way would she let Auntie G down.

"I'm here and I'm willing," she said. "The kids need me and they know me." She raced on before he could start objecting again. "Honestly, I have a plan and it's a good one. This house has seven bedrooms and only four people live here now—including the twins."

After his parents died, Daniel and Lillie had raised his seven surviving siblings right there in the Bravo family home. All the Bravo siblings had moved out now, though. Except for Grace. A junior at Reed College in Portland, Grace still came home for school breaks and between semesters. She had the only downstairs bedroom, an add-on off the kitchen.

Keely forged on. "I can take one empty upstairs room for a bedroom and one for my temporary studio—specifically, the two rooms directly across the hall from the twins' playroom and bedroom. It's perfect. And most nights, once you're here to take over, I'll probably just go home." She had a cute little cottage two blocks from the beach, not far from her gallery. "But if you need me,

I can stay over. With a studio set up here, I can work on my own projects whenever I get a spare moment or two. I have good people working at Sand & Sea, trustworthy people who will pick up the slack for me."

He leaned back against the counter, crossed his big arms over his soft flannel shirt and considered. "I don't know. I should talk to my sisters first, see how much they can pitch in."

Besides Grace, who would be leaving for Portland day-after-tomorrow, there were Aislinn, Harper and Hailey. Aislinn worked for a lawyer in town. She couldn't just take off indefinitely to watch her niece and nephew. As for Harper and Hailey, who'd been born just ten months apart, they were both seniors at U of O down in Eugene and wouldn't be back home until after their graduation at the end of the semester.

And what was it with men? Why did they automatically turn to their sisters and mothers-in-law in a childcare emergency? Daniel had three brothers living nearby. Keely *almost* hit the snark button and asked him why he didn't mention asking Matthias, Connor or Liam if they could pitch in, too?

But she had a goal here. Antagonizing Daniel would not aid her cause. "Well, of course everyone will help out, fill in when they can. But why make your sisters scramble when I'm willing to take on the main part of the job?"

"It just seems like a lot to ask."

"But, see, that's just it. You're not asking. I'm offering."

"More like insisting," he muttered.

"Oh, yes, I am." She put on a big smile, just to show him that he couldn't annoy her no matter how hard he tried. "And I'm prepared to start taking care of Frannie and Jake right away. I'll move my stuff in tomorrow, and I'll take over with the kids on Sunday when Grace leaves to go back to school."

He scowled down at his thick wool socks with the red reinforced heels and toes. Daniel always left his work boots at the door. "There's still Gretchen to think about. If you're busy with the kids, who's going to be looking after her until she can get around without crutches again?" Keely's uncle, Cletus Snow, had died five years ago. Auntie G lived alone now.

"She's managing all right, and I will be checking in on her. And that's not all. She's called my mom."

One burnished eyebrow lifted toward his thick dark gold hair as Daniel slanted her a skeptical glance. "What's Ingrid got to do with anything?"

It was an excellent question. Ingrid Ostergard and Gretchen Snow were as different as two women could be and still share the same genes. Round and rosy Gretchen loved home, children and family. Ingrid, slim and sharp as a blade at fifty, was a rock musician who'd lived just about all her adult life out of her famous purple tour bus. Ingrid had never married. She claimed she had no idea who Keely's father was. Twenty years younger than Gretchen, Keely's mother was hardly the type to run to her big sister's rescue.

Keely said, "Mom's decided to change things up in her life. She's coming home to stay and moving in with Aunt Gretchen."

Daniel stared at her in sheer disbelief. "What about the band?"

Pomegranate Dream had had one big hit back in the nineties. Since then, all the original members except Ingrid had dropped out and been replaced, most of them two or three times over. "My mother pretty much *is* the band. And she says she's done with touring. She's talking about opening a bar here in town, with live music on the weekends."

He just shook his head. "Your mother and Gretchen living together? How long do you think that's going to last?"

"There have been odder odd couples."

"Keely, come on. Those two never got along."

She picked up the bottle of scotch and poured them each another drink. "How 'bout we think positive?" She raised her glass. "To my new job taking care of your adorable children—and to my mom and your mother-in-law making it work."

He grabbed his glass. "I would insist on paying you the going rate." He looked as grim and grouchy as ever, but at least he'd essentially accepted her offer.

"Daniel, we're family. You don't have to—"

"Stop arguing." He narrowed those silvery eyes at her. "It's only fair."

Was it? Didn't really matter. If he had to put her on salary in order to agree to accept her help, so be it. "Go ahead then. Pay me the big bucks."

"I will." He named a figure.

"Done."

He tapped his glass to hers. "Here's to you, Keely. Thank you." He really did look relieved. "You're a lifesaver." And then something truly rare happened. Daniel Bravo almost smiled.

Well, it was more of a twitch on the left side of his mouth, really. That twitch caused a warm little tug in the center of her chest. The man needed to learn how to smile again, he really did. Yes, he'd caused Lillie pain and Keely resented him for it.

But Lillie, diagnosed with lupus back in her teens, had craved the one thing that was most dangerous for her. She'd paid for her children with her life and left her husband on his own to raise the sweet babies she just had to have.

Life wasn't fair, Keely thought. At least there should be smiles in it. There should be joy wherever a person could find it. Jake and Frannie needed a dad who could smile now and then.

"What are you looking at?" Daniel demanded, all traces of that tiny twitch of a smile long gone.

Keely realized she'd been staring at Daniel's mouth for way too long. She blinked and gave an embarrassed little cough into her hand. "Just, um, thinking that you ought to smile more often."

He made a growly sound, something midway between a scoff and a snort. "Don't start on me, Keely. You'll give me a bad feeling about this deal we just made."

It was right on the tip of her tongue to come back with something snippy. *Do not get into it with him*, she reminded herself yet again. They would be living in the same house at least some of the time, and they needed to get along. Instead of a sharp retort, she gave him a crisp nod. "Fair enough."

Claws clicking gently across the floor, Lillie's sweet basset hound, Maisey Fae, waddled in from the family room. The dog stopped at Keely's feet and gazed up at her longingly through mournful brown eyes.

"Aww. How you doin', Maisey?" She knelt to give the dog a nice scratch under her jowly chin. "Where's my sugar?" She pursed her lips, and Maisey swiped at her face with that long, pink tongue.

When Keely rose again, Daniel was holding out a house key. "I'll give you a check tomorrow to cover the first week."

"Thanks. I'll be here nice and early with my car full of clothes, equipment and art supplies."

"I can't wait," he said with zero inflection as she headed for the front door. "What time?"

"Eight," she said over her shoulder.

"I'll come over and help."

"No need." She waved without turning. "I've got this."

The next morning, as Keely was hauling her prized Bernina 1015 sewing machine out to her Subaru in the drizzling rain, Daniel pulled up at the end of her front walk in his Supercrew long-bed pickup.

He emerged from behind the wheel, his dark gold hair kind of scrambled looking, his face rough with beard scruff, wearing a heavy waffle-weave Henley, old jeans and the usual big boots.

"I told you I can handle this," she reminded him as he took the sewing machine from her.

"You're welcome. Happy to help," he said, and for a split second she imagined a spark of wry humor in those ice-blue eyes.

She remembered her manners. "Thank you—and be careful with that," she warned. "Those aren't easy to find anymore, and they cost a fortune." She swiped at the mist of raindrops on her forehead, then stood with her hands on her hips watching his every move as he set the machine carefully in the back seat of his truck. When he shut the door again, she asked, "So Grace has the kids?"

"Yeah, they're with Grace. Let's get the rest." He headed up the walk, his long strides carrying him to the front porch of her shingled cottage in just a few steps.

She hustled to catch up. "You want some coffee? I can make some."

"I had two cups with breakfast. Let's get this done."

Half an hour later, all her equipment, including her spare Bernina—a 1008 model—a raft of art and sketching supplies and the giant pegboard loaded with industrial-sized spools of thread in just about every color known to man, was either in the rear seat of his crew cab or tucked in the long bed beneath the camper shell. He'd loaded up her two collapsible worktables, too, and the smaller table she liked to keep beside her easel. That left only her suitcase to go in the Subaru. She'd figured it would take three trips to get everything up to the Bravo house. Thanks to Daniel, they would get it done in one.

"See you back at the house." He climbed in his truck.

"Thank you. I mean that sincerely."

With a quick wave, he started the engine and drove off.

She locked up and followed him, leaving the mist-shrouded streets of town to head up Rhinehart Hill into the tall trees and then along the winding driveway that led to the beautiful old Bravo house, with its deep front porch flanked by stone pillars.

Keely stopped behind Daniel's truck in the turn-around in front of the house. She grabbed her biggest suitcase and hauled it inside and up the curving staircase to the room she planned to use for sleeping whenever she stayed over.

He emerged from the other room to meet her as she

headed back down. "I'm putting your sewing stuff in the white room." He shot a thumb back over his shoulder. "You're using it for work, right?"

"How'd you guess?"

"It has better light than the other one. You want me to get the bed and dressers out of there?"

"I can use the dressers for storage, if that's all right. Are they empty?"

"I think they've got a bunch of old clothes nobody wants in them. Just clear out the drawers, and I'll take everything away."

"Thanks." *Note to self: be nicer to Daniel.* He really was a handy guy to have around when a girl needed to get stuff done. "And as for the bed, yes, please. I would like it gone."

"I'll have it out of there before dinnertime." And off he went down the stairs to bring up the next load of her stuff.

She peeked into the kids' bedroom and also the play-room before following him. Nobody there. Grace must have them downstairs somewhere.

Working together, they hauled everything up to her two rooms, bringing the big thread pegboard up last.

"You want this board mounted on the wall?" he asked.

"That would be terrific."

"I'll get to that tonight. Once we get the bed out, we can set things up pretty much like the room you were using at your place."

It was exactly what she'd hoped to do, and she got a minor case of the warm fuzzies that he'd not only pitched in to help move her things, he'd also given real thought to making her as comfortable as possible in his house. "Totally works for me. Thanks."

With the barest nod of acknowledgment, he pulled a folded scrap of paper from his pocket—a check. "First week's pay." She took it. "I need to go on up to Warrenton," he said. Valentine Logging operated a log sorting and storage yard, deep water and barge cargo docks, and a log barking and chipping facility in nearby Warrenton at the mouth of the Columbia River. The company offices were there, too. "You planning to look in at the gallery today?"

"I am, yes. But I'll be back in the afternoon, ready to take over with the kids."

"No rush. Grace is here until tomorrow. She'll watch them today and tonight so you can get settled in."

That didn't seem fair. Grace had spent her whole week helping with the kids. "I'm fine on my own with them."

His regular frown got deeper. "Grace'll be here. In case you need her."

She considered the wisdom of arguing the point further. But his mouth was set and his eyes unwavering. Maybe not. "See you later then."

With a grunt, he turned and went down the stairs.

From the docks in Warrenton, Daniel called a handyman he trusted to haul the bed from the white room down into the basement. He'd been feeling pretty desperate yesterday when Keely showed up to save his bacon on the childcare front.

True, her offer had seemed like a bad idea at first. He'd been afraid they wouldn't get along. In the last years of Lillie's life, as his marriage unraveled, Keely had never said a mean word to him directly. But he got the message in her disapproving glances and careful silences whenever he happened to be in the same room with her. She'd been firmly Team Lillie, no doubt about it. Still, for the twins' sake, she'd stepped up to provide the care they needed.

It was important to do everything he could to make her happy in his house. He planned to be home for dinner and then to help her get everything just the way she wanted it.

But the day came and went. By late afternoon, he still needed to go through the stack of paperwork he hadn't managed to get to during the week. After a short break to grab some takeout, he headed for the office, ending up by himself at his desk until after seven.

When he finally pulled his truck into the garage, he caught Grace, in tight jeans and full makeup, as she was coming down the stairs from the inside door. She flashed him a smile and tried to ease past him on the way to her car.

"Hold on."

"Daniel." She made his name into a serious complaint. "I have to go. I'm meeting Erin at—"

He caught her arm. "We need to talk."

"But—"

"Come on."

She let out a groan, but at least she followed him back into the house. "What? Can you please make it quick?"

"Let's talk in my study." She trudged along behind him to his home office off the foyer. Once they were both inside, he shut the door. "The kids and Keely?"

There was an eye roll. "Jake and Frannie are already in bed. Keely's upstairs, putting her stuff away, fixing up her room and her workroom. She said it was fine for me to go."

A hot spark of anger ignited in his gut. But when he

got mad, Grace just got madder. He reminded himself to keep his cool. "The agreement was that you would give Keely a hand tonight, help her get comfortable, pitch in with the kids." He kept his voice level. Reasonable.

Still, Grace's eyes flashed blue fire. "The kids are in *bed*. Got it? And what agreement? You told me what to do as you were going out the door."

"Grace, I—"

"No. Uh-uh. I talked to Keely. I *asked* her if she needed me. She said go, have fun."

"Of course she would say that."

Grace looked up at the ceiling and blew out a furious breath. "You know, some people go to Cancún for their spring break. Me, though? I come home and help your mother-in-law look after your kids. And then when she trips over Jake, it's just me. Until Keely stepped up— which I totally appreciate. Keely's about the best there is. But me, I've got one night. One night of my spring break to myself. A few hours with my friends, and then I'm on my way back to school."

When she said it like that, he felt like an ogre. A litany of swear words scrolled through his brain. Playing stand-in dad to his own sisters and brothers should be more rewarding, shouldn't it? How come so much of the job just plain sucked?

She's the last one at home, he reminded himself. He was pretty much done with raising his siblings.

Too bad he still had a couple of decades ahead with his own kids.

"Come on, Grace. Don't exaggerate. You've spent time with your friends this week."

"Not much, I haven't."

"You went out last night, remember?"

Another giant sigh. More ceiling staring. "For like two hours."

"I want you to stick around tonight in case she needs you."

"But I promised Erin—"

He put up a hand. "You're needed here. And that's all I have to say about it."

If looks could kill, he'd be seared to a cinder. He waited for the yelling to start, dreaded the angry words about to erupt from her mouth—*I hate you, Daniel* and *Who died and made you king?* and the worst one of all, *You are not my father.*

As if he didn't know that. As if he'd *asked* for the thankless job of seeing that his brothers and sisters made it all the way to fully functioning adulthood without somehow crashing and burning in the process.

But this time, Grace surprised him. "Fine," she said way too quietly. And then, shoulders back and head high, she marched to the door, yanked it wide and went out.

He winced as she slammed it behind her. And then, even with the door shut, he could hear her boots pound the floor with each step as she tramped through the downstairs to her room off the kitchen—and slammed that door, too.

Chapter Two

Daniel scrubbed both hands down his face. And then he stood stock-still, listening for cries from upstairs—Jake or Frannie, startled awake by Grace's slamming and stomping. He didn't breathe again for several seconds.

Finally, when he heard nothing but sweet silence, he stuck his head out the door and listened some more.

Still nothing.

By some minor miracle, Grace had failed to wake up the kids.

Daniel retreated into the study and quietly shut the door. He really ought to go straight upstairs to see how Keely was managing.

But Grace might still have angry words to hurl at him. He would check his email now, hide out for a few minutes. If Grace came flying back out of her room again loaded for bear, he didn't want to be anywhere in her path.

* * *

Keely was in her bedroom, putting her clothes in the dresser when she heard a door slam downstairs, followed by the loud tapping of boots across hardwood floors.

Grace. Had to be. Keely tucked a stack of bras into the top drawer, quietly slid it shut—and winced as another downstairs door slammed.

Apparently Daniel had come in before Grace could escape.

Keely felt a stab of guilt. Daniel had made it abundantly clear he intended for his sister to stay home tonight. If Keely had only asked Grace to stick around, the confrontation that had so obviously just occurred downstairs could have been avoided.

But come on. Grace had a right to a little fun with her friends now and then. And Keely really didn't need her tonight.

The question now: Should she leave bad enough alone and stay out of it?

Yeah, probably.

But what had just happened was partly her fault. At the very least, she could offer Grace a shoulder to cry on.

Still not sure she ought to be sticking her nose in, she tiptoed out into the hall, down the stairs, past the shut door to Daniel's study and onward to the back of the house, into the hall off the kitchen. She tapped on Grace's door.

After a minute, a teary voice called, "Go away, Daniel!"

Keely tapped again. "Grace, it's me."

Silence. Keely steeled herself to be told to get lost.

But then she heard footsteps in there. Grace opened the door with red-rimmed eyes and a nose to match.

Keely held out a tissue. "I come in peace."

Grace took the tissue and wiped her nose. "Where is he?"

"Still in his study, I think."

"Jake and Frannie?"

"Not a peep."

Grace sniffed again. "Come in." She stepped back. Keely entered and followed her to the bed where they sat down side by side.

Keely made her apology. "He told me this morning that he expected you to stay in. I should have warned you that he seemed kind of dug in about it."

"He's kind of dug in about everything." Grace stuck out her chin. "You know it's true." Keely didn't argue. Why should she? She agreed with Grace on that. "He treats me like I'm a borderline delinquent. I'm twenty-one years old, getting decent grades in school, doing a perfectly fine job of adulting, thank you so very much. I could just get up, get in my car and go."

"But you won't. Because you are sweet and helpful. You love your brother, and you want to get along with him. You know he's got way too much on his plate, and so you try your best to be patient with him."

Grace let out a reluctant snort of laughter. "Yeah, right."

"I want to make a little speech now. It will probably annoy you, but I hope you'll listen anyway."

"Go for it."

"When he was your age, he was married, working, fitting in college classes as best he could and raising you and your brothers and sisters—and probably getting zero nights out with his friends."

Into the silence that followed, Grace shot her a surprised glance. "That's it. That's the speech?"

"That's all."

Grace seemed to consider. "I know you're right. He hasn't had it easy. But he still drives me crazy. I mean, does he *have* to be such a hard-ass *all* the time?"

Keely put her hand over Grace's and gave it a pat. "I'll go talk to him."

Grace scoffed, "Like there aren't a thousand ways that could go horribly wrong."

"Trust me."

"I do. It's *him* that I'm worried about."

Daniel was still holed up in his study, reluctant to venture out and possibly have to deal with his sister again when the tap came on the door.

Grace? Doubtful. Probably Keely. He didn't really want to listen to whatever she had to say right at the moment either. Chances were she'd only come to give him a bad time about Grace.

There was another knock.

He gave in and called out, "It's open."

Keely pushed the door wide and then hesitated on the threshold. She wore what she'd had on that morning— jeans rolled at the ankles, a black-and-white-striped shirt half-tucked-in and hanging off one shoulder, with high-tops on her feet. Her hair was naturally reddish blond, but she liked to change it up. Today, it fell in fog-frizzed brown waves to her shoulders. Her big, wide-set green eyes assessed him.

He leaned back in his swivel chair and cracked his neck to dispel some of the tension. "Go ahead. I'm listening."

She braced a shoulder in the doorway, stuck her hands in her pockets and crossed one high-top in front of the other. "I really did tell Grace I didn't need her, and I urged her to go out and have a little fun."

Women. They always knew how to gang up on a man. "All right."

She pushed off the door and straightened her shoulders. "All right, she can go—or all right, you heard what I said and I should get lost?"

He stared at his dead wife's cousin and reminded himself all over again that he was really grateful she'd come to look after his children, even if she did consider him to blame for all that had gone wrong between him and Lillie.

And maybe he *was* to blame.

When his parents had died suddenly on a second honeymoon in Thailand, he was eighteen. The most important thing then was to keep what was left of his family together. He'd stepped up to take care of his three surviving brothers and four sisters. Lillie, a year behind him in school, stepped right up with him. He and Lillie had been together—inseparable, really—for two years by then. They'd agreed to get married as soon as Lillie graduated high school.

A born nurturer just like her mother, Lillie was only too happy to take over as a second mom to his big brood of siblings. She always claimed that choosing a life with him and his ready-made family was the perfect solution for her. She could have the kids she longed for and not risk her health.

But as the years passed and his brothers and sisters grew up and moved out, her yearning for babies of their own only got stronger. He didn't share that yearning. No way. An empty nest. That was what he'd looked forward to. He'd thought they might travel a little, get to know each other all over again...

"Daniel? You all right?" Keely was waiting for him to answer her last question.

He shook himself and put his regrets aside. "Sorry." *Grace.* He needed to smooth things over with Grace. "You're sure you don't need her?"

"Positive."

He got up. "I'll go talk to her."

Grace opened the door at his knock. "What now?"

"Grace, I'm sorry we got into it."

"It's all right," she said flatly. He got the message. It was not all right. It was anything but.

"Listen, go ahead. Go meet Erin. Enjoy your last night home."

She almost smiled. But she was still too pissed at him for that. "Thanks."

Don't stay out too late. He closed his mouth over the words. She was an adult after all. He had trouble sometimes remembering that. She'd been a sweet little six-year-old in pigtails with two missing front teeth when George and Marie Bravo decided they needed a romantic getaway in Thailand. They got there just in time for the tsunami that killed them. And Grace had had to grow up without them.

No, he wasn't his baby sister's father, but sometimes he felt like it. He liked it when she stayed home—and not only because she helped out with the kids. He wanted her safe, damn it, wanted all of them safe. Life was too dangerous. Anything could happen. He knew that from hard experience.

"Have a good time." He pushed the words out of his unwilling mouth.

"I will," she said obediently and then lifted her arms in a limp offer of a hug.

He gathered her close, but only for a moment. She pulled free quickly, and he left her to go offer Keely some help setting up the white room for her studio.

By a little after eleven, they had the thread pegboard hung and covered with giant spools. He'd put up some shelves for her, ones he'd found down in the basement. The shelves used to be in his brother Matthias's room way back before Matt moved out. She had two worktables set up, one for sketching and one for her sewing machine. There was an easel in the corner and another, smaller table next to it piled with paint and brushes.

"This is looking good, Daniel. Thank you."

"What else needs doing?"

"That's it." She hid a yawn behind her hand. "We are finished."

"You sure?"

She pushed in the chair at her sewing table. "Yep."

He felt the oddest reluctance to head for his own room. After Grace left for her night out, it had been pretty much a no-pressure evening. He'd felt useful, helping Keely get the room the way she wanted it. And besides that, it was kind of good just to hang with her. Kind of companionable.

He hadn't had much of that, of companionship. Not for a long time. Not for a couple of years at least. Not since he'd found out that Lillie was pregnant.

And really, since before that, even. More like five

years, since about the time Lillie started really pushing him to try for a baby of their own.

"Okay, what'd I say?" Keely asked.

"Huh? Nothing. Why?"

"You looked… I don't know. Faraway. Unhappy."

He tried for a laugh. It came out as more of a grunt. "I always look unhappy. Ask anyone who knows me."

"Now, see. I want to say that's not true. But, Daniel, it kind of is."

He had the absolutely unacceptable urge to start talking about Lillie, about how angry he still was at her after all this time, for betting on her life. And losing.

What was the matter with him? To even consider spilling his guts about Lillie to Keely, of all people? That would be a bad idea of spectacular proportions.

Wouldn't it? Why did he have this powerful feeling that Keely would understand?

Didn't matter. He just wasn't going there. No way.

And he needed to get out of there. Now.

He rubbed the back of his neck. "What can I say? Except, yeah, I'm a gloomy guy. And since you're good to go here, I'll see you in the morning."

She didn't reply for several seconds, just looked at him, kind of thoughtful and sad, both at once. A soft sigh escaped her. "All right then. Night."

"Night—come on, Maisey. Let's go." The dog, stretched out by the window, got up and followed him from the room.

With Maisey trotting along behind, he went down the stairs to let her out before bed. He walked fast, too, just in case Keely got it in her head to try to stop him, to start asking questions he saw no win in answering.

* * *

Daniel got in bed around midnight. He had trouble sleeping until a little after two, when he heard Grace come in. Relieved that she was home safe, he finally drifted off.

He woke to the sound of one of the kids crying. Maisey was already out of her dog bed and sniffing at the door. She gave a worried little whine, urging him to hurry as he yanked on track pants and a frayed Go Beavers T-shirt. When he opened the door, she pushed out ahead of him, leading the way along the hallway to the twins' bedroom.

The door stood open, dim light spilling out. Maisey went in first.

Keely was already there, Frannie in her arms. She was pacing the floor in the muted light from the little lamp on the green dresser. She turned when he entered, her hand on the back of Frannie's head, stroking gently as Frannie sobbed against her shoulder.

He felt that familiar ache his chest, the one he got when one of his own was hurting. A quick glance at Jake's crib showed him his boy was still asleep. That miracle wouldn't last long. "Let me take her," he whispered.

Keely kissed Frannie's temple. "Here's your daddy," she murmured, keeping it low, probably hoping Jake wouldn't wake up.

Yeah. Good luck with that.

Daniel held out his arms. With a sad little cry, Frannie twisted in Keely's hold and fell toward him. "Da-Da!" she wailed. He caught her and gathered her in. She dropped her head against his chest. "Ow. Ow, ow, ow."

Keely moved in close, the soft sleeve of her flannel pajama top brushing his arm. He got a faint whiff of sweetness—her shampoo? Her perfume? "Ear infection?" she whispered.

He felt the back of Frannie's neck as she sobbed against his chest. "She seems kind of hot."

"I thought so, too."

"We should take her temperature."

"I'll get the thermometer."

"It's the one that says *rectal* on the case," he advised over Frannie's unhappy cries. *Rectal.* Story of his life. Rectal thermometers and never enough sleep—and did Keely know where to look? "Cabinet in the big bathroom," he added. "On the left, second shelf. Just to be sure it's sterile, clean it with alcohol and a little soap and water."

"You got it." She disappeared into the hallway. Really, she was a champ, that Keely.

About then, Jake woke up with a startled cry. "Da?"

"It's okay, big guy."

"Fa-Fa?" It was Jake's name for his sister.

"She's not feeling so good."

Jake stood up in his crib. "Fa-Fa?" he called again.

Frannie answered, "Day!" She couldn't make the *j* sound yet, and she tended to drop hard sounds at the ends of words, so the *k* got lost, too, and she called her twin Day. "Ow, ow, ow!"

"Shh." Daniel soothed her. "It's okay…" Gently, he laid his wailing daughter on the changing table. As she wiggled and whined, he took off her one-piece pajamas and her diaper. Meanwhile, Jake jumped up and down in his crib, calling out "Fa-Fa, Fa-Fa!" in frantic sympathy, followed by a bunch of nonsense words to which Frannie replied with nonsense of her own—well, maybe not nonsense to the two of them. They had their own language that only they understood.

Keely came back with the thermometer in one hand, a bottle of liquid Tylenol and a dosing syringe in the other. "We'll probably need it," she said, meaning the Tylenol. Chances were way too good she was right.

He held out his hand as Frannie continued to cry and squirm. Keely passed him the thermometer—and Jake let out a wail from his crib.

"I'll get him," she said. "Tylenol's right here." She set it on the shelf above the changing table and went to reassure Jake.

The thermometer registered 102 degrees. He put a fresh diaper on Frannie and dosed her with the Tylenol as Keely sat in the corner rocker, soothing the worried Jake.

Once he had Frannie back in her pajamas, he walked the floor with her until the Tylenol seemed to kick in. She went to sleep against his shoulder.

He kissed the top of her sweaty little head and glanced over to find Keely watching him.

She mouthed, *Sleeping?* At his nod, she nodded back, pointing at Jake, who was curled up against her, sound asleep, too.

It was only a few steps to Frannie's crib. He carried her over there and slowly, gently, laid her down. She didn't stir as he tucked the blanket in around her.

Across the room in the other crib, Keely was tucking Jake in, too. She turned off the lamp, and they tiptoed from the now-quiet room together.

"Psst. Maisey," he whispered. The dog lurched to her feet and waddled out after them. Daniel closed the door. "Whew."

Keely leaned back against the wall next to her bedroom and said hopefully, "Maybe they'll sleep the rest of the night and Frannie will be all better in the morning."

"Dreamer. And what rest of the night? It's already morning, in case you didn't notice."

"Don't go overboard looking on the bright side there, Daniel." She glanced through the open door to her room and blew out her cheeks with a weary breath. "Sadly enough, though, you're right. The clock by my bed says it's almost five. Tonight is officially over."

"Let's hope we get lucky and they both sleep till, say, eight."

"As if." She laughed, a sort of whisper-laugh to go with their low, careful whisper of a conversation. The low light from the wall sconces struck red glints in her brown hair, and she looked sweet as a farm girl, barefoot in those flannel pajamas that were printed with ladybugs.

He thought of Grace suddenly, knew a stab of annoyance that kind of soured the companionable moment between him and Keely—and there it was again, that word: *companionable*. He'd felt companionable with his dead wife's cousin twice in one night, and he didn't know whether to feel good about that or not.

"What?" Keely asked. "Just say it."

He went ahead and admitted what was bugging him. "Grace. She's got one of the baby monitors in her room, so she had to hear what was happening. But she didn't even come check to see if we needed her."

"Yeah, she did. She came in the kids' room before you. I knew she'd been out late and could use a little sleep, so I said I could handle it and sent her back to bed."

He hung his head. "Go ahead. Say it. I'm a crap brother."

Maisey chose that moment to get comfortable. She

yawned hugely, stretched out on the floor and lowered her head to her paws with a soft doggy sigh.

Keely said, "You love Grace. She loves you. Ten years from now, you'll wonder what you used to fight about."

"Uh-uh. I'll remember."

"Maybe. But you'll be totally over it." Would he? He hoped so. She said, "When I was little, living with the band on my mother's purple bus, I used to dream of a real house like this one, dream of having sisters and brothers. Family is hard, Daniel. But it's worth it. And I think you know that it is."

"Yeah," he admitted. "You're right."

Family was everything. But that didn't stop him from fantasizing about totally non-family-related things. Partying till dawn, maybe. A game of poker that went on till all hours, with a keg on tap and all the guys smoking stinky cigars, telling politically incorrect jokes. A one-night stand with a gorgeous woman he'd never met before and would never see again, a woman who only wanted to use him for hot sex.

Now there was a big *as if.* He'd been with one woman in his life and was perfectly happy about that—until the past few years anyway. He just wasn't the kind of guy who went to bed with women he hardly knew. The one time he'd tried that, six months ago, he'd realized at the last possible moment that sex with a stranger just wasn't for him. His sudden change of heart had not endeared him to the lady in question.

And Keely was watching him again, a hint of a smile on her full mouth.

"I'm going to work on thinking positive," he promised her, because she did have a point about his negative attitude.

She gave a whisper-chuckle. "Anything is possible."

He clicked his tongue at Maisey and she dragged herself up on her stubby legs again. "Night, Keely." He turned for his room at the end of the hall.

"Night, Daniel," she whispered after him.

When Keely woke up it was ten after eight Sunday morning and no one was crying. She put on her vintage chenille robe over her pajamas and looked across the hall.

Both cribs were empty.

Downstairs in the kitchen, she found two smiling cherubs eating cut-up pancakes off their high chair trays and both Daniel and Grace at the breakfast table, neither one scowling.

Yes. Life was good on this beautiful, foggy-as-usual Sunday morning in Valentine Bay. She poured herself coffee.

Grace said, "I'm here till two, Keely, so if you need to run errands, go for it."

"Keewee!" crowed Jake, pounding on his tray.

Keely stepped over and kissed his gooey cheek.

"Kiss, kiss, Keewee!" Frannie pounded her tray, too, and smacked her rosebud lips.

Keely kissed her as well, and then returned to the stove where a stack of pancakes waited. She put a couple of them on a plate. "Thanks, Grace. I'll run by Sand & Sea and stop in to check on Aunt Gretchen."

The gallery opened daily at eleven. Keely arrived at nine thirty. Her top clerk, Amanda, promoted temporarily to manager, joined her five minutes later. They went through the books and discussed the schedule. Sand & Sea was 3500 square feet of exhibit space on Manzanita

Avenue, in the heart of Valentine Bay's downtown historic district. With a focus on Oregon artists, Keely offered contemporary work in just about every form imaginable, from painting to printmaking, sculpture to woodworking. She displayed and sold artisan jewelry, furniture, textiles and photography.

Sand & Sea also hosted receptions and special events. Every month or so, she featured an individual artist or a group of artists in a themed joint show. The first Friday in April, she would hold an opening for a new group show with several top Pacific Northwest artists working in various mediums on the theme of the ever-changing sea. Everything was on schedule for that one so far. Amanda was knowledgeable, organized and more than competent, and they had almost three weeks until the opening. Keely needed to find help with Frannie and Jake for the opening-night reception party and the few days before it. But that should be doable, one way or another.

Feeling confident that Sand & Sea wouldn't suffer while she focused on Daniel's twins, she left the gallery at eleven thirty to check in on her aunt.

Gretchen still lived in the house she'd shared with her husband, the house where she'd raised her precious only child, Lillie. Keely considered the four-bedroom craftsman-style bungalow her childhood home, too.

Yes, she'd spent most of her growing-up years living on the tour bus. But now and then, Ingrid's career would get a boost and the tour schedule would get crazy. Those were the times that Ingrid took Keely to Valentine Bay to live temporarily with Aunt Gretchen and Uncle Cletus. Keely loved when that happened. She was constantly begging her mother to let her live with the Snows full-time.

When Keely was fifteen, Ingrid finally gave in. Keely moved in with her cousin. At last, she got the settled-down life she'd always dreamed of in the seaside town she considered her true home.

Keely knocked on the green front door, but only to be considerate. She had a key and she used it, sticking her head in the door, calling, "It's just me! Don't get up!"

"I'm in the kitchen!" Gretchen called back.

Something smelled wonderful. Keely followed her nose to the back of the house. She found her aunt balanced on her good foot, one hand braced on the counter, as she pulled a tray of cookies from the oven.

Keely waited until Gretchen had set the tray on top of the stove and shut the oven door to scold, "You're not supposed to be on that foot."

"Sweetheart!" Gretchen turned and hopped toward her.

"You are impossible." Keely caught her and hugged her, breathing in the familiar, beloved scents of vanilla and melted butter. Her aunt not only always smelled delicious, she was still pretty in a comfortable, homey sort of way, with smooth, pale skin and carefully styled hair she still had professionally colored to the exact Nordic blond it used to be when she was young.

Gretchen laughed. "You know you need cookies."

Keely grabbed a chair from the table and spun it around. "Here. Sit."

"Oh, don't fuss." Gretchen held on to Keely for balance as she lowered herself into the chair.

Keely tried to look stern. "You will stay in that chair. I mean it."

Gretchen swept out a plump arm in the direction of the big mixing bowl on the counter. "I have two more cookie sheets to fill."

"Stay where you are. I'll do it." She grabbed another chair and positioned it so that Gretchen could put her foot up. "There. Want coffee?"

"Please—and where are my babies?"

"At Daniel's." Keely filled a cup and set it on the table next to Gretchen. "Grace isn't going back to Portland until this afternoon, so she's watching them."

"I miss them already."

"I'll bring them by during the week."

"You're a good girl. The best."

Keely got to work dropping spoonfuls of dough onto a cookie sheet. "Looking after Frannie and Jake is no hardship. You know how I always wanted babies." She'd been married once. A hot and charming driftwood artist, Roy Varner had come to town six years ago, before Keely opened Sand & Sea. Another local gallery had given him a show. Keely went to his opening. The attraction was instant and mutual. Roy swept her clean off her feet. They'd married within weeks of that first meeting. Roy traveled a lot to various art shows all over the west. Slowly Keely figured out that all the traveling wasn't only about selling art. When he traveled, Roy behaved like a free man in every way. Including sleeping with other women. Keely had divorced him four years ago.

"Don't you worry," said Gretchen. "You've still got plenty of time. A good man and babies will be yours."

Keely sent her aunt a fond glance over her shoulder. "Love you, Auntie G."

"Love you more."

"Heard from Mom?"

"Not since the other day."

"So we still don't know exactly when she's coming?"

"Keely, I am managing just fine—and what about you? All settled in at Daniel's?"

She considered mentioning Frannie's earache. But the little girl had seemed fully recovered this morning, so why worry Gretchen? "It's going great. And I'm all set up. I've got a bedroom across from the twins, and I'm using the room beside it as a work area—and you know, I've been thinking that we could get you some live-in help. Or you could move to Daniel's temporarily."

"I like my own house."

"But—"

"Don't start. I mean it. I've hired the boy next door to handle the yard. His sister will come in and clean when I need her. I'm having my groceries delivered. I'm used to doing things for myself, and I like my independence. Plus, in the Bravo house, all the bedrooms except Grace's are upstairs. That's not going to work with this foot."

Keely scooped up another spoonful of dough. "I'll call Mom, pin her down on when she'll be here."

"Don't you dare. I will handle this. You've got enough to do, and you know it."

"Auntie G, it's just a phone call," she said into the bowl of dough.

"Put down that spoon and look at me."

Keely dropped the spoon back in the bowl and turned to face her aunt. "Yeah?"

"Your mother *is* coming, but she'll be doing that in her own good time. That's how she rolls and don't we all know it."

Keely stifled a laugh. "How she *rolls*?"

Gretchen's blue eyes twinkled. "You know it's true.

Ingrid makes her own rules and sets her own schedule. Trying to change her at this late date? Never going to happen."

Keely picked up a cooling cookie, took a bite and groaned in appreciation. "You shouldn't be up making cookies. But these are *so* good."

"I made lunch, too. It's in the fridge. Don't ruin your appetite."

"No chance of that. Not when it's your cooking—and were you on your feet to make the lunch?"

"Don't nag, sweetheart. Nagging is not attractive."

"What am I going to do with you?"

"Finish your cookie, get the rest of them in the oven—and then serve us both the amazing crab salad and crusty rolls I threw together."

Keely got back to the Bravo house at a quarter of two, and Grace left for Portland a few minutes later. As usual, Daniel had stuff to do at the office. He promised to be back by dinnertime.

She stood on the porch, one twin on either side of her, waving as Daniel headed off down the driveway. The sun had made an afternoon appearance, so for a while she took the kids out back, where there was a big wooden playset that had been there for as long as she could remember. They played in the sandbox, slid down the slide and she swung them on the toddler-friendly swings.

Back inside, she gave them a snack and took them upstairs for diaper changes and nap time. They went down like little angels, reaching for kisses, settling right in and closing their eyes.

She got a full hour in her new studio, bent over her

precious Bernina before Frannie started crying. When Keely went to check on her, she had a fever again.

That night, poor little Frannie didn't sleep much. Neither did Keely or Daniel. Or Jake, for that matter. Frannie's ear hurt, and nothing seemed to make it feel better.

The next day, one of the ladies from Gretchen's church came by to watch Jake so that Keely could take Frannie to the pediatrician. Diagnosis: ear infection. Keely picked up the antibiotic and eardrop prescriptions on the way home.

Frannie had another bad night. All day Tuesday, she fussed and cried. Tuesday night, though, she only woke up crying twice.

"I think she's better," Keely whispered to Daniel when they tiptoed from the kids' room for the second time that night.

"I hope so." He had dark circles under his eyes. "We could all use a good night's sleep."

Wednesday morning, Frannie woke up smiling.

When Keely said, "I think you feel better, honey," the little angel replied, "I fine, Keewee. I goo."

And she really did seem fully recovered. After breakfast, Keely took both kids to see Gretchen, who still had no idea when Keely's mom would be showing up. But Auntie G was all smiles to get to spend an afternoon with her beloved babies. She held them on her lap and sang the nursery songs she used to sing to Keely when she was little and staying with the Snows.

On Thursday, Jake got sick.

It was some weird flu bug. There was vomiting and a lot of mucus. Keely called the pediatrician, who suggested a humidifier, cool baths, cough medicine and

Tylenol for fever. No need to bring Jake in, the doctor had said, unless his fever hit 104 or he wasn't better within a week.

The next three nights were hell. Jake woke up crying and that woke Frannie. Keely and Daniel took turns looking in on them. The weekend went by somehow, not that Keely even cared what day it was. Making art with her sewing machine? Not even happening. And as for the original plan that she might go back and forth between the Bravo house and her cottage?

She never once made it home. In fact, she had to call a neighbor to water her plants.

She was exhausted, run ragged—and she found herself beginning to seriously admire Daniel. He worked all day and then stayed up with her all night to help with the kids. So what if he wasn't the happiest dad on the planet? The man was dedicated to the well-being of his children. He mopped up vomit and changed diapers with the best of them.

By late Sunday, Jake had weathered the worst of it. He coughed less frequently and the mucus factory seemed to be shutting down. The sweet little guy was definitely on the mend. Sunday night, Keely actually slept straight through. The kids didn't wake once, from bedtime until six the next morning.

Monday, Daniel woke her with a tap on her door.

"Ugh?" She blinked and yawned. "It's open."

He peeked in the door, looking almost rested for once. "Sorry to wake you."

She yawned again. "It was bound to happen sometime. What's up?"

"I'll get them up and downstairs if you'll start the breakfast."

"Deal."

She was at the stove when he came down with the little ones. She glanced over her shoulder to see him wiping Frannie's streaming nose. They stared at each other across the gorgeous expanse of the soapstone island. "Oh, no," she whispered, as though if she didn't say it too loudly, Frannie wouldn't be getting the bug Jake had just recovered from.

"No fever," Daniel said. He didn't add *yet*, but it seemed to her the unspoken word hung in the air between them.

By that afternoon, Frannie's nose ran nonstop. By dinnertime, she'd thrown up twice and a persistent cough seemed to rattle her little bones. By then, she also had a fever. It hovered at around 101.

Keely and Daniel spent another night taking turns waking up to soothe a sick baby. Really, they were getting the nighttime nursing care down to a science, as though they had radar for whose turn it was. Keely barely stirred when it was his turn, and the master bedroom door remained shut when it was hers.

Once that night, she woke when it was his turn.

"This one's mine," he mumbled when she stuck her head out into the hall.

"Unh," she replied and went back to bed.

On Wednesday, a week and a half into the endless string of illnesses the twins had been suffering, Daniel had a timber owner he had to go meet with. It was a small grove of Douglas firs ready to harvest, and Daniel would walk the grove with the landowner, explaining how Valentine Logging would maximize each tree to its full potential. The landowner wanted to meet at eight in the morning and Daniel wanted the contract, so at a quarter after seven he staggered out of the house, bleary-eyed, armed with a giant travel mug of coffee.

Keely spent the morning alone trying to keep her eye on Jake while doing what she could to ease poor Frannie's misery. She dosed the little girl with over-the-counter meds, kept the humidifier running and gave Frannie cold-water sponge baths at regular intervals.

The day never seemed to end.

Finally, at around two in the afternoon, she got both kids down for a nap. To the soft hissing of the humidifier, she tiptoed from their room with Maisey at her heels. Across the hall, both of her doors were open. She cast a despairing glance toward her studio room. *As if.*

Right now, her beloved Bernina was the last thing she wanted to cuddle up with. The bed in the other room, though...

Nothing had ever looked so beautiful.

She dragged her tired body in there and fell gratefully across the mattress as Maisey flopped down on the rug right beside her. Blessed sleep settled over her.

She dreamed of walking the foggy beach not far from her back door—with Daniel of all people. They didn't talk, just strolled along the wet sand, side by side but not touching, the waves sliding in, foaming around their bare feet.

"Keewee! Da-Da!"

"Wha—huh?" Keely shuddered, instantly wide-awake.

"Da-Da!" Frannie cried from the other room, followed by a long wail of sheer misery.

Keely shoved herself backward off the bed, raked her hair out of her eyes and hustled for the other room. Frannie was standing up in her crib, sobbing and coughing, snot running down her flushed little face.

"Oh, honey…"

"Keewee! Ow!"

Keely ran over and lifted the poor sweetheart into her arms. "Frannie. Oh, now. It's okay…" She settled her on her shoulder.

At which point, Frannie threw up. It went down Keely's back. That caused Frannie to wail all the louder.

"It's okay. It's all right," Keely promised, though clearly it was anything but. Gently, she peeled the little girl off her shoulder. "Shh. Shh. Let me…"

It was as far as she got. Frannie hurled again, this time down Keely's front. "Oh, bad!" Frannie wailed.

"No, no," Keely promised her. "It's not bad, honey. It's okay."

That was when Frannie threw up again, all over herself. She wailed even louder, "Keewee, I sowwy. I sowwy, sowwy, sowwy."

From his crib, Jake cried, "Fa-Fa? Fa-Fa, oh, no!"

"She's okay," Keely promised and wished it were true. "Jakey, she's going to be fine."

Maisey appeared in the doorway to the hall. She moaned in sympathetic doggy distress.

Keely carried Frannie to the changing table and quickly got her out of her soiled clothes. "Jakey, we'll be right back," she promised the increasingly agitated little boy as she grabbed the little girl and a clean diaper. Holding both out and away from her vomit-soaked body, she stepped over Maisey and carried baby and diaper across the hall to her room, moving straight through to her bathroom, which had a traditional tub-and-shower combination.

Shoving the shower curtain aside, Keely lowered the little girl into the tub. "Here. We'll get you all cleaned up."

"'Kay." Frannie sniffed.

Keely turned on the water. Once she had it lukewarm, she grabbed a washcloth and rinsed Frannie off.

Frannie was quiet, sniffling a little, watching her through wide eyes, as Keely dried her off and carried her—held out and dangling—to her own bed, where she put on the diaper.

"You feel better now, honey?"

Frannie solemnly nodded, eyes wide and wet. Keely scooped her up again and put her in the playpen she kept set up in the corner for any time she needed to corral the kids in her room.

"Fa-Fa? Keewee?" Jake cried from the other room.

"Coming, Jakey. Just a minute!" Keely called back.

A plush pink squeaky kitten lay waiting in the playpen. Keely squeezed it and it meowed. Frannie took it and hugged it close.

"I'm just going to go into the bathroom to clean up. I'll be right back. Okay, honey?"

For that, she got another somber nod from Frannie. Though still flushed, her eyes red and her nose running, Frannie did seem much calmer at least.

Thank God, the vomiting bout seemed to be through.

Jake called again, "Keewee?"

"Just another minute, Jakey. I'll be there. I promise!" Peeling off her smelly shirt as she went, Keely darted for the bathroom. Standing on the bathroom rug by the tub, she wiggled free of her bra, kicked out of her shoes and shoved down both her jeans and panties at once.

"Keewee!" Jake shouted.

"Jakey, I'm right here! Just a minute!" she called, as she hopped around in a ridiculous circle, whipping off one sock and then the other. Flipping on the taps, switching the flow to the showerhead, she got in under the still-cold spray and yanked the curtain closed.

Three minutes, tops, she was in there. Jake called her name repeatedly. Once or twice, Frannie did, too. Keely got the mess off, rinsed in record time, flipped off the tap and shoved the shower curtain wide.

She'd stepped, dripping wet to the bath mat, and reached for her towel before she happened to glance through the open bathroom door to the bedroom.

Jake in his arms and Maisey at his feet, Daniel stood by the playpen staring at her with his mouth hanging open.

Chapter Three

Keely grabbed her towel, whipped it around her, stepped to the bathroom door and shoved it shut.

Only then did she sink to the toilet seat and hit her forehead with the heel of her hand. Never in her life had she been so embarrassed. Not even the day she wore white jeans on the tour bus and got her first period. Except for her and her mom, everyone on that bus was a guy. Keely just knew all those rockers had seen her shame—and okay, on second thought, that might have been worse.

But this was plenty bad.

The look on his face. Like someone had just dropped a safe on his head.

God. Daniel had seen her naked. That was so wrong. In all the ways that really counted, she was Lillie's sister and a man ought never to see his wife's sister naked.

Seriously. Would it have killed her to shut the damn bathroom door?

But she'd thought they were alone—just her, the kids and Maisey. She'd wanted to be able to hear them while she cleaned up, just in case…

Just in case, *what*? Come to think of it, she had no idea.

It's not the end of the world, Keely. No one will die from this. Get over yourself.

Daniel tapped on the door. "Keely? You okay?"

"Fine! Really!" Her voice had the tinkling brightness of breaking glass. "We, uh, had a little accident."

"But…you're okay?"

Oh, hell, no. "Yes. I'll be out in a few minutes."

He made a nervous throat-clearing sound. "I'll just take the kids into the other room."

"Great! Be there in a few."

"Uh. Take your time."

She started to call out something frantic and cheerful. "Righto!" or "Absolutely!" But she shut her mouth hard and folded her lips between her teeth so that not one more ludicrous word could escape.

Fifteen minutes later, she found Daniel and the kids in the bedroom across the hall. He sat in the rocker, holding Frannie, who looked like a slightly flushed angel, all curled up in his arms, sucking peacefully on a baby bottle half-full of water. He'd dressed her in a cozy pair of pink pajamas.

Jake lay on the floor nearby, gumming a plastic teething pretzel, one plump arm thrown out across Maisey, who lay at his side. He took the pretzel from his mouth and gave her his most dazzling smile. "Keewee. Hi there."

"Hey, honey."

"Da-Da home."

"Oh, yes, he is."

Jake stuck the pretzel back in his mouth and chewed some more. Maisey nuzzled him, and he gave a lazy little giggle around the toy in his mouth.

The puddle of vomit on the rug was only a damp spot now, and the room smelled of the all-natural cleaner they used around the kids, a citrusy scent.

She made herself raise her gaze and look at Daniel. Those sea-glass eyes were waiting. She made herself speak. "You're home early."

"I was worried about Frannie and thought maybe you could use a break or at least another pair of hands."

She forced a smile. "Thank you. I see you cleaned up the mess already."

"Seemed like the least I could do." Gently, he stroked Frannie's fine gold hair, his rough hand big enough to cradle the whole of her little head. He pressed a kiss to her temple. "She's cooler. I think the fever might have broken."

"Wonderful."

He rocked slowly, back and forth. In his arms, Frannie looked so peaceful. Safe. Content. "I am sorry." His fine mouth twisted, and a hot flush swept up his thick neck. "For barging in on you. I should have knocked. But Jake was calling for you and for Frannie. I picked him up and he pointed at your room…"

Did they really need to talk it over?

Maybe. After all, it could be good, right? To be frank and open about it? They could clear the air, so to speak.

"I left both doors open. It's not your fault. Of course you came right in." How red was her face? As red as his? *Oh, God.* "It's not a big deal, Daniel."

"You're right," he said and swallowed hard. "Not a big deal at all."

And it wasn't.

Oh, but it *was*.

For Daniel anyway.

Nothing had changed. But for every minute of the rest of that day, Lillie's cousin was suddenly very much on his mind.

Not to mention wreaking havoc lower down.

His longtime sexual abstinence had never felt so painful. Could he *be* more inappropriate? All of a sudden, he was a man obsessed. Who did that? Who *thought* like that?

He needed to stop. Stop thinking of her, fantasizing about her, imagining what it might be like if they...

No. Uh-uh. That wasn't going to happen. Ever. And it *shouldn't* happen.

She was family. She was great with the kids. He no longer felt that she judged him for the troubles between him and Lillie during the last years of her life.

They were, well, *friends* now. Weren't they? He counted on Keely, enjoyed talking to her. Liked having her around.

No way would he mess with that.

He wasn't even considering messing with that.

Uh-uh.

He needed to focus on the positive and forget the smooth white curves of her shoulders shining wet from her shower, not think about those full, tempting breasts, her dusky pink nipples puckered and tight. He needed to block out the memory of that tiny, shining rivulet of water sliding down the center of her, filling her navel, spilling over and dribbling lower, into the water-beaded landing strip of red-brown hair that did nothing to cover the ripe swell of her mound.

Yeah.

Right.

All that. He needed to damn well forget about all that. To focus on what mattered.

Family. The kids. Not rocking the fragile boat of their lives, a boat that had finally steadied after almost capsizing with the loss of Lillie.

By that evening, Frannie seemed fully recovered. She ate a big dinner and kept it down. Both children slept straight through that night and the next night and the night after that, too.

Daniel could go to the office or out on a job in the morning and concentrate on both his bottom line and the potentially dangerous work that needed doing. His kids were safe and well with Keely. He needed her, and he was grateful to her.

And he was not going to jeopardize all the good she brought to his family by doing something stupid like putting a move on her.

That Sunday, he picked up Gretchen and brought her over for dinner. She'd baked a chocolate cake for their dessert, and though she was still using a walker to get around, she claimed she felt better every day.

She praised Keely's pot roast and fussed over the kids. "I do miss taking care of them."

"Now that they're both recovered after the mystery

bug from hell, I'll bring them to your house this week," Keely promised.

"What day?" Gretchen demanded.

"Tuesday, for lunch—my treat. That means I'm bringing the food along with the children," Keely lectured. "Don't you dare fix a thing." Daniel watched her plump lips moving, admired the shine to those wide green eyes, wondered what it would feel like to press his mouth to the smooth white skin of her throat, to stick out his tongue and learn the taste of her skin.

"Right, Daniel?"

He blinked and stared at his mother-in-law. "Er, what was that?"

Gretchen chuckled. "I swear, you are a thousand miles away. I hope you're not letting work run you ragged."

"Uh, no. I was just, you know, thinking…" *About Keely. Naked.* "But anyway, what was the question?"

"Well, I only said that it wouldn't be right, not to at least have some cookies ready Tuesday when Keely brings the twins over. The babies love my cookies." She aimed a chiding glance at Keely. "*Keely* loves my cookies. I'll send some home for all of you to share."

"Cookies!" Jake pounded his high chair tray and then shoved a hunk of potato into his mouth.

"She needs to stay off that foot," Keely grumbled. "Auntie G, that cake you brought looks fabulous, but cake and cookies are not necessities. For you to take care of yourself, that's what matters."

Gretchen pursed her lips. "I've worked out a way I can sit down to do most of the work."

"Oh, please. Like I believe that one."

"It's true. I'm very careful of my injured foot, and it's healing quite nicely, thank you very much. And part of taking care of myself is doing what makes me happy. Baking makes me happy, and one way or another, I am bound to bake."

"Bound to bake." Keely pressed her lips together. In the two weeks she'd been living in his house, Daniel had already learned to read her expressions. Right now, she was trying to stay stern, trying *not* to burst out laughing. She glanced toward the ceiling as though calling on a higher power. "What am I going to do with you?"

"Not a thing." Gretchen drew her plump shoulders back. "Just be my sweet girl and stop trying to tell me how to live my life."

Keely glared, but then she gave it up. "All right. Fine. Bake your heart out."

"I intend to."

Keely focused on her dinner. Daniel recognized the move for the ploy that it was. She pretended to let the argument go, but she was only regrouping before trying again. After carefully chewing and swallowing a bite of pot roast, she set down her knife and fork. "I have to ask. What about Mom?"

"What about her?" Gretchen replied way too sweetly.

"She's supposed to be with you, helping you as you recover. Have you heard from her? Have you called her? Do you know when she's coming?"

Daniel considered interrupting, suggesting that Keely leave it alone. Really, Gretchen seemed to be managing pretty well on her own. But then again, siding with his mother-in-law against the woman he needed to take care of his kids... Well, that wouldn't be very smart, now, would it?

If he was going to mess things up with Keely, he

might as well just make a pass and take a chance she might say yes—not that he would do that.

Never.

Uh-uh.

Not going to happen.

"Ingrid will come when she comes," declared Gretchen.

"That does it." Keely's eyes had gone flinty. "I'm calling her tonight."

While Daniel drove Gretchen home, Keely straightened up the kitchen and then took the kids upstairs. She watched them in the playroom for a while and then hustled them to the hall bathroom and knelt by the tub to supervise as they splashed and giggled and even allowed her to swipe at them with a washcloth now and then.

"Clean children. My favorite kind," said Daniel from behind her in the doorway. Keely glanced at him over her shoulder. Their eyes met and a hot little shiver slid through her.

Hot little shivers? She'd been having those a lot lately, ever since the day she left the doors open and he saw way more than he should have seen.

It was so crazy, this growing awareness she had of him now, as a man. Like a secret between them, that was how it felt. A secret that created a forbidden intimacy, an intimacy that, really, was only in her mind. She *imagined* he felt it, too.

But she had no real proof of that.

None. Zero. Zip.

As a matter of hard fact, she kept telling herself, this supposed secret intimacy between them didn't even exist. It wasn't real.

So why did it only seem to get stronger, day by day?

"Da-Da!" Jake crowed and waved his favorite rubber duck.

Daniel came and stood over her where she knelt by the tub.

She looked up, over his long, strong legs in dark blue denim, past the part of him she really needed *not* to focus on, to his broad, deep chest, his thick tanned neck, his sculpted jaw. All the way to those eyes staring down into hers.

A weakness swept through her, delicious and hot. She wanted to reach up her arms to him, have him pull her to her feet and tight against his chest. She wanted his mouth on her mouth, hard and deep.

Seriously, what was the matter with her?

Why couldn't she stop imagining what it might be like—if he touched her in a man-woman way. If he kissed her. If he took off all her clothes and took his off, too.

It had to stop.

Nothing was going to happen between them.

She really needed to let this crazy new yen she had for him go.

"Go ahead and call your mother." He dropped to the bath mat beside her. "I'll finish up here."

"Great. Thanks." Did she sound breathless? If she did, she didn't think he noticed. She pushed herself to her feet and turned for the door.

As she went out, Frannie demanded, "Kiss, Da-Da. Kiss," followed by Frannie's usual lip-smacking sound.

Keely stifled a jealous groan. Oh, to be Frannie, to demand kisses of Daniel and have them instantly bestowed.

Not that she would be satisfied with the innocent kisses he gave his daughter. She would want deep kisses, wet and slow and long.

The kind of kisses she was never going to share with him, the kind of kisses she was not going to think about anymore.

Starting now.

She marched to her bedroom and grabbed her phone, punching up the contact for her mother and hitting the call icon.

It went straight to voice mail. She was leaving a quick, angry message asking Ingrid to call her back the minute she got this when the phone rang in her hand.

After Daniel put the kids to bed, he went looking for Keely.

He didn't have to go far. He found her sitting at her sewing machine in her workroom and tapped on the door frame to get her attention. She turned and gave him a strange little smile.

"You busy?" he asked.

She looked at the length of fabric in her hand as though wondering how it got there. And then she smiled at him—God, that smile of hers. It lit up her face. "Let's get a drink and sit out on the back steps," she said.

Warmth filled him. Even if he wasn't ever having sex with her, it was damn good to have her here in his house with him, someone smart and interesting and pretty to talk to after the kids went to bed. "Deal."

At the wet bar in the family room, he poured himself a scotch and she asked for cranberry juice with ice and a splash of vodka.

Outside, the air was damp and cool, mist creeping in

around the thick branches of the evergreens, shimmery and soft-looking in the golden glow of the in-ground lights dotted here and there around the yard. They sat on the deck, with their feet on the steps. Maisey, who'd come out with them, flopped down a few feet away.

Keely shivered, and he almost forgot himself and wrapped an arm around her.

Almost.

But not quite.

Instead, he grabbed a faded afghan off one of the deck chairs and draped it across her shoulders.

"Thanks," she said as he dropped down beside her again. She gathered the afghan close and sipped her drink. "Much better."

He stared off past the playset, along the bluestone path that wound through the clumps of landscaping out to the woodshed and the tree fort his father had built for him and his second and third brothers, Matthias and Connor, back before any of his sisters were born, when he wasn't much older than Frannie and Jake. "Did you talk to your mother?"

"Yeah." She said it on a sigh.

"Is she really coming?"

Keely nodded. "A week from Wednesday, she said. She got hold of a real estate agent, some friend of hers from way back, and bought the Sea Breeze." The landmark pub on Beach Street had been closed for several months now.

"She bought it sight unseen?"

"Yeah. She says the price was right and that it's been her dream for the last decade or so to come home someday and open her own place, that when she pictured that place it was always the Sea Breeze. She's going to settle in with Auntie G and fix up the bar, get it ready for business. She's aiming for a grand opening over the Fourth of July."

"Your mother is something else."

She nudged him with her shoulder. "And you mean that in the best possible sort of way, am I right?"

He was still kind of marveling. "Just like that, she buys a bar."

"She always knew what she wanted and how to get it—not to mention how to manage her money. No, she never got rich, but she's a good businesswoman. She paid for more than half of my college education. And I wouldn't have Sand & Sea or my cottage if she hadn't written me big fat checks when I needed them the most."

"All because of that band of hers?"

"Because of *her*, Daniel." Ingrid not only sang and played lead guitar. She was the owner and manager of Pomegranate Dream.

"I know. But still..."

"When members of the band dropped out, she replaced them and went on. When Pomegranate Dream stopped drawing big crowds, she booked them into county fairs, casinos and smaller clubs. She got her commercial driver's license and started driving the bus herself. She runs everything out of the bus. That keeps the overhead low."

"I thought you hated being raised on that bus."

"It wasn't all bad. Yeah, I always dreamed of a more settled kind of life than my mother ever gave me and sometimes she gets on my last nerve, but she's a dynamo and I admire her." Keely held up her glass and he tapped his against it.

He offered the toast. "Here's to Gretchen and Ingrid making it work."

She laughed. The sweet sound played along his nerve endings, stirring up all that yearning and hunger he kept trying to quell. When she put her glass to her lips, he drank, too.

And then he stood. Maisey got up, as well.

Keely tipped her head back and looked at him. "Going in?" He stared into those moss green eyes that he'd been seeing in his dreams lately.

"A few things I need to catch up on." Actually, those things could wait. But the temptation to touch her would only get stronger the longer he sat there. "I'll be in my study if you need me."

How about if I need you right now? Keely thought but didn't say. "Fair enough." She gave him a nod, then turned back to the fog-shrouded yard again. A moment later, she heard the back door open and the tapping of Maisey's claws on the floor. The door clicked shut.

The week went flying by. Keely had that opening at the gallery on Friday night. Daniel called the nanny service and got a woman to watch the kids all day Thursday and Friday, so that Keely could be at the gallery, making sure the group show was ready to go. And he came home from work early Friday to take over kid care from the temporary nanny. Keely was able to work straight through, grabbing a break at six in the evening to run home to her own little house by the beach and change into her favorite vintage teal blue cocktail dress and kitten heels.

By eight that evening, the gallery was packed with artists and their friends, supporters and family. Plenty of paying customers came by, too. The show did brisk business. Keely sipped a nice Oregon Pinot Noir, nibbled great finger foods provided by her favorite local caterer and enjoyed the party.

Aislinn Bravo, one of Daniel's sisters and Keely's longtime BFF, dropped by. Keely was older than Aislinn by four years, but she'd got to know all the Bravos back when Lillie married Daniel. From the first time they met, Keely and Aislinn had hit it off. The age difference hadn't mattered, even way back then. They'd always liked to hang out together. Then when Keely opened Sand & Sea, Aislinn had worked in the gallery for a while and the two of them had grown even closer.

Aislinn had a house not far from the beach. She raised Angora rabbits and made jewelry in her spare time, beautiful pieces that Keely was proud to showcase at Sand & Sea. But jewelry making was only a hobby for Aislinn. She liked variety in her work. She'd done everything, worked on local ranches and at the used-car lot on the south end of town. She'd even worked for Daniel at Valentine Logging, running the office for a while. Now she was essentially a legal secretary.

"So how's the law business?" Keely asked her.

Aislinn wrinkled her nose. "Boring. I think I need a job outside next. Maybe fishing, something on a salmon troller."

"Oh, I can just picture that."

"Hey. I'm a fast learner, and I'm not afraid to get my hands dirty—and how's it going playing nanny for my niece and nephew?"

"I adore them. They have me wrapped around their tiny pinkie fingers."

"Consider this my offer to babysit any weekend day or night that you need me."

"Thanks. I might take you up on that one of these days. So far, though, we're making it work."

"Daniel treating you right?"

"He's been great." *And lately he's driving me wild with unsatisfied lust.*

Aislinn laughed. And then she leaned closer. "You have a funny look on your face. What's going on?"

"Funny how?"

"Evasive much?"

Should she tell Aislinn? Ordinarily, Keely never held back with her best friend. But Daniel *was* Aislinn's brother and, well, it felt somehow awkward. Maybe even wrong.

Because really, wasn't it just a little bit strange for her to suddenly get a wild, burning yen for Daniel Bravo? Not only had he belonged to her beloved Lillie, he was not her type, all stalwart and solid. She went for the artsy guys, the charmers, the fast-talkers, guys like her ex-husband, Roy.

Aislinn watched her, narrow eyed. "That does it. You're hiding something. We need to talk. Lunch, I think. A *long* lunch. Next week's no good. They're running me ragged at the office with a couple of big cases. But the week after that...?"

Why not? By then, she might be totally over this bizarre fixation on Daniel. At the very least, she'd have plenty of time to decide how much to say. "Sure. I can get a sitter from the nanny service. Let's say tentatively Wednesday after next?"

"You're on."

Keely got back to Daniel's at a little after midnight that night. Slipping off her shoes as soon as she got inside, she locked up and turned to find him standing in the open doorway to his study, wearing his usual jeans and a flannel shirt with the sleeves rolled to the elbows, his shoulders a mile wide, muscled arms crossed over his chest, his eyes cast into shadow by the chandelier high above.

Like if Paul Bunyan was a sex god.

Nope. Not her type, no way.

Not her type, but…

More.

So. Much. More.

"How'd it go?" he asked.

"Really well. Good sales. A great crowd. Everyone talking and laughing at once. The kids?"

"We played a lot of peekaboo. I'm worn-out."

She laughed. She'd come to love his dry sense of humor, which she'd never even noticed he had until she'd come to live with him and the twins. "And then, after the peekaboo, the bath that never ends."

"All that splashing." He pretended to grumble.

"Exactly. And then you have to read to them."

"And they just *have* to turn the pages for you."

Maisey's claws tapped the floor behind him. She appeared at his side, plunking down on her haunches right there in the doorway.

Keely wanted to ask him to maybe go out back with her, sit on the deck. It was a clear night. They could count the stars, pick out a few constellations.

She might make a move on him.

Oh, God. She just might.

And where would that take them?

Somewhere wonderful—or straight to disaster?

"Good night, Keely," he said. Did she hear regret in his voice?

Or was that only in her coward's heart?

"Night, Daniel." She flipped her shoes back over her shoulder and headed for the stairs.

Ingrid arrived that Wednesday.

Keely took the kids over to Gretchen's to help out while Ingrid got moved in. Her mom had streaked her graying auburn hair with pink and blue. She looked good, Keely thought, slim and straight and strong as ever, in a giant purple Pomegranate Dream T-shirt with the arms ripped off over a sports bra and tropical print leggings, all that pink-and-blue-striped auburn hair piled in a sloppy updo, red Converses on her feet.

Gretchen started right in, ragging on her about her hair and her clothes. "Honestly, Ingrid. You're fifty years old. Your rock and roller days are over and that outfit is simply not age appropriate."

Keely's mom took her big sister by the shoulders and planted a kiss on her plump cheek. "My rock and roller days will never be over. And don't cramp my style. You know that never goes well—Keely, leave the kids in that playpen and help me carry a few things in from the bus…"

For the next few hours, Keely fetched and carried while Gretchen fed Frannie and Jake too many of the cookies that she never should have been on her feet baking in the first place.

Actually, it wasn't that bad. The kids didn't seem to mind sitting in the playpen while Gretchen fed them and fussed over them. And Ingrid sang as she worked, all the great old songs she and the band used to cover when they toured—"Wanted Dead or Alive" and "Crazy on You" and "Purple Rain." More than once, Keely found herself singing along.

As they made the bed in Ingrid's new bedroom with sky blue sheets and a fuchsia duvet scattered with gold stars, Keely's mom said, "How's it working out, the whole pinch-hit-nanny thing?"

"Really well." *Except for this insane burning lust I've developed for Daniel.*

"The gallery?"

"Runs like clockwork, no problems. I have a great manager, Amanda. And I get by there to check in and help out with whatever needs doing almost every day. I like it. I'm keeping busy."

"You always had a lot of energy."

Keely gazed across the brightly made bed at her mom. "I get that from you."

"As long as you're happy."

"I am."

"But you do seem a little on edge."

No way she was touching that. Keely plumped the hot-pink pillows and grinned like she didn't have a care in the world.

Ingrid let it go. "Well, all right. I'm here whenever you want to talk."

Uh-uh. Not happening.

She followed her mother back out to the bus to haul in more stuff and tried not to think about Daniel and this feeling she had for him that kept getting stronger. Denial wasn't working. Her body seemed to hum with yearning—to touch him. To get close enough to breathe in the scent of his skin.

Every morning she woke up freshly resolved to stop

this silliness. It was all just in her mind, and she'd had enough of it.

But then she'd go downstairs and there he would be at the breakfast table, spooning scrambled eggs onto the kids' high chair trays, answering, "Yeah, Jake," and "Okay, Frannie," at every new imperiously delivered toddler demand. Somehow, the guy who wasn't her type had slowly become the most desirable man in the world.

And her resolution to stop this idiocy?

Out the kitchen window every time.

That night, at eight thirty with the babies tucked in bed, Keely and Daniel sat in the kitchen, drinking coffee that would probably keep them awake way too late. It was raining out. Keely watched the raindrops hit the kitchen window and slide down like tears.

They'd been talking about mundane things—the lumber business, how she would need to have the part-time nanny back a few times this week. She'd got a couple of commissions to make wall hangings. One for a customer's living room and one for a bank in town that liked to support local artists.

And then they were quiet, both staring toward the dark, rainy window.

He said, "Lillie always loved the rain."

Keely nodded. "She said it made her feel cozy and safe, to be inside looking out at the rain coming down."

Another silence. She thought of the wedding portrait that hung in the upstairs hall—Lillie gorgeous in white lace and Daniel so handsome and young in a tux. Two people full of love and hope, with no idea of the ways they would hurt each other.

Keely realized she was holding her breath. With slow care, she let that breath go.

Daniel broke the quiet. "I would have said yes, to the kids, to Lillie getting pregnant. It wasn't…what I wanted. But I did want her to be happy."

Keely sucked in another breath and had to remind herself again to breathe out. It was one thing to talk about Lillie lightly, to remember her fondly—the things she loved, her habits, her quirks.

But what Daniel had just said? Not a light thing. Apparently he'd decided to stumble toward something deeper.

That should feel dangerous, shouldn't it? Or maybe just wrong.

But it didn't.

It felt…honest. Real.

Now Keely longed to reach across the table, to lay her hand over his. "She was *born* to be a mom. I mean, I've always wanted children, but if I never have them, I'll be okay. There's so much to life. I love my gallery, the work I do. My family. Friends. There are a lot of babies to love in the world, even if they aren't my own. But for Lillie, it was an imperative. A yearning in the blood."

"I know."

"Daniel, it was just so wrong that the one thing she wanted above anything was the thing she couldn't have."

A muscle twitched in his square jaw. "Sometimes in life you just don't get what you want. And given that having a child could kill her, I wasn't budging. No kids. We'd already lost my parents and one brother."

The lost brother's name was Finn. He was the fifth born, after Aislinn. He'd vanished on one of those trips that Daniel's parents were always taking. In Siberia, of all places. The family still had investigators searching for him. But a lot of years had gone by, so it didn't look all that likely that Finn would ever be coming home.

Daniel said, "I couldn't do it, couldn't stand to chance losing Lillie, too." He looked across at her, ice-blue eyes piercing. "I've always wondered…" Keely knew what he was about to ask. And then he did ask, "How much did she tell you?"

She couldn't lie about it. Not now. "A lot."

He fisted those big hands on the table between them. "I thought so. I…felt it. In the way you looked at me sometimes. Like you thought I was a real rat bastard, but I was family, so you were going to have to put up with me after all."

She shouldn't have chuckled. But she did. "I was mad at her, too. That she couldn't just accept that her body wouldn't do what her heart wanted so much."

His eyes. They saw inside her. They knew too much and they demanded to know more. "Keely. Tell me what she told you."

"That you were going to have a vasectomy, but she talked you out of it—and looking back, I don't know why that made me mad at you. Except that she also said you didn't want children. It really pissed me off that you didn't want what she wanted more than anything."

He shut his eyes and swore low, with feeling. "'You never know how things will turn out,' she said to me. 'Someday I might not be here.' I said I didn't care. I'd *had* my kids. I'd raised my brothers and sisters as my own. It was enough. I'd done my bit playing dad. I was done. But she kept after me not to do it. It seemed so important to her that I still be able to change my mind in some far, distant future, if something happened to her. So I let it go. I never got around to actually having the procedure." He stared at his own dark reflection in the rainy window. "I should have known what she was up to."

Keely's hands kept trying to reach for him—and then she just gave in. She reached.

And so did he.

They held hands across the table. His were big and rough and warm, and she wanted to feel them, touching her, running over her skin, learning the secrets of her body—and later, afterward, when they were both satisfied, she wanted his arms around her, holding her close.

He said in a low rumble, "I'm still so damn mad at her."

"I know." It came out in a whisper because her throat had clutched.

"I need to forgive her, but I can't forgive her. When we first got married, we used condoms and she used a diaphragm, too. We were so careful. But then her rheumatologist approved her for the low-dose estrogen pill. She was on it for years. I thought it was safe not to use anything else. She didn't tell me she'd stopped taking it until she was already pregnant. I thought the pill had failed and I was furious. I was going to go after her doctor, to sue the guy. That was when she admitted she'd stopped taking the pill. She tricked me. And it killed her."

Keely wanted to hold on to him forever. But if she kept holding on, well, how would she ever make herself let go?

Carefully, she eased her hands away. She wrapped them around her almost-cold coffee and sipped the bitter dregs. "There's no win in not forgiving her. You get that, right?"

"Win? What's any of this got to do with winning?"

"Daniel, what I'm saying is…" Okay, really. What *was*

she saying? She tried again. "I mean, you know about forgiveness, right?"

"What about it?" he demanded, gruff. Impatient.

"It's not for the forgiven. It's for the one who forgives. Until you forgive, you're a prisoner of your anger and resentment, at the wrong that's been done to you. But when you forgive, you don't have to be eaten up with anger anymore. When you forgive, you are set free."

"Who told you that?" He sounded almost angry.

She held his gaze. "My mother."

"The crazy rock chick who dragged you all over the country when all you wanted was to come home to Valentine Bay?"

"Ouch."

His expression softened. "Sorry. That was harsh."

"But also true. My mom does what she wants to do, and people get fed up with her. But she really does know stuff. She tells the truth as she sees it. And about forgiveness, well, I think she's got forgiveness right."

He pushed back his chair and carried his empty cup to the sink. "I'm going to bed."

Let me come with you...

Ha. Like that would ever happen. *She* might give in, definitely. But Daniel? Even if he really did want her as much as she wanted him, he would see all the ways things could go wrong. He wasn't the kind of man to take dangerous chances.

She gave him a soft good-night and sat alone for a while, thinking of Lillie, who loved the rain.

Lillie, who had betrayed her husband's trust to get what she wanted more than her life.

Chapter Four

Friday, Keely had the temporary nanny, Jeanine, watch the kids for the whole day. Keely worked all morning on the art-quilt hanging for the bank and gave Jeanine a break for lunch. When the nanny returned to take over with the kids, Keely went to the gallery for a couple of hours.

She stopped by Gretchen's before returning to Daniel's house. Ingrid was at the Sea Breeze, getting a start on the renovations she had planned.

Auntie G brought out the cookies, poured Keely coffee and complained about her housemate. "At least she's finally moved the bus to the bar parking lot. This is a *neighborhood*, Keely. People don't want giant purple vehicles cluttering up the street where they live—especially not when they have half-naked, pot-smoking women painted on the side."

Actually, the half-naked woman was Ingrid herself. More than twenty years ago, she'd talked the famous cartoonist R Crumb into drawing her—in ratty cutoffs and a low-cut tank top, clearly braless underneath, playing her Telecaster and smoking what looked like a big fat cigar, but according to Ingrid was a giant doobie. She'd had the image blown up bigger than life-size and used it to decorate her tour bus.

"I love your mother," added Auntie G, "but she can be so thoughtless sometimes. She plays her guitar at *night*. That's not right. I had to ask her this morning to please just go to that bar she bought when she has to… bang out a riff, or whatever it is she calls it when she beats on that old acoustic guitar of hers and wails at the top of her lungs."

Keely asked gingerly, "What are you telling me?"

Gretchen raised both hands out to the side and glanced toward heaven. "Sweetheart, what do you think I'm telling you? Your mother makes me insane."

"Are you worrying it won't work out, with her living here?"

Her aunt blinked in obvious surprise. "Whatever makes you think that?"

"Well, you do sound pretty annoyed with her."

"Of course I'm annoyed with her. She's very annoying, and she always has been. I knew that when we decided she would be coming home to live. It doesn't mean I don't want her here. She's my sister and I love her and she's going nowhere. We are going to learn to get along and support each other in our waning years."

Keely winced. "'Waning years'? I hope you don't use that term around Mom."

A sly smile curved Gretchen's pale lips. "Oh, but I

do and she hates it, too. She claims it makes her want to scream—"

"Wait." Keely put up a hand. "Let me guess. Because she's *only* fifty and about as far from 'waning' as a vital, brilliant woman can get?"

"Sweetheart." Auntie G's sly smile now had a smug edge. "I do believe that you know your mother almost as well as I do."

"So...no plans to kick her out then?"

"None. Don't you dare tell her I said so, but life is so much more interesting when your mother's around."

Sunday morning, Keely's mom called while she and Daniel and the twins were having breakfast. Keely barely got out a "Hi, Mom," before Ingrid was off and running.

"Gretch has got some potluck thing at her church this afternoon. She asked me to go."

"Well, that sounds—"

"Boring? Stifling? Mind-numbing? Tedious? All of the above?"

"So, then. Let me guess. You're not going?"

"You bet your sweet ass I'm not. I told her that you invited me to dinner up there at Daniel's. And then after I told her that, I realized it was a great idea. So what time are we eating?"

"Hold on." Keely muted the call and turned to Daniel, who was wearing a blue-and-black-plaid button-down, the blue of which made his eyes look like oceans— oceans she could happily drown in.

"What?" he asked.

She shook herself. "My mother wants to come to dinner tonight."

"Sure. Gretchen, too?"

"No, she's got something at church." Keely unmuted the call and said to her mother, "We like to eat with the kids, so it will be early."

"I knew when I decided to move home that nothing in my life would ever be civilized again."

"I'm rubbing my fingers together," Keely teased. It was an old joke between them. As a child, whenever Keely would whine about this or that, Ingrid would rub her thumb and middle finger together to signify the smallest violin in the world playing "My Heart Bleeds for You."

Ingrid released an audible sigh. "I raised you to be wild and free and sophisticated in a boho sort of way, to drink deep from life's bounteous cup. Instead, you live in the same small town where I was born, and you spend your days taking care of your cousin's toddlers."

"Hey. I own an art gallery and my work has been written up in *Oregon Art Monthly*. That's kind of sophisticated."

"I rest my case. What time?"

"Come at four, earlier if you want to. We'll eat at five."

"I'm driving Gretch to the potluck, dropping her off and then picking her up. The church gig is from four to six thirty, so the timing is perfect. I'll bring wine. Two bottles. Red or white?"

"You choose. We're having chicken."

"White then. See you about four."

Ingrid came early, armed with the promised bottles of Oregon Sauvignon Blanc. She joined Keely and the twins in the kitchen.

"It's pouring rain out there." She set the wine on the counter and then smoothed little tendrils of damp pink-

and-blue-streaked hair back from her forehead. "I'll just put these in the fridge, keep them cold for dinner." She grabbed up the two bottles again. "Where's Daniel?"

"He had to run out to the office." Keely slid a beautiful, plump roaster chicken into the oven. "Some minor detail he needed to deal with on a job that starts tomorrow. He'll be back in time for dinner."

Ingrid leaned over the playpen to give kisses to the twins.

Jake held up his arms to her. "Out. Pwease."

And she asked, "Is it okay if I release them from prison?"

Keely opened the cupboard to grab the rice. "As long as you watch them."

Ingrid took the kids out of the playpen and sat on the floor with them while Keely cooked. When they lost interest in the toys Keely had brought downstairs for them, Ingrid turned for the cupboards. She soon had a wide array of pots and pans, lids and utensils out on the floor and she was tapping spoons on the pans and banging pot lids together.

Keely watched her fondly, remembering her own little-girlhood, when Ingrid would use any object she could get her hands on to make music. Keely used to love that, banging things together to make loud sounds.

So did Frannie and Jake. They pounded and banged, laughing and shouting, while Maisey sat in the doorway to the family room, watching through those droopy eyes of hers and occasionally even throwing her head back to howl along with them.

Daniel came in at four thirty. He took over with the kids, and Keely's mom set the breakfast-nook table.

Everything was going so well, her mom chatting easily

with Daniel about how his various brothers and sisters were doing. He asked about the bar, and she filled him in on her plans to put a roll-up door in the wall that faced the beach so she could fully open the place up to the outdoors in good weather. Daniel uncorked the wine, and Keely put the kids in their chairs and tied their bibs around their necks. She gave them rice and cut-up chicken and cooked carrots in bowls along with spoons, because sometimes they actually managed to scoop food onto a spoon and get it into their mouths. She handed them their sippy cups of milk.

The adults sat down. Wine was poured and bowls were passed. The kids were focused on their food and acting like little angels. The conversation flowed easily—for a while anyway.

At what point did Ingrid start darting looks back and forth between Keely and Daniel?

Keely wasn't sure.

But when her mother asked, "What *is* this?" tipping her head to the side, eyes narrowed, like she had the scent of something she hadn't quite named yet, Keely got that sinking feeling.

Whatever her mom was thinking, Keely dearly wished that Ingrid might keep it to herself. Her mother often had intuitions and when she had them, they were usually right—and also mostly about the things no one really wanted to talk about.

"Chicken, Mom," she said, going for the obvious, hoping against hope that Ingrid really was only wondering about the food. "It's chicken and mushroom rice. I added a teaspoon of curry to the rice, to change it up a little."

"I don't mean the dinner, which is delicious." Ingrid gestured grandly at the meal before them and sipped her wine. "But no. This is not about the food." She lifted her glass in a silent toast, first to Daniel and then at Keely. "This is about the two of you…"

"Who two?" Keely demanded, though of course she already knew.

Ingrid sweetly smiled. "Oh, yeah. I'm getting a very strong vibe that you two are having some hot sexy times."

Daniel made a distinct choking sound. Keely sent a frantic glance his way as he coughed into his napkin. "Sorry," he croaked out, looking nothing short of stricken.

Keely longed to jump up and run out into the driving rain, run and run and never come back. Sadly, escape wasn't any kind of option. Besides, she'd done nothing wrong and had nothing to be ashamed of. Her mother was the one who was out of line. She yanked her shoulders back and took a valiant stab at outright denial. "Mom. Come on. Where do you get these crazy ideas?"

"Crazy? I think not. You should see your face. You look like a landed trout…" Ingrid widened her eyes and let her mouth fall open, an apparent imitation of Keely's expression. Then she actually had the nerve to laugh. "And now you are blushing. Oh, yeah. I'm right. I know I am." She reached across and patted Keely's hand. "Baby, come on. Lighten up. I'm on your side. I think this is simply wonderful, really! Daniel deserves a little pleasure in his life, and so do you."

Keely stuck with denial. "You're wrong, so wrong. And you're being ridiculous. Not to mention, you are embarrassing me."

Ingrid sipped more wine and refused to stop smiling. At least she was quiet. For the moment.

Too quiet. The faint sound of the rain coming down outside seemed to swell to fill the silence. Even the kids just sat there, little fists full of chicken and carrots, staring from one adult face to the other, not sure what was going on, let alone how to react to it.

Daniel spoke up then. "Oh, come on, Ingrid." His eyes still had that freaked-out look, but his voice? Wonderfully calm and assured. "Your imagination is running away with you. Keely's been amazing, taking over with the kids, doing a terrific job with them. We get along great, she and I. But that's it. That's all that's going on here."

Ingrid gave a lazy little one-shoulder shrug. "Well, if you're not having lots of fabulous sex together, you should be."

"Mother," Keely muttered. "Shut. Up."

But Ingrid just went blithely on. "Make hay while the sun shines, I always say. And I mean, whoa!" She pointed at Daniel and then at Keely and then back to Daniel again. Before Keely could remind her how rude pointing was, she let out a loud hissing sound. "Ssssssmokin'. You two could burn the house down with the heat you're generating."

Jake chose that moment to crow in delight. He grabbed his spoon, pounded it on his high chair tray and imitated his great-aunt. "*Sssssss!* Moke!"

Frannie took her cue from her twin. "*Sssssss!*" she hissed, then burst into giggles and pounded her hands on her tray. Rice and pieces of chicken went flying.

Ingrid laughed. "See? Even the kids know."

"You are out of your ever-lovin' mind."

"Oh, baby." Ingrid had the sheer gall to cluck her tongue. "Don't be ashamed."

"Ashamed? I'm not—"

"Sex is natural and right, and far too many of our

social norms are nothing more than ways to sap all the joy from life. You know that. I taught you that."

"Can you just drop it? Please?"

But Ingrid was on a roll. Keely purposely refused to even glance at poor Daniel as her mother replied, "No. No, I will not drop it. Not until I remind you both that life is too short *not* to do what comes naturally, and that it's nobody's business but your own if you find a little pleasure along the way—and wait."

Jake clapped his hands. "Wait!" he crowed, and Frannie clapped too.

"Is it Gretchen?" demanded Ingrid. "You're worried about Gretch?"

"Gwet," repeated Frannie experimentally and let out tiny cackle.

Ingrid huffed out a breath. "You think she's going to judge you for somehow 'betraying' Lillie?"

"Ingrid." In a careful, level tone, Daniel tried again to call a halt to this insanity. "Come on. The kids don't need to hear this."

"Oh, please. No harm is being done here. They're too young to understand anyway. As long as we keep the language clean and our attitudes civil, this conversation is totally kid-friendly—and where was I? Right. Gretch. If she's going to judge you for finding what joy you can in this life, well, that is just wrong and she will need to get over it. Lillie was a lovely woman and the world is emptier without her in it. But frankly, she's dead. Gretchen needs to accept that—not that I would ever say a word to my sister about any of this. What you two do in private is none of Gretchen's business anyway. It is nobody's business but your own—and did I already say that? Well. If I did, it bears repeating."

Silence.

Again.

At last.

Keely longed to throw in a snide remark to the effect that if it was their private business, what the hell was Ingrid doing butting in about it? But Keely knew her mother much too well. To challenge her would only set her off again. Thus, Keely settled on a soft-spoken "Tell us you're done, Mom. Please. Just tell us you're done."

Something wonderful happened then. Ingrid nodded. "Yes. I have said what I needed to say. The rest is up to you. Now, lighten up and pass the wine."

Ingrid kept her word. She didn't bring up the subject of Keely and Daniel and their "smokin'" attraction again.

She stayed for dessert, helped clear the table and played with the kids for a few minutes after that. And then it was time to go pick up Gretchen from church. Ingrid kissed the kids, hugged Keely, bade a fond goodbye to Daniel and breezed out the door.

Keely was thinking they would put the kids to bed and then maybe they could talk about her mother's cringeworthy behavior. She would advise him not to take her mom too seriously, reassure him that it really wasn't a big deal. They could clear the air about the whole thing.

But the minute Ingrid walked out the door, Daniel suddenly remembered he needed to go to the office again—at six twenty on Sunday night.

"Sorry," he said, his gaze skittering away from hers. "I know it's not right to leave you here to deal with the kids alone on Sunday night. You deserve a little time to yourself, but this is something I really should get handled before—"

"The kids are no problem, honestly. I'll put them to bed."

"I just forgot a couple of important things, and I really ought to get back over there and make sure that—"

"Daniel." She put up a hand. "It's okay. Just go."

And he went—practically at a run. It would have been funny if it wasn't so awkward and depressing.

No, Keely didn't really blame him for fleeing the scene. Of course, he would want to get away after the Sunday dinner from hell that her mother had just put him through. Really, he'd been a prince not to just get up, grab the kids and get out the moment her mother started in on them.

Maybe they would talk about it later. Or maybe they wouldn't. In any case, Ingrid had essentially promised not to bring the subject up again. She'd damn well better keep her word about that.

The kids sat on the kitchen floor gazing up at her expectantly.

"Bath time," she said.

"Baf!" Frannie sang out, and Jake let out a happy cry.

Keely took them upstairs, gave them a long bath and then let them loose in the playroom for a while, getting down on the floor with them, joining in as they played with their toys. As bedtime approached, she led them into her room and cuddled up with them on the bed to read them a few of their favorite stories.

By eight thirty, they were both asleep, one on either side of her. She took Jake across the hall first and tucked him into his crib, then went right back and got Frannie. Neither of them made so much as a peep as she crept from their room and silently shut the door behind her.

Without the kids to keep her busy, the house seemed

way too quiet. She stood there in the hall, listening to the distant roar of the rain outside, like a whispered secret in the quiet of the night.

What now?

Thoughts of Daniel came rushing in—the sadness in his eyes the other night when they spoke of Lillie. The freaked-out expression on his face tonight when her mother wouldn't shut up about the hot sex he and Keely ought to be having. The way he wouldn't even look her in the eye before he left tonight.

When would he be home? When he did come back, should she try to talk to him?

Or just let it be?

Until tonight, she'd pretty much convinced herself that he didn't need to know about this crazy crush she had on him, that she could take care of his babies and be his friend for as long as he needed her.

Really, she'd been thinking that this yearning she had for him would eventually fade. Sooner rather than later, she hoped.

Well, it wasn't fading. And tonight had been like that day he saw her naked all over again. She felt stripped in the worst kind of way. Revealed.

And she really didn't know how *he* felt. Sometimes, the way he looked at her, she was absolutely certain he had it bad for her, too.

But that could so easily be wishful thinking. He'd never even hinted that he wanted more than her help with the kids and maybe someone he could talk to. In fact, tonight at the dinner table, he'd laid it right out there. He'd told her mother that he appreciated her stepping up with the twins, that he enjoyed her companionship...

And nothing more.

She needed to stop obsessing about this.

Maybe she should work.

She wandered into her studio room and sat down at her sewing machine where her current project waited. With her index finger, she traced the shapes of flowers and starbursts she'd sewn into the fabric, flattening her palm on the material, feeling the metallic thread scratch at her skin.

How long had she been the twins' nanny? About a month. So quickly, she'd settled into a life here at Daniel's.

And her original plan to go home most nights? She'd given that up right away when the babies got sick—and then, after they got well, it had just seemed so much easier and more convenient to continue living here.

Convenience wasn't all of it, though. Not by a long shot. She loved it here in the big Bravo house among the tall trees on Rhinehart Hill. She loved taking care of Jake and Frannie, hanging out with Daniel for an hour or two every night, waking up in the morning to find him downstairs fixing breakfast, the twins already in their high chairs, waving their fat little fists full of Cheerios at her, demanding morning kisses.

With a wry smile, she rose and wandered to the window. Through the pouring rain, she stared out at the backyard, lit in smudges of gold by the lights dotted here and there amid the bushes, along the paths—one leading to the side gate and another that wound its way farther back, toward the rear fence. Way back there, a light glowed by the door to the woodshed.

Keely shut her eyes and leaned her forehead against the cool glass. Time to face the truth. The twins were not her children. And Daniel was not her man.

She didn't need to talk with him about the silly things her mom had said. She just needed to tell him he would have to start looking for someone else to watch the kids full-time.

As for working tonight?

Not happening. Her work required a steady hand and concentration. Right now, her mind was a hot stew of yearning and regret, and she felt shaky with emotions she had no business feeling.

No working. No waiting up to talk to Daniel. She'd have a nice long bath and take a good book to bed with her.

And tomorrow, she would tell him it was time for her to go.

With a soft cry, Keely sat up in bed.

The juicy hardcover romance she'd been reading flopped to the mattress and shut with a snap. She'd left the lamp on. She shoved her hair back off her forehead and glared at the clock.

Ten past midnight—and she'd heard something, hadn't she?

A strange sound had jolted her from sleep.

The kids?

She sat completely still, willing her racing heart to slow a little, not even daring to breathe, as she listened.

No sound from across the hall—let alone from the baby monitor right there at her bedside by the clock.

Not the kids then.

Thump-thump.

There. That. It was coming from the backyard.

Another thump, followed by a clatter.

Distant. Rhythmic.

Thud-thud. And then that faint clattering noise, like bowling pins toppling in on each other.

The thudding and clattering continued as she pushed back the covers and went to the window she'd left open a crack to let in the moist night air and the soothing, constant whisper of the falling rain.

She gazed out on essentially the same view she'd had from her workroom—the dark backyard, the bright smears of garden lights through the veil of the rain.

Thunk-thunk. Clatter...

Her gaze tracked the path through the trees, seeking the source of the sound.

She saw him then. Daniel. There. Revealed in the light by the woodshed door, shirtless and wielding a splitting maul in the pouring rain.

Thud. Thud. Clatter. The log sheared down the center and the two pieces tumbled from the chopping block into the mounds of split wood on either side.

Daniel...

No, she couldn't see him all that clearly, but she knew him by his height, by the breadth of his shoulders, the proud shape of his head.

And who else would be chopping wood in the backyard in the middle of the night?

Those poor logs. He attacked them without pause or mercy.

A tiny stab of guilt pierced her. She shouldn't be watching this. She should leave the man alone, let him work out his obvious frustration in his own way, undisturbed.

But, well, what else could be driving him but her mother's utter tactlessness at dinner?

Maybe something at work?

Yeah. That was more likely. Ingrid's big mouth might have embarrassed him, but shouldn't he be past that by now?

Whatever it was, she just couldn't stand to see him punish himself this way. And maybe, if she went to him, they could actually talk it over, get it out in the open, whatever it was.

Because however he felt or didn't feel about her as a woman, and whatever happened tomorrow when she told him she was leaving, he *had* called her a friend and she truly believed that he'd meant it. What kind of a friend was she if she just left him all alone out at the woodshed in the middle of the night? The least she could do was go to him, ask if he needed someone to talk to and then listen if he said yes.

Decision made, she whirled from the window, yanked an old green zip-up hoodie from the dresser and pulled it on over her pajama top. Barefoot, she opened her door to find Maisey right there, looking up at her expectantly.

"What? You want to go out?" She got a hopeful whine for an answer. "All right," Keely whispered. "Let's check the kids."

She tiptoed into their darkened room and leaned over one crib and then the other. Both slept like little angels— angels who were unlikely to wake up anytime soon. And she would be back within minutes, hopefully dragging the dripping, shirtless Daniel along behind her.

Off she flew, along the upper hall, down the stairs, to the kitchen and the mudroom beyond, Maisey trotting along behind her. Her red rain boots with the white polka dots were right there by the door. She shoved her feet into them, pulled the green hood up over her head and ran out across the back deck. Maisey trailed her down the wide stairs but stopped to sniff the bushes by the walk.

Keely went on alone, racing down the lighted path to the back fence.

Her boots made splashing sounds, but Daniel didn't seem to hear her coming. He just kept raising and lowering that maul. He was like a machine, turning to grab a log, plunking it on the block with a thud, cleaving it with a single perfect stroke—and turning for the next one as the pieces fell. Never once did he look up.

Dear sweet Lord, he was a gorgeous man, the beautiful, water-slick muscles of his shoulders and arms shifting and bunching beneath his skin as he set and attacked each log.

She stopped not ten feet away from him, her hoodie already soaked through, her pj's clinging wet. Still, he didn't look up.

"Daniel!" she shouted as he turned and bent to grab the next log.

He froze in midreach. And then, slowly, he rose to his height and faced her. Those ice-blue eyes found her, pinned her where she stood.

"Keely." His voice was a low, rough rumble, dredged up from the deepest part of him.

That did it. As he gazed at her, unblinking through the pouring rain, she knew the truth at last.

It was more than just her own wishful thinking and vivid imagination.

She wasn't alone in her need and her yearning.

Daniel wanted her, too.

Chapter Five

Daniel stood in the rain and stared at the soaking wet woman who'd made his house a home again, the woman he wanted now. Beyond all reason.

Of all the crazy things that could happen in life.

He wanted Keely, Lillie's little cousin, with the wide-set eyes and the soft mouth and the smattering of pale freckles across her pretty nose. He wanted Keely, wanted her so bad he'd cut and run after dinner because of the scary, true things that her mother had said.

Run off like a candy-ass to the office, where he sat for more than three hours, alternately staring at the far wall and playing "Space Invaders" on his phone.

Wanted her so much he'd come straight to the wood-pile when he got home, hoping to chop that want away.

It hadn't worked. Not even a little bit.

And now she stood there in her soggy pj's, drooping

hoodie and shiny polka-dot rubber boots, her eyes locked to his—and he wanted her even more now than he had when he ran away from her after dinner.

It was a whole conversation they shared, with not a word spoken, in the space of a few seconds, standing in the pouring rain.

She wanted him, too.

If he'd had any doubts on that score, the look in those big eyes when he glanced up and saw her standing there blew them clean away.

She wanted him. He wanted her.

And now, well, what the hell? Ingrid was right.

Nothing stood in their way. Why shouldn't they have each other?

The maul was heavy in his hand now. He almost dropped it where he stood. But the habits of a lifetime took precedence. A man looked after his tools. Afraid if he broke the hold of her gaze, she might just vanish— disappear like a dream, melt away in the rain—he backed to the woodshed, elbowed the door open a crack and set the maul inside, out of the wet. He pulled the door shut then, until he heard the latch click.

The rain beat down on her, but she didn't move. She had her head tipped up, watching him from under the soggy green hood, but she hadn't spoken except for that one word—his name.

Well, okay. Words were unnecessary at this point, anyway. She'd told him all he needed to know by the simple act of coming for him, of standing right there on the path back to the house, calling his name.

And he was tired. So damn tired of resisting, of coming up with reasons why having her wasn't right.

His shirt was around here somewhere. Where had he thrown it? He had no idea and really didn't care.

Keely. *She* was what mattered. He took a step toward her. She blinked but held her ground.

The rain beat down on him and he welcomed it. His body burned and each cool drop felt so good.

Another step. She swallowed, but she stayed where she was, watching him, unmoving, as though mesmerized by the energy that zapped back and forth between them.

Two more steps and he was there with her, staring down into those wide green eyes of hers. Slowly, in order not to spook her, he lifted his hand.

"Daniel." She said his name for the second time, in a whisper, giving it only her breath, but no real sound.

"Keely." And he touched her, touched the high, wet curve of her cheek. "Like velvet," he said. "I knew it would be."

"I, um, don't know if—"

"Shh." He pressed his finger to that mouth of hers, that mouth he was going to kiss all night long. "You do know."

"Oh, Daniel…" Her breath around his finger, sweet and warm. He wanted his tongue in there, in the heat and the wet. When he kissed her, he would coax her mouth to open for him, take that warm, sweet breath of hers into himself. "I don't know—"

"Yeah, you do. Come on, your mother knew it. We both know and we have known. Since that day you pushed back the shower curtain and stepped out of the tub without a stitch on."

"I shouldn't have left that door open."

"I shouldn't have barged right in. But so what, at this point? We did what we did."

"I was thinking, earlier, that maybe it's time I—"

"No."

"No?" She looked adorably bewildered.

"Forget about earlier." He eased his fingers under the soaked hoodie, along the silky curve of her neck, around to her nape, which he cradled in the palm of his hand.

"Forget?"

He nodded. "Let's just think about right now."

"Um. Okay." A soft, surrendering moan escaped those beautiful lips as she tipped her mouth up for him. "Okay," she repeated as his mouth closed over hers.

It was perfect, that first touch of his mouth to hers, the softness of her cold lips, the warmth inside, slick and welcoming, so good.

She smelled of some faint, tempting perfume and she tasted so damn sweet. Her nose was cold and her hair dry at her nape under the hoodie, like silk against the back of his hand, short little wisps of it curling under his fingertips.

Glad. He was so damn glad.

Glad in the way he hadn't been for years and years. Years of doing what needed doing. The right thing. The careful thing. Looking after everyone else, putting his own selfish desires aside.

Not tonight. Tonight, he would be selfish. He would take what wanted, and he wouldn't feel bad about it.

Because she wanted it, too.

The rain beat down on them, trickling out of his hair and into his face, his mouth. And hers. He could stand here just kissing her forever.

But really, a dry, warm room. A cozy bed.

That would be better.

Reluctantly, he broke the kiss. Pressing his forehead to hers, he asked her, "Come inside? With me, to my room, into my bed?" He thought his heart might explode as he waited for her answer.

"Yes," she said, and he could breathe again. "Yes, Daniel. Please. Take me inside."

"Done." He put a hand at her back and one under her knees and scooped her right up off the ground.

She let out a little screech of surprise, grabbing for him, wrapping her arms around his neck. And off they went along the winding path and up onto the deck, where Maisey waited under the deck cover, out of the rain. She bumped in ahead of them when he pushed open the mudroom door.

Once inside, he let Keely down so they could both toe off their boots. He took off his socks, too, and she draped her sopping hoodie on a free peg.

When she turned to him, he grabbed her hand and pulled her after him, through the kitchen, along the short hall to the living room, into the front entry and on up the stairs. They paused at the kids' room, just long enough to glance in and see that both of them were sleeping soundly. Maisey had a bed in there. She headed for it.

"Come on," he whispered and pulled Keely along to the big room at the end of the hall, tugging her in there, closing the door and then pressing her up against it to steal another kiss.

She moaned into his mouth, a needy little sound. Everything about her thrilled him, her soft, curvy body, her wet hair, the sweet, sexy sounds she made, the scent of her skin. He kissed his way down over her chin and licked the rain off her throat as she clutched at him, sighing, whispering, "Yes. Oh, yes..."

"I want to see you." He scraped his teeth down her neck, licked the tight, sweet flesh over her the points of her collarbone. "You taste so good. I can't believe this is happening." He fumbled with the pink buttons on her soggy pajama top. "I really need to get you out of these wet pj's..."

"Let me help you." But instead of getting to work on her own buttons, she went for his belt buckle.

He froze and looked down in total wonder at her soft, pretty fingers as they undid his belt and whipped it away, dropping it to the floor at their feet. When she glanced up, he would have kissed her again.

But then she asked, "Is your monitor on?" They had three receivers—one in her room, one in his and a third downstairs somewhere.

He commanded, "Do not move from this spot."

She laughed and gave him a playful shove. "Go. Do it."

He was back in a flash. "The damn thing is on. Now, about all these buttons..."

"What, these?" She went to work on the row of pink buttons down her front. Quick work it was, too. A moment later, he was sliding the soggy pajama top off her shoulders, revealing more gorgeous expanses of beautiful, smooth skin.

He said, "Beautiful." And he bent his head and took one dusky nipple into his mouth.

"Oh!" She wrapped her arms around him and pulled him close as he drew on the tightened bud, using his teeth just a little, flicking at her with his tongue.

But then she interrupted him, taking his head between her hands and pulling him up so they were face-to-face.

"What?" he complained.

"I forgot." She bit her lower lip and he wanted to take that mouth again, to kiss her right there where her teeth sank into the plump, tempting flesh. "We need condoms."

"I have some—and don't look so surprised."

"You're just so…"

He tried to glare at her but didn't succeed all that well. "Say it. I'm so what?"

"Upright?" she suggested. "Stalwart? Not a guy who has condoms handy, that's for sure."

He groaned, "You're killin' me here. And if you have to know, several months ago, I tried Tinder."

"No. Really?"

"Yeah."

"Daniel." She spoke in a hushed little whisper, like they were sharing a secret too delicious for anyone else ever to know about. "You hooked up with someone?"

"I made a date. As it turned out, the hooking up didn't happen, but I did get the condoms."

She giggled. He loved when she did that. Her whole face lit up. "You have to tell me all about it."

"Later," he growled at her. "Right now, I'm kind of busy." And he swooped down and covered those sweet lips with his.

That kiss went on forever. Her hands stroked his shoulders, gliding upward to wrap around his neck. She threaded those soft fingers into his hair.

And he? He got to go on touching her, first framing her wonderful face in his hands for a long kiss. But he didn't stop there. He needed to touch her. He needed to get intimately acquainted with every perfect, womanly inch of her skin.

He ran his eager hands along her neck, over the damp velvet flesh of her shoulders, down her arms and back up again. He palmed her waist. And when he pulled her in close and wrapped his arms around her, he got to feel those beautiful breasts against his chest as he traced the delicate bumps of her spine.

Her wet pajama bottoms were in his way. He shoved at them, impatient to be rid of them. The elastic waistband couldn't hold out against him. Down they went.

She was shivering as she stepped out of them.

He lifted his mouth from hers. "Cold?"

"Um," she replied, which could have meant anything. And then she surged up on tiptoe to capture his lips again.

"You're cold," he accused in the middle of that kiss. He clasped her waist and lifted her. Her bare legs went around him. He groaned at the feel of that, her thighs spread wide against his fly, his aching hardness pressing into the heat and wet of her, so close to where he couldn't wait to be.

Were they really doing this?

If this was a dream, please, please let him never wake up.

He kissed her as he carried her to his bathroom, set her down on the rug and groped for a towel.

She allowed him to dry her off, standing there without a stitch on, smiling at him, her eyes moss green and glowing as he used the towel on her hair first and then the rest of her, pausing now and then in order to scatter quick kisses across her skin.

He knelt to dry her thighs, to rub the towel a little

longer than necessary along the backs of her knees and down to her slender feet with their purple-painted toes.

When she stopped shivering, he tossed the towel aside. Sinking back on his bent knees, he looked up her body as she gazed down at him.

How could he resist a long, thorough touch? He trailed a slow hand up her shin, over her knee, along the firm skin of her thigh to the soft white pillow of flesh where her thighs joined. She was just so pretty. With that neat strip of hair, that tempting pink cleft.

He eased a finger into the wet heat of her. She sighed and a low moan escaped her. "More, please," she said, sweet and soft and oh, so tender.

Daniel gave her more, slipping another finger in, using his other hand to grasp her waist, to hold her in place while he touched her at will. And then, wanting even more, he leaned into her and used his mouth, too.

She signaled her approval with a hungry little cry as she widened her stance for him. He took full advantage, kissing her, touching her deeply, moving his fingers within her, trying to pick up every cue her body gave him, trying to show her how much he wanted her through sheer attentiveness to her needs.

It was amazing. It had been such a long time for him, years, since sex had been like this—a glow that got brighter, a hot shiver that kept getting stronger, burning wetter, quivering harder, a feeling of wonder, a pleasure so deep.

His body ached to have her, his hardness painful against the prison of his fly. But he wanted to make it last, take his time with her, to caress every inch of her, drink every drop.

Life could be so cruel sometimes. He might never get this chance again.

She came on his tongue. It was straight-on amazing, her smooth thighs wide, fingers fisted in his hair, her head thrown back, her slim neck straining as she moaned and begged him, "Please, yes. That. Like that…"

He stayed with her, drinking her, until the pulsing within her settled to a faint throb.

And then he commanded her, "Again."

She gasped. "Daniel. I can't."

"Yeah, you can," he insisted. "You are so beautiful, Keely. Like some miracle I never thought to find. And tonight, here you are. And I want to see you. All of you. How you are. What you do. Come for me. Again."

A wild laugh escaped her, followed a few seconds later by a plaintive little cry.

And then she was rising a second time as he played her, as he caught the rhythm she liked with his fingers. Shameless, he used everything he had—his lips and tongue and even his teeth to get her there, to make her go over, lose herself completely to his touch and the wet press of his hungry mouth.

That time, as the pulsing faded, he swept upward, catching her as she started to crumple. He gathered her into his arms and carried her to his bed, setting her on her unsteady feet just long enough to throw back the covers, then scooping her up again and laying her down.

She stared up at him, her damp hair spread out on his white pillow, her mouth soft and vulnerable, eyes full of stars.

Reaching into the bedside drawer, he found the strip of condoms he'd been absolutely certain would be out-of-date before he ever had a chance to use them. He tore one off and set it in easy reach. Then, with a grateful sigh, he ripped his fly wide and pushed down his boxer briefs along with his jeans, letting out a relieved sigh as his erection sprang free.

Stepping out of the tangle of soggy pants collapsed around his ankles, he went down to the bed with her.

"Daniel." She reached for him.

He stretched out beside her and pulled her close. "Kiss me, Keely."

And she did, a perfect kiss. The slow kind, nipping and teasing to start, then going deep and wet.

She touched him, running her hands over him, showing him that she felt as he did, that she couldn't get enough of touching his body. Perfection. There was no other word for this, just lying here with her, touching her as she touched him.

Talk about a dream come true.

Her fingers strayed over his hips and around to his butt. She grabbed on and squeezed so hard. Chuckling, he buried his nose in the velvety curve of her neck.

And then he bit her, right there where her neck met her shoulder. She was so ripe and tender, he needed a taste.

"Ouch!" She slapped him sharply on the shoulder.

"Sorry. I can't control myself. I just want to eat you right up."

"You already did."

They laughed together.

And then she took him by the shoulders and pushed him away enough to meet his eyes. "Daniel. I don't think I've ever heard you laugh before. At least, I haven't for a very long time."

What was he supposed to say to that? He had no idea.

So he said nothing, just cradled her head in his two hands to hold her in place for another kiss.

She wrapped her fingers around his aching length and she stroked him, slow strokes, her grip nice and tight. But he wasn't going to last long if she kept that up.

"Too good," he groaned at her and gently peeled her hand away.

She was the one who reached for the condom. He let her deal with it. She seemed to know what she was doing. Holding him in place, she rolled it down over him.

"Eyes on me," he whispered, taking her shoulders. Pushing her down to the pillows, he rose up over her and settled between her thighs.

This. Now. It was a moment to remember. Those green eyes holding steady on his, shining with heat and pleasure as he came into her.

She felt so good. Tight, giving way to him slowly, so he had to take his time. But slow was fine with him. Slow was just right—no, better than right. Pure perfection, the pleasure rolling over him, through him, threatening to take him down way before he was ready.

He guided a damp curl of hair away from her cheek. "You're so beautiful, Keely."

"Daniel. Is this real?"

He nodded at her slowly, holding her gaze. "I want to make it last forever. But I don't think that's going to happen."

She lifted her hips to him, drawing him deeper.

He groaned at the pleasure as it shimmered all through him, a pleasure that somehow skimmed the sharp, delicious edge of pain.

"Wait," he whispered. "Just for a moment. Just for a

little while, I want to be with you. Just for a little while, don't even move."

She licked those sweet lips of hers. And when she did that, well, he had to kiss her. He lowered his head and plundered her beautiful mouth.

And the stillness?

It just couldn't last. As he kissed her, she was shifting restlessly under him, raising her legs and wrapping them around him, pushing herself up him as he pushed into her.

They rolled, and she had the top position. He captured her face in his hands, holding her still so that at least she had to look at him, *know* him in this intimate way, feel him in her and with her as she rocked against him slow and deep, her folded legs pressed tight along his sides now, her breath all tangled, eyelids drooping.

"Keely. Look at me."

And she did. She looked right at him.

His finish barreled at him much too fast. "I don't think I can wait for you."

And then she gasped. Her eyes went wide. "Daniel!" He felt her climax throb around him.

That did it. With a strangled groan, he joined her, pushing up into her, hard and tight, as his release arrowed down his backbone, undeniable now.

What could he do but give himself up to it?

With a guttural shout, he surrendered, let his finish roll through him, let her sweet, pulsing heat take him down.

Chapter Six

Keely loved the tender way Daniel pulled the covers up and settled them around her, as though she was infinitely precious to him.

He made her feel special. Treasured, somehow.

Daniel, of all people.

She'd just...never known.

He kissed the tip of her nose. "I know I'm being selfish, but I want you in this bed with me. I want you to stay here with me. I want to wake up beside you in the morning. And the next morning. And the morning after that. I don't want you to get up and go."

"I don't want to go either." But they were in uncharted territory here. Yes, they were both single and had every right to find comfort and pleasure together. Still. He'd belonged to Lillie for so many years. Keely just didn't know how the family would react. Lillie had died more than a year and a half ago, but for Gretchen, the pain of losing her only child lingered—and always would. How would she take it to see Daniel moving on? And with Keely, of all people? How would his brothers and sisters see it? She really couldn't predict what their reactions would be. With families, well, you just never could tell.

"So you'll stay?" He looked so hopeful. And very sexy, with his bedhead and his beard scruff and that mouth she wanted to kiss again and again.

"I'll stay," she said. "But I really think, at least for the time being, that as for telling the family that we're spending our nights together..." She sought the right words.

He found the words for her. "They don't need to know." And he laughed. For the second time that night. "You should see your face. I've surprised you?"

"Well, yeah. I mean, that was exactly what I was about to say. But I guess I was kind of afraid you would take it wrong."

"No. Uh-uh. This is between us." Now he sounded a little bit grim and a whole lot stalwart, very much the nonsmiling, laughter-averse Daniel she knew best.

She admitted, "It's only, well, I could do without another rant on the wonders of sex from my mother. And I have no idea how Aunt Gretchen will react, but at the moment, I'm not ready to find out. I can't see why we even need to deal with the family about it. Not right now at least. Not while it's all so new."

He smoothed a few errant strands of hair behind her ear. "It's just better..."

"If we keep it between the two of us."

"Da? Da-Da? Da-Da, Da..." It was Jake's voice in a lazy singsong coming from the baby monitor, luring Keely from sleep.

"Da-Da! Keewee!" Frannie joined in more insistently. "Up!"

Keely opened her eyes to find a sleepy Daniel watching her from the other pillow. He reached out, brushed the hair from her eyes and traced the curve of her ear with a lazy finger.

She gave him a slow smile. Wonder of wonders, he smiled back.

And to think, last night she'd been about to tell him it was time for her to go.

Well, forget that. As of this morning, she was going nowhere.

Everything had changed with that first kiss in the rain.

Now she knew that he wanted her, too. Hadn't he proved it in the most spectacular way?

She wasn't giving him up. Not until…

When? She had no idea. And she refused to get all tied in knots about how things would end up.

Right now, it was only beginning and it was glorious.

"What?" he asked gruffly.

"I was thinking that you and I have a thing now. A secret thing, just between the two of us. It's exciting. Also, kind of crazy."

He wrapped his big hot fingers around the back of her neck. "Just as long as you're not trying to tell me you've changed your mind."

A lovely shiver quivered through her. "No way. I'm in."

"Da-Da, now!"

"Coming!" he called, loud enough the kids could probably hear him even through the solid-core bedroom door. And then he spoke low again, just for her.

"I would love to lie around in bed with you for the rest of the day…"

"Me, too. But the kids are hungry and Valentine Logging isn't going to run itself."

That evening after they put the twins to bed, Daniel led her to his room again.

The night before had been spectacular. Keely hardly thought it possible that it could get any better.

But oh, my. It did.

Daniel was the very best kind of lover—attentive and patient. Kind of bossy, too. He could be tender, and he could be just a little bit rough. She loved the way he touched her, the way he said her name as he caressed her and when he was inside her.

As though she was everything.

As though there could never be anyone but her.

He kissed her as though he could never get enough of the taste of her mouth. And he smelled so good, clean and manly, like cedar branches, like the forest right after the rain.

Later, when they settled in with the light off, she stroked her hand down the beautiful muscles of his arm and asked about the woman he'd met on Tinder.

"What can I say, Keely? We both swiped right."

"But you said it didn't happen…" Her hand strayed downward, to his wrist, over the back of his big hand.

He spread his fingers, and she slipped hers between them. "You're sure you want to hear this?"

"Yes, please."

He made a low sound in his throat. "It's not all that interesting."

"Tell me," she demanded.

He muttered a bad word, but he did give in enough to mutter, "So we got on chat together."

She coaxed him. "And then?"

"She seemed nice. I bought condoms, and we met for a drink at the Hotel Elliott in Astoria." A port city near the mouth of the Columbia River, Astoria was about fifteen miles northeast of Valentine Bay. "I liked her," he went on. "She said she liked me, too, and she'd already taken a room. We went upstairs." He buried his face against her neck. "Never mind," he muttered, his breath so warm, his mouth brushing her skin in a way that made her want him desperately all over again. "I'm not telling the rest."

She pushed him away enough to look at him, to hold his gaze. "It can't be that bad."

He rolled onto his back and pulled her down on top of him, guiding her head to rest on the powerful bulge of his shoulder. She felt his lips against her hair. "I went into her room with her and she started to undress and I knew it wasn't happening. I put up both hands. 'Whoa,' I said. 'Hold on a minute.' She stared at me like maybe I'd lost my mind. And I said I was sorry, but this was a bad idea and I had to go."

"And...that's it? You left?"

"Yeah. She called me a few ugly names as I was ducking out the door..."

"Oh, Daniel." She pressed a kiss to his shoulder, and she felt his big hand on her head, gently stroking her hair.

"I should have known better. Because I couldn't, that's all. With a stranger, like that? That's just not me. I've been with Lillie. And now you. I need a woman I can talk to, a woman I can trust. I'm thinking that makes me kind of a dweeb."

She kissed his shoulder again. "Naw."

"Yeah."

Stacking her hands on his chest, she rested her chin on them. "Daniel, no dweeb looks like you."

"I'm a dweeb *inside*, where it counts." He petted her, running his hand down her hair some more, catching a random curl and wrapping it around two of his fingers. "God. You are beautiful."

"You're blinded by lust."

He wrapped her hair around his whole hand and then guided her up so her mouth was an inch from his. "You're beautiful. Don't argue with me."

"You are so bossy."

"And I think you like that."

"It is just possible that I might."

He kissed her. For a man who'd been with only two women, he sure knew what he was doing with that mouth of his.

The kiss led to yet more spectacular lovemaking. They didn't get to sleep until almost two.

"You look tired, honey." Gretchen slid the plate of snickerdoodles closer to Keely's elbow.

Keely took one. "You're a cookie pusher, Auntie G. You know that, right?"

"Enjoy, sweetheart." Gretchen had Frannie on her lap. Jake lay sprawled on the floor, hugging his favorite stuffed rabbit, staring dreamily up at the ceiling. "Your mother said she had a great time at dinner Sunday night."

Keely ate a bite of cookie and tried to judge how much Ingrid might have told her aunt—not a thing, she decided. First, because Ingrid knew nothing. And second, because Ingrid had clearly stated that whatever was or wasn't going on between Keely and Daniel, it was none of Gretchen's business.

"Mom seems happy," she said, "about how things are going with her plans for the bar and about living here with you."

Frannie dropped the rubber frog she'd been chewing on. Gretchen caught it and gave it back to her. Frannie stuck it in her mouth again, leaned back in her grandmother's arms and closed her eyes. "All in all, your mother and I are doing just fine. How about you, honey? You've been juggling kids and work and the gallery for five weeks now."

"It's going really well. I don't get home to my place much, but I've got my workshop set up at Daniel's and we found a dependable woman who fills in for me when I need her. I get in to the gallery several hours a week."

"Are you sure you don't need a break?"

"Absolutely."

"Because I'm getting around without the walker now, and I would be happy to start watching the kids again."

Keely hardly knew what to think. Here she and Daniel had this secret thing going on—and all of a sudden, Gretchen wanted to take over with the kids again? "Just give your foot the full eight weeks to heal," she said gently but firmly. "Then we'll talk."

Frannie was fading off to sleep. She dropped the rubber frog again.

Gretchen caught it and set it on the table. "I have to confess that I'm beginning to feel guilty. I'm afraid we're taking unfair advantage of you."

Keely asked cautiously, "We?"

"Daniel and me. Daniel, because you watch his children. And me, because I'm the one who roped you into this."

"I wasn't 'roped' into anything. You asked me to step in and I was happy to. I'm *still* happy to. I love watching the kids. Daniel pays me well. Honestly, I see no reason to fix what isn't broken."

Gretchen was frowning. "Sweetheart, you've always wanted a family of your own. How are you going to find the right guy if you're living at Daniel's, running yourself ragged taking care of my grandchildren?"

Keely tried not to scowl at the woman who was truly a second mother to her. Seriously, did Gretchen somehow *know* what was going on with her and Daniel?

But that made no sense. If Gretchen knew, she would say so. Wouldn't she?

"How many ways do I have to say it?" Keely pasted on a smile and put real effort into keeping her tone even and low. "I love taking care of your grandchildren. I'm not feeling overworked in the least. And what's this all about anyway?"

Gretchen's blue eyes seemed guileless. "This?"

"Aren't you the one who's always telling me I have plenty of time for marriage and a family?"

"Well, of course you do. It's only, as I said, I'm beginning to feel guilty, that's all."

"Don't. I mean it. There is absolutely nothing for you to feel guilty about."

"But you have your own life, and how can you live it if you're up there at Daniel's all the time? It's not right."

"Auntie G, I'm perfectly happy. I have everything I need up at Daniel's. If things get to be too much for me, I will tell you. I promise."

"Has something got you upset?"

"What? No, of course not." *Except I'm having a totally*

torrid, amazing love affair with your son-in-law, and I don't know how you'll take it if you find out.

Gretchen had said she felt guilty. Well, Keely did, too. And there was absolutely no logical reason for her to feel that way.

Her aunt looked at her sideways. "You're sure you're all right?"

"I am. Truly."

"Daniel can be…difficult, I know. He's such a self-contained sort of fellow, so hard to get to know."

"He and I get along great. I mean that." *In more ways than you need to know.*

Careful not to jiggle the sleeping toddler, Gretchen reached across the table and laid a soothing hand on Keely's arm. "You know you can always talk to me about anything that's bothering you."

"Thanks," Keely said, trying really hard to mean it. "I love you, Auntie G, but there's nothing to tell."

The next day, Jeanine came to watch Jake and Frannie from eight to three.

Keely headed straight for her doctor to get a prescription for the pill. From there, she went to her hairdresser for a cut and a color change to strawberry blond. Then at noon, she met Aislinn for lunch at Fisherman's Korner, a cozy diner on Ocean Road.

They both had the fish and chips—the absolute best anywhere—and tall iced teas.

Keely had just swallowed her first incomparable bite of beer-battered Albacore tuna when Aislinn started in on her.

"I love your hair that color. It really sets off your

eyes—and, Keel, why do I have a feeling you've met someone?"

Keely tried her best to look totally unconcerned. "I have no idea what you're talking about."

"You've got one of those faces."

Keely ate a french fry. "One of *what* faces?"

"An honest face. An open face. A face that currently has a definite I-am-getting-it-good sort of glow."

Keely let out a groan. "'Getting it good'? Ew."

"Well, you do. Now. Tell me everything."

Keely had to press her lips together to keep from doing just that. No, she did not want Gretchen to know, but she *did* want to confide in Aislinn. She'd had three true, forever friends in her life so far, the kind of friends to whom she could bare her soul: Lillie, lost to her now. Meg Cartwell, who'd recently moved to Colorado and married the love of her life. And Aislinn.

But Aislinn was not only her BFF, she also happened to be Daniel's sister. Keely had promised Daniel she wouldn't say anything to anyone in the family.

But maybe if she just didn't say *who* the guy was…

Aislinn shook malt vinegar onto her fish. "Come on. You know you're dying to tell me." She set down the vinegar and sipped her tea. "And I'm not leaving this booth until you come clean."

"Okay, fine." Keely leaned closer across the Formica tabletop and confessed gleefully, "There's someone—and that's all I can say."

"Ha! Yes! I knew it. Who?"

Keely picked up another crunchy-crusted, perfect piece of fish. "What did I just say? I can't tell you."

"Omigod!" Aislinn burst out. "No!"

Keely flinched back. "What?"

"I just had a horrible thought."

Keely groaned, "Aislinn. What thought?"

"Is he married? Is that it?"

Keely was still clutching the uneaten piece of fish. Now she dropped it back in the basket without taking a bite and grabbed a napkin from the dispenser at the end of the table. "Married?" She wiped the grease from her fingers. "Please. After what Roy did to me, do you actually think I would turn around and do that to another woman? You know me better than that."

Aislinn slumped against the red pleather seat. "I'm sorry. You're right. Forget I asked. That question was more to do with me than you." A few years back, Aislinn had fallen for a married man. Nothing had happened between them, but she'd been totally nuts for the guy and miserable over it. "Of course, you would never get involved with a married guy."

"Damn right I wouldn't—and you didn't either, so stop beating yourself up about it." Keely picked up the piece of fish again. They ate in silence for a few minutes.

But Aislinn hadn't given up. "Come on. Tell me. Who *is* this guy you're seeing?"

"I *can't* tell you. Not right now."

"Why?"

"It's all new, you know? We just want to be private. That's all. For now." Did that sound lame? Yeah. Maybe. A little.

And Aislinn wasn't buying it. "Okay, I get that you don't want to wander down the street talking about the guy to complete strangers. But you can tell *me*."

"Aislinn, come on. What I will say is that I'm crazy about him and he's terrific. He's steady and good. And totally hot."

"Steady?"

"Well, yeah."

"But you never go for the steady ones."

"Hey. Give me some credit. I'm thirty years old. About time I grew up and fell for a responsible, trustworthy human being for once."

Aislinn's eyebrows had scrunched together. "I know him, right? If I didn't know him, why not just tell me who he is?"

"Ais, stop. I told you I can't say—"

"Wait." Aislinn picked up a french fry, studied it as though for clues and then bit it in half. "Really, with the kids and the commissions and the gallery, you don't have *time* for a man." Now she was sounding way too much like Gretchen.

Keely tried to look stern. "I can see I shouldn't have told you anything."

"Get outta town." Aislinn plunked her half-eaten french fry back in the basket, leaned forward and peered hard at Keely as though she couldn't believe what she saw. "No." She sat back again.

"No, what?"

"No, it can't be."

"What are you babbling about? Will you chill?"

Aislinn stared at her piercingly and accused, "It's Daniel, isn't it?"

Keely barely escaped choking on the bite of fish. She swallowed hard and washed it down with a big gulp of cold tea before launching into a stammered denial. "No. Uh-uh. I don't, um… No. Not Daniel. Absolutely not."

Aislinn so wasn't buying it. "Uh-huh. Daniel. Has to be. Makes total sense. You're around each other all the time. You *live* together. And I can see how you two would be good for each other. You can help him lighten up a little. And for once, you've found a guy with both feet on the ground, a guy you can actually count on. I mean, it was probably bound to happen, if you think about it."

"What? No. Wrong—I mean, not necessarily."

Aislinn laughed. "You are blushing. It's so cute. Cop to it. It has to be Daniel. You're all alone in that big house together every night after the twins are in bed. And you told me at the gallery a week and a half ago how *great* he is." Keely opened her mouth to spout more denials, but Aislinn just shook her head. "Don't lie to me, Keel. It will only hurt my feelings, and I won't believe you anyway."

Keely let her shoulders slump. "I don't *want* to lie to you."

"Hey." Aislinn reached across the table. Keely stared at her outstretched hand. "C'mon." Aislinn wiggled her fingers. "Gimme." With a giant sigh, Keely reached back. They laced their fingers together, palms touching. As they stared at each other, Keely felt acceptance settle over her, that her best friend had figured it out, that it wasn't a *bad* thing, that Aislinn knew her so well—far from it. Keely was grateful to have such a good friend. After a long moment of mutual silence, Aislinn asked softly, "You really like my big brother?"

"I do. I really do."

"Well, all right then." One corner of Aislinn's mouth kicked up in a half smile. "Let's finish our fish." They focused on the food until Aislinn glanced up again. "He *is* a good guy."

Keely nodded. "The best."

"Too bad he's got that poker up his butt."

"Stop!" Keely slapped at her friend with her napkin.

"Hey. It's only the truth. Maybe with you, he can relax, enjoy life a little."

"It's all really new, Ais. We're kind of feeling our way along as we go."

"I just want you to be happy. Both of you."

"Thank you—and I really don't want anyone else to know."

"Keely, I promise you. Nobody's going to hear a thing about it from me."

As soon as the kids were in bed that night, Daniel did what he'd been waiting all day to do. He took Keely's hand and led her down the hall. In his room, he shoved the door shut with his foot and reached for her.

Her happy laughter filled his head as she kissed him. He walked her backward toward the bed. But before they got there, she pushed him into the bedside chair.

He caught her hand. "There is no escaping me." With a tug, he pulled her down across his lap. She laughed again and wrapped her arms around his neck. He couldn't get over how right it felt—the two of them, together. After too many years of just doing what he had to do, he had something really good to come home to at night. He had Keely.

And that was pretty damned amazing.

He nuzzled her neck and breathed in the perfect scent of her skin. She was wearing way too many clothes, though. And she didn't need that big clip holding her hair off her neck. He undid it and set it on the bedside table. Her hair drifted down in soft waves to her shoulders.

"I like this new color," he whispered, combing his fingers through the red-gold strands.

"It's pretty close to my natural color."

"I know. And it suits you." He caught her chin on his finger and guided her closer for a kiss, claiming that mouth he couldn't seem to get enough of. She tasted as good as she smelled.

When the kiss ended, she rested her head on his shoulder. "I had lunch with Aislinn today."

Something off in her tone alerted him. "She okay?"

"She's fine. But she, um, knows about you and me."

Aislinn knows.

It wasn't anger he felt, exactly. More like frustration. He wanted this thing with Keely to be just theirs, for the two of them alone and no one else. The family owned him. It was all about them and had been ever since he was eighteen years old.

With Keely, for the first time in forever, he felt free. He didn't want the family butting into that, bringing demands, making judgments, feeling cheated or disapproving that he was crazy for Lillie's little cousin and wanted to spend every moment he could with her.

He just wanted to come in this room with her and have the world disappear. At least for a while, he wanted her all to himself, wanted everyone to leave them the hell alone.

She pressed two soft fingers to the space between his eyebrows. "You're scowling at me."

He took care to keep his voice level when he answered her. "I thought we agreed that, for now, we won't tell the family."

She hunched her shoulders, put her hands between her knees and chewed her lower lip a little. "I didn't tell her. She figured it out." He wasn't sure what to say to that, so he didn't say anything. Keely chided, "Aislinn's not only your sister—she's my best friend, Daniel. She knew there was someone, and she guessed it had to be you. And I just couldn't outright lie to her. So I didn't. She promised to keep our confidence. I believe her."

He really couldn't blame her for breaking their agreement. He *didn't* blame her. She and Aislinn were tight. "Okay, then."

"What does that mean?"

"It means I see your point." He traced the line of her hair where it fell along her cheek. "You can't go telling lies to your best friend. Aislinn *is* someone who keeps her word, so she's not going to say anything. And I'm being completely selfish anyway. I want you all to myself."

She looked at him then, that mouth he couldn't get enough of kissing soft and pliant, eyes so bright. "I kind of feel the same. Like this should be *our* time, just you and me. Most people get a little space to get to know each other when they start something together. The families don't enter into it until things get serious."

Serious.

To him, this *was* serious. He didn't really know how to be any other way.

"There's something else," she said.

"You're frowning." He pulled her closer, kissed her cheek, nuzzled the tender corner of her delicious mouth. "Whatever it is, it can't be all that bad."

"It's not. Not really. But I didn't tell you yesterday, and it's been bothering me. I took the kids to see Gretchen."

"You mentioned that."

"Yeah, but what I didn't say was that she got after me to let her take over again with Jake and Frannie. She even said she felt guilty, that she was taking advantage of me."

He had to order his arms not to lock tight around her.

No one was taking her away from him, not Gretchen. Not anybody.

But she *had* been taking care of his children for weeks now. It had to be getting old. So really, Gretchen had a point. He made himself ask, "Maybe it's getting to be too much for you?"

That got him an eye roll. "Of course not. I love it here. I love the kids. I'm getting everything done that needs doing, with my work and at the gallery. It's all going great for me."

Suddenly, he could breathe again. But was he being unfair to her? "You're sure?"

She turned a little, caught his face between her hands and kissed him quick and hard. "Yes, I am sure."

"Well, all right then." He caught her hand, opened her fingers and pressed his mouth to the soft center of her palm.

But when he looked up, a frown still crinkled her forehead. "There's more. It wasn't only that Gretchen said she worried about taking advantage of me. She also started talking about how she knew I wanted my own family. She asked how I thought I was going to accomplish that while taking care of your kids and living in your house. I don't know. I couldn't help wondering if she suspects that we're together and she doesn't like it."

"She's pretty outspoken. If she knew, I think she would say so."

"You're right. It was just odd, that's all. Think about it. You and I get together. We decide to keep what we have to ourselves, to have a little time just for us—and suddenly Gretchen, who asked me to take care of the kids in the first place, thinks I should be moving on."

He hated what he knew he had to say next. "Okay.

Maybe we're handling this all wrong. Maybe we're just going to have to be up-front about what's going on between us after all. Let anyone who's going to get weird about it go ahead and have at it. Then we can move on from there."

Her gorgeous smile bloomed wide. "I love that you said that. But you know what? I just don't want to do that. Not yet. Do you?"

"Hell, no," he replied with feeling.

"Well, then. It's decided. We'll go on as planned— for a while, at least. And we'll reevaluate as necessary." She snuggled close again.

"Deal." He rested his cheek against her hair and felt way too relieved they weren't immediately inviting the family into the middle of their business.

She fiddled with the top button of his shirt, her head tucked nice and close, over his heart. "This weekend should be interesting…"

It was Easter weekend. Grace would be home Friday. And Sunday, they were planning the kids' first egg hunt, with a big family dinner in the afternoon.

Keely tipped her head back to meet his eyes. "I'm assuming you don't want to tell Grace about us yet?"

"Please no," he answered fervently. "If we tell her, she's way too likely to blab to everyone. Or get mad at me."

"Why would she get mad at you?"

"As if she needs a reason. One way or another, Grace always ends up pissed off at me."

Her soft mouth twitched. A definite tell. She wanted to lecture him but didn't know how it would go over. "Grace is young and she wants to be free, and to her it seems like you're the one holding her back."

"I *am* holding her back. She doesn't need to be free until she's at least forty—preferably fifty."

Keely gaped. And then she giggled. "Daniel. You actually do have a sense of humor."

He put a finger to his lips. "Do not tell a soul. I have a certain image to uphold."

"You mean the one where they all think you're crabby and uncompromising?"

"And narrow-minded and controlling—oh, and did I mention I never crack a smile?"

That had her grinning. "What in the world do I see in you?"

"I'm handy around the house, good with babies and amazing in bed."

Her cheeks got pinker. He loved to watch her blush. "True." She nodded. "On all counts. And we're agreed that we're not telling Grace yet?"

"We are agreed, yes."

She slipped his top shirt button from its hole. Finally. "You know that means I won't be staying all night with you while she's here? We'll have to be careful or she'll find out, whether we're ready for that or not." She undid the second button.

"That does it." He took her hand and guided it down to button number three. "I changed my mind. We're telling Grace."

"No, we're not." Button number three gave way, and four and five, as well. "We deserve our privacy for as long as we want to keep what we have just between us. And it's only for Friday and Saturday. She goes back to Portland Sunday." She undid the last button. "At which time we can go back to being secret lovers in a full-time kind of way." She sat up enough to work the shirt off his shoulders.

"I don't know. Waking up without you..." He took her red knit top by the hem and pulled it up. "I don't think I can do that." She raised her arms so he could pull it off over her head. Underneath, she wore a pretty pink bra. He made short work of that, undoing the hooks at the back and tossing it aside. Her breasts were so beautiful. He cradled them, felt her hard little nipples pressing into his palms. She moaned—and jumped off his lap. "Get back here," he commanded.

"So bossy..." But she did come back, swinging one slim thigh across him, straddling him, so his growing hardness pressed right where he most wanted to be— well, except that her jeans and his jeans and two sets of underwear barred the way. He cradled her breasts again. "Oh, Daniel..." She was suddenly breathless. He loved that about her, when she got breathless and wanting, when she looked at him through heavy-lidded eyes the way she was doing now. He rolled those pretty nipples between his thumbs and forefingers, and she let her head drop back, all that glorious red-gold hair tumbling down behind her. "Daniel..."

"Yeah?"

"Um. What were we talking about?"

"Not a clue," he said rough and low, sliding his hands to her waist, lifting her as he stood and setting her on her feet long enough to get rid of her jeans and her panties, her shoes and socks.

He *had* to kiss her. As much of her as possible. Gathering her close again, he pressed his lips in the center of the five freckles on her left shoulder that seemed to him to make the points of a star. He scraped his teeth along her collarbone, licked his way up the center of her throat, over her strong little chin until he reached that plump mouth of hers. She opened for him on a happy sigh.

But only for one too-brief moment. And then she was dropping away from him, folding to her knees in front of him.

She had his jeans undone and down around his ankles in seconds. The woman amazed him. How could he have thought he knew her for all these years and years?

He'd known so little.

And she was so much more.

He put his hands in her shining hair, holding on for dear life as she took him inside that warm, wet mouth of hers. All the way in, right down her smooth throat. How did she do that?

Not that he cared how. What mattered was that she was here, in his room, with him. What mattered was that touching him, kissing him, taking him inside herself, driving him crazy with want and need, seemed to please her every bit as much as it pleased him.

It was too much in a very good way, what she did to him. He didn't last very long. His mind shattered along with his body, into a thousand happy, smiling pieces.

He forgot about everything—all the bits of his life and his family's lives that he was responsible for. He let it all fade away, the million and one little things he had to keep a constant eye on so that no new disaster could strike those he loved.

With her, he could just let go. With her, at last, he knew what it felt like to be free.

Chapter Seven

Grace arrived on Friday at ten in the morning.

She burst into the kitchen where Keely had the kids in their high chairs for a morning snack.

"Munchkins, I am home!" Cheeks pink and white-blond hair windblown, Grace dropped her giant shoulder bag and overstuffed pack to the floor.

The twins beat on their tray tables in glee at the sight of her. "Gwace! Gwace! Kiss, kiss!"

She went to them for hugs and sticky kisses. Then she turned to Keely. "Oh, look! It's my favorite nanny." She whipped Keely's sketchbook and colored pencil right out of her hands and plunked them on the table.

"Hey!" Keely laughed in protest. But Grace only pulled her out of her chair and waltzed her once around the kitchen, not letting her go until they were back at Keely's chair again.

"God. I'm starved," Grace announced as she knelt to give Maisey a good scratch and a hug.

Keely picked up her sketchbook and pencil and reclaimed her seat at the table. "You want breakfast?"

"Had that, thanks."

"There's tuna salad in the fridge."

"Dave's Killer Bread?"

"Got that, too."

"I love you, Keely. You have all the right answers to the most important questions." Grace got busy gathering what she needed for a fat tuna sandwich, including Tillamook cheddar slices, tomatoes, lettuce and dill pickles. "Old Stone Face at work?"

"Yep."

"How you holding up watching the little darlings day after day?"

"So far, spectacular."

Grace popped a hunk of pickle into her mouth. "I can't believe you're still here, that you've yet to run screaming into the night."

Keely chuckled as she added shading to the mountains in the background of the wide, green field she was sketching, the artist in her hard at work planning how she might create a similar, but more striking effect with fabric and thread. "What can I tell you? I have zero complaints—how's school?"

Grace launched into a monologue about the co-op she lived in, how much she loved studying Shakespeare's relevance to the modern world and how the guy she'd met last Saturday might be driving up to party with her and her friends this weekend.

By the time she finished her sandwich, scooped up her stuff and disappeared into her room, the kids were getting restless in their high chairs. Keely wiped their gooey hands and faces, and took them and Maisey outside for a while.

When she came back in, Grace had emerged from her room. She offered to watch the kids. Keely took her up on it. Promising to return by two, she grabbed her purse and headed out to check in with Amanda at Sand & Sea.

She left the gallery at one and swung by Gretchen's. Keely's aunt was baking like a madwoman in preparation for the family get-together Sunday. Ingrid was nowhere in sight.

Gretchen waved a flour-dusted hand. "She's off at that bar. Have you been by there?"

"No. I keep meaning to stop in."

"Well, go anytime. Your mother will be there. Not that I'm complaining. We get along best, your mom and me, if we're not around each other too much—and have you given any more thought to what we talked about the other day?"

"If you mean my finding someone else to watch the twins—"

"That is exactly what I mean—have a cookie, sweetheart."

Keely took one. They were chocolate with chocolate chips. "Amazing. I think I gained ten pounds just from this first bite."

"You look great. You can afford a cookie or two—and I do still want you to think about letting me fill in with them at least some of the time."

"What did we already decide? You get the go-ahead from your doctor, then yes. I would love a few hours off every once in a while."

Gretchen released a long, drawn-out sigh. "I do worry about you, honey. You deserve a break now and then."

"I have plenty of time to myself."

"Not enough. I'm going to have to talk to Daniel about it."

That did it. Keely knew she had to speak up. "Auntie G, don't you dare."

Gretchen sent her a wounded look, her pink mouth drawn down. "You don't have to snap at me. I have your best interests at heart."

Keely took her aunt by the shoulders and turned her around so she could look her squarely in the eye. "You and I both know how Daniel is."

Gretchen wiped her hands on her apron. "What do you mean?"

"He takes on everybody else's burdens. And that means he has plenty to deal with. He doesn't need you whispering in his ear about how I want him to find someone else for the kids. It isn't true, and it will only worry him. That's just not right."

"I would hardly be whispering," Gretchen muttered. Then she sniffed and lifted her round chin. "I only want what's best for you."

Keely's heart seemed to expand in her chest. It was an ache, but a good kind of ache. "Auntie G…" She wrapped her arms around Gretchen. "I know you do."

Gretchen sniffed again. "You're going to get flour all over that pretty sweater of yours."

"I don't care." She pulled back enough to give her aunt a smile. "And you have to let it be. *I'm* the one who gets to decide what's best for me. And I mean it when I say that I'm enjoying myself with Frannie and Jake. I will have no problem telling you and Daniel when and if I've had enough."

"But…you're happy? You mean that?"

"Yes. I'm very happy with the way things are right now, and I have no plans to make a change."

They made it halfway through dinner that night before Daniel and Grace got into it.

It was the same thing they always fought over. Grace wanted to go out with her friends, and Daniel wanted her to stay in.

"Gracie," he said, and Keely tried to take heart that at least he spoke in a mild tone. "You just got here. We've missed you. It's not going to kill you to stay home tonight."

Grace let out an exaggerated groan. "God. You drive me insane. I've *been* home all day, and I haven't seen Erin or Carrie in weeks. Plus, there's this guy I met in Portland. He and a couple of his friends are driving up, meeting us at Beach Street Brews." The brewpub on Beach Street served local craft beers.

"What guy?" Daniel's voice had gone distinctly growly.

Grace blew out an angry breath through her nose. "His name is Jared Riley. He goes to Reed. I like him, all right? Daniel, come on. He's a great guy and he's driving all the way up here and I'm looking forward to seeing him. And Erin. And Carrie. Okay?"

"I just think—"

"Don't." Grace leaped to her feet. The twins startled in unison at her sudden move. "Just don't. I do not want to hear it." And with that, she shoved back her chair, whirled on her heel and ran across the kitchen, straight to her room, slamming the door good and hard when she got there.

The slammed door scared Frannie. She burst into tears. Jake saw his twin crying and let out a yowl.

Keely and Daniel rose as one. She took Jake. Daniel took Frannie. They both delivered soothing reassurances and comforting hugs until the kids stopped fussing and were ready to go back into their high chairs.

Daniel returned to his seat. Keely stayed right where she was. He didn't notice she'd remained on her feet until he'd picked up his fork again.

"Okay." His fork clattered back to his plate. "What?"

"I've got to say something." She took extra care to make her voice even and drama-free. "You need to give this up, Daniel."

"Give what up?"

As if he didn't know. "This...overprotectiveness with Grace."

"I'm not—"

"Could you just not go straight to denial, please?" Keely waited to make sure he was listening. After he'd glared at her for a solid ten seconds, she continued, "Yes, you *are* overprotective. I get that it's for all the right reasons and you love her and you want her safe. I get that she's the last of your brothers and sisters to strike out on her own and that even if you can't wait for that to happen, you're still going to miss her when she goes."

"I—"

"Uh-uh. Not finished."

He took a long drink of water. "Right. Wrap it up."

"Thank you," she said and tried to mean it. "I get that you want to protect her, that you feel it's your job to keep her safe. But then again, she *is* twenty-one. She sets her own hours and takes care of business just fine while she's in Portland. The first thing she did when she arrived today was offer to watch the kids so I could run errands. It's not right that you still treat her like a child when she comes home."

"I don't…" That time he caught himself in middenial. He drank more water as Jake let out a string of nonsense syllables. Daniel set down his glass—and surrendered in a growl. "All right. I'll talk to her after dinner."

"Wonderful." Keely sank to her chair. As she smoothed her napkin on her lap, she heard a door open. Grace appeared, unsmiling but composed. She returned to the table and sat down again.

"I'm sorry I lost my temper, Daniel," she said. "I promised myself I would stop doing that."

"Ahem," Daniel said stiffly. "I came on pretty strong. Apology accepted."

"Thanks." Grace sat up straighter. "And I *am* going out after dinner."

Daniel scowled. Keely braced for him to start barking orders again. Instead, slowly and carefully, he cut a bite of pork roast. "Just be safe," he muttered, adding with great effort, "and…have a good time."

Grace left at a little after eight. By eight thirty the kids were in bed, and Keely enjoyed a glorious few hours in Daniel's bed.

He caught her arm when she tried to get up to go at a quarter of midnight. "Stay. I don't like it here without you. Grace probably won't come in until after two, and there's no reason she'll come up here when she does."

"Uh-uh. Either we tell her or we don't. Setting ourselves up to get caught is just beyond tacky. She doesn't need that and neither do we."

"Sometimes you're too damn reasonable," he grumbled.

She chuckled and cuddled in close, just for a minute more, nuzzling his broad chest with its perfect light dusting of gold hair and that wonderful happy trail she wished she could stick around and follow to her favorite destination. Again.

He tipped up her chin and kissed her. She savored the moment. And then, with a playful shove, she rolled away from him and out from under the covers.

He braced up an elbow and watched her pull on her jeans and shirt. His eyes, silvery in the lamplight, sent shivers down the backs of her knees.

"Don't look at me like that," she chided.

"Like what?"

"Like you're thinking about all the naughty things you're going to do to my body."

"But I *am* thinking of all the things I want to do to your body. Come on back here. Let me show you."

Somehow, she made her bare feet carry her to the door. "Night," she whispered as she slipped from the room.

Her bed felt huge and empty with just her in it. It took her a long while to get sleep. She wondered if she and Daniel were doing the right thing to make a secret of what they had together. And she marveled that everything about what she had with him felt so good and real and right. As though they were perfectly suited, each to the other. As though this was a love affair that would never wear itself out.

Saturday night Grace went out again. Keely and

Daniel stole some precious time alone. She left him at midnight for her too-empty bed, where she lay awake again, missing him, though he was just down the hall— missing him and hoping that this thing between them would never have to end.

Was she being ridiculous? They'd only been lovers for a week.

Didn't matter.

She knew her own heart, knew she was falling. Falling hard.

And scary-deep.

Easter morning, Gretchen and Ingrid arrived at ten thirty with a big basket full of old-school dyed eggs, a cake and a few dozen cookies, plus an array of side dishes to go with the prime rib roast Keely would serve for the main course.

Keely and Daniel helped the sisters bring everything in from the car as Keely tried not to let nerves get the better of her. She dreaded that her mother might start in about the "smokin' hot" chemistry between her and Daniel.

But Ingrid never uttered a single embarrassing word or cast Keely so much as a meaningful smirk. She must have actually meant what she'd said last Sunday night— that what went on between Keely and Daniel was nobody's business but their own.

Gretchen kept the kids entertained while Ingrid, Daniel and Keely hid the eggs out in the foggy backyard.

Aislinn arrived with a salad at eleven, about the same time Grace emerged, sleepy-eyed in pajamas and a giant floppy sweater. Outside, the fog had thinned a little.

Grace poured herself a mug of coffee and followed the rest of them out back.

At first, Frannie and Jake seemed unsure of the whole egg-hunting concept. Ingrid and Gretchen led them around pointing out the bright eggs, many of them in plain sight. And the twins would look up at their grandma and great-aunt, their faces simultaneously curious and confused.

But eventually, they seemed to catch on, laughing and holding up their prizes as they found them. The hunt went on for over an hour, mostly because the twins tended to get distracted. They would plunk down on the grass and put their fingers in their mouths until Gretchen or Ingrid got them up and moving again. By noon, they'd started fussing. Keely took them inside for a little lunch and a nap, leaving Aislinn and Grace to gather the rest of the eggs.

More Bravos arrived. Harper and Hailey, who shared Aislinn's rambling beach cottage with her when they were home, hadn't made the three-hour-drive back to Valentine Bay for the holiday, but Daniel's brothers, Matthias, Connor and Liam, appeared. There was also a great-aunt and uncle, the eccentric brother-and-sister duo, Daffodil and Percy Valentine. The two were the last of the Valentines, the founding family for which Valentine Bay had been named. Neither Aunt Daffy nor Uncle Percy had ever married, and they both still lived in the house where they'd been born. A slightly crumbly Italianate Queen-Anne Victorian, Valentine House sat on a prime piece of real estate at the edge of Valentine City Park. Aunt Daffy kept a beautiful garden, and Uncle Percy considered himself a genealogist as well as something of an amateur detective.

At two, when they all sat down at the long table in the dining room, Keely felt wonderfully relaxed and happy. All her life, she'd dreamed of a big family around her. This, now, today? It felt a lot like her dream come true.

Gretchen said grace. When the soft *amens* echoed around the table, Keely couldn't help but look to Daniel first. He gave her the most beautiful, private, tender smile. She glanced away quickly, so no one would see.

That evening, Grace returned to Portland and Keely slept again in Daniel's bed.

By Wednesday, Keely had been on the pill for a full week. After they put the kids to bed that night, she and Daniel had the contraceptive talk. He'd only been with Lillie and Keely. And she'd been tested after she broke up with her last boyfriend two years ago. They agreed it would be safe to go without condoms.

But then Daniel shook his head. "I would just feel better if we used both." He looked kind of sad when he said it.

And she understood. After Lillie's betrayal, Daniel was unlikely to trust his partner to take responsibility for contraception. They continued to use condoms, which was totally fine with her.

The next week, at the very end of April, Daniel left for Southern Oregon to meet with timber owners near the California border and to look in on several jobs in progress along the way. It started out as a two-day trip, but there were issues at one of the mills and with a few employees in key positions on two current jobs. Two days stretched to three and then four.

Gretchen insisted she was well enough to help out with the kids, and she did seem to be walking just fine without even a cane. She came every day and stayed for three or four hours, giving Keely a break to work in her studio or stop in at Sand & Sea. On the fourth day, Ingrid pitched in, too, so that Keely could concentrate on getting everything ready for a new show opening at the gallery on Friday.

With her aunt and mom helping out, Keely had no trouble keeping on track workwise. The nights were lonely, though. She missed the delicious, perfect pleasure of Daniel's big hands on her body, not to mention the addictive wonder of his kiss and the feel of his muscled body, so warm and solid, right there beside her as she slept.

And yes, she spent her solitary nights in his bed. Somehow, it wasn't quite as lonely in his room as in hers down the hall.

Thursday night he called to say he wouldn't be home until Saturday. They talked for two hours—about his work and hers, about Frannie and Jake, about how well it was going for her because she had Gretchen and Ingrid taking up the slack.

"I want to take you out," he said. "Find out what night Jeanine's available, and then I'll make dinner reservations. There's this great place in Astoria…"

Astoria. Because as long as they were keeping their true relationship from the family, they'd be safer to take date night somewhere out of town. Same as he had with the woman he'd met on Tinder—and yes, she knew that what she had with him was so much more than a hookup.

They really needed to talk about coming out to the family. The secrecy was starting to wear on her nerves.

"Miss you," he said gruffly as they were ending the call.

I love you. The three little words filled up her mind and created a sensation of radiating warmth in the center of her chest. But she didn't say them out loud. A first *I love you* should not be said on the phone.

"Miss you, too," she replied. "See you Saturday…"

She felt the absence on the line as he hung up and she wanted to cry, of all the self-indulgent reactions. He would be home in two days. It was nothing to cry over. She grabbed his pillow from his side of the bed and pressed her face into it. It still smelled faintly of him, kind of piney and fresh.

With a groan, she tipped her head toward the ceiling. "Get ahold of yourself," she commanded out loud, tucking the pillow behind her head and dropping onto her back, feeling mopey and bereft and achy all over.

Hormones? Not likely. She was on the pill now. Her periods on the pill tended to be regular and pretty much mood-swing, bloat- and pain-free.

And it wasn't her placebo week anyway. There were two more weeks to go until her mild, pill-controlled period was even due.

She ordered herself to stop being a big baby and put all thoughts of weird hormone swings from her mind.

Friday, she ran around like a madwoman, handling the hundred and one final details before the new gallery show. It was all worth it, though. The opening went off beautifully.

Saturday, Daniel came home while she and Gretchen were out in the backyard with the twins. Gretchen hung around until dinnertime and then stayed to eat.

Which meant that at seven thirty that night, when Gretchen finally left, Keely still hadn't felt Daniel's big arms around her or enjoyed the taste of his mouth on hers.

They all—Daniel, Keely and the twins—stood at the front door, waving as Gretchen drove away.

The twins loved to wave goodbye. It was, "Bye-bye, Gwamma! Wove you!" from Frannie.

And "Bye-bye, bye-bye!" from Jake.

As Gretchen's enormous silver Escalade sailed off down the driveway, Daniel shut the door. "For a while there I was scared to death she planned to stay the night." Every inch of Keely's skin seemed to spark and flare at the way he looked at her—like she was everything, like he couldn't wait to get her alone and take off all her clothes.

"Baf!" demanded Frannie.

"Baf now!" Jake concurred.

Which was great. Wonderful. The sooner the twins had their baths, the sooner they could all go to bed— Jake and Frannie, to sleep.

Daniel and Keely, to make up for lost time.

They all went upstairs together and straight to the big bathroom. The kids were out of their clothes and into the tub in record time.

"I can't stand it," Daniel muttered.

"What?" Keely sent him a worried glance as he rose from the side of the tub, grabbing Keely's arm and pulling her up with him. "Not having you in my arms."

He hauled her close and kissed her forever, melting her heart and incinerating her lady parts, while Frannie and Jake laughed and splashed and demanded kisses of their own.

A great moment, Keely thought, one that almost made up for not being free to run to his arms that afternoon,

when he'd first stepped out on the back deck to tell them
he was home.

With obvious reluctance, he let her go. The kids finished in the tub. Daniel and Keely dried them, diapered
them and put on their pj's.

The twins were pros at the pulling of heartstrings.
As soon as they had their pajamas on, they wiggled and
squirmed, demanding, "Dow! Now!"

Once on their feet, they ran to the bookcase, each
returning with a stack of favorite kids' stories.

Daniel sat in the rocker, one child on either arm, and
read them four stories.

Finally, by the end of *Goodnight, Goodnight, Construction Site*, the twins could hold out no longer. They
slept in that endearing way little kids do, heads hanging
like wilting flowers on a stem, lower lips sticking out,
drooling just a little down their pajama fronts.

"We have to go ahead and tell them, tell the family,"
Keely said breathlessly ten minutes later.

They were in Daniel's room by then, with the door
shut at last. He'd already whipped her shirt up over her
head and taken away her bra and was in the process of
pushing her denim skirt to the floor, her panties along
with it. She kicked off her shoes and she was naked.

"God, I missed you." He grabbed her close.

She wanted to get closer. He helped by picking her
right up off the floor so that she could wrap her legs
around him. He braced her against the door and kissed
her until she feared her lips might fall off. And oh, she
could feel him, so hard and ready, pressed against her so
intimately, but with his pants and boxer briefs in the way.

She wanted him naked, too.

But she *needed* him to listen to her first. She really did have a point, and she was going to make it.

Fisting her hands in his hair, she yanked that amazing mouth of his away from her. "Listen." She tried to glare at him in a purposeful manner, but she knew her cheeks were flushed and her eyes low and lazy. Even her breathing betrayed her. It came in ragged, hungry little gulps. "I mean it."

"You're so beautiful. I need to kiss you. Kiss you all over. Come back here…"

Somehow, she managed *not* to give in to him. She kept that tight grip on his hair and turned her lips away so he couldn't take them. "When are you going to be ready to tell the family about us?"

"Soon," he said, and a strangled groan escaped him. And well, how could she resist that, when he groaned that way, as though it would kill him stone-dead not to have his hands and mouth all over her?

"Daniel," she moaned. And that did it. He claimed her lips again. And oh, she had missed him, and they had a lot of lovemaking they needed to catch up on. Days' worth, seriously.

She was practically love starved. They needed to get busy making up for lost time.

With another moan, she pressed her mouth to his.

Incendiary, that kiss, a hot tangle of breath and seeking tongues. It went on forever as she unbuttoned his shirt and pushed it off his shoulders. He had a white T-shirt on underneath, darn it. She wanted him closer, needed skin on skin.

Grabbing a fistful of T-shirt on either side of him, she scraped it upward. He let her down to the floor again so she could drag the shirt off over his head.

"There now. Better." She sighed as she pressed her hands to his broad, hot chest, gliding them upward to clasp behind his neck. She dragged that mouth of his down to hers again.

They kissed some more—endlessly, gloriously—as she went to work on his belt and his pants.

Finally they were naked—except for his socks. Luckily, socks had no bearing on what she was after.

He lifted her again. Neither of them could wait. He slid right into her, right there against the door.

Heaven. Paradise. Her arms around him, holding him tight, joined with him at last.

He groaned, broke their never-ending kiss and pressed his forehead to hers. "Forgot…"

She remembered, too, then. "The condom."

"I shouldn't have…" He let that thought trail off. Another low groan escaped him. "Keely. You feel so good." He kissed her chin, the side of her throat. "It should be okay." He kissed the words onto her skin. "Right?"

She was on the pill. Of course, it should be fine.

"Okay?" he asked again—well, more like pleaded, really.

She took him by his square jaw. "Yes." And she kissed him, kissed him so deep as he moved within her. "Missed you," she whispered against his mouth.

"Keely. Me, too. I missed you so much…"

And then all actual words were lost to them. They rocked together, with her wrapped tight around him. They rocked and swayed in perfect rhythm.

Nothing else mattered then. Except that he was holding her, so close, so perfectly.

Her climax came spinning at her, rolling like a river

of heat and wonder, down her spine to the core of her where she held him, rocked him, home with her at last.

Alone together, Keely and Daniel.

Right where they belonged.

Chapter Eight

The days went by.

Full days. Happy ones.

Friday night Jeanine came to babysit, and Daniel took Keely to dinner in Astoria. The meal was lovely. He ordered a nice Oregon Pinot Noir. Her stomach had been acting up on and off for the past few days, so she didn't have more than a sip or two. Daniel teased her about being a lightweight and she shrugged and agreed with him.

After dinner, they strolled the Riverwalk, holding hands like lovers do, watching the big boats out on the majestic Columbia, even wandering out onto the East Mooring Basin boat ramp to get a look at the lazy sea lions that had taken over the docks there. It was wonderful.

They didn't get home until after midnight. They

thanked Jeanine and sent her on her way, then went upstairs hand in hand, to check on the kids, who slept like little angels, feathery eyelashes fanned across their plump cheeks.

An hour later, tucked up nice and cozy together in his big bed in the dark, Keely said, "I want to tell the family that we're a couple. I know it will probably be awkward. But, Daniel, we really need to do it."

Daniel agreed with her. "We *will* do it. Soon." He went on, "Sometimes it feels like all my life, I've never had anything that was just mine. Everything's about the family, and it has been since I was eighteen. You and me, here, now, in this room with the door closed? It's just us, Keely. You and me and no one else. I'm jealous of that. Protective of that."

She captured his hand under the covers and wove her fingers with his. "It's only that I'm getting tired of lying, you know?"

"We're not lying. We're just…not sharing."

She laughed at that and then she warned, "Before you know it, Grace will be home for the summer and living in this house with us. If we're not telling her, we'll have to start sneaking around again. No more waking up together every morning."

He kissed the tip of her nose. "We've got two weeks till then. Don't rush me, woman." With a low growl, he pulled her closer and bit her lightly on the chin. "Give me a kiss."

She laughed again and kissed him and that led where kissing him usually went—to more kisses and endless caresses and a satisfying ending for both of them.

Later, as she held him close and listened to his breathing even out into sleep, she decided that she would stop pushing him to tell the family about the two of them. He wasn't ready yet, and she needed to give him time. She would leave the subject alone until he brought it up.

She grinned to herself in the darkness. He just needed the proper motivation. Once Grace got home and he got a taste of sleeping alone again, she had a feeling he'd see telling the family in a whole new light.

The following Saturday, they went out again. Jeanine wasn't available that night. But they got someone else from the nanny service instead. Daniel took her to a great seafood place in Cannon Beach. She watched his beloved face across the table from her as they waited for their food. He looked relaxed. Happy.

She was happy, too—except she was in her placebo week on the pill now and her period hadn't come. It didn't mean anything. It would probably come tomorrow or the next day. She felt kind of puffy and crampy and that was a good sign that everything was on schedule.

Except that she'd never got preperiod cramping when on the pill in the past.

She just wanted to tell him about her silly worries. Just open her mouth and say it. *My period's a couple of days late and I'm a little concerned about that...*

He probably wouldn't look all that happy then.

No. Uh-uh. Not doing that.

She would wait. Her period would come. If it didn't come, she would buy a test and take it before she brought it up to him. Then she could joke about it. *Guess what? I had a pregnancy scare! Isn't that hysterical?*

She had a feeling he wouldn't find even a scare all that humorous. He loved his kids, but they hadn't been his idea. Not by a long shot. He'd wanted a little freedom at last now his brothers and sisters were grown. But Lillie had got pregnant anyway—and then lost her life for it. The poor guy had some serious baggage around having babies.

That she might have to tell him they had another baby on the way?

Uh-uh. That fell squarely into the category of things she very much did not want to do.

And why was she fixating on this? She wasn't pregnant. She was a few days late, that was all.

Thursday, her period still hadn't put in an appearance.

At eleven, her mom came over to watch the twins for her.

Ingrid took one look at her and demanded, "Okay. What's wrong?"

"Wrong?" There was nothing wrong. Okay, yeah, she was maybe obsessing over the possibility that she might be pregnant. Just a little. But how in the world could her mother sense that? She stared at Ingrid's high green ponytail and deep purple bangs. "I'm fine. A little tired, I guess."

"You're lying. I can tell. I always could."

"No, I am not lying," she lied.

"Yeah, you are. But you don't want to talk, I get that. When you do, I'm ready to listen. You know that, right?"

"I do, Mom. And I'm grateful."

Ingrid fiddled with her bangs. "You like the purple and green?"

"I do. Purple and green works for you."

"Gretch hates it." Ingrid chuckled.

"And that means you love it even more, right?"

"No, I love it because it looks super bad in a very

good way. Gretch hating it is just a little extra bonus that makes me smile."

"I do not understand your relationship with Auntie G."

"And there's absolutely no reason you have to understand, so don't worry about it." Jake toddled over and held up his ragged stuffed bunny. Ingrid scooped him into her arms. "You are the handsomest little man, Jakey."

"Kiss my wabbit." Ingrid kissed the ugly stuffed toy on its matted face.

Keely bent to pet Maisey, who was always following her around. "Okay, I'm outta here." She picked up Frannie, planted a kiss on her cheek and set her back down. "Bye, Frannie-Annie."

"Bye, Keewee. Wove you."

"Back by three," Keely promised.

"No rush," said her mother as she bent to let Jake down.

Keely ran errands, including a quick trip to Safeway, where she bought three pregnancy tests.

No, she did not think she might be pregnant. But if her period didn't come by the weekend, she would take the tests just to prove to herself there was nothing to worry about. She bought three because it never hurt to triple-check, and if the first test came up positive, triple-checking was exactly what she planned to do.

So what if false positives were extremely rare? Negative or positive, she would test and test again, just to be sure.

At lunchtime, Keely sat across from Aislinn at Fisherman's Korner and longed to tell her best friend everything.

But she just couldn't, not about this.

Daniel was Ais's brother after all. Once he knew—*if* it turned out there was anything *to* know—then she could confide in Aislinn. Until then, laying her crazy worries about possibly, *maybe* being pregnant on Daniel's sister felt beyond unacceptable.

Keely had been kind of afraid that Aislinn, like Ingrid, would know she had something on her mind.

But Ais seemed distracted. And Keely was the one who ended up asking, "What's wrong?"

"It's that weird old Martin Durand. Remember, I told you about him?"

"I remember." Durand owned a horse ranch, the Wild River Ranch, inland on the Youngs River. Aislinn had worked there as a stable hand one summer, back when she was still in college.

"He called me—Martin Durand did—this morning, at Deever and Gray." That was the law firm she worked for. "I had no idea the old guy even knew I had a job there. I mean, I've seen him like twice since that summer I worked for Jaxon at the ranch." According to Aislinn, Jaxon Winter, the nephew of Durand's deceased wife, had been responsible for the actual running of the ranch for years. Jaxon also just happened to be the married man Aislinn had fallen so hard for once.

"What did Durand want?"

"He said, 'Hello, Aislinn. This is Martin Durand. Jaxon's divorce is final, in case somehow you didn't know.'"

"Jaxon Winter got divorced?"

"Yeah. Over a year ago."

"You already knew?"

"So?"

"Well, I just thought—"

"Keel. I told you. There was nothing between us. It was all in my mind—now, is it okay with you if I tell you the rest?"

"You don't have to get mad at me."

Aislinn huffed out a breath. "You're right. I'm sorry. I'm just freaked about that call and overreacting is all."

Keely reached across the table of their booth to clasp Aislinn's arm in reassurance. "It's okay. What else did he say?"

"He laughed. Like Jaxon's marriage not working out is funny, somehow. And he said, 'It's been final for a year, Aislinn Bravo. Just in case you might not have heard.' He put this weird emphasis on *Bravo*. 'Aislinn *Bravo*,' he says, like I'm living under an assumed name or something. I mean, that's creepy, right?"

"So Martin Durand knew that you had a thing for Jaxon Winter?"

Ais flinched. "I guess so, but I don't have a clue how he knew. Keely. I swear to you. I mean, it was five years ago. Jax was *married*. Nothing happened."

"Of course it didn't."

"I worked for him for eight weeks one summer. That's it. Once the job was over, Jax never called me. And I never called him. Yeah, I really, um, liked him. I got the feeling maybe he liked me, too, but I think I just wanted to think that, because of how I felt. When I heard he got divorced, it just seemed better to leave it alone—and what business is it of Martin Durand's anyway?"

"It's not his business, not in the least." Keely wiped her greasy fingers on her napkin.

"I hardly knew that old man, never exchanged more than a few words with him. But he always used to look at me funny—kind of like he was keeping an eye on me, you know, waiting for me to sneak in the house and steal the silverware or something? And I swear, he let poor Jax do all the work. Old Mr. Durand would get up at noon and sit on the front porch of the main house in his bathrobe. One of the other hands told me that Jax is his heir because Durand and his wife never had kids of their own and the ranch belonged to Mrs. Durand in the first place and Jax was *her* nephew, so at least Jax gets something eventually."

"I'm happy to hear that. And you know, maybe the old guy was just trying to help out."

"Help out how?" Aislinn demanded, scowling.

"Whoa." Keely patted the air between them. "Back it up. I mean, maybe he was kind of playing cupid a little."

"When he called today, you mean? Ew."

"Hey. I'm just trying to look on the bright side here."

"There is no bright side. That old man is scary." Ais set down her tea glass harder than she needed to. "And I do not feel *helped* by him, let me tell you."

Keely said gently, "You're acting like a guilty person, and you know there is nothing at all for you to feel guilty about."

Aislinn had hold of her straw now. She poked the ice chunks in her glass. "I do feel guilty."

They'd been speaking quietly, but now Keely lowered her voice even more. "I know you didn't do anything, Ais. Stop beating yourself up."

"He was *married*. My heart just didn't care. I felt... I don't know, like he was meant to be mine. And so I really, really *wanted* to do something."

"But you didn't. That's what counts. And is that—

your guilt, I mean—why you've never followed up with him now that he's free?"

"Excuse me, but he's never followed up with me either. And there's no reason that he would. There really was nothing between us. It was all in my mind."

"You do get that you're trying way too hard to convince yourself of that?"

"Look. Like I said, it's just better this way."

"But, Ais, you're not acting like it's better."

Aislinn opened her mouth as if to speak—and then drank more tea instead.

Keely dared to suggest, "Just call him."

"I'll think about it—and can we change the subject? Please?"

They talked about Keely's next show at the gallery, which opened in mid-June. They discussed how Aislinn was really getting tired of Deever and Gray, news that was no surprise to Keely. It always went that way with Aislinn and a new job. She loved it at first, when it was all new and she had lots to learn. Once she'd mastered the work, though, she got bored and started wanting a change.

Aislinn said how happy she was that Keely and Daniel were together and when would that stop being a secret?

"Soon, I hope," said Keely.

"He's holding off, right? He wants you all to himself."

It was pretty much what Daniel had said. "How did you know that?"

"He's my brother and you're my best friend. You think I can't see that you're wild for each other? You're the best thing that's ever happened to him, and he doesn't want anyone else butting in."

Keely didn't know how to feel. There was the unlikely pregnancy she couldn't stop obsessing over. And all the family members Daniel didn't want to tell. But still, Aislinn's joy in what Keely had with Daniel was a definite spirit lifter. "We're that obvious? No one else seems to have figured out what we're up to."

"It's only obvious to me. I mean, I did finally get you to admit he's the one. So when I see you together, I already know what's going on. And it looks to me like what's going on is very, very good."

Keely thought of Lillie, of how much Lillie and Daniel had loved each other once. And now Lillie was gone forever...

Suddenly Keely's spirits weren't so lifted anymore.

"What?" demanded Aislinn. "And on second thought, you don't have to say it. I get it. Lillie, right?"

"How did you know that?"

Aislinn shrugged, as if to say "How could I not?" "He did love her. A lot. But they were so young to have so much piled on their shoulders. They were sort of married by necessity. It's not the same as you and Daniel. You're older now, both of you. You've each been married already, and you can choose each other with your eyes wide-open."

"Are you saying you think Lillie was the wrong choice for him?"

"No. Absolutely not. I'm saying that what you have with him takes nothing away from what he once had with her. It's two different things. You have to see that, Keel. Accept it. Let yourself be happy with the man that you love."

Keely felt her face go hot. She pressed her hands to her cheeks in a failed attempt to cool them. "I never said the word *love*. You know I didn't."

"Doesn't matter what you said or didn't say. You *are* in love with my brother, and he's in love with you. I think that's terrific, so I do not get why you're all tied in knots about it."

Again, Keely couldn't help longing to tell Aislinn about the might-be baby. But no. Not yet. "You just… never know how things will work out, that's all."

Aislinn scoffed at her. "Is that supposed to be news? Stop worrying about what could just possibly, *maybe* go wrong and enjoy everything that is clearly going so right."

"I'll do that."

"Ha!"

Keely pointed her last french fry at her friend. "As for you, Ms. Bravo. Pick up the phone and give Jaxon Winter a call."

Aislinn glanced away. "I'll think about it."

Keely knew she wouldn't, and that made her sad all over again.

Back at Daniel's an hour later, Keely left the three pregnancy tests in the car until after her mother had gone.

Then she dithered for a while about where to put them. She ended up sticking them in the empty suitcase under the bed in the room where she never slept, ready in case she needed them.

Which, of course, she would not.

Her period did not show up that day, or the next.

On the day after that, Saturday, Grace arrived home for the summer. She put her things away in her room, helped with the twins and pitched in to fix dinner.

When they all sat down to eat, Grace said, "I'm leaving at seven. Carrie's picking both Erin and me up. I can't wait to see them."

Keely caught Daniel's eye and gave him a minuscule shake of her head before he could even think about objecting. He did take the hint about Grace going out—but he just had to ask, "Any luck on the job front yet?"

Grace pushed a string bean around on her plate. "I'm working on it."

"I can put you to work at the front desk, answering the phones—and we can use a clerk in Payables and Receivables."

Grace left the string bean alone and went to work poking at a bite of oven-browned potato. "Thanks, Daniel. I have something I'm working on, though, a job I think would really be fun and interesting."

"What job is that?"

"I'm going to need a few days to see if it pans out, okay?"

"Some reason you don't want to tell me about it?"

"Daniel." Grace set down her fork. "I want to work it out for myself. And *then* I'll tell you about it."

"Summer doesn't last forever," he warned in a ridiculously dire tone. He was close enough that Keely could have given him a good, sharp kick under the table. But she'd interfered enough. He and Grace needed to figure out ways to get along without Keely constantly stepping in to referee.

"Just give me till Monday." Grace ate the bite of potato she'd been torturing.

"Till Monday. And then what?"

"If I can't make it happen by Monday, Valentine Logging, here I come."

* * *

Daniel made a point not to say anything critical to Grace through the rest of the meal.

He knew Keely had it right, that he was being over-bearing and too protective, and he needed to give his baby sister her freedom as an adult. He had to let her make her own choices. Still, it got him all itchy and pissed off that he couldn't just make the right decisions for her.

The end of her school year had kind of crept up on him. He wasn't ready for it, for Grace to be home all the time. And not only because he worried she would end up wasting her summer sitting around the house and hanging out with her friends.

There was also what he had with Keely. With Grace living in the house, they either needed to tell her that they were together or sneak around.

Sneaking around wasn't something he approved of. It showed a certain lack of integrity. Sneaking around had seemed excusable back at Easter, when he and Keely had just found each other and Grace was only home for three days.

But now?

No. Now, sneaking around was cheap. Unacceptable.

He and Keely hadn't said the words yet. But he meant to say them, and soon. She was *his* in the deepest way. He wanted what they had to continue. Forever, if possible.

And to get forever with her, he was going to have to get honest, not only with Grace, but with the rest of the family, too. Keely was more than ready for that. She'd pushed him repeatedly to come out with the family—though she seemed to have given up on that lately.

He didn't know if he liked that, her giving up. Yeah,

he'd felt pressured when she kept after him about it. But her pushing meant she saw them as a couple, as two people with a future together. Her giving up could mean any number of things, some of them not good.

No, he didn't want the family in their business. But the family *was* their business.

So there wasn't a choice in the matter, not really. Telling the family had to be done.

He waited until Grace left and they'd put the kids to bed.

Then he took Keely to his room, shut the door and backed her up against it for a long, sweet kiss. When they came up for air, he caught her hand and led her to the bed. "Okay, I've been thinking." He pulled her down beside him.

She gave him the side-eye. "This sounds ominous."

He might as well just come out with it. "We need to tell the family about us."

"Finally." She laughed. He loved her laugh. It was an open laugh, musical and free. However, he wasn't all that sure he cared for it right at that particular moment.

He turned her hand over, smoothed her fingers open, then curled them shut again. "You do still want to tell them then?"

"You thought I didn't?"

"Well, you stopped pushing for it."

"Daniel." She turned her body toward him so she was fully facing him. "Pushing wasn't exactly getting me anywhere."

"Hey." He wrapped his arm around her, pulled her close and pressed his lips to the smooth, cool skin of her forehead. "I'm an ass."

She glanced up at him, that mouth he never tired of

kissing curling in a hint of a smile. "On occasion, you are most definitely an ass." Before he could act insulted that she'd agreed with him, she went on, "But you're still the best man I know—and you're mine." She whispered that last part, and his heart beat a faster, triumphant rhythm.

"Yeah. As you are mine." It felt so good to say it. He wanted to say more. *I love you, Keely.* The words sounded damn fine in his head. But was it too soon for that?

He lost his chance to go big when she added, "So yeah. We need to get honest with them. It's Gretchen and Grace I'm most concerned about."

"I agree. Aislinn already knows. Your mother made her position on the subject very clear that first Sunday she came to dinner. My brothers and Harper and Hailey have their own lives."

"Exactly." She rested her head on his shoulder. "I think they'll all just be happy for us. And really, Grace should be fine, too, as long as we're up-front with her."

He stroked her hair, rubbed his hand down her arm. Touching her soothed him. Plus, he was reluctant to put it right out there about his mother-in-law. It had to be said, though. "So, it's Gretchen we're talking about really. She's the one who might not be happy to learn we're together."

She nodded against his shoulder. "It's hard to say how she's going to react. Yeah, Lillie's gone forever and you're single now. But you and me together…"

"There are just too many ways Gretchen could see that as a disloyalty to Lillie's memory," he finished for her. "Too many ways it could stir up all the loss and the grief for her all over again."

Daniel hadn't forgotten how bad it had been for

Gretchen when they lost Lillie. His mother-in-law had tried to put on a brave face, but for almost a year, she'd rarely smiled. And she didn't bake a single cookie for thirteen months. That had freaked him out the most. For Gretchen, baking was an act of joy and love. He'd never felt so relieved as the day she showed up at the house to watch the twins with a smile on her face and a big plastic container full of butter pecan sandies.

"We have to tell her, Daniel. We should tell her first of all, privately, just Auntie G and you and me. Then Grace. And then the rest of them, which shouldn't be a big deal. I'll tell my mom, and however you want to tell your other brothers and sisters, that's fine with me."

"Agreed." Still, he dreaded it. He would miss having her all to himself. He knew he was being an idiot. She'd just called him *hers*. No way she was going anywhere. But he felt anxious and jumpy nonetheless. "So, as for telling Gretchen. When?"

"As soon as possible."

"Tomorrow then?"

"No. Tomorrow she'll have all kinds of church stuff going on. Monday night is bingo night at the senior center and Tuesday she plays bridge. How 'bout this? I'll call her, ask her to watch the kids Wednesday, in the afternoon. Then I'll suggest that she can just stay for dinner. We'll tell her then."

"But what about Grace? Chances are, she'll be here for dinner on Wednesday, too."

"We'll work it out, wing it, you know? Get Grace to take the kids upstairs after we eat and tell Gretchen then, maybe. Then once Auntie G knows, we can just tell Grace that night."

He swore under his breath. "Isn't this getting way too complicated?"

"Maybe. But I really think we need to tell Auntie G first. No matter how she reacts, she'll at least know we came to her specifically, that we love and respect her as Lillie's mom and your mother-in-law and the woman who has always treated me as a daughter."

"Okay. Wednesday. We'll try for that."

"In the meantime, we have to be careful. I really don't want Grace to find out by accident, to see me sneaking out of your room or to knock on the door when I'm in here in bed with you. It could upset her, not only because we didn't trust her enough to tell her what's going on, but also because of the problems between the two of you. You're the classic overprotective big brother, and yet you're fooling around with the nanny behind everyone's back."

Okay, that was kind of insulting—to both of them. "I'm not fooling around with the nanny, I'm fooling around with *you*."

She dimpled. How could she be so damned adorable while simultaneously pissing him off? "I think you just made my point for me."

He was getting a headache. "Keely. You can't control everything."

"Says the man who won't let his grown-up baby sister go out on Saturday night."

"I did let her go. I'm working on that. And why would Grace come wandering up here at night out of the blue? We're taking care of the twins, the two of us. She doesn't have the baby monitor in her room anymore. There's no reason for her to come upstairs."

Keely leveled those green eyes on him and chided,

"She lives here, Daniel. There's no reason for her *not* to be upstairs whenever she feels like it. I just think it's better if we don't sneak around, period."

Okay, he truly did not like where this was going. "You mean, we're not sleeping together until after we tell Gretchen and Grace that we *are* together?"

Now her eyes widened, kind of pleading with him. But her soft mouth was set. "I really think it's the best thing to do, the *right* thing to do."

He didn't. He thought it was crap. "I get that you won't spend the night with me until all this is settled. But for a few hours after the kids are in bed, we could at least— "

She cut him off with a shake of her shining red-blond head. "It's only until Wednesday. It's not like we'll die from four nights apart."

"Four nights?" He scowled at her. "You mean tonight, too? Come on. Grace won't be home till late. We have hours yet."

She pressed her cool, smooth hand to the side of his face. "I just want to do this the best way, the *right* way…"

"I don't like it." The nights with her were everything. He didn't want to lose a single one. Fate was a real bitch sometimes. You never knew what might happen. A man needed to grab what he wanted and hold on good and tight.

"Oh, Daniel." She kissed him then, a lingering kiss that only served to remind him of all the reasons he needed her here with him—tonight, and every night.

"Don't go."

Gently, she pushed him away. "I think we're doing the right thing."

"But—"

She stopped him with a finger to his lips. "Good night, Daniel." And then she was up and out the door before he could convince her how much he needed her to stay.

Silently, Keely shut the door to the master suite and tiptoed along the upstairs hall to her own room.

Four nights without his big arms around her. She could do that. She'd already done it while he was traveling at the end of last month. *Only* four nights. And then she wouldn't have to leave Daniel in the middle of the night again—not that she *had* to leave him, she reminded herself. She was choosing to leave him in order that Grace would have less chance of finding out they were together until they were ready for her to know.

And really. Did Daniel have it right? Was she making this whole thing way too complicated?

Uh-uh. No. This was the right way to handle it. For everyone—especially Gretchen, who'd already suffered way more than enough. Telling Gretchen first was the right thing to do. And until they told Gretchen, nobody else should know, not even by accident.

In her room, Keely took a long bath to relax. It didn't help much. She ended up lying there alone in the dark, trying not to think about what waited for her in the suitcase under the bed.

The last couple of days, her breasts had felt swollen and sensitive. Her stomach continued to be just a little bit queasy.

The signs were there and her placebo week was over without a period to show for it. But really, she just wasn't ready to know for sure.

And no way was she ready to tell Daniel. She would

get through telling Auntie G that she and Daniel were together. After that, she would need to stop being a big fat chicken and pull that suitcase out from under the bed.

Chapter Nine

In the morning, Keely came downstairs to find Daniel at the breakfast table and the kids in their high chairs.

"Sleep well?" he asked, and she felt the knot of tension in her belly unwind. He didn't seem mad or even annoyed at the way she'd left him last night.

"Grace?" she asked, with a glance toward the short hall that led to his sister's room.

"Still sleeping is my guess."

Keely couldn't resist. She needed the contact. She stepped close and bent down to him. They shared a quick kiss. "Missed you," she whispered.

The tender look he gave her made everything right.

She poured herself a scant cup of coffee. For the past week, she'd been allowing herself one small cup a day just on the off chance that she might actually be pregnant. Setting her coffee on the table, she grabbed her phone and autodialed her aunt.

Gretchen answered on the first ring. "Sweetheart. I'm just on my way out the door to catch the early service."

"I won't keep you, but I was hoping maybe you could come over Wednesday around two and watch the kids for a couple of hours."

"Happy to."

"You're a lifesaver. And how about staying for dinner, as long as you're here?"

"I would love it."

They chatted for a couple of minutes more and then said goodbye.

"We're set," Keely said to Daniel as she hung up the phone.

"Good." He caught her hand and pressed his wonderful lips to the back of it as Jake let out a string of nonsense words and Frannie shoved a fistful of Cheerios into her mouth.

Keely bent close to give him one more quick kiss. She'd barely brushed her lips against his when Grace emerged from her bedroom in sleep shorts and a giant Reed College T-shirt.

Her heart lurching into overdrive and her stomach performing a scary pitch and roll, Keely pulled out the nearest empty chair and dropped into it.

Had they just been busted?

Grace went straight to the coffeepot and poured herself a cup. When she turned, she sipped her coffee and announced, "Brace yourselves. It's happened." Her slight grin turned to a full-on smile. "I've found my summer job."

Keely's heart slowed to a more sedate rhythm, and she breathed a careful sigh. Grace hadn't seen a thing.

"Good news," said Daniel, and he even put on one of his low-key Daniel-style smiles. "Where are you working?"

"At the Sea Breeze." She beamed at Keely. "I had an interview with your mom set for tomorrow, but she was out at Beach Street Brews last night, sitting in with the band they had playing. We started talking between sets, and she said of course I had a job with her if I wanted it. I start tomorrow. Nine to five, Monday through Friday until she opens for business."

"Terrific." Keely got up again and gave her a congratulatory hug.

Grace laughed. "I think it's going be fun. Your mom's the best."

Daniel asked, "What *is* the job, exactly?"

Grace picked up her coffee again. "A little bit of everything. Light construction, helping plan and set up for the grand opening, and playing general all-around gofer for now. Then I'll be a waitress when the place opens in July."

Daniel had that stern look he got when he was about to tell someone something they probably didn't want to hear. Grace's smile fell. But at the last possible second, he must have remembered that he was supposed to be letting her run her own life. All he said was "Sounds good."

Grace's face lit up again. "I think so. Ingrid's paying me twelve an hour to start." She tipped her chin higher, as though still anticipating some sort of criticism. When Daniel only nodded, she went on, "I'll make more when we open. I'll work nights then. Tips should be good."

"Gwace!" Jake made a bid for his favorite aunt's attention. "Hey there!"

"Hey there, Jakey." She went to him and kissed him on his puckered little mouth. "How's my favorite boy?"

"I goo." He offered her a Cheerio.

She took it and popped it in her mouth. "Delicious. Thank you."

Jake jabbered out something that was probably meant to be "You're welcome."

Keely watched the interaction with a giant grin on her face. She wanted to jump up and kiss Daniel for working so hard to let his sister go. Right now, though, she needed to keep a serious lid on the PDAs. She settled for sending him a quick secret glance of love and approval, feeling a little glow inside herself that Grace had a job she wanted for the summer and Daniel had let her go about finding it in her own way.

Daniel felt good about things with Grace—at least he did for the rest of the day.

But their hard-won peace didn't last. After dinner, Keely took the kids upstairs, and he and Grace cleaned up after the meal. Once that was done, his sister vanished into her room. He went to his study off the front hall to check email on his desktop before heading upstairs to help with the baths and the bedtime stories.

He'd left the study door open or he wouldn't have caught Grace on her way out the front door.

Okay, he should have just let her go. Keely would want him to let Grace have her freedom, and Keely was probably right.

But he was out of his chair and calling, "Grace!"

before he could remind himself that he had to let his little sister make her own mistakes.

"What now?" She let go of the door handle and turned on him. In a skimpy metallic top, tight jeans and red high-heeled sandals, she had to be headed for another party night. "Erin's waiting out in front for me."

He felt he had to say something. "Doesn't your job start tomorrow?"

Grace flipped her hair back over her shoulder and braced her hands on her hips. "Rhetorical question much? Yes, Daniel. My job starts tomorrow."

"Well, it seems to me that it would be smarter for you to stay home tonight and get a good night's sleep, that's all." He put a lot of effort into sounding more helpful than critical.

Too bad Grace did not seem the least grateful for his wise advice. "I told you. Erin's waiting."

"Don't you want to be rested for your first day of work?"

"God. Listen to yourself. You're like some old mother hen."

"Grace. Come on. I'm just trying to—"

"Stop." She showed him the hand. "I'm going. Please don't worry. I won't stay out late, and I'll be on time for work tomorrow."

"I think this is unwise."

"I know you do. I'm going. Good night, Daniel." She pulled open the door and went through it before he could muster another objection.

Once she was gone, he stood rooted to the spot, listening to the sound of voices out in front, of a car door opening and shutting, and then the engine revving as Erin drove away. He scrubbed his hands down his face, rubbed the tension knots at the back of his neck and returned to his study long enough to shut down his desktop and turn off the light.

Upstairs, Keely had the kids in the tub.

He leaned in the doorway and watched her with them as they splashed her and giggled and played with their tub toys. She was something amazing, all right. With her bright smiles and her easy ways, juggling the kids, her gallery, her mom, her aunt and those quilt things she made. And somehow finding time to fill his nights with magic, too. With her, it was all worth it again, to get up in the morning and go to work every day. To come home to the demands of a whole new family. He could do that, even enjoy that.

As long as she was there, too.

And they were young yet, really, he and Keely. The kids were almost two. Another sixteen years or so and they would head off to college. He and Keely would have the whole house to themselves. They could go where they wanted when they wanted without having to consider who would watch the kids. It was a long time off, but it wasn't forever.

And in the meantime, well, he didn't mind things just as they were—or as they would be, come Wednesday night.

Until then, he'd be miserable sleeping without her. It was his own damn fault, though, and he owned that. He'd been the one who put off telling the family about them.

But as of last night, when she left him to sleep alone, he damn well couldn't wait to break the big news to Gretchen. However that went off, at least once it was over, nobody and nothing could keep him and Keely apart.

"Da-Da!" cried Frannie, holding up a red rubber monkey. She gave it a squeeze and it squeaked at him.

He entered the room, skirted Maisey, who was stretched out on the floor a few feet from the tub, and knelt beside Keely.

She leaned his way and butted him with her shoulder. "Did I hear you and Grace downstairs just now?"

"Yeah," he confessed.

"Are you trying to avoid admitting that once again, you failed to keep your mouth shut?"

"We got into it. She went out with Erin anyway."

"Da-Da!" Now Jake had the monkey. He squeaked it several times in succession. Daniel stuck out a hand and tickled his round little belly. Crowing in delight, Jake splashed wildly, flinging water at Daniel, getting Keely wet, too.

Keely laughed. "Look at it this way. You made your point with her, right?"

"I spoke my mind, yeah."

"Perfect. You made your point, and she did what she wanted to do. It's a win all the way around."

Screw keeping his hands off her. Nobody here but the four of them anyway—five, counting Maisey. He yanked her close and kissed her while the twins screeched, "Kiss! Da-Da! Keewee!" and splashed water everywhere.

Later, after they'd tucked the kids in, Daniel managed to steal a few more kisses.

But when he tried to coax her into his room, she balked and shook her head. "Tonight and two more nights. Then I am yours—but right now, I'm going to get a little work done in my studio."

Reluctantly, he left her to it.

He went to bed alone and couldn't sleep, missing

Keely beside him, hoping Grace was exercising good judgment while staying out way too late.

At 2:46 a.m., he heard her come in. Relieved in spite of his aggravation with her, he turned over and shut his eyes.

In the morning, Grace joined them in the kitchen at a little before eight. She had dark circles under her eyes and a scowl on her pretty face.

He knew that he needed to keep his damn mouth shut. The words got out anyway. "Looking kind of ragged there, sunshine."

She pointed a finger at him. "Just don't start. I'm not in the mood."

Keely said unnecessarily, "Coffee's ready."

With one last dirty look in his direction, Grace headed for the coffeepot.

He had to know. "You still going to work?"

Grace took her time filling her cup. She turned to him slowly, enjoying a long sip before grumbling at him, "Of course I'm going to work. I'm looking forward to this job and I take my responsibilities seriously."

When he left for the office, Grace was still taking her sweet time getting ready in the downstairs bathroom. With his sister occupied behind a shut door, Keely allowed him a quick kiss as he was leaving.

He said, "Call me if she decides to stay home."

For that, she gave his shoulder a playful slap. "Not on your life."

"Nobody does what I tell them to around here."

Keely only smiled sweetly and pushed him out the door.

Keely felt relief when Grace emerged from the bathroom dressed in old jeans, a chambray shirt and a worn pair of black Converse, her hair pinned up out of the way. "Your mom said to wear comfortable clothes, that there might be painting to do today. You think this is all right?"

"As long as you don't mind getting paint on anything, it's perfect."

Grace leaned close. "Has the ogre left the building?"

"Your brother is gone for the day, yes."

"He's such a—"

"Uh-uh." Keely put up a hand. "Don't go there." She pressed her hand to Grace's smooth cheek. "Have a great first day of work." Grace had the strangest look on her face. "What? You okay?"

She seemed to shake herself. "Yeah, sure. I'll take overtime if Ingrid offers it, so don't count on me for dinner."

"No problem. There will be plenty of leftovers to heat up if you have to work late."

"You're the best." Grace gave her a quick hug and headed for the inside door to the garage.

She'd been gone about half a minute when Frannie, on the floor with Jake a few feet away, let out a wail.

Jake had grabbed a stuffed giraffe from her. Keely moderated the dispute, reminding Jake to share and offering him his favorite ratty rabbit in exchange for Frannie's toy. A few minutes later, they were playing as happily as ever together.

Daniel called at ten. Keely reported that, yes, Grace had gone to work on time, and then she said goodbye quickly, annoyed with him for promising to back off his sister and then calling Keely to check up on her.

At eleven, she fed the twins. At one, she put them in their cribs for a nap.

And then, before she could invent more pathetic excuses not to face the truth, she marched into her bedroom and pulled the suitcase out from under the bed.

She took two of the three tests. They both told her what she already knew.

As for when to tell Daniel, she was finished stalling. Tonight, as soon as the kids were in bed, she would break the news that they were having a baby.

She was dropping the second test wand into her bathroom wastebasket when the doorbell rang downstairs.

Quickly, in hopes that whoever it was wouldn't have time to ring again and increase the likelihood of waking the twins, she rushed out into the upper hall and ran down the stairs. Through the etched glass on the top of the door, she could see who it was.

Gretchen. Keely recognized her by the set of her plump shoulders and the halo of carefully arranged blond hair around her head.

But she couldn't see her aunt's expression until she pulled the door wide-open. "Keely. Hello." She looked… irritated, maybe? Her eyebrows were pinched together, her mouth all pursed up.

"Gretchen? Are you all ri—"

Her aunt cut her off. "May I come in?"

"Of course." Keely stepped back. "Come on to the kitchen." She gestured toward the arch that led to the back of the house.

"The babies?"

"Napping at the moment—and it's warm out. How about something cold to drink?"

"No, it's fine. Daniel's at work?"

"Yes."

"It's just us?"

"That's right."

"Good. We need to talk." Gretchen turned and headed for the kitchen. Keely just stood there and stared after her, wondering what in the world was going on. Her aunt paused just past the arch to the living room and aimed an impatient glance over her shoulder. "Well? Are you coming?"

"Sure." Keely hurried to catch up. In the kitchen, she gestured at the table. "Have a seat. I can make some—"

"No. Nothing. Really." Gretchen went and stood by the island. Not sure what to do next, Keely followed her over there. Her aunt stared at her for a long, very uncomfortable string of seconds before announcing, "I just feel I have to say something. It's about Grace."

"Grace?" Keely's stomach lurched. "Is she all right?"

Gretchen wrung her hands, blinked and looked down at them. Shaking her head, she smoothed the ruffles on the front of her shirt and tugged on the side seams of her A-line skirt. "She's making things up. That's what she's doing. Hurtful lies."

Dread crept over Keely, like a cold fog on a dark night. "What lies?"

"Well, I just dropped in at the Sea Breeze to see how things were going. And there was Grace, painting the wood trim on the door to the restroom hallway. She said Ingrid had run out for more paint but would be back soon. I decided to wait and we started chatting, Grace and I. And then, out of nowhere, she asks me if I know about you and Daniel."

Keely blinked. There was a sudden buzzing sound in her ears. She put her hand on her stomach and prayed that everything in there wasn't on the verge of coming up. "What about me and Daniel?"

As if she didn't know.

Dear, sweet Lord, this was the exact wrong way for Gretchen to find out that she and Daniel were a couple. It was supposed to be done on Wednesday, done kindly, with love and respect.

We never should have kept the secret in the first place, said an accusatory voice in the back of her head.

But they had. And now came the part where they got to live with their bad choices.

"Grace said she saw you and Daniel kissing, right here in this kitchen, yesterday morning." Her aunt touched her then. She reached out and gently squeezed her shoulder. All Keely could do was stare. "Sweetheart. Don't look so crushed."

"I'm not, I—"

"Because of course, I don't believe a word of it. I just really felt that you should know that Grace is, well, she's spreading tales about you. It's a problem, a big one. She has all these…issues with Daniel, though the good Lord knows why. He's been a saint, we all know that. With Grace, with *all* of his brothers and sisters. He and my Lillie, what they did to keep that family together…"

"Auntie G—"

"No. Wait. I haven't finished. I ask you, where would Grace be if not for Lillie and Daniel? She could have ended up in foster care. Anything might have happened. I just don't understand what has got into her, to speak so disrespectfully about Daniel. About *you*. It's an outrage and—"

"Auntie G." Keely took her arm. "Come on. Please. Sit down." Gretchen allowed Keely to lead her to the table, pull out a chair for her and ease her down into it. "Now, how about some ice water?"

"I—yes. All right. Ice water. Good."

By rote, Keely went through the motions of getting down a glass, adding crushed ice from the dispenser, filling it the rest of the way with water, all the while knowing the moment for exactly what it was.

The moment of truth. All her careful plans to break the news to Gretchen just so, after a nice dinner, in a gentle, reasonable way?

Right out the kitchen window.

It was happening now, like it or not. With Auntie G already upset and saying cruel things about poor Grace. It was happening without Daniel here, with no time to prepare.

"Here you go," she said to her aunt.

"Thank you, honey." Gretchen took the glass and had a long drink. "It's only… I suppose I'm overreacting. But that girl has no right to speak of you and Daniel that way."

Keely pulled out the next chair over and lowered herself into it. Where to start?

The answer was painfully simple.

Start with the truth. Nothing would make the news go down easy for Gretchen. And looking at her aunt's red face, Keely doubted that it would have gone much better on Wednesday night.

Better to just say it straight-out. "Auntie G, I'm sorry if this upsets you. But Grace wasn't lying. She did see me kissing Daniel yesterday morning."

Gretchen set down her glass. "What are you…?" She forced out a tight little laugh. "Oh. I understand. An innocent, friendly kiss that Grace has blown all out of proportion then?"

Keely's heart seemed to bounce off the walls of her

chest. It was beating so hard. "No. Grace saw what she said she saw. I kissed Daniel. It was a real kiss."

"A real...?" Gretchen scoffed. "Sweetheart, you can't be serious."

"Yes. Yes, I am. Daniel and I have...feelings for each other. We're in a relationship, Auntie G."

Gretchen's flushed face went white. "No."

"Yes. We should have told you sooner. I'm so sorry that you had to find out in this way."

"Sorry." Gretchen spit the word.

"Yes. We...we didn't know how things would work out at first, so we kept our feelings to ourselves. But then, well, we do want to be together. So we were going to tell you Wednesday."

"Sorry," Gretchen repeated, as if she hadn't heard a word of what Keely had just said. "You're *sorry*." She slapped the table hard enough that her glass bounced. "How could you, Keely? After everything, after all the years, all that I've done for you. All *Lillie* did. We *loved* you. Like a daughter. Like a sister. We took you in, gave you a real home, provided the stability my sister never gave you, the settled family life you always longed for."

Keely's heart no longer felt like it would burst out of her chest with its frantic beating. Now it felt heavy as lead, aching. And out of that ache, she felt fury rising, adrenaline spurting. Hurtful words to match Gretchen's rose to her lips. It took all the will she had to swallow those words down, to try to speak reasonably. "Auntie G—"

"No."

"Please don't—"

"I don't want to hear your ridiculous, unacceptable excuses. I will not accept your apology. You are supposed to be *helping* here, not taking advantage of poor

Daniel's loneliness, sneaking around behind everyone's backs. I tried, you know I did, to talk you into letting me take over again. I tried weeks ago, at Easter. But no. You were too *happy* here. You just wouldn't go. And now I know why, don't I? Now I know what you have been up to. It's unacceptable, Keely. Unforgiveable and so cruel."

Keely's carefully banked fury tried to spike again. "You really should hear yourself. You're telling me you *plotted* to keep Daniel and me apart."

Gretchen blinked several times in rapid succession. "Plotted? There was no plotting. How could I plot? I had no idea what you were up to. I was only trying to take the pressure off you—and you wouldn't let me because you were having a secret affair with my son-in-law." Gretchen's eyes had glazed over with tears. "How dare you?" she demanded. "How *could* you?"

Keely said nothing. She let the last of her own defensive fury sputter and die. Now she felt only sadness as she waited to be sure her aunt had finally run out of steam.

"Well?" Gretchen swiped away tears, hitched up her chin and glared.

Keely asked, just to be certain, "Are you finished?"

"I… What? What in the world can you possibly have to say for yourself?"

"Well, first of all, you're wrong."

"Wrong? No. No, I have it right and you know that I do."

"No, you do not. I'm sorry this hurts you, but most of what you just said? All wrong. You say 'secret affair' as though Daniel and I are cheating on Lillie somehow. You haven't accepted yet that Daniel is a single man now. You need to do that. You need to accept in your heart that Lillie is truly gone from this world. We loved her. We lost her. And our lives have to move on."

"Excuses," insisted Gretchen, looking down at the table, shaking her head. "These are flimsy, cowardly excuses you are giving me."

"No. That's not true. Daniel loved Lillie very much and would never have betrayed her. Neither would I. You know me, Auntie G. And you know very well I never would have done such a thing. But Lillie really is dead, and Daniel and I are both single adults with every right to find a little comfort in each other."

"Comfort," Gretchen uttered the word as though it disgusted her. "That's not what I would call it." She shoved back her chair, her face starting to crumple all over again. "And I…I cannot stay here one minute longer. I can't… I just… I really do have to go." And with that, she was turning, striding out of the kitchen toward the front of the house.

Keely just sat there, staring at Gretchen's half-finished glass of water until she heard the sound of the front door closing hard.

That did it.

Her stomach went beyond merely roiling. It completely rebelled.

Leaping up, she ran for the downstairs half bath, making it just in time to drop to her knees and throw back the toilet seat before everything came up.

Chapter Ten

Once the vomiting had finally stopped, Keely wandered upstairs to brush her teeth and check on the twins. Maisey, who'd been napping in Keely's studio room, wanted to go outside. Keely took her down and let her out into the backyard. Then she went upstairs again and stretched out on her bed. Maybe a nap would help.

But within five minutes, she knew she would only lie there and stew over the absolutely rotten things Gretchen had said. She got up again, went back downstairs and let Maisey in. The dog stretched out on the kitchen floor as Keely put some crackers on a plate and poured herself a ginger ale.

As she was resolutely chewing a saltine, Grace came running in from the garage all spattered in paint, with red-rimmed eyes. "Keely! Are you…okay?"

Maisey looked up with a worried whine. Keely only shrugged and finished her saltine.

Grace darted over and stood at the table, clutching the back of a chair. "She was here, wasn't she—Gretchen?"

"Yeah." Keely took a careful sip of her ginger ale. "She was here."

"Oh, God." Grace burst into tears.

Keely couldn't bear to see her so miserable. "Hey. Come on…" She got up, went around the table and gathered Grace close.

"Oh, Keely…" Grace hugged her hard—for a moment. And then she pulled away. Her nose was red and tears streamed down her face. "Gretchen said she was coming straight over here. I should have stopped her. I should've kept my damn mouth shut."

"Hold on." Keely went to the island, grabbed the tissue box she kept there and brought it back to Grace, who blew her nose and swiped at her eyes. "I'm so sorry. Oh, Keely. I hate myself. I…" She let out a moan. "I should have talked to you or Daniel—well, not Daniel. Every time I talk to Daniel, I just want to scream. But I *can* talk to you. And I *didn't* talk to you…"

"So you did see me kiss him yesterday morning?"

Grace yanked out the chair, collapsed into it and whipped another tissue from the box. "I did. And I pretended I didn't because… Well, I don't really know why. And before that, I kind of figured there might be something going on between you two. It was nothing specific. Just, you know, the way you look at each other. And then there's Daniel. Other than treating me like I'm still in diapers, he's been…different lately. Happier. I know that's because of you. And now, look what I've done. I've ruined *everything*." That brought on a fresh spurt of tears. Keely, still right there beside her, clasped her shoulder and waited for the tears to play themselves out. Finally, Grace grabbed yet more tissues and dabbed at her eyes. "You should probably hate me—yeah. No doubt about it. I deserve your disgust."

Keely moved squarely behind her so she could put both hands on Grace, one on either shoulder. "No way."

Grace let her head drop back. They shared a long look. Then Keely gave Grace's shoulders one more good squeeze and returned to her chair. She ate another cracker and sipped her ginger ale.

Grace drew herself up and said, "I knew what I was doing when I told Gretchen. I was *trying* to cause trouble. I knew it, and I did it anyway. I went straight to the one person who was likely to have issues with Daniel moving on. What is the *matter* with me?"

"Nothing is the matter with you. You're frustrated with your brother, so you did something mean. Now you're doing what you can to make amends."

Grace sniffed. "I told your mom everything."

"Good."

"She sent me here to explain what I did, to tell you I'm so sorry—which I am—and to make sure you're okay."

"I am. I'm okay." Keely almost believed it as she said it. "And yes, it would have been much better if you'd come to me or Daniel about it when you saw us kissing. But, Grace, it's really not the end of the world. You're not the only one who could have behaved better. Gretchen is no saint in this. And Daniel and I shouldn't have kept our relationship a secret from the family. It was one of those things, you know? You start out keeping a secret and then the longer you keep it, the harder it gets to tell the truth."

"But it was awful with Gretchen, wasn't it?" Grace burst out. "Just admit it!"

Keely hated to see Grace so miserable. But she didn't want to lie either. "It was pretty bad."

"I knew it!" Grace wailed. "I'm a complete bitch, and everything's all my fault."

"Gracie, come on," Keely soothed. "Quit beating yourself up. It's all going to work out." Would it? Really? Keely had no idea. But Grace was hurting and Keely couldn't bear to add to her suffering.

Maybe another hug was in order. Keely got up again. With a cry, Grace rose, too. They met midway between their two chairs and wrapped their arms around each other.

Grace grabbed on tight and whispered, "I love you, Keely."

"And I love you."

"Daniel doesn't deserve you." Grace sniffed.

Keely pulled back enough to cradle Gracie's pretty face and smooth her pale hair away from her eyes. "Don't say mean things about your brother."

"Not even if they're true?"

Keely laughed. And then Grace laughed, too, right through her tears.

"Keewee?" called a small, sweet voice from the baby monitor Keely had left on the sideboard by the door to the dining room. That was Frannie.

Jake joined in. "Up, Keewee! Up!"

Keely let go of Grace as the twins babbled to each other over the monitor in the special language only they understood. "Nap time is over, I'm afraid."

Grace nodded. "I need to get back to work anyway."

"Do me a favor?"

"Anything."

"Come home from work right at five?"

"Absolutely."

"If you would watch the kids so that Daniel and I can talk about what to do next…?"

"Of course—he's going to kill me, isn't he?" Grace face-palmed with a drawn-out groan.

"No, he is not." Once Keely told him about the baby, getting mad at Grace would be the last thing on his mind.

A half hour later, Ingrid called. By then, Keely had got the kids up, changed their diapers and turned them loose with their toys in the upstairs playroom.

"Just checking on you," said her mother.

"I'm okay."

Ingrid gave a snort of laughter. "Oh, please. I do know what's going on. And I also know you're about as far from okay as a girl can get."

"Yeah. Well." Keely reached down to Maisey, who lay at her side. She gave the dog a quick rub on the top of her head, followed by a couple of long strokes down her back. At a time like this, having Maisey to pet really did help. "It's been one of those days." Jake wandered over with his ratty rabbit. He held it out. Keely bent and kissed it. The smile he gave her melted her heart to a puddle of mush. She stared after him as he toddled away again.

"I'm so sorry that Gretch has made a damn fool of herself," Ingrid said. "The woman has a dark side. I suppose I should have warned you, but I kind of hoped you'd never have to see it. You always adored her, and now she's let you down. Do you need me to slap her silly?"

"No, Mom. But I appreciate the offer."

"How 'bout some motherly support? I can be there

in ten minutes. I'll make you peanut butter and jelly on white bread with the crust cut off."

Keely smiled at that. When she was little and living on the purple tour bus, crust-free PB&J was her go-to comfort food. "Sit tight. Have the peanut butter ready. I'll keep you posted after I talk to Daniel."

"What? You think he's going to get all up in your case about it for some reason? Well, he'd better not or he will be dealing with me."

"Back it down, Super Suzie." "Super Suzie" was a Pomegranate Dream song about a reluctant superheroine named Suzie, who took on all the small-minded bullies in her hometown.

"I'm here," said her mother. "You just need to know that."

Keely shut her eyes and swallowed the sudden lump in her throat. "Love you, Mom."

"Call me."

"You know I will."

Grace got home as promised, at ten past five. Keely had dinner all ready.

She spoke to Grace about how things would go. "If possible, I would like to put off talking about what happened today until after dinner. If you would take the kids upstairs as soon as we're through eating, I'll talk to Daniel privately in his office."

"Works for me. Then if he wants to yell at me, you take over with the kids and he and I can go a few rounds somewhere they can't hear us fighting."

Keely chided, "Don't go planning for trouble."

"I don't need to plan. Trouble between me and Daniel happens naturally, no matter what we do."

Daniel came in at five thirty. Keely had worried that Gretchen would track him down and confront him, too—that she might have called Valentine Logging or shown up at the office unannounced. But if she had, Daniel gave no sign of it. Which was great. Perfect. Keely didn't want to get into it with him until Grace took the kids upstairs.

Grace put the twins in their high chairs while Daniel filled the water glasses and Keely brought the food to the table.

Neither Keely nor Grace felt much like conversation, but the twins kept up a steady chatter, partly in English, partly in twinspeak. Their bright voices filled up what might have been uncomfortable silence.

Daniel asked Grace how she liked working for Ingrid.

Grace put on a bright voice and talked about the job itself. "Already I love working there. Lots of variety. I painted woodwork, ran errands and helped Ingrid rearrange her office in back. We experimented with a couple of possible signature cocktails, and she taught me the POS system she's going to be using."

"I'm glad it's working out." Daniel sounded sincere.

"Yeah," said Grace, both awkward and strangely hopeful at once. "Me, too."

The meal ground on, with Frannie waxing poetic over her love of peas. "Peas! Yummy, yum, yummy, in my tummy!" And Jake chortled maniacally at intervals, beating his spoon on his chair tray, sending food flying.

When it was finally over, Grace wiped up the kids and swept them off upstairs. Daniel cleared the table as Keely loaded the dishwasher.

She'd just set the cycle and pushed the dishwasher door shut, when Daniel said, "Okay. What's going on?"

Her heart kind of stuttered in her chest and then became a warm little ache, that he *had* noticed something was off. That she loved him so and she really had no idea how he would take all that had gone down that day—with Grace, with Gretchen and with two of the tests from under the bed.

"Keely." He moved in closer, smelling of cedar and soap and everything good. Tipping up her chin, he brushed the sweetest, softest kiss across her mouth. "Tell me."

"Let's go into your study?"

He ran a slow finger down her cheek to her chin, stirring up sweet sensations, causing the ache in her heart to deepen. "Sure." His finger trailed along the side of her throat, out to her shoulder and down her arm. He took her hand.

In his study, she eased free of his grip and shut the door.

He went to the sofa against the inside wall, folded his powerful frame down onto the cushions and patted the space beside him. "Come on. Whatever it is, tell me everything."

She approached with caution, hardly knowing where to begin. He reached up a hand to her. She took it but stiffened her knees to stay on her feet when he tried to pull her down next to him.

"Damn, Keely. What?" He searched her face.

She opened her mouth, and the words kind of tumbled out all over each other. "Gretchen, Grace and my mom all know about us. Grace and Mom are fine with it. Gretchen is furious. She came over here today and she—"

"Hold it." He squeezed her hand—and then let go.

Keely wrapped her arms around herself and stepped back. "What?"

"How did they find out?"

She kept her shoulders square and looked down at him steadily. "Yesterday, in the kitchen at breakfast...?"

He knew then. His pale blue eyes went icy. "Grace did see us kissing."

"That's right."

He unfolded to his full height. "I knew it. Grace." He started for the door.

"Daniel," she said forcefully. At least he stopped walking and turned back to her. Good. She wasn't about to let him go after Grace. Not until he'd heard all she had to say. "I'm not finished yet."

A muscle twitched in his jaw. "I'll be back. I want to hear it from Grace, though, okay?"

She clutched her arms tighter around her middle. "No, Daniel. It's not okay. I want you to hear me out, please. Then you and Grace can talk."

"But—"

"No *buts*. I have things to say, and I intend to say them. Grace isn't going anywhere. She'll be here when I'm finished."

A stare down ensued. She didn't feel much relief when he gave in. "Fine, then. Go ahead."

Now it was a face-off between them. She stood by the couch, clutching her middle for dear life. He loomed a few feet from the door. Not the way she'd wanted to begin this difficult discussion.

But no way was she backing out now. "The way it happened, Gretchen stopped by Mom's bar. Mom was out. Grace and Gretchen started talking. Grace told Gretchen that she'd seen us kissing. Gretchen didn't believe her and came running over here to tell me how awful and unappreciative Grace is of all you've done for her. I set Gretchen straight, after which she accused me of betraying Lillie's memory and seducing you in your loneliness and a whole lot of other crappy things that I think I've already blocked from my memory. Then she stormed out."

"I'm sorry," he said. And then he went to his desk, crossed behind it, pulled out his big leather chair and dropped into it. "What a mess."

She stared at his bent head and went on, "Grace came home next. She'd already confessed to my mom what she did. Mom had sent her to me. Grace knows she did wrong, and she feels terrible about it. Your jumping all over her on top of her own disappointment in herself isn't going to help the situation in the least."

His head came up. He cracked his powerful neck, raked his thick hair off his forehead, the beautiful muscles of his arm flexing and bulging as he moved. "Nobody's talked to Gretchen since then?"

"Why should we? I may never talk to her again."

"Keely." His voice was velvety soft, coaxing. He pushed to his feet, but this time he came around the desk to her and reached for her. With a grateful sigh, she let herself sway against him. "You don't mean that." He kissed the words into her hair.

She rested her head on his giant rock of a shoulder. "Right at this moment? Oh, yes, I do."

"Well. We'll work it out." He clasped her arms. When she looked up at him, he bent for a kiss, a slow one. Not deep, but so comforting—and then he ruined it by setting her away from him and announcing, "In the meantime, I'm going to go talk to Grace."

Like hell he was. "I'm still not finished yet."

A frown formed between his thick eyebrows. Apparently he'd noticed she wasn't all that happy with him and his bullheaded insistence on making this disaster all about Grace. "You're kidding." At least he tried to lighten up a little. He made a real effort to speak teasingly. "There's more?"

Oh, is there ever. "Listen. I get that you're worried about Auntie G. I am, too. Even though I want to wring her neck right now, I know she's suffering, that she's still not over losing Lillie. I mean, really, who is? Lillie's death isn't something any of us who loved her are ever going to get over. But we do need to learn to go on, to make the most of a world without her in it. So Gretchen's reaction didn't really surprise me. And I do hope she'll get past this. But she *was* in the wrong, Daniel. This is more about her than it is about Grace."

He backed up enough to hitch a leg up on the corner of his desk. "I don't think so. Grace was purposely stirring up trouble and that's what I want to talk to her about."

"She *knows* that. You don't have to tell her. Why don't you try surprising her for once and being a little bit understanding?"

That muscle in his jaw was back, twitching away. He asked in a flat voice, "What else did you want to tell me?"

Her body kind of went crazy on her—throat-clutching, breath-catching, stomach-churning crazy. She worried she would have a choking fit or maybe throw up on him. "I, um…"

"Just say it." He reached for her hand again.

She flinched. She knew if he touched her, she would lose it completely.

"Keely, what in the—"

"I'm pregnant." The words burst from her mouth like a volcanic eruption.

His eyes seemed to tilt back in his head. "What? I don't—"

"It's for sure. I've been feeling strange and bloated and kind of crampy for a while now. My period should have come last week. It didn't. And in the past several days, I've been having... I don't know. All the signs? Breast sensitivity, feeling sick to my stomach. I finally took a test this morning."

"A test," he echoed, as though the word made no sense to him.

She nodded frantically, her head bouncing up and down like a bobblehead doll's. "Two tests, actually. They were both positive. So it's real. It's happening. I'm having a baby."

He'd frozen there, like a statue, one leg on the desk, one arm bent on his thigh. "But we always used condoms except the past few times. You're on the pill."

"It was probably that first time we were together or one of the times right after that. Before I started on the pill or before it started working. Back when we were using just condoms. One of them must have been faulty. Torn, maybe. Or broken." He was still in statue mode, staring straight ahead at her. But also right through her. She threw up both hands. "Daniel. Could you just not look at me like that? We've always used birth control, and I don't know how it happened. I did not plan this, and if you're thinking that I did because of what happened with..." She caught herself. This wasn't about Lillie, and she refused to bring her lost cousin into this. She tried again. "If you're thinking I tricked you somehow, well, I don't know what to say. I would never do that. But I *am* pregnant. It did happen. We're having a baby."

He kept looking right through her.

Something was going wrong with her heart. It seemed to be breaking. A roaring sound filled her ears. Maybe she was drowning.

Drowning in heartbreak.

What kind of silly idiot was she anyway? There was no way to explain herself, no way to get through to him. Not about this. Not when the last thing he'd ever wanted was another child.

"Daniel. I'm sorry, I am. I did not mean for this to happen. But I do want this baby. And I am keeping it. That doesn't mean I expect anything from you. I am fully self-supporting and completely capable of raising a child on my own. And I will, if that's how you want it. You can, you know, think it over. There's plenty of time for you to decide how involved you want to be. My mother raised me on her own, and it worked out just fine." Her throat locked up again, and she swallowed convulsively. "Ahem. So…okay, then. You think about it. Take your time. You don't have to decide anything today."

Daniel watched Keely's mouth move. She looked too pale. The freckles stood out on her adorable nose and twin spots of bright red stained her cheeks.

She thought he was blaming her.

He wasn't, not one bit. He was only struck speechless.

It was way too damn much to take in.

Straighten up, you idiot. Pull yourself together, yelled a frantic voice in the back of his mind. He needed to snap out of it, say the comforting, supportive words she had every right to hear from him.

But…

Another baby.

More years to add on before he got his empty nest, before he finally knew what it felt like to be free. How many more years? Three, maybe? Four?

"Daniel," she whispered on a bare husk of breath. "You are breaking my heart. I really am sorry, but this is just bad. All wrong, you know? You take the time you need. I'm…well, I'm just as stunned by this thing as you are. I need some time to think, too. I'm guessing Jeanine will fill in where you need her until you can find somebody permanent. If she can't, you'll just have to work it out, because, really, I've gotta go."

"Go?" He blinked, shook his head, brought himself back into the moment. "What are you saying to me?"

"Daniel. I'm saying I'm going to pack a few things and go."

"No."

She stood up straighter. "Yeah."

"You're leaving?"

"Yes, I am."

"Just like that? You can't leave." He got up from the desk. "We have to work this out, damn it. We have to decide what to do next." He reached for her.

But she only jerked back another step. "No, we do not. We don't have to decide a thing right now. For me, this has been one never-ending train wreck of a day, and I'm in no condition to decide anything. Right now, I need a break. I need to get away."

"Get away?" he echoed numbly.

"Yeah." Now her chin hitched up. She'd set her mouth in defiance.

"Get away where?"

"I haven't decided yet. I'll…call you. Let you know."

Could this actually be real? "This isn't happening."

"Yes, Daniel. It is. I don't like it. I'm not happy." She darted around him and went to the door. "But right now, I just need to go."

What could he say to make her reconsider? "If you walk out that door, I'm not going to follow you."

"Terrific. Please don't." She pulled the door open, went through and shut it behind her.

Keely called her mother as she paced back and forth, grabbing stuff she thought she might need and tossing it into her suitcase.

Ingrid skipped the hellos and went straight to "Are you okay?"

"I need a break, Mom."

"And I'm just the one to make sure you get it."

"Meet me at my house?"

"I'm on my way."

Keely ended the call, stuck the phone in a pocket and finished packing. She zipped the suitcase, grabbed her big shoulder bag and headed for the door. From down the hall, she could hear Grace in the bathroom with Frannie and Jake. Grace said something, and Jake laughed.

Frannie giggled. "Mine!" she announced.

Keely's heart just seized up at those sounds.

Maybe they weren't her babies, but her silly heart had somehow claimed them. She left her purse and suitcase in her room and went down the hall and through the open bathroom door.

Jakey called, "Keewee!" and splashed with both hands.

Grace turned from the tub. She knew instantly that

something had gone very wrong. "Bad?" was all she asked.

Keely nodded. "I'm taking off for a while. Sorry to leave you on the hook, but I can't stay here right now."

"It's okay." Grace levered back on her heels and came for her, grabbing her, pulling her close.

Keely hugged her back, hard. "If he makes you too crazy, come stay at my house. And if I'm not there, I'll text you where I put the key."

"Oh, Keely. What do you mean, if you're not there? Where are you going?"

"Hell if I know."

"Keewee!" called Frannie.

Grace released her and she went to them. She knelt to kiss their wet cheeks and whisper, "Bye-bye. Love you."

"Wove you!"

"Bye-bye!"

Their beautiful, wet faces almost changed her mind, made her stay.

But then she thought of Daniel, of the words he didn't say and the bleak, distant look in those cold blue eyes. She pulled herself to her feet.

With a last nod at Grace, she marched back to her room, grabbed her suitcase and her purse and dragged them down the curving staircase and out the front door.

Chapter Eleven

Ingrid was already there, as promised, sitting on Keely's porch, her hair a red never seen in nature—candy apple, fire-engine red. It perfectly matched the paint on Keely's front door.

Keely pulled into the pebbled driveway, jumped out and ran to her mother's waiting arms. Grabbing on tight, she sobbed, "I love your hair," as she burst into tears.

"Come on. It's all right." Ingrid held her tighter. She smelled of sandalwood and a hint of weed. The silver bangles on her wrists jingled against each other as her hands moved, soothing and stroking, over Keely's shoulders and down her arms. "Let's go inside." She didn't wait for Keely's answer, just turned her gently and guided her to the red door.

In the kitchen, Keely sat at the table as her mother made tea. Outside, dark was falling, fog creeping in.

When she sat very still, she could hear the sigh of the ocean, down the hill and across the rolling dunes from her back porch. She'd always loved that sound, like the great Pacific shared a secret just with her. It was the main reason she'd chosen the cottage, snared on a short sale for a ridiculously low price. Ingrid put the steaming cup in front of her, and Keely sipped it slowly.

Her mother took the chair across from her. "Tell me."

And Keely did, starting with the pregnancy tests she'd taken that afternoon, moving on to all the bad stuff Auntie G had said and ending with the awfulness that had happened in Daniel's study. When she was finished, her mom poured them more tea.

Keely stared into the steaming cup. "I don't believe how Daniel reacted. When I told him about Auntie G, he blamed Grace. And then, when I said there would be a baby, he looked at me like I'd hauled off and punched him in the face."

"He's a good man. He'll recover. You'll work things out."

Would they? She just wasn't sure. She wrapped her arms around her middle and the new life growing there. "I left most of my stuff up there at the house, my Berninas included. I dread going back for everything."

"Stop. Your sewing machines will be there when you need them. Don't get ahead of yourself."

"Oh, Mom. I still don't really believe it, you know? A baby…"

"It's fabulous," declared Ingrid. "You're going to be an amazing mom. And babies bring good luck. You're living proof of that. Best thing I ever did, having you."

Keely answered her mom's broad smile with a wobbly

one of her own. But then she thought, *Daniel*, and that brought the misery crowding in on her again.

Ingrid said, "Have you told him you're in love with him?"

How did her mother know these things? "It seemed too early, you know? Too soon."

"Forget that. You're having a baby. You two will get nowhere until you face how much you mean to each other."

"Until today, I kind of thought we *had* faced it. No, we hadn't said the words. But I *believed* in us, that we were really together, you know? That we had what I've been looking for all my life. Now, though, I'm not so sure."

"Give it till tomorrow. You'll feel better. You'll be ready to talk to him again."

Keely let her head drop back and groaned at the ceiling. "Mom. I don't want to think about tomorrow, about what will happen next. And right now, I'd just as soon never talk to Daniel again."

"You don't mean that."

"I just want to get away, okay? I want to take off, like we used to when I was little, get on the road in the Pomegranate Dream bus. I want to drive up to Seattle, see Dweezle." Dweezle Nitweiler had been the band's first bass player—or maybe the second? Keely wasn't absolutely sure. "And then we could maybe head on to Boise, see what Wiley Ray and Sammy are up to." Wiley Ray was a drummer. His wife, Sammy, had sung backup and played the marimba. Last Keely had heard, Wiley Ray and Sammy had five kids. She sent Ingrid a sharp glance. "Don't you dare say I'm running away."

"Wouldn't dream of it."

"So…?"

"You want to go, baby girl? We are outta here."

Her spirits didn't lift exactly. But the awful pressure in her chest seemed to ease just a little. "You mean it? Really?"

"I'll call Grace, put her in charge at the bar while we're gone."

"That's a lot to ask of her. She just started today."

"I'm my own boss. If nothing gets done until we get back, I'll reschedule the opening. Not a big deal, but you'll need to get in touch with Amanda about the gallery."

"And Aislinn. I'll call her, too. She'll help out wherever she can." Keely leaned across the table and held her mother's gaze. "I mean it, Mom. I don't want to dither around about this. We're leaving tomorrow."

"You got it." Ingrid pulled her phone from her pocket. "We'd better start making calls."

Twenty minutes later, Amanda had said she could handle the gallery no problem. Aislinn, Keely learned, had just quit Deever and Gray. She would be picking up the slack wherever Amanda needed her.

Grace had instantly agreed to take over at the bar. She said that, yes, she could meet Ingrid there in half an hour to get emergency instructions on being the boss.

When Keely took the phone to see how she was holding up, Grace reported that the kids were in bed and Daniel had been surprisingly civil. "I'd just put the kids in their cribs, about half an hour ago. He came upstairs as I was going down, just said good-night and went on up to his room."

The ache in Keely's chest intensified as she pictured him, alone in the room that had become both of theirs.

To reclaim her resolve, she closed her eyes, sucked in a slow breath and focused on the goal, which was to get out of town. "Mom has a key to my house. She'll give it to you, just in case you need a place to get away."

"Thanks, Keely. Be safe."

They said goodbye. Keely handed her mom back her phone, and Ingrid left to meet Grace and stop in at Gretchen's to pack a bag for the trip.

"Don't even talk to her," Keely advised with a sneer as Ingrid was leaving. "She'll only say rotten things you don't need to hear."

Her mom just chuckled. "Sweetie, don't worry. I've been dealing with your aunt a lot longer than you have."

It was after ten, and Keely had just finished repacking her suitcase for their open-ended tour of the Great Northwest and beyond, when Ingrid returned.

Keely ran out to the living room when she heard the front door open. "How'd it go?"

Ingrid rolled her Frida Kahlo Skull Art spinner suitcase in the door and then shut it behind her. "Grace is up to speed. As for Gretchen, I told her everything."

Keely felt slightly breathless suddenly. "What do you mean, everything?"

"That you and Daniel had words and you need a getaway, so we're going on the road, you and me, up to Seattle, probably over to Boise and after that, wherever the wanderlust takes us. She was outraged, she said, that I could even think about taking you on the road at a difficult time like this."

"That sounds just like her."

"My sister is remarkably consistent in her opinion of a nice road trip. So I said that a time like this is exactly the right time to go on the road, after which I asked her what was *wrong* with her to begrudge you and Daniel a chance at happiness?"

"What did she say to that?"

"I didn't give her time to say anything to that. I just told her where she could stuff her self-righteous attitude, after which I broke the big news that you and Daniel are having a baby."

"Omigod, Mother." Strangely, Keely felt nothing but relief that Gretchen knew about the baby. "What did she say?"

"Not a word. I have to admit I found her silence supremely satisfying."

Keely sank to the couch. "All of a sudden, I'm hoping she's okay. I mean, I wanted to strangle her this afternoon, but I do love her and I don't want her to be suffering or worrying about us."

Ingrid came and sat beside her. "It's all going to work out."

"You keep saying that."

She hooked an arm around Keely and pulled her close. "I'm your mother. That's what mothers say."

Keely surrendered to her mom's embrace. She let her head rest on Ingrid's shoulder. "I'm so tired, Mom."

Ingrid stroked a hand down her hair. "We don't *have* to go anywhere, you know."

A weakness stole through her, to give in to her own misery, to go to her room and cry for a while. And then maybe tomorrow, to head up Rhinehart Hill to try to work things out with Daniel…

But then her belly knotted, and she ground her teeth at just the thought.

No way.

She wasn't working anything out with him if he

couldn't accept the baby. She hadn't meant to get pregnant, but now that she was, well, she *wanted* her baby. If he didn't, that was his loss. She couldn't be with a man who refused to love and welcome his own child. "I need this trip and I am going. Don't you dare back out on me now."

"Baby doll, I'm in if you're in."

"Good."

Rising, Ingrid took Keely's hand and pulled her to her feet. "Come on then. Let's get some sleep. I want to get an early start in the morning."

Daniel went to bed at a little before eleven, an exercise in futility if ever there was one. He spent the night staring into the darkness, afraid he'd lost Keely forever.

No, he argued with himself. That could never happen. The words had not been said, but they lived inside him.

He loved her.

And he knew she loved him—or at least, she had until she'd witnessed his reaction when she told him about the baby. Was it actually possible that he'd killed her love stone-dead?

He didn't know what to do, how to make it up to her. Somehow, he had to figure out what to say to her, how to tell her, how to prove to her that she was everything while also convincing her that he was happy about the baby...

The baby.

Every time he thought about the baby, he went numb. He needed to cope with that, with the reality of that. If he didn't, he had a sneaking suspicion he would only blow it all over again when he tried to make it up with her.

* * *

The kids woke up at six thirty as usual. The monitor by the bed came to life as they called to him. "Da-Da, Da-Da!"

"Keewee!"

"Up! Now."

As Daniel dragged himself out of bed and reached for his jeans, Jake's said, "Gwace! Up."

And Grace answered, "Hey, sweet monkeys. Good morning to you." She must have taken a monitor to her room last night so she could go to them if they needed her—and so she could give him a break this morning.

Daniel sank to the side of the bed, his chest gone tight, his jeans still in his hands.

Grace. Keely had it right about her. Grace was a good kid. She helped a lot. And she deserved to be treated as an adult.

He'd been way too hard on her. That had to change. He pulled on his pants along with yesterday's wrinkled shirt and headed for the playroom.

"Grace," he said, when he stood in the doorway to the playroom.

"Morning." She handed him Jake and picked up Frannie. "Let's get some breakfast."

"B'eafus. Yum!" Jake decalred and stuck his fingers in Daniel's mouth.

Daniel pretended to chew on them, which made Jake chortle in glee.

Downstairs, Grace poured kibble and fresh water for Maisey and got the kids their fruit and dry cereal. Daniel scrambled eggs and fixed toast for all four of them.

When they sat down to eat, Grace revealed that Keely

and Ingrid had gone on a road trip. "I'm temporarily promoted to manager of everything that needs doing at the bar, which unfortunately means there's no way I can watch the kids today."

Where did they go and when will they be back? he longed to demand. Instead, he said, "Congratulations on the promotion. As for the kids, you've been a lifesaver, always helping out with them. Don't worry about today, I'll figure something out." Aislinn probably had to work. Harper and Hailey were still at U of O until the second week of June. He would try the nanny service. If they couldn't help him, he would take a damn day off from the office. Gretchen would most likely come running if he asked her to watch them, but over the past sleepless night he'd realized he was seriously pissed off at his mother-in-law. He wouldn't be reaching out to her until his anger had cooled a little.

Grace set down her fork with a bite of scrambled egg still on it. "Did you just say I'm a lifesaver?"

"I did. And you are. And I'm going to do my best to respect your, er, adulting skills and be a better big brother to you."

She just looked at him for several seconds, her blue eyes suspiciously moist. "Thanks," she said in a husky little whisper. At his nod, she added, "They went to Seattle first. And she does have a phone, you know. You need to just call her."

"Yeah," he said with a half shrug.

Grace shook her head at him. "You're not going to call her, are you?"

He didn't answer her. She made one of those my-brother-is-an-idiot faces and let it go at that.

* * *

Aislinn had to work at Keely's gallery that day. The nanny service had no one to send on the spur of the moment, so Daniel stayed home.

The sun came out early. He took the kids for a walk, letting them lurch along beside him until they got cranky and then tucking them both into the double stroller to push them back home. He took them up to the playroom, changed their diapers and then stretched out on the playroom floor to keep an eye on them as they played with their toys.

The twins alternated between using Maisey as a pillow and decorating Daniel with various toys, placing them on his chest and stomach, then grabbing them up and wandering away, only to return with some other toy to set on him.

Frannie bent over him and asked, "Keewee?" causing his heart to pound like it wanted to burst from his chest and go searching for the woman he didn't want to live without.

He replied, "She went on a little trip."

"Back soo'?" demanded Frannie.

He didn't know how to answer that and settled for the painful truth. "I don't know."

With a snort and a sigh, Frannie dropped to her butt beside him. She reached out and patted his shoulder with her fat little hand. He stared at her, loving her, as Jake plunked down on his other side.

"Da-Da," Jake said and lay down next to him.

They weren't close enough. He gathered Frannie in with one arm and Jake with the other. They settled, tucked right where he needed them, on either side of his heart.

For a minute, maybe two, he knew the sweetest sort of peace.

He thought of Lillie, and for the first time, the anger didn't come. He felt only gratitude and tenderness, that if she had to go, she hadn't left him alone. She'd given him these two little ones, not as an eighteen-year sentence to struggle through.

But as a gift. The greatest gift.

What was freedom, really? He'd never had much of it, and he'd believed that he hungered for it.

But freedom was nothing. Not compared to his children, not stacked up against Frannie and Jake.

And the new baby, his and Keely's baby?

What a jackass he'd been.

He wanted the new baby, too. He truly did.

That guy who wanted freedom? He, Daniel Bravo, wasn't that guy and he would never be. He was a dad and a damned good one. He wanted his woman back, so he could be a husband, too. He wanted it all with her—the two of them together openly, with the family around them, raising Jake and Frannie and the new baby, as well.

Downstairs, he heard the front door open.

Keely?

His heart raced with hope. Maisey perked up her floppy ears as the kids wriggled free of his hold and sat up. Footsteps mounted the stairs.

Gretchen appeared in the open doorway to the upstairs hall.

"Gwamma!" Frannie got up and went for her.

Gretchen scooped the little girl into her arms, kissed her once on her forehead, then propped her on her hip. "My sister and Keely have gone to Seattle."

"I know. Grace told me."

"What is the matter with you, Daniel? I can't believe you let Keely go." She scowled down at him.

"What are you doing here?" Toys dropping off him and clattering to the rug, he rose. "I thought you were furious with her—and with me."

"I was." Frannie squirmed, so she let her down. Both kids headed for the toy box as Gretchen continued, "And I was wrong—don't look at me like that, Daniel Bravo. I'm capable of admitting when I'm in the wrong. I love you. And I love her. She's the only daughter I have left. And she took off with Ingrid in that embarrassing purple bus, took off to Seattle to visit someone named Dweezle. I know it's your fault, Daniel. I behaved very badly, and I realize that now. But she wouldn't leave just because of me. What did you do to her? What did you say?"

Shame rolled through him. He confessed, "All the wrong things."

"I knew it." Gretchen sagged in the doorway. But then she seemed to catch herself. She drew herself up. "I've been trying to call them. Both of them. My calls go straight to voice mail."

"Maybe they don't want to talk to you."

She made one of those faces women were always making at men, as though they can't help wondering how one-half of the species could be so thoroughly aggravating and hopelessly dense. "No kidding. Have *you* tried calling them?" When he didn't answer, her expression turned smug. "Coward."

He couldn't let that remark stand—even if it did happen to be true. He grabbed his phone from where he'd left it on the kids' dresser and autodialed Keely.

And got voice mail.

As he waited through her recorded greeting, he tried to decide what the hell to say.

He had nothing. Whatever he managed to sputter out would be hopelessly inadequate.

And what good would leaving her a message do anyway? He needed to be there. He needed to see her beautiful face when he told her all the ways he'd been a thickheaded jerk and begged her to please, please forgive him.

When he ended the call without leaving a message, Gretchen rattled off Ingrid's number. He tried that, too.

"Voice mail," he admitted, as he hung up.

"We need to stop wasting time and go get them," Gretchen cried. "We have to apologize and mean it and beg them to come home."

He completely agreed with her—in theory anyway. "Go get them how, exactly?"

"I know what route they took."

"How do you know that?"

"Ingrid told me. The Coast Highway to I-5."

"Why would she tell you that?"

"Why does my crazy sister do anything?" A determined gleam lit her eyes. "You think we can catch up with them?"

We? "How 'bout this. If you'll stay here and look after Frannie and Jake, I'll—"

"You can stop right there," she cut in before he could finish. "I have apologies to make, too, you know. I'm going with you. And I'll thank you not to argue with me. Arguing will only waste valuable time."

They took Lillie's minivan. It had plenty of room. Gretchen sat in the first row of back seats between the kids' car seats, armed with snacks and toys to keep them happy through the drive. Maisey went, too. She claimed the front passenger seat. Daniel rolled down her window so she could let her ears flop in the wind.

"I know we're going to find them," Gretchen kept saying as the miles rolled by. Daniel didn't share her certainty. They crossed the bridge at Astoria and entered Washington State, heading north along the coast, at first with the mouth of the mighty Columbia on one side of them and then, as they aimed true north, other, smaller rivers and then Willapa Bay. Once past the bay, they headed slightly inland again, where the trees grew thick and the banks at roadside were covered in moss and sword ferns, sometimes with green meadows stretching toward the mountains to the east.

The longer they rode, the more certain he became that Gretchen was kidding herself. That damn purple bus with the giant cartoon of Ingrid playing her Telecaster emblazoned on each side was probably miles and miles ahead of them. Depending on when the two women had set out, they could have reached Seattle by now—or changed their route or got off the highway for a bathroom break just long enough for the minivan to roll right on past.

They were approaching South Bend, and he was about to tell Gretchen they needed to give it up and go home when they rounded the next curve of the highway and he saw it—the butt end of the giant metallic-purple vehicle rolling along at a majestic pace about a hundred yards ahead.

Gretchen made a low noise in her throat, a sound both self-satisfied and triumphant. "What'd I tell you? There they are."

* * *

Ingrid was up to something. Keely had no doubt about that.

So far, they'd pulled over to the side of the road a total of six times since they left home. It had not escaped Keely's notice that her mother only thought she had engine trouble when there was enough of a shoulder that to stop wouldn't be illegal or dangerous. Only then would she start complaining that the engine was knocking or maybe it was one of the tires going flat as she eased the giant vehicle to the generous space at the side of the road.

Then she would get out and check the tires and go around to the back of the bus to look in on the engine. Each time, she took forever about it. When she came back, she would shake her head and say how everything seemed okay after all. She would start the bus up again, and they would get back on the road.

After the most recent of her pointless inspections, she'd insisted that before they moved on, they might as well have some of the tea and muffins she'd brought along.

Keely didn't want tea or muffins. She sat on the bench seat next to the door, holding her phone, hoping Daniel would call.

And he did call. Once, at a little after ten, causing her pulse to race, her whole body to catch on fire and her tummy to heave alarmingly. She almost answered that call. But she let it go to voice mail. Better to just hear what he had to say before she decided whether to talk to him or not.

He hung up without bothering to leave her a message.

And they drove on. And stopped. And drove on. And stopped.

After four hours on the road, they were just now approaching South Bend, Washington. The shoulder was wide and clear on one side. Any minute, her mother would start in about the engine knocking and when she did, Keely was going to throw back her head and scream.

Behind them on the road, someone honked. People did that all the time. The bus was big and purple, after all. And there was also the famous R Crumb cartoon of her mother playing guitar and smoking suggestively plastered on both sides. Keely craned her head to check the road behind them in the giant side mirror just as whoever it was honked again.

"A white minivan," she murmured to herself. Her heart started racing again. "That's Lillie's van! Mom, it must be Daniel."

"About freaking time," muttered her mother, as she smoothly turned the big wheel and eased the bus to side of the road.

"You planned this, didn't you?" Keely accused.

The hydraulic brakes hissed as they stopped. "Let's just say I planted the seeds. I told your aunt what route we were taking. Gretch did the rest—and she took her own sweet time about it, too."

"I'll go first," proclaimed Gretchen as Daniel pulled in and stopped behind the bus. "You stay here with the babies. Once I've made my apologies, it will be your turn. I'll bring Ingrid back here, and we'll watch the babies while you and Keely have some time alone in the bus."

He wanted to argue with her. Unfortunately, her plan made a scary kind of sense.

"Wish me luck," she said briskly and eased out between

the two car seats with surprising flexibility. She slid the door shut and walked quickly to the door on the right front side of the bus. Her gait was even and steady, without a trace of a limp left over from the injury that had broken four bones in her right foot and given him the chance to get to know Keely. To learn to love everything about her, to find what he hadn't realized he needed most: the right woman to stand beside him, the truest kind of freedom, the kind he found in her arms.

He had both front windows down and heard the bus door open. Gretchen disappeared inside.

Keely watched in the side mirror as her aunt got out of the minivan.

From behind the wheel, her mother was watching, too. "Gretchen's coming this way."

"I know. I can see her."

"She looks determined."

"Oh, yes, she does."

"Shall I let her in?"

"Yes." Keely rose and went through to the galley area. She couldn't make herself sit down for this, so she just stood by the table. "I'll talk to her in here."

The door opened with a wheezing sound. Keely heard her aunt's footsteps on the stairs.

"I would like to speak with Keely," Gretchen said stiffly.

"Through there," her mother replied.

And then Gretchen came and hovered in the doorway, her head high and her plump shoulders back. "I'm sorry," she said. It came out in a whisper as her shoulders drooped and her blue eyes filled with tears. "I had it all wrong. I said terrible things, and I have no excuse for them. I really thought I had made my peace with losing Lillie, but now I see I still have a ways to go on that. But I didn't want to let you leave without saying that I love you so much, sweetheart. And I am sorry for the rotten things I said to you. They were born of my own pain, untrue and completely unfair to you, to Grace and to Daniel, too. You and Daniel have every right to find happiness with each other. I hope that you do. I hope you can get past all the trouble I've caused and somehow find your way back to each other. I...well, I..." A tear escaped and trickled down her cheek. She sniffed, swiped the tear away and held her head high again. "I guess that's all. I'm sorry. I love you. Someday, I hope, you'll find a way to forgive me."

Keely's heart ached so bad. But it felt a little lighter, too. And there was only one thing to do now. "Of course I forgive you. I love you, Auntie G." She held out her arms.

With a soft cry, Gretchen came to her and grabbed her close.

In the back seat, as Daniel waited, the twins babbled to each other, amazingly content even after more than two hours in the car. Maisey, beside him, gave a little whine. He got out, went around to her side, let her out to do her business and then gave her a boost back in.

He'd just settled in behind the wheel again when Gretchen emerged from the bus. Ingrid, her hair a blinding cherry red, stepped out right behind her. They marched toward him.

Ingrid went to the driver's door, Gretchen to the passenger side. The sisters leaned in the windows.

Ingrid said, "You're up. Make it good."

His heart went wild inside his chest. But somehow he spoke calmly. "I'll give it my best shot." He turned to his mother-in-law. She'd clearly been crying. Her eyes and nose were red. "Did she accept your apology?"

Gretchen gave him a brave little smile. "She did. And I'm grateful."

"I'm glad for that," he said.

She nodded. "I do love that girl."

The next move was his. He got out. Ingrid took the seat behind the wheel. Gretchen put Maisey in the back and then came and sat next to her sister.

"This may take a while," he warned.

"Not a problem," replied Ingrid.

"We've got water and snacks and toys for the babies," said Gretchen. "Take as long as you need to show her how much you love her. We'll be waiting right here."

Ingrid had left the bus door open.

His heart in his throat and his pulse roaring in his ears, Daniel mounted the steps and went inside.

"Keely?"

"In here."

He found her sitting in the galley, on the long seat across from the table, wearing a little white T-shirt, faded bib overalls and white Keds. She rose as he went to her.

Tired. She looked tired, those green eyes sad, her bright hair gathered in a messy bun on the top of her head. His arms ached to hold her. He kept them tight at his sides.

"I did everything wrong," he said.

"No." Her lush mouth curved in the saddest little smile. "You did so much right. Almost everything. But, Daniel, I can't be with you."

"Because of the baby?" When she bit her lip and nodded, he clarified, "You think I don't want our baby."

For that, he got another nod, a tiny one, the barest dip of her pretty chin, as her face flushed deep red and her eyes shone with tears. It gutted him to see those tears, to know he was the cause of them.

"Keely. Don't you cry." His hands lifted of their own accord—but he lowered them when she fell back a step. He went on with his confession, "I found out today that I'm not who I thought I was." She frowned, like he'd spouted some nonsensical riddle. He said, "I've been bitter. I've believed that my freedom had been stolen from me."

"You *believed*?" She seemed to ponder the word. "Are you saying it isn't true?"

"That's right. I had it all wrong, what I want. What I need. And what you saw when you told me we were having a baby—that was the man I *thought* I was coming up against who I really am. In my bitterness, I'd convinced myself that what I wanted, what I *needed*, was freedom. I couldn't wait for Frannie and Jake to be grown, to get my so-called freedom at last. It took your leaving me to make me see that I'm not that guy. I'm a family man and I will always be. Everything I really need, I already have. Or I did, until yesterday, when I chased you away."

She searched his face. "Are you telling me, then, that you're okay with the baby?"

"More than okay. I've been stupid and blind. But the truth is I *want* our baby. I love you, Keely. I want us to be a family—all of us—you, me, Frannie, Jake, the little one that's coming—and more babies, if that happens, if you want them. I want to marry you. With you, I have everything. The family I need and the right person to talk to, the one I want beside me when things are good *and* when times get tough, the one who makes me free in all the ways that matter."

She stared up at him—hopeful and yet cautious, too. Proud and beautiful and true. "Daniel, I do love you, so very much."

She loves me. His heart beat at the wall of his chest, urging him closer. "Keely…" Again, he would have reached for her.

But she put her hand up between them. "You really mean this? I need to know. I need the brutal truth from you. If your heart isn't open, if you still have doubts about taking on another child, I need you to tell me."

He captured her raised hand, brought it to his chest and pressed it close, at the spot where his heart beat so hard for her. "No doubts. No regrets, not a one. Not anymore. I hate that you left, Keely. But I understand why. You were right to leave. It put the fear of God in me, let me tell you. It showed me the hard truth, that I've been a complete ass in a whole bunch of ways. It showed me that I could actually lose you.

"I couldn't stand that," he said. "I want you and I want our baby. I want us all to be together. I love you, and I want to spend the rest of my life with you." He lifted her hand higher, bringing it to his lips so he could kiss the tips of her fingers, one by one. "Just think about it, okay? Go ahead with your mom, up to Seattle and wherever else you need to go. Just, while you're away from me, know that I will be waiting, hoping that when you come back, you'll be coming home to me, that someday you'll say yes and be my wife."

She lifted her other hand and pressed it to his cheek. So cool and soft, that hand, soothing him, easing the painful pounding of his heart, a balm to the ache of long-ing in his soul. "Daniel." She said his name in a breath as she lifted her sweet mouth to him.

A kiss, so slow and tender, growing wet and deep. It ended far too soon.

She sank back to her heels again. "I love you, Daniel. And yes, I will marry you. As for the road trip, I don't need it anymore. I'm ready to go home."

Eight weeks later, on the last Saturday in July, Keely married Daniel in the backyard of their house on Rhine-hart Hill. The whole family attended, all the Bravo brothers and sisters, Great-aunt Daffy and Great-uncle Percy, and Ingrid and Gretchen, of course. There were a lot of family friends as well, including several of the musicians who used to play with Pomegranate Dream—Dweezle, Sammy and Wiley Ray among them. Meg Cartwell McKenna, Keely and Aislinn's mutual BFF, came too. She and her husband, Ryan, had driven in from Colorado.

Keely wore a vintage fifties' white lace dress that came to midcalf with a short veil. She was already show-ing, her stomach noticeably rounded, as she walked the petal-strewed grass between the rows of white folding chairs, her eyes on the man waiting in front of an arbor covered in roses.

When Daniel smoothed back her veil and took her hands in his, Jakey shouted from the front row, "Da-Da! Keewee!" and everybody laughed.

Keely said her vows, strong and proud. Daniel's voice was rougher, lower, the words meant for her ears alone.

And when he took her in his arms for the kiss that sealed their bond, each to the other, she knew she had found the love and trust that mattered most between a man and a woman. She felt such joy and gratitude, that he would be hers and she would belong only to him.

From this day forward.

They held the reception right there in the backyard, including dinner and champagne toasts and, later, a four-tier cake. Ingrid and her former bandmates played music on the grass.

And after dark, when Keely stood on the upper deck outside the master bedroom to throw her bouquet in the glow of endless strands of party lights, she took careful aim before she flung the lush bunch of sunflowers, orange dahlias, baby's breath and daisies into the waiting crowd below.

The flowers sailed out, bright and hopeful, full of the promise of love-to-be. They landed right where she wanted them.

In Aislinn's outstretched hands.

* * * * *

EXECUTIVE: EXPECTING TINY TWINS

BARBARA HANNAY

CHAPTER ONE

SHE was wearing white, for crying out loud.

Jack Lewis grimaced as the elegant figure stepped down from the tiny plane while clouds of red dust slowly settled on the airstrip. The same red dust covered his ute, his riding boots, and practically everything else in the outback, and yet Senator Elizabeth Green had chosen to arrive on Savannah cattle station dressed from head to toe in blinding, laundry-commercial white.

Her elegant sandals were white, her crisply ironed trousers, her matching linen top and even her floppy-brimmed hat. The only non-white items were her accessories—swanky dark glasses and a pale green leather shoulder bag that clearly held a laptop.

Where did she think she'd flown to? The flaming Italian Riviera?

Jack muttered a soft oath, audible only to Cobber, the cattle dog at his heels. 'I suppose we'd better go and say g'day.'

Shrugging off an uncomfortable sense of martyrdom, Jack set out across the stretch of dirt, moving with a deliberately easy amble, his faithful dog close behind him.

He was mad with himself for allowing his boss, an

eighty-year-old widow, to bully him into hosting this visitor. Kate Burton regularly tested Jack's patience by directing her business via long-distance phone calls from her top-price-tag retirement home in Melbourne.

'I owe Lizzie a favour,' Kate had told him breezily. 'She won't be any trouble, Jack. She just wants to rest up and take in the country air, and she needs to retreat from the public eye for a spell. You understand, don't you?'

After a lifetime of getting her own way, Kate hadn't given Jack the chance to protest that no, he didn't understand, that he was managing her cattle station not a hotel, that the mustering season had started and he was planning to join the team.

For her part, Kate made no attempt to explain why a high-profile senator, the darling of the Canberra media, was suddenly diving for cover in distant North Queensland.

Kate had left Jack with no choice but to send out the mustering team while he remained behind at the homestead. This morning he'd dutifully rounded up the horses grazing in this paddock, and he'd flattened the anthills that had popped up on the airstrip since the last time a light plane had landed here.

Now, as he approached his guest, she straightened her shoulders and lifted her chin—her very neat and determined chin.

Her shady white hat and dark glasses hid the top half of her face, but Jack sensed her surprise, as if he wasn't quite what she'd expected.

He was having the same problem—madly readjusting his assumptions. Up close, Senator Elizabeth Green was a bombshell.

He'd seen photos of her in newspapers, of course, and he was aware of her classic Italian good looks, but he'd expected the real-life version to be closer to Iron Maiden than Sophia Loren. Surely this woman was too soft and sensuous to be a federal politician?

Jack could see curves beneath her crisp white linen clothes—old-fashioned, reach-out-and-touch-me curves.

Her dark hair was tucked up under her hat, but silky wisps had strayed onto her nape, drawing his attention to her super-smooth, pale skin with a dusky hint of the Mediterranean.

As for her mouth...

Whoa. Her mouth was wide and full and soft and sultry, quite possibly the sexiest mouth Jack had ever met.

Her mouth moved. 'Mr Lewis?'

It took Jack a second or two to get his brain on the right track.

'Good morning, Senator.' He spoke a little too loudly. 'Welcome to Savannah.'

He wondered if she was going to offer her hand. Her big hat and sunglasses hid so much of her that he found it hard to pick up clues, but he sensed she was still checking him out, trying to make as many correct assumptions as possible.

When at last she offered her hand, it was cool and slim, her grip firm.

'I have luggage.' Despite the faint Italian accent, when the senator spoke she was Iron Maiden through and through.

Reassured that he knew what he was dealing with, Jack waved to the pilot. 'I'll get the luggage, Jim.'

In the hold, he found two large and perfectly matched green leather suitcases—*Louis Vuitton, of course*—and a matching leather holdall filled with books. When he hefted the strap over his shoulder, the books weighed a ton.

'I see you plan to do a little light reading,' he said, offering her a grin.

The senator gave a slight shrug, as if it was obvious that she'd have little else to do out here except improve her mind.

Reducing his grin to a resigned smile, Jack waved to the pilot, then picked up the suitcases. Hell, judging by the weight of them, she planned to move in to Savannah for six months. Or longer. Kate Burton had been vague about the length of this visitor's stay.

'We'd better get going before Jim takes off and creates another dust storm.' Jack nodded in the direction of his parked ute. 'The limousine's this way.'

Again, Senator Green didn't acknowledge Jack's attempt at a joke. Instead, she looked over at the vehicle covered in dust and then gazed slowly about her, taking in the wide and empty red plains dotted sparsely with clumps of grey-green grass, and at the sky, huge, blue and cloudless. Boundless.

A lone crow's cry pierced the stillness. *Ark, ark, ark!*

Watching his guest closely, Jack saw her take a breath as if she were bracing herself for an ordeal. He had no interest in her problems or why she'd come here, yet to his dismay he felt a faint pang of sympathy.

They set off for the ute and by the time they reached it—a matter of sixty metres or so—Senator Green's sandals were filmed with red dust and a faint red rim showed at the bottom of her pristine trousers.

Her mouth pursed with sour-lemon tightness as she watched Jack set her glamorous luggage next to bales of fencing wire in the tray back of his battered ute.

'Hope you weren't expecting anything too flash.' He opened the passenger door, saw dog hairs on the seat, and, despite an urge to leave them there, swept the seat clean with the brim of his Akubra hat.

'Thank you,' the senator said in a princess-speaking-to-the-footmen tone.

Jack wished he hadn't bothered.

'How far is it to the homestead?' she asked.

'Not far. A couple of kilometres.'

She nodded, but chose not to comment.

'In the back, Cobber,' Jack ordered, and his dog obediently jumped up beside the pale green luggage. 'And you'd better fasten your seat belt,' he told his passenger as he swung into the driver's seat. 'It's bound to be a bumpy ride.'

Lizzie sat in grim silence as the ute set off across the trackless ground. She was grateful that Jack didn't try to carry on a conversation, yelling above the roar of the motor. He seemed happy enough to drive while she clung to the panic handle, which she needed more to steady her nerves than because the ride was rough.

She needed to calm down, to throw off the alarming schoolgirl thrill that had flared inside her the instant she'd set eyes on Jack Lewis.

Good grief. It was ridiculous. Laughable. She hadn't felt such an instantaneous, unwarranted reaction to a man for almost a decade. She'd thought she'd developed immunity.

For heaven's sake. It was absurd and distressing to feel this fireworks-in-her-very-veins excitement at the sedate age of forty. It was a joke. She would put her reaction down to surprise. She'd expected Jack Lewis to be older, several decades older, actually.

After her conversation with Kate Burton, she'd had an image of the manager of Savannah as a mature and kindly, grey-haired man of the land. He'd be a little shy perhaps, as rural folk were reputed to be. Reliable, dependable, salt of the earth. A fatherly figure, possibly a bit like her dad.

Lizzie couldn't have been further from the mark.

Jack was young, younger than she was, for sure, and he

had all the attributes of a hunky pin-up boy—height, fitness, muscles, glowing health. Throw in sun-bleached hair and sparkling green eyes and a smile that would melt granite, and the man was borderline dangerous.

The silly thing was, Lizzie had met oodles of good-looking men without going weak at the knees, but there was something else about this fellow, something elusive.

Perhaps it was the slow and easy way he moved. She thought about the way he'd approached her with a leisurely, loose-hipped stride, and the effortless way he'd hefted her luggage as though it held nothing but tissue paper. Even the way he drove was relaxed and easy—guiding the steering wheel with one hand, while his other hand rested lightly on the gear stick.

Sex appeal in spades.

No doubt the young women for miles around were all in love with him.

Good grief. She had to stop thinking like this. *Now!*

Jack Lewis wasn't her type. Not remotely. She was a federal senator, earnest and conscientious—busy, busy, busy. Everything about Jack—his lazy smile and his easy, laid-back body language—showed that his whole attitude to life was different from hers.

Of course, Lizzie knew she shouldn't react to superficial appearances. She'd learned early in her career that if she genuinely wanted to find ways to help people, she had to look below the surface. Things were rarely as they appeared. The truth was always hidden.

As a woman, she also knew that she had a bad habit of falling for the wrong man. Twice in her life, she'd met someone she'd found instantly attractive. Twice she'd been burned, almost reduced to ashes.

Never again. With good reason—two very handsome

reasons—she'd made a conscious decision to keep her private life a male-free zone. Men. Just. Weren't. Worth. It.

She'd been relieved to finally step off the dating-relationship merry-go-round, and she couldn't believe she'd wasted so many years trying to choose a life partner. Now she embraced the freedom of going it alone, just as her mother had. In fact, she was taking her independence one step further than her mother had.

The ute bounced and rattled over a cattle grid and Lizzie automatically placed a protective hand over the tiny bulge below her navel.

Her baby.

Hers and only hers.

The past three months had flown so quickly, and, according to the pregnancy books that Lizzie had studied in depth and learned by heart, her baby was already the size of half a banana. It would have tiny fingerprints now, and if it was a little girl, she would have about two million eggs in her ovaries.

'Are you OK?' Jack sent Lizzie a quick look of concern that took in the protective hand on her stomach.

'I'm fine, thank you.' She spoke brusquely. Tension made her brittle and she quickly lifted her hand and fiddled with a stray wisp of hair, tucking it under her hat.

The last thing she wanted was to draw attention to her growing baby bump. Kate Burton had promised not to mention her pregnancy to Jack, and Lizzie certainly didn't want to explain until she got to know him better.

Come to think of it, Lizzie couldn't imagine taking Jack into her confidence. Surely there would be someone else at the homestead, perhaps a kindly housekeeper, who would be happy to indulge in heart-to-heart chats over a cup of tea. She should have asked Kate Burton more questions.

Looking out at the endless stretch of red plains, Lizzie felt her spirits swoop. She was planning to spend at least a month out here in the back of beyond. She needed the break, for the baby's sake, and for sanity's sake, and she surely needed to escape from the hound dogs in the press gallery.

If they caught a sniff of Jack, I'd be in trouble.

The isolation should keep her safe, however, and somehow she would cope.

She planned to keep busy, of course, staying in touch with her office in Brisbane and her parliamentary colleagues in Canberra via her laptop and her mobile phone— her *new* mobile phone, with a number that she'd only shared with a discreet circle of people she could trust.

In her spare time she would work her way through the supplementary reading matter she'd brought with her. She'd always complained that she never had enough time for reading for pleasure, although once upon a time she'd liked nothing better than losing herself in a good book.

She'd also imagined going for pleasant country walks, except this flat, parched land didn't look very inviting.

'Here's the homestead,' Jack said, pulling up at a gate and pointing ahead through the dusty windscreen.

It was a timber building, long and low, and painted white. It had a dark green, corrugated iron roof, and there were several smaller buildings scattered around it. Sprawled beneath the harsh outback sun, the collection of buildings made Lizzie think of a sleepy dog with a litter of puppies.

Jack sent her a sideways glance loaded with expectation, and she realised she was expected to say something. But what?

There was no garden to admire, although the curving lines of stones cemented together suggested that there might have been gardens in the past. She supposed she would be comfortable enough here, but the house looked very lonely sitting in the middle of the flat empty plains.

She said, 'The house looks...very...nice.'

There was a glimmer of impatience in his glance. *What is his problem?*

'Do you think you could get the gate?' he asked, super-politely.

The gate?

'Oh-h-h...the gate.' Lizzie gave a shaky laugh to cover her shock. In Canberra, she had a swipe card that opened doors or gates in a split second, or her staff went ahead of her, smoothing the way. 'You'd like *me* to open it?'

He gave her a wry smile. 'It's sort of bush tradition. Driver stays at the wheel. Passenger opens the gate. So, if it's not too much trouble.'

This gate proved to be a great deal of trouble.

First Lizzie had to wrestle with the door handle, then she had to clamber down from the ute into several inches of fine red dust that once again covered her sandals and seeped between her bare toes. Finally, she spent an embarrassing age at the gatepost, wrestling with a heavy metal loop and a complicated piece of rusty wire.

Pride wouldn't allow her to give in, but she hadn't a clue how to get the thing open.

A deep and very annoying chuckle brought her whirling around. Jack Lewis had left the truck and was standing close behind her, grinning. 'I guess I'd better show you how it works.'

'I guess you'd better,' she snapped. 'This is the most ridiculous gate I've ever seen. What's the point of making it so difficult? Why can't you have a normal latch?'

'That'd be too easy. Even the cattle could work out how to open it.'

Her response was a disdainful sniff, and she watched him with tightly closed lips as he tilted the metal loop, and, with the swift ease of a conjuring trick, slipped the wire hook free, letting the gate swing easily open.

He winked at her. 'Did you get that?'

'Of course,' she said stiffly, unwilling to admit that she wasn't completely sure how he'd done it.

'Good-o. I'll take the ute through, and you can close it after me.'

'Wait!' Lizzie commanded as he headed back to the truck.

Jack turned super-slowly, an ambiguous smile lurking in his eyes.

Her shoulders stiffened and her chin hiked higher. 'You didn't show me how to close it.'

With a lazy shake of his head he ambled back to her, and she couldn't tell if he was smiling at her expense, or trying to be friendly.

Unfortunately, he stood too close as he refastened the gate, and Lizzie found herself distracted by the play of muscles in his tanned forearms and the deft movements of his brown fingers.

'You tilt it at two o'clock,' he said, showing her twice. 'Here, you have a go.'

Their hands brushed, making her skin flash with ridiculous heat, but at last she had the hang of it, and, of course, it was dead easy once she knew.

Back in the truck, they trundled on till they reached the front steps, and Jack retrieved Lizzie's luggage with the same easy economy of movement that she found so unsettling. This time she tried very hard not to watch.

At the top of the steps he turned to her. 'I guess you'd like to see your room first.'

'Thank you.'

'It opens off this veranda.'

His blue cattle dog curled in a pool of sunlight on the veranda, while Lizzie followed its master, carrying her laptop, and shamelessly watching the man from behind, noting the way his broad shoulders stretched the seams of his blue cotton shirt, and his faded jeans rode low on his lean hips.

Good grief, Lizzie. Give it a miss.

Jack turned through French doors into a large, airy room and set Lizzie's bags on the beige carpeted floor beside the big bed with old-fashioned brass ends and a soft floral spread. He watched Lizzie look about her, inspecting the pale pink walls and fine, white spotted curtains.

'This is the room Kate uses when she visits Savannah,' he told her.

Lizzie nodded. 'I could well believe that. It's just like Kate—comfortable, relaxing and no-nonsense.'

And you're damn lucky to have it, he thought. *It's the best room in the house.*

Lizzie looked at the painting above the bed, a water-colour of a flock of birds taking off against a soft pink dawn.

'Kate thought you'd like it in here,' he said.

'It's very kind of her to let me use her room. I do like it. Very much.'

OK. One hurdle over, Jack thought.

But then two vertical lines creased Lizzie's forehead. 'Is there an en suite?'

He shook his head, and took perverse glee in saying, 'The bathroom's down the hall.'

'Oh, right.' Lizzie lifted her limp shirt collar away from her neck. 'I don't suppose there's air-conditioning?'

'The ceiling fans are adequate. It's not summer. You'll

be OK.' He pointed to the large, silky oak table next to the window with a view across the paddocks. 'Kate said you needed a desk, so I put this here for you.'

'Thank you.' Lizzie sent a final queenly glance around the room, then slipped her laptop bag from her shoulder and set it on the desk, giving the laptop an affectionate pat, as if it was her best friend—or her lifeline.

Then she removed her sunglasses and set them beside the laptop, and took off her big white hat, which should not, of course, have been a big deal.

But *hell.*

Jack's body reacted as if Lizzie had launched into a striptease.

She'd accidentally dislodged her hairpins, and her hair—thick, lustrous, shiny and as dark as midnight—spilled to her shoulders, and suddenly he was having difficulty breathing.

Which was probably just as well. If he'd been able to draw breath, he might have spoken, might have said something crazy, like telling her she was out-of-this-world beautiful.

Because—damn it, she was. She was stunning. Her eyes were the most amazing hazel, with flecks of earthy brown and mossy green stippled with gold. As for her face, framed by all that silky dark hair—

Jack could feel the muscles in his throat working overtime as he stood there like a fool, staring. At her.

Until she frowned, then looked worried. Nervous.

Somehow, he dragged in a necessary breath, and switched his gaze to the desk, forced his mind back to business. 'I—I believe you—you've brought your own Internet connection?'

'Yes.' Lizzie also took a breath, and she lifted her shirt collar again, pulling it away from her flushed skin. 'I—um—have a wireless broadband mobile card.'

'Sounds brilliant.'

'It's handy for travelling.'

She took another breath, deep and slow, then began to twist her hair back into a safe, neat, spinsterish knot.

Jack rammed his hands hard into the pockets of his jeans and looked about him—anywhere but at her. 'So what would you like to do? Unpack and settle in here? Or take a gander at the rest of the house?'

Lizzie hesitated, dismayed that her mind was so fuddled she found the simplest decision difficult. Given the amount of work she had to do, she should unpack her laptop and get started immediately.

'Perhaps you need a cuppa first,' Jack suggested slowly, almost reluctantly.

There would be a housekeeper in the kitchen. Someone sensible and cosy to provide a reassuring buffer between Lizzie and this disturbingly attractive, but highly unsuitable man. She found herself saying, 'Tea would be lovely, thanks.'

Once again, she followed Jack, this time down a narrow hallway and through a large living room filled with deep squishy lounge chairs and low occasional tables, with two sets of French doors opening onto a veranda. Casting a quick glance around the room, she gained an impression of casual relaxation and carelessness.

Cushions had been left in a tumbled pile at one end of the sofa, clearly for the comfort of the person who'd lain there watching television. Sporting magazines and empty coffee cups were strewn about, and an overturned beer can lay on the floor beside the sofa. The housekeeper was obviously as casual as Jack.

Lizzie thought fondly of her minimalist, twenty-first-century apartment and her super-efficient cleaning woman, and sighed.

They reached the kitchen.

'Pull up a pew.' Jack nodded to one of the mismatched chairs gathered around a huge, scrubbed pine table that had one end cleared, while the rest was littered with magazines, newspapers, an assortment of mail, a hammer, nails and a leather strap with buckles that might have been part of a horse's bridle.

To Lizzie's surprise, he went to the sink and filled a kettle, turned on the gas and set it on the stove.

Where was the friendly, pink-cheeked, country housekeeper, waiting with a warming teapot and a batch of scones just out of the oven?

'Is it the housekeeper's day off, Jack?'

He frowned. 'What do you mean?' His eyes narrowed as he sent a puzzled look around the shabbily out-of-date kitchen. 'Is there something wrong?'

With growing dismay, Lizzie watched him reach up to a shelf above the stove for a caddy of loose-leaf tea. He did it automatically, with the familiar ease of someone who'd done this a thousand times. 'You do have a housekeeper, don't you?'

Jack shook his head. 'No need. There's just me in the main house.' He sent her a wry quarter-smile. 'Kate said you wanted a retreat. She didn't say anything about luxury.'

'I'm not asking for luxury.'

Jack's eyebrow rose, but he spoke quietly, 'That's all right, then.'

He poured a little hot water into the teapot, swirled it around and then tipped it into the sink before he added tea leaves. Once again, Lizzie watched his hands—strong, long and capable, with golden, sun-bleached hairs on the backs.

Damn. She shouldn't have been watching Jack Lewis's

hands. She was over men. Twice bitten, permanently shy. Besides, Jack was much younger than she was—and she'd come here to escape, to retreat in peace and quiet: optimum conditions for a healthy pregnancy. Already, she felt agitated and edgy. It was Jack's fault. No, it was hers. She simply had to control her reactions.

Of course, if she told Jack she was pregnant, she would clear the air instantly. Such news would quickly kill that sexy sparkle in his eyes, and she might be able to let her hair down without the world coming to a standstill.

She could get on with her plan to relax at Savannah while her baby grew healthy and strong.

She opened her mouth, already tasting the words: *By the way, Jack, I'm pregnant.*

But suddenly she knew she wasn't going to tell him. She'd come to this outpost to avoid giving explanations about her pregnancy to a pack of hungry journalists. There was no need to tell Jack. Not yet.

Maybe later.

Maybe never. He was a stranger, after all, and Lizzie's pregnancy was none of his business.

Very soon, her hormones would settle down and this inappropriate sense of attraction would die a natural death.

CHAPTER TWO

'DO YOU do all your own cooking?' Lizzie asked Jack, forcing her mind to practical matters.

'Not usually. Most of the time there's a station cook, but I sent him out with the mustering team.' Jack poured boiling water into the teapot, replaced the lid and set the pot on the table with two blue striped mugs.

'Is there a muster on at the moment?'

He nodded. 'We always muster as soon as the wet season's out of the way.'

'Does that mean I've inconvenienced you?'

His shrug was a beat too late. 'The team can manage without me.'

'But you're the manager. Are you supposed to be supervising?'

His back was to her now and he spoke as he reached for milk and sugar. 'I have a satellite phone. I can stay in touch.' He turned, and his green eyes regarded her steadily. 'You should know that, Senator. After all, you'll be running the whole country from here.'

It was a not-so-subtle dig—and she realised that Jack probably resented her sudden arrival.

She said, 'I suppose you're wondering how a federal

senator can retreat into the outback without reneging on her responsibilities.'

'Not at all. I leave politicking to politicians.' Jack's face was as unreadable as a poker player's as he poured tea into a mug. 'Do you take milk? Sugar?'

'Thank you.' She helped herself to a dash of milk and half a spoon of sugar. 'I hope I haven't spoiled too many of your plans.'

'Most plans are easy enough to change.' Jack sat and, now that he was level with Lizzie, she was reacquainted with the superior breadth of his shoulders.

He looked across the table at her, trapping her in his steady gaze. 'That goes for you, too, Senator. No one's holding you here if you find that this place doesn't suit you.'

Something in his gaze set fine tuning-fork vibrations inside her. Quickly, she looked down at her mug. 'Please, you mustn't keep calling me Senator.'

'What should I call you? Elizabeth?'

'My family and friends call me Lizzie.'

'Lizzie?' Jack repeated her name without shifting his gaze from her face. 'Now that's a surprise.'

'Why?'

His mouth twitched as he stirred sugar into black tea. 'Seems to me, a woman called Lizzie is a very different kettle of fish from an Elizabeth.'

'Really? How?' As soon as the question was out Lizzie regretted it. It wasn't appropriate for her to show so much interest in this young man's theories about women and their names. And yet, she was desperately curious to hear his answer.

'When I think of Elizabeth, I think of the Queen,' Jack said.

'My mother would be pleased to hear that. It's why she chose Elizabeth as my name.'

'She named you after the Queen?'

'Yes. She named all her daughters after strong women. I have a younger sister Jackie, named after Jackie Onassis, and then there's Scarlett, named after Scarlet O'Hara.'

'Yeah?' Jack chuckled. 'No maternal pressure or anything.' He lolled back in his chair, legs stretched under the table. The man sure had a talent for looking relaxed. 'Your mother must be proud of you. A federal senator. That's a pretty big deal.'

'Yes, I'm sure she is proud.'

'But she still calls you Lizzie.'

Lizzie… *Cara*…

With a wistful pang Lizzie remembered her mother's tearful reaction to the news she'd shared just last week, when she'd flown back to Italy, to her hometown of Monta Correnti. Her mother's tears had been happy, of course, and accompanied by fierce and wonderful hugs.

Lisa Firenzi was thrilled that her eldest daughter was about to become a mother at last, and she'd been surprisingly OK with the unexpected news that her grandchild's father was an unknown donor. But then, Lisa Firenzi had never bowed to convention.

Like mother, like daughter…

Lizzie took a sip of her tea, which was hot and strong, just as she liked it, and she pushed aside memories of the end of her visit home, and the unhappy family row that had erupted.

Instead, she asked Jack, 'Why do you think Lizzie is so different from Elizabeth? What kind of woman is a Lizzie?'

Jack laughed out loud and the flash in his eyes was most definitely wicked. 'I'm afraid I don't know you well enough to answer that.'

For heaven's sake, he was flirting with her. She had to stop this now. She was most definitely not looking for any kind of relationship. Apart from the fact that she'd given up on men, she was pregnant, for heaven's sake. Besides, Jack was probably the kind of man who flirted with any available female.

Lizzie froze him with her most cutting glare. It was time to get serious. Really serious. She hadn't come to the outback for a holiday, and she certainly hadn't come here for romance. She had a stack of paperwork to get through and she should set Jack Lewis straight. Now.

And yet...she couldn't help wondering...who was she really? An Elizabeth? Or a Lizzie?

A small frown settled between Jack's brows and he stood abruptly. 'We should talk about meals,' he said. 'The pantry's well stocked and so is the cold room, but we're the only ones here to do the cooking, so—'

'We?' Lizzie interrupted, somewhat startled. 'You're not expecting me to cook, are you?'

He slid a sideways glance to the big country stove, then back to Lizzie. 'Excuse me, Senator. Perhaps you weren't aware that lesser mortals actually prepare their own meals?'

'Of course I know that,' she snapped, aware that he probably planned to call her Senator whenever he wanted to put her down.

Jack narrowed his eyes at her. 'Can you recognise one end of a saucepan from another?'

She rolled her eyes to the ceiling to show her exasperation, but, truth was, in recent years she'd been far too busy to dally with anything remotely domesticated. Admittedly, since she'd become pregnant, she'd been conscientious about breakfast—making a smoothie from yoghurt and fruit—but her PA brought her a salad from the deli for lunch, and her diary was filled with evening engagements—

charity functions, political dinners, business meetings—so she often ate out.

On the few occasions she ate at home, the meals had mostly been takeaway, eaten at her desk with little attention to taste or texture. She couldn't remember the last time she'd eaten alone with a man in a private home.

'I don't have time for cooking.' Lizzie added a dash of ice to her tone.

Not in the least intimidated, Jack leaned his hips against a cupboard and eyed her steadily. 'Then you'll have to risk your digestion with my cooking.'

'Is that a threat?'

His eyes held the glimmer of menace. 'I guess you'll soon find out, won't you? Otherwise, you could go solo and make your own meals. No skin off my nose. Or we could take turns at the stove and share what we cook.'

'Share?' Lizzie set her mug down before she spilled its contents. She hadn't shared a house, taking turns in the kitchen, since her carefree university days.

Back then, when she'd shared a house and a kitchen, she'd also fallen in love. With Mitch.

Her mind flashed an unbidden memory of her younger, laughing self, teaching Mitch to test spaghetti by throwing it against the kitchen wall to see if it stuck. As always, he'd had a better idea, and they'd shared a spaghetti strand between their linked mouths, eating until their lips met. And then, of course, they'd kissed…and, quite probably, they'd gone to bed. She'd been so madly in love back then.

But it was such a long time ago.

'No worries.' Jack gave her a crooked grin. 'I'm no chef, but I guess I can look after the cooking. I hope you like steak.'

'Steak's fine,' Lizzie said, and then, to her astonishment, she found herself adding, 'but I'm sure I could brush up on a few old recipes.'

When Jack looked uncertain, she supplied her credentials. 'After all, my mother owns a restaurant.'

'A restaurant?' His eyes widened, suitably impressed. 'Where?'

'In Monta Correnti. In Italy.'

'An Italian restaurant!' Jack sent her an eye-rolling grin and rubbed his stomach. 'I love Italian tucker. I bet the talent for cooking runs in your family.' His grin deepened. 'And here I was thinking you were just a pretty face.'

As Lizzie unpacked her suitcases she refused to think about Jack Lewis. She especially refused to think about his throwaway line about her pretty face.

For heaven's sake, he was a young man, barely thirty, and she was pregnant and practically middle-aged, and she'd long ago learned to ignore comments about her looks.

Female politicians were fair game for the media, and from the moment she'd hit parliament journalists had paid far too much attention to her appearance, her dress sense, and her hairstyles. It had been beyond infuriating.

Since Lizzie's university days, she'd had her heart set on working hard to better the lives of ordinary, everyday Australians, but the reporters only seemed to notice what she was wearing, or which man she was dating.

There'd been one infamous photo, early in her career, of her coming out of a restaurant, arm in arm with a male colleague. Her hair was loose, blowing in the wind, and she was wearing a shortish skirt with knee-high Italian leather boots. The boots were dark red, and the photo had found its way onto the front page of every metropolitan daily in the nation.

"Boots and all" the headlines had announced. It was as if she'd dropped IQ points simply because she'd worn something sexy.

After that, Lizzie had chosen to keep her hair in a tidy bun and to dress sedately and she'd schooled herself to ignore the unwanted attention of the press gallery.

Jack's comment was no different. It was water off a duck's back.

Of course it was.

She concentrated on colour-coding her clothing as she hung it in the old-fashioned wardrobe with an oval mirror on the door. Her undergarments and nightwear went into the Baltic pine chest of drawers.

She arranged the ten good books she'd brought on her desk, and set up her laptop, checked that the Internet connection worked—yes, thank heavens—and downloaded a raft of emails from her office.

Out of habit, she answered them promptly, although she would have loved to ignore them today and to wander down the hall to the old-fashioned bathroom, to take a long soak in the deep, claw-foot tub she'd spied there. Just as she would have loved to take a little nap on the big white bed, with the French doors open to catch the breeze blowing in from the paddocks.

She couldn't slacken off on her very first day. It was important to prove to herself and to her colleagues that this month-long retreat would not stop her from working.

With business emails completed, Lizzie sent a quick message of thanks to Kate Burton, telling her that she'd arrived safely. She considered gently chiding Kate for not warning her about Jack's youth, but she decided that even a gentle protest might give Kate the wrong idea.

She also sent a quick note to her mother and another,

warmer message to her cousin Isabella in Monta Correnti, telling her about the move to Savannah.

During Lizzie's latest trip to Italy, Isabella had surprised everyone by announcing her engagement to Maximilliano Di Rossi. But to Lizzie's dismay, the exciting news had been rather overshadowed by the terrible animosity that flared up, worse than ever, between her mother and Isabella's father, Luca.

There'd been ongoing tensions between the two families for decades now, fuelled by the fierce rivalry between their restaurants, "Sorella" and "Rosa", which stood next door to each other in Monta Correnti.

Lizzie, however, had always been close friends with Isabella, and she was determined to keep in touch with her now as an important step in her plan to build bridges across the family divide.

In her private life and her public life Lizzie Green planned to become a stress-free zone...

And with her duties accomplished, the big white bed still beckoned.

Really, she found herself asking, what was the harm? She'd been fighting tiredness ever since she'd first become pregnant—and there'd been an embarrassing occasion when she'd nodded off during a senate enquiry into the cost of roadworks in new mining areas.

Now, she was here in one of the remotest corners of the big empty outback, amazingly free to adjust her schedule in any way she liked, and next to no one would be any the wiser.

After years of relentless hard work and a punishing schedule, the sudden freedom was scary.

But it was real.

Wow.

Yes, she really was free. Out here, no one would know

or care if Senator Elizabeth Green took a long, relaxing bath in the middle of the afternoon. There were no journalists lurking outside the homestead, and Lizzie was free to contemplate the miracle happening inside her.

· As always, her spirits lifted the instant she thought about the tiny little baby growing in her womb.

She was so, so glad she'd gone along with her plan, in spite of all the worry, and the doubts voiced by her friends.

'A sperm donor, Lizzie? You've got to be joking.'

Her girlfriends hadn't understood at first, and Lizzie couldn't really blame them. For years it hadn't bothered her that she was the only woman in her circle of friends who was still single and babyless. She'd been almost smug, proud that she was an independent thinker, a New Age woman who didn't bow down to the pressure to follow the crowd. She was focused on a higher calling.

Unfortunately, the smugness hadn't lasted.

At thirty-eight pushing thirty-nine, almost overnight, something had clicked inside her. She'd been gripped by a sudden, deep and painful yearning for the precious, warm weight of a baby in her arms. Not a friend's baby. Not a niece or a nephew.

Her baby.

The longing had become so powerful it had pressed against Lizzie's heart, becoming a constant ache, impossible to ignore and she'd faced the alarming truth that her body was a ticking time bomb…counting down, down, down…to a lonely and childless future…

Of course, the lack of a potential father for her baby had posed a hiccup. The scars left first by Mitch, and several years later by Toby, were deep and painful. Still.

Even so, Lizzie had tried dating. Truly, she had tried. But all the decent guys were already married, and she wasn't prepared to settle for Mr Good Enough, and there was no way she would leap into a convenient marriage just to have a baby. Where was the morality in that?

Besides, Lizzie had learned at her mother's knee that a woman could embrace independence and single mother-hood with dignity and flair.

So she'd settled on a sperm bank, but it had taken twelve nail-biting months before a viable pregnancy was confirmed. By that time, Lizzie had been so fraught and nervous that Kate Burton had kindly insisted that she spend some time at her outback cattle station, where she could enjoy being pregnant out of the spotlight.

Lizzie had accepted with gratitude.

She knew only too well that eventually there would be questions, and all kinds of fuss about the sperm-bank decision. People would say that she'd kissed her political career goodbye, but for now she wanted to give her baby its best chance to be born healthy. Already, she loved it fiercely.

After the birth, she'd find a way to continue her career and raise her child.

Lizzie Green always found a way.

But right now, on this sunny autumn afternoon, she was a forty year old woman, pregnant for the first time, and feeling just a little lonely. And more than anything she was tired.

So why shouldn't she take that bath? If for no other reason than because she needed to get rid of the gritty red dust between her toes. Already she could picture the soothing ritual of running water, adding a swoosh of the scented salts that Kate had left. A glug of luxurious oil, then sliding down for a long soak.

And then afterwards, why not a nap?

* * *

At six o'clock, Jack tapped his knuckles on the door to Lizzie's room to tell her that dinner was ready.

When there was no answer he cleared his throat and called, 'Senator Green?' And then, another knock. 'Lizzie?'

Still there was no answer, and he wondered if she'd gone for a walk.

He'd come to her room via the veranda, so it was a simple matter to lean over the railing to scan the yard and the home paddock, but he saw no sign of her.

Surely she hadn't wandered off? Damn it. Was she going to be a nuisance on her very first day here?

He supposed there was no point in searching elsewhere without checking her room first, so he stepped through the open French doors, and his heart almost stopped beating when he saw her.

Asleep. Like a modern-day Sleeping Beauty.

Jack knew exactly what he should do—turn smartly on his heel, march straight back out of the room and knock again loudly, and he should keep on knocking or calling until the senator heard him and woke up.

Pigs might fly.

No way on this earth could he move. His feet were bolted to the floor, and his eyes were glued to Lizzie as she lay there.

She'd changed into soft and faded low-rise jeans and a pale green, sleeveless top with a low neck and little ruffles down the front. The way she was lying, curled on her side, exposed a good six inches of bare midriff.

Hey, senator, you're not so bad when you're asleep.

Not so bad? Who was he kidding?

Sleep hadn't only stolen Lizzie's haughtiness; it had left her defenceless and vulnerable. Out-of-this-world sexy.

With the attention of an artist commissioned to paint her portrait, Jack took careful note of details.

The soft light filtering through the curtains washed her with warm shadows, highlighting the intricate pattern of fine veins on her eyelids, the dusky curve of her lashes, and her dark hair rippling like water over her pillow.

Her mouth was a lush, full-blown rose, and the scooped neckline of her blouse revealed a little gold cross winking between the voluptuous swell of her breasts. His hands ached to touch her, to trace the cello-like dip and curve of her waist and hip.

Even her bare feet resting with one pressed against the other were neatly arched and sexy.

Far out. He had to get out of here fast. This sleeping beauty might look like every temptation known to man, but he knew damn well that the minute she woke she would morph straight back into the officious and cold city senator. So not the kind of woman he'd ever get involved with.

Jack forced himself to take a step back. And another. Problem was, he was still watching Lizzie instead of where he was going, and he backed into a chest of drawers, sending a hairbrush clattering to the floor.

She was instantly awake, sitting up quickly, dark hair flying about her shoulders, eyes and mouth wide with shock.

'I'm sorry.' Jack threw up his hands, protesting his innocence. 'Don't scream. It's OK.'

She was breathing rapidly, clearly frightened and disoriented, but even so she clung to her dignity.

'I'm not in the habit of screaming,' she said haughtily, while she tugged at the bottom of her blouse with both hands in a bid to close the gap of bare midriff.

No, Jack thought wryly as he bent to retrieve her silver-backed hairbrush and set it on the chest. Of course she wasn't a screamer. She was too cool. Too tough.

'I was trying to call you from the veranda, but you were out like a light,' he said, forcing himself backwards towards the door. 'I just wanted to let you know that dinner's ready when you are.'

'Dinner? Already?' She sent a hasty glance to the fading light outside, then frowned as she reached for the wrist-watch on the bedside table. When she saw the time, she let out a huff of annoyance. 'I've been asleep for hours.'

'Half your luck.'

Clearly Lizzie didn't agree. Already she was off the bed, shuffling her feet into shoes while tying her hair into a tight, neat knot. 'Your steaks will be overcooked,' she said.

'At ease, Lizzie.'

She went still and frowned at him and Jack wondered what she would do if she knew how amazing she looked at that moment. In the shadowy twilight, with her arms raised to fix her hair, her breasts were wonderfully rounded and lifted, and the luscious gap of creamy skin at her waist was on show once more.

Jack forced his gaze to the floor. It was clearly too long since he'd had a girlfriend.

'We're not having steaks tonight,' he said. 'There's a stroganoff and it's simmering away nicely, so you've no need to rush.'

'Stroganoff?' Lizzie's eyes widened. 'You're serving stroganoff?'

'It's no big deal.' Jack shrugged, and began to head back along the veranda, calling over his shoulder, 'I'll see you in the kitchen. No hurry. Whenever you're ready.'

In the meantime he would go chop firewood, although it wasn't yet winter. Or he'd make a phone call to his dentist and volunteer to have all his teeth drilled, even though they were cavity-free. Anything to take his mind off his sexy, out-of-bounds houseguest.

To Lizzie's surprise, the stroganoff was really good. The beef was tender, the mushrooms plump and sweet, and the sauce super-smooth and tasty. She found that she was hungry—ravenous, in fact, with a new interest in food that had begun when she'd reached the end of her first trimester. As soon as her morning sickness had stopped, her appetite had blossomed.

Along with her libido. Which no doubt explained the difficulty she was having keeping her eyes off Jack. She didn't understand how she could find a man who'd slaved over a kitchen stove so incredibly attractive.

Lizzie respected successful, career-driven men, powerful politicians, or business magnates at the top of the corporate ladder. An unambitious cowboy, who managed a remote cattle property for an imperious old lady, held no appeal whatsoever.

And yet…she'd never seen blue jeans sit so attractively on a man, and Jack's shoulders were truly sensational. As for the easy way he moved and the lively sparkle in his eyes…and his smile…

He made her feel girly and soft.

Clearly, pregnancy hormones had depleted her common sense and awakened her earthier instincts.

It was an unsettling problem, and it wasn't going away.

'This is an excellent meal,' she admitted, in a bid to keep her mind on the food. 'I'm impressed.'

From across the table, Jack accepted her praise with a nonchalant smile. 'Glad you like it.' He drank deeply from a glass of beer.

'I suppose it was just a little something you threw together?'

'More or less.'

Lizzie didn't return Jack's smile. Her enjoyment of the meal was somewhat spoiled by her competitive instincts. Already, she was wondering how she could match Jack's culinary efforts when it was her turn to cook, and she wished she could remember the finer points of her mother's favourite recipes.

'I've heard that country folk are exceptionally resource- ful,' she said. 'I imagine you're probably a mechanic, a cook, a cattleman and a businessman all rolled into one.'

'Something like that.' Jack's green eyes narrowed. 'That's how most city people see us, at any rate. Jack of all trades and master of none.'

Lizzie was surprised that easy-going Jack was suddenly touchy. Clearly she'd hit a raw nerve.

Practised at calming touchy politicians, she said, 'A senator has to be a bit like that, too. Economist one day, social worker the next. You get to be a minor expert in one hundred and one areas of policy.' A moment later, she asked, 'Have you always lived in the outback?'

Jack took his time answering her. 'Pretty much. Except for the years I spent at boarding school.'

'And did you grow up always wanting to work on the land?'

This question should have been perfectly harmless, but again it seemed to annoy Jack. Leaning forward, elbows on the table, he twisted his glass between his hands. 'Did you grow up always wanting to be a politician?'

'Oh—' Lizzie wasn't normally thrown by sudden about- turns, but tonight she was off her game. She responded too quickly, 'Not really. Politics was something I sort of fell into.'

Jack's eyes widened with understandable surprise.

Unhappily, Lizzie set her knife and fork neatly together on her empty plate, sank back in her chair and let out an involuntary sigh. Why on earth had she made such a revealing confession to this man? She gave a dismissive wave of her hand. 'Everything changed when I went to university.'

He sent her a teasing grin. 'Don't tell me that you fell in with the wrong crowd?'

'I suppose you could say that,' she replied icily. 'I met a group of hardworking, committed idealists.'

Jack pulled a face as if to show that he wasn't impressed. Then he rose, and took their plates to the sink.

'Well…thanks for dinner.' Lizzie stood, too. It was time to get back to the work she'd missed while she'd napped. 'The stroganoff was delicious.'

'Hey,' he called as she headed for the door, 'Don't hardworking, committed idealists help with the dishes?'

Lizzie's cheeks grew hot. She hadn't given dishwashing a thought. Now she imagined standing with Jack at the sink, side by side, chatting cosily, possibly brushing against each other while they washed and dried their dishes.

'I'll wash up when I cook tomorrow night,' she said, and, without another word, she made a dignified, if hasty, exit.

Instead of watching TV as he did most nights, Jack spent the evening in the machinery shed, tinkering with the old station truck. The brakes were dodgy and needed fixing, and he seized the excuse to stay well clear of the homestead, well clear of Lizzie.

Unfortunately, staying clear of the senator didn't stop him from thinking about her. He kept remembering the way she'd looked when she was sleeping, kept thinking about her mouth, and how it would taste if he kissed her.

When he kissed her.

He was an A-grade fool.

He should be remembering how the senator turned starchy as soon as she woke, and the snooty way her lush mouth tightened when he asked her to do a simple thing like help with the dishes. Elizabeth Green was light years away from the kind of girl he was used to. She didn't even belong on a cattle property.

He couldn't imagine why Kate Burton had sent her here. Surely she must have known that Lizzie wouldn't fit in?

Jack had lived in the outback all his life and everyone he knew, even the hoity-toity grazier's wives, pitched in to lend a hand. On a working cattle property, people pulled their weight with everything from opening gates and helping with the dishes, to cooking, gardening, caring for children, mending a fence, or joining the cattle muster. Jack could remember one occasion when his mother had even helped to fight bushfires.

If the senator thought he was going to run around waiting on her, she had another think coming. She'd waltzed onto Savannah at an extremely inconvenient time, and she certainly couldn't expect kid-glove treatment.

If he had his way, he'd bring her down a peg or two.

Problem was, even though Lizzie was out of place here, and even though she was bossy and citified and bloody annoying, she *was* incredibly sexy. Maddeningly so. Those lips of hers and those alluring curves were driving Jack crazy. Already, after half a day.

An entire month of her presence on Savannah was going to be torture.

If Jack thought it would work, he'd ignore Kate's request to play host to Lizzie, and he'd ring the contract mustering plant on his satellite phone and offer to trade places with Bill Jervis, his cook.

Bill was sixty, and a grandfather, and he could keep an eye on Lizzie Green as easily as Jack could, and he could prepare top-class meals for her every night. Jack, on the other hand, could be out on the muster with the stockmen. They had a difficult task, clearing three thousand head of cattle out of some very rough country, and his intimate knowledge of the Savannah terrain would be a definite asset.

The swapping scheme was beautiful in its simplicity. There was only one problem with it. Jack might be a good stockman, but he'd have a mutiny on his hands if he tried to deprive the ringers of Bill's cooking.

Which brought him back to square one—he had no choice but to stay put and to grin and bear Lizzie Green's presence here.

It was ten o'clock when he left the truck's innards lying in pieces on the machinery shed floor and went to the laundry to scrub off the worst of his grime. The laundry was a simple wooden lean-to attached to the back of the house—a very basic and functional bachelor affair. Tonight, however, it was filled with white linen clothes soaking in sparkling suds, and wispy bits of lingerie dangled from a tiny line suspended above it.

Jack groaned as the fantasies fuelled by those scant scraps of fabric caused a whole new set of problems.

CHAPTER THREE

THE strident laughter of kookaburras woke Lizzie. Disoriented, she lay still, staring about her, taking in the soft grey morning light that crept through an unfamiliar window. Slowly, she remembered her arrival at Savannah yesterday, and why she'd come here.

She smelled bacon frying, which meant Jack was up.

Dismayed, she washed and dressed and hurried to the kitchen. It would be her turn to cook dinner this evening and already the task was looming in her mind as The Great Kitchen Challenge. She wanted to catch Jack before he took off for some far-flung corner of the property, to ask him about the contents of Savannah's pantry.

He was still at the stove, fortunately, tending to a frying pan, and looking far more appealing than any man had a right to look at such an early hour.

He was wearing a blue cotton shirt, faded from much washing, and old jeans torn at the knee. His fair hair was backlit by the morning sun and his skin was brown and weather-beaten, and he looked astonishingly real, and vitally alive. Impossibly attractive.

But I don't want to be attracted. I can't believe I'm reacting this way. It's bizarre.

He turned and smiled, and Lizzie's insides folded.

'Morning, Senator.'

'Good morning, Jack.' Good heavens. She sounded ridiculously breathless.

'Hope you slept well?'

'Quite well, thank you.'

She cast a deliberately cool glance at the contents of the frying pan and suppressed an urge to enquire about Jack's cholesterol levels.

'You're welcome to share this,' he said.

'No, thanks.' She gave a theatrical shudder. 'I usually have yoghurt and fruit.'

'Suit yourself,' he said smoothly. 'The fruit bowl's on the table. Feel free to take whatever you like. I'm pretty sure Bill keeps yoghurt in the cold room.'

'The cold room?'

With a lazy thumbing gesture, Jack pointed to a door in the opposite wall. 'Through there.'

Good heavens. What kind of host expected his guests to hunt for their own meals? Lizzie was distinctly put out as he turned off the heat and loaded up his plate, leaving her to march into the huge cold room in search of yoghurt.

Admittedly, the cold room was very well organised, and she found, not only a small tub of biodynamic berry yoghurt, but the cuts of meat she needed for the evening's meal.

'I've made coffee,' Jack said, sending her a smile when she returned. 'And there's still plenty in the pot.'

'I'm afraid I can't drink coffee.'

His eyebrows rose high. 'You don't like it?'

'Not—at the moment.' The doctors had warned Lizzie to avoid coffee while she was pregnant. 'I'll make tea,' she said, guessing he was unlikely to offer. Then, 'So what are your plans for the day?'

'I'll be bleeding the brakes on the old truck we use to cart feed around the property.'

'Bleeding brakes? That sounds tricky.'

'It is, actually. I decided to give the truck an overhaul while the men are away, and I started last night, but the brakes are even worse than I thought.' His green gaze held hers. 'I'm afraid I'm going to need a hand.'

Lizzie frowned. 'But there's no one left here to help you, is there?'

Across the table, he flashed a grin. 'That's why I was hoping you'd offer to help.'

'Me?' Lizzie's jaw dropped so quickly she was surprised it didn't crack.

'I'd really appreciate it.'

Stunned, she shook her head. '*I* can't help you. I'm far too busy, and I don't know the first thing about trucks. I've never even changed a tyre.'

'You don't need to *know* anything. You just have to press the brake pedal a few times.'

Clearly, Jack was one of those people who thought politicians only worked when parliament was in session. Lizzie was used to colleagues who treated her heavy workload with due reverence, but Jack didn't give a hoot about her investigations into fairer private health incentives.

'I have a mountain of important documents to read through this morning.' *And I have to spend this afternoon cooking.*

'You could spare a few minutes.'

Shocked, Lizzie stared at him, angry at his lack of respect. That is, she wanted to be angry. She intended to be angry, but his naughty-boy smile was like sun thawing frost.

She heard herself saying, feebly, 'I—I suppose I might be able to spare ten minutes. No more.'

Which was how she found herself in the machinery

shed a quarter of an hour later, balanced on the front bumper of a rusty old truck, breathing in diesel, while she stared helplessly at a bewildering tangle of metal cylinders, knobs, pipes and rubber hoses.

'I have to get fluid through the system and air out of the lines,' Jack said.

'So what do I have to do?'

'I'll need your help just as soon as I've poured this fluid down the brake line.'

'Where's the brake line?'

'Over there to the right, next to the carburettor.'

Lizzie hadn't a clue where the carburettor was, but she couldn't help admiring the concentration on Jack's face as he poured the fluid, very carefully, not spilling a drop.

That done, he told her to hop behind the wheel, ready to work the brakes, and then he promptly disappeared beneath the truck.

Fine prickles darted over Lizzie's skin as she watched him. There was something so very earthy and unsettling about seeing a grown man—a gorgeous, broad-shouldered, lean-hipped grown man, no less—on his back, on the ground, easing himself under a mass of machinery.

Jack's head and shoulders disappeared first, and she found herself staring at his torso and legs…at the bare tanned skin showing through the tear in his jeans—not a designer tear, but a proper work-worn rip—at the battered leather plait threaded through his belt loops…and the very masculine bulge beneath the zip in the centre seam.

Her mouth went dry as she actually imagined lying there beside him, on top of him, under him, their bodies intimately entwined.

'Right,' Jack called. 'Press the brake down steadily with an even force.'

'Oh.'

Caught out, she had to scramble to get into the truck's cabin.

'OK,' she called, a flustered minute later. 'I'm pressing the brake now.'

'Sing out "down", when you've pressed it as far as it will go. And then take it off when I call "up".'

It wasn't easy to depress the brake fully. Lizzie had to sit on the very edge of the seat, but at last she called, 'Down!'

It was ages before Jack called, 'OK. Up!'

Relieved, she let the brake off, but then Jack called, 'Can you do that again?' And the process was repeated over and over, while he patiently tested and retested the first brake, and then the brakes connected to each of the truck's wheels.

She couldn't believe he'd dragged her all the way down here just to call out 'down'. The process took much longer than ten minutes, and she was angry about the precious time she was wasting…

And yet, to her immense surprise, she actually enjoyed the strange back-and-forth communication with his disembodied voice. She liked the sense of teamwork…and she had to admit that brakes *were* vitally important… Men's lives relied on them.

Besides…she kept picturing Jack on his back beneath the massive vehicle…kept remembering how breathtaking he'd looked down there.

Oh, no. Not again.

How could she be obsessing about a man who was at least ten years younger than her? A man who had no idea that she was pregnant?

It was all very disturbing. And surprising. This time yesterday she'd been chairing a last-minute face-to-face meeting to discuss the Renewal Energy Amendment Bill.

Today she was perched behind the wheel of a truck in an outback machinery shed, breathing in diesel fumes, and having a disjointed conversation with a man lying beneath the vehicle.

It was almost as if she'd been teleported to another planet.

Finally, Jack shouted, 'OK, that's it. All good.'

Relieved, Lizzie scrambled down from the truck, and Jack slid out from beneath it, wiping blackened hands on an old rag. He jumped to his feet with easy grace.

'Thanks,' he said. 'I couldn't have done that without your help. You were brilliant.'

He was looking into her eyes and his smile was so genuine, Lizzie became flustered and dismissive. 'Don't be silly. It was nothing.'

Jack laughed. 'I suppose you're used to putting your foot down.'

Her smile stiffened. 'It's a very necessary part of my job. Now, if you'll excuse me, I must get straight back to that job.'

'By all means, Senator. I'll walk with you to the house. I need to make a phone call to Kate Burton.'

Walking with Jack hadn't been part of her plan. She'd been hoping to escape his knowing smile, and those ripped jeans, the rumpled shirt, and the smear of grease on his jaw.

As they left the shed and emerged into dazzling sunlight Jack asked in a conversational tone, 'So how long have you known Kate?'

'Oh, for quite a few years.' Lizzie couldn't help smiling. 'Kate's hard to miss. She's involved in so many organisations. Quite a mover and shaker. On the national board of several charities. She got me onside to help with funding for additional places in aged care.'

Jack grinned. 'That sounds like her cup of tea.'

'Actually, it was a tall order. We needed to increase the budget for the aging by a third, but Treasury was blocking it. In the end I had to get support from both houses to allow the passage of a new bill. Kate was very grateful.'

'No doubt.' Jack's voice was strangely rough, and his mouth had twisted into a complicated smile.

'What about you, Jack? How long have you known her?'

He shrugged. 'Since I was a kid. She and my mother have always been friends.'

Lizzie expected further explanation, but they'd reached the homestead steps.

'I'd better let you get to work,' he said, moving ahead of her, taking the steps two at a time, then swiftly disappearing inside, and leaving Lizzie to wonder if she'd said something wrong.

In his study, Jack raked a shaky hand through his hair.

He picked up the phone, dropped it down again, paced to the window and looked out, shocked by the confusion churning inside him. He fancied Lizzie like crazy, but she was the last woman on the planet he should chase.

Why would he want to? It didn't make sense. Why would an outback cowboy even dream of getting together with a high-profile federal senator, who had the power to affect the course of their nation?

She wasn't remotely his type. She was ambitious, and driven. The kind of person he'd always steered clear of. Too much like his father.

Jack's stomach clenched tighter as he thought about his old man.

Ambition, boy. That's what you need. A man's nothing without ambition.

Sure, Dad.

To please his old man, Jack had chosen his life's goal at the age of six. Together they'd watched Air Force training exercises—sleek, super-sophisticated monsters ripping across the outback skies—and Jack had decided that as soon as he finished school, he would be in the cockpit of a fighter jet.

To impress his dad, he'd spent his boyhood trying to excel in the usual outback activities, but no matter how many pony races or calf-roping events he'd won, his father had always found something to criticise.

Just remembering the boxing lessons he'd taken sent a wave of resentment through Jack. He'd never satisfied his old man. He was constantly criticised for not having the killer instinct, for standing back if an opponent slipped, or for holding back on a knockout.

He'd put up with it all, however, because he knew that one day he'd finally make his father proud.

Then he'd sat the recruitment exams. Jack had known he had the necessary co-ordination and fitness, and he'd scored good grades in the required subjects, so he'd gone into the final tests brimming with confidence.

He'd come out devastated.

He'd passed every section with ease, except the most important of all—the psych test.

The recruiting officers had been diplomatic, but Jack got the message. He wasn't cut out to fly their devastating weapons into battle. They wanted someone with a ruthless streak, with hard arrogance and a get-out-of-my-way attitude…

The kind of man his father had pushed him to be… The kind of man he could never be…

It had taken Jack years to accept this, and to finally be comfortable in his own skin. Now, his awareness of his strengths and weaknesses only made it plain as day that he and Lizzie were polar opposites. He had no doubt that she'd trampled on people as she scaled the heights of parliament.

She was pushy and powerful. She had to be. OK, maybe she was driven by an urge to help people, but maybe she was also just hungry for success.

Bottom line—they had nothing in common. He was a strumming guitar. Lizzie was the whole brass band. Why was he lusting after a woman like that? And why the hell couldn't he simply talk himself out of it?

By six o'clock, Lizzie was ready to crawl into bed. Instead she had to face a mountain of washing-up.

She was out of practice at this cooking caper, and she'd gone overboard, of course.

Inspired by fond memories of her Grandmother Rosa's ossobucco in a heavenly vegetable sauce, she'd thrown herself into the task. She'd been so sure it would be the perfect meal to impress Jack, so she'd hunted on the Internet for a recipe that closely matched her memories of Rosa's dish, and she'd followed it to the letter.

The first part hadn't been too bad. She'd already found the meat she needed in the homestead's cold room and she'd tied string around each ossobucco, then lightly floured them on both sides, but not around the edges.

While they were browning, she'd cut zucchinis, carrots, onion and celery—all of which she'd found in a surprisingly well-maintained kitchen garden at the back of the house.

With the casserole in the oven, however, Lizzie had begun on the special vegetable sauce that had made her grandmother's dish out of the ordinary. Four different vegetables—peas, beans, carrots and celery—all had to go into separate bowls of cold water and soak for half an hour. Each vegetable then had to be boiled in its own pot, then they were blended together before being added as a smooth sauce to the casserole.

Honestly, Lizzie knew it was ridiculous to go to such lengths for a simple evening meal with Jack Lewis. He'd managed to throw together last night's meal with a minimum of fuss, and he'd only used one pot, for heaven's sake. She, on the other hand, had used practically every saucepan and dish in the kitchen.

With too much to fit in the dishwasher she was still up to her elbows in detergent suds when she heard Jack's footsteps approaching.

'Honey, I'm home!' he called in a pseudo-American accent, rippling with humour.

She spun around, outrageously pleased to see him fresh from the shower, damp strands of dark blond hair flopping onto his forehead, and smelling of sexy aftershave.

He was smiling and he looked so genuinely pleased to see her that her heart seemed to tilt in her chest.

'How's the truck?'

Jack smiled. 'I took it for a test-drive this afternoon and it runs as smoothly as a sewing machine. The brakes are perfect.' He sent a curious glance to the stove. 'I'm faint with hunger, and that smells amazing. Is it Italian?'

'Yes.' Lizzie took a breath to calm down. 'It's ossobucco.' *Oh, dear.* She sounded far too proud of herself, didn't she?

'Ossobucco?' Jack's eyebrows lifted. 'That's authentic. Did you have any trouble finding everything you needed?'

'Not at all.' She wondered how he could look at her with such thrilling intensity and discuss food at the same time. 'There are so many different cuts of meat in the cold room, and all sorts of vegetables in the garden.'

'All thanks to Bill,' Jack admitted.

'Is he the cook who's out with the mustering team?'

'The one and only.' Jack saw the huge pile of dishes in front of her. 'Hey, you knew you only had to cook one meal tonight, didn't you?'

Lizzie bit her lip. 'You weren't supposed to see this mess. I wanted it all cleared up before we ate.'

'But what have you been up to? Cooking for a whole week?'

'No,' she said tightly, turning back to the sink, highly embarrassed by the amount of mess she'd made.

Jack snagged a tea towel. 'I'll give you a hand.'

'No!' This time she almost snapped at him. 'Please, don't bother. I—I'll have these dishes done in no time. Dinner won't be ready for another ten minutes, or so. Why don't you go and—and—'

'Count kookaburras?' he suggested with a knowing smile.

'Watch a bit of television,' she supplied lamely.

Shrugging, he crossed the kitchen, opened the refrigerator and selected a beer. 'I'll feed the dog,' he said as he snapped the top off the beer.

Lizzie felt strangely deflated when he left the room. Lips compressed, she finished the dishes and set the cleared end of the table, took the casserole from the oven, and cut the strings from around the meat before setting it aside to rest.

When Jack wandered back, he was carrying a dusty bottle of red wine. 'I found this in the cellar. I thought your meal deserved something better than beer.'

Lizzie forced a smile.

'You'll join me, won't you?' he said, reaching into an overhead cupboard for wine glasses.

'Um…I'm not drinking alcohol at the moment.'

Jack's green eyes widened. 'This retreat of yours requires abstinence?'

'Yes.'

With a puzzled grin, he held out the bottle. 'But this is a great vintage, and it's Italian vino.'

'I'm sure it's lovely, Jack.' She forced lightness into her voice. 'But you can't tempt me to the dark side. I won't have wine tonight, thanks.'

He turned the bottle in his hands, frowning at the label. 'I don't want to drink it alone. Guess I'll stick with beer.'

'I'm sorry. Normally, I'd love a glass of wine, but I'm—'

The word *pregnant* died on Lizzie's lips.

Annoyed with the situation, she picked up a fork from the table and rubbed at it against a tea towel as if she were removing a spot.

'No worries.' Jack was as easy-going as ever.

But Lizzie *was* worried. She shouldn't feel bad simply because she hadn't told Jack about her pregnancy. He didn't need to know. It wasn't any of his business. Except…unfortunately, she knew there was another reason she was clinging to her secret.

Her news would kill the playful warmth in his eyes, and, for reasons that made no sense at all, she didn't want to break the bewildering thread of attraction that thrummed between them. She hadn't felt anything like it for ages. She didn't want to feel anything like it. She'd deliberately distanced herself from such feelings.

And yet, even though she knew this attraction was highly inappropriate, it was also spectacularly thrilling.

She set the casserole dish on a mat on the table and lifted the lid.

Jack let out a soft groan. 'This is too good to be true.'

'What is?' She was tense as a violin string. The flash of heat in his eyes seemed to scorch her, but it disappeared as quickly as it had come, and he offered her a lopsided smile.

'Beauty, brains and a talent for cooking. You're quite a package, Senator Green.'

'Don't be too rash with the compliments until you've tasted the meal.'

Using a serving spoon, she lifted two ossobucci smothered in vegetable sauce onto Jack's plate. The smell was the same rich and appetising aroma she remembered from her grandmother's kitchen, and even though the meat probably wasn't young veal, it was tender and falling away from the bones, just as it should.

With a sense of relief Lizzie sat down to eat, but she couldn't completely relax until Jack had taken his first bite. To her dismay, he sat staring at his plate.

'Is something wrong, Jack?'

'No.' He picked up his knife and fork and sent her another crooked smile. 'I wondered where these bones had got to.'

'These bones?' she repeated in horrified alarm.

Jack grimaced, clearly embarrassed, and he shook his head. 'Don't worry. It's nothing. Shouldn't have mentioned it.' Immediately, he began to eat. 'Mmm. Lizzie, this is amazing.'

'But what were you saying about bones?' She couldn't eat until she knew.

'Don't worry about it. I shouldn't have said anything. Just relax and enjoy the meal. You've gone to a lot of trouble and it's sensational.'

'But I shouldn't have used these ossobucci, should I?'

Jack dropped his gaze to his plate. 'Well, I've never heard them called *that* before,' he admitted.

'What do you call them?'

His eyes were apologetic. 'Shin bones. We—er—usually keep them for the dogs.'

Caro Dio. Lizzie clasped a hand over her mouth. Tears stung her eyes.

'Lizzie.' Jack reached across the table and touched the back of her hand. 'It's OK. The meal's fabulous.'

'But you wanted the bones for your dogs.'

She sniffed. It would be ridiculous to cry.

'I didn't realise you could make a meal out of tough old bones, and, heaven knows, the dogs don't need them. Don't give it another thought.'

Jack's eyes sparkled at her, enticing from her an answering smile.

'I suppose it serves me right,' she admitted. 'I was trying too hard.' She gave a shaky laugh and a roll of her eyes. 'All those pots and pans.'

'This meal is worth every one of them,' Jack said, tucking in.

Lizzie ate, too, and she had to admit that the food tasted very good, but she could have saved herself an awful lot of work if she'd cooked something simple like spaghetti.

Why was it so hard for her to remember that she'd stepped out of the political circus ring? She didn't have to compete any more. She was here to relax. To slow down. Loosen up. Let go.

As they ate Jack encouraged her to talk, but, while most people expected her to talk about some aspect of her political work, he wanted to know more about her childhood in Italy, and she found herself unwinding as she recalled those happy times.

Many of her memories involved her little sisters, Jackie and Scarlett, and when she let her mind roll back she could almost hear the echoes of their laughter bouncing off their neighbours' houses as they chased each other down the cobbled streets. She could hear their girlish squeals as they ran up the hill, brushing past bushes of rosemary, catching its scent in their skirts, ducking beneath thorny branches in the lemon grove.

She told Jack about the sky in Monta Correnti, the unbelievable deep, deep blue of hyacinths, and the buttery sunlight that fell on ancient stone walls as she walked to school, clutching her mother's hand. She told him about the tangle of wild olive trees on the mountainside, the winding paths rimmed with autumn crocuses, her grandmother's cat asleep in the ivy.

Suddenly, she realised that Jack was staring at her, no longer easy-going, or relaxed, or smiling, but with an emotion that set her pulses racing.

'So beautiful,' he said softly.

Lizzie swallowed a gasp. She was almost certain he was talking about her, but this attraction thing was getting out of hand. She found it undeniably exciting, but it was wrong. Misplaced. She shouldn't allow Jack to speak to her like this.

'Yes, Italy's beautiful,' she said, pretending that she'd misunderstood him. 'But Australia's beautiful, too. Every country's beautiful in its own way.'

By now they'd finished their meal, and Lizzie stood to take their plates to the sink.

With a wry half-smile, Jack stood, too.

To her relief, he didn't try to repeat his compliment.

'Thank you,' he said instead. 'That was a memorable meal.'

'I'm glad you enjoyed it. I really liked your stroganoff last night.' Lizzie set the plates in the sink. 'I thought men were supposed to be messy cooks but you tossed that meal together so easily, *and* you only used one pot.'

From the sink, she threw a glance back over her shoulder to see Jack's reaction to this admission, was surprised to find him looking sheepish.

'Maybe that's because I only had to reheat the stroganoff,' he said.

Lizzie frowned. 'Excuse me?'

Standing there, with his hands shoved in his pockets, he looked like a little boy caught out for cheating in a spelling test. 'Bill, the cook, left the stroganoff in the freezer. I just had to heat it up.'

Lizzie's jaw dropped. 'But you let me think you'd made it from scratch.'

He shrugged. 'I didn't actually say I'd cooked it, but you seemed so impressed and I was happy to leave it that way.'

'Jack!' She couldn't believe he'd tricked her like that. How annoying.

Jack sent her a teasing smile. 'I should have known you'd turn the meals into a competition.'

'But I didn't!'

'Of course it was a competition, Lizzie.' Jack was moving towards her now. Laughter shimmered in his eyes as he came slowly, easily, across the kitchen, closer and closer. 'You can't help being competitive.' His voice was slow, deep, and teasing. 'Your mother named you after the Queen, and now you have to be top dog in everything.'

'That's not true.' As protests went, it was very weak. Lizzie threw up her hands in frustration.

Jack caught her wrists and held them fast.

Her breath was trapped in her throat. He was holding her by her wrists alone, and yet she felt pinned against the sink by the sheer force of his sexy masculinity. Looking up at him with a kind of fascinated awe, she could see that he wasn't smiling now.

She recognised the serious intent in his eyes. She'd seen it before, in other men, and she knew he wanted to kiss her. Oh, heavens, Jack was so very attractive and she could feel herself weakening, but she couldn't allow it. She was pregnant, for heaven's sake.

Their situation was precarious—a man and a woman alone in the middle of nowhere with a dangerously simmering attraction. Lizzie felt poised on a tightrope, about to fall, but she had to cling to common sense. She couldn't afford this kind of complication.

'Jack, you're invading my personal space.'

'Are you objecting?'

'Most definitely.' She spoke in her steeliest senatorial tones.

The light in Jack's eyes died. He let her wrists go and took a step back from her. For tense moments neither of them spoke, but they stared at each other, unhappily aware that a thrilling but reckless opportunity had been offered and rejected.

'So,' he said quietly, 'what would you like to do now?'

'I have to wash up.'

'You've washed up. It won't take a moment to throw these few things in the dishwasher. What then? Do you want to watch TV?' His mouth tilted in a half-mast smile. 'I'm assuming you'd like to keep up with the news.'

Lizzie imagined watching television with Jack, pictured him sprawled on the sofa, jeans stretched tight over solid, toned thighs. She knew she would spend the evening checking him out, and then he would know for sure how impossibly attracted she was.

She should keep her distance, calm down, get her head

straight. The news of the world would have to wait. She could always keep up with it via the Internet.

'No TV tonight, thanks,' she said as she headed for the door. 'I need to catch up on my emails.'

CHAPTER FOUR

SHE'D almost let Jack kiss her.

She'd *wanted* him to kiss her.

She'd very nearly jumped into his arms.

Lizzie stood at the doorway of her room, looking out across the front veranda to the quiet paddocks and the silvery trunks of gum trees, shocked by how close she'd come to wrecking her careful plans.

She'd come to Savannah to escape the pressures of the city, mostly to escape the pressure of journalists who'd just love to discover her pregnancy and turn it into a scandal. Yet tonight she'd been on the brink of creating a hot, new scandal.

With Jack.

She could imagine the headlines.

'Senator's Outback Love Nest.'

'Senator Takes a Cowboy.'

She'd wanted Jack to kiss her. Heaven help her, she'd practically *prayed* for amnesia. She'd wanted to forget her political responsibilities, and to forget she was forty and off men, and that she *always* picked the wrong men anyway. She'd wanted to forget that she was only here for a few short weeks, forget that her focus was on becoming a mother to an anonymous man's baby.

She'd wanted to forget everything…except the sexy sparkle in Jack's eyes and the alluring promise of his lips.

How scary it was to know she was so hopelessly weak. After years of self-discipline and hard work, after carefully weighing the pros and cons of single motherhood, tonight she'd wanted to risk it all while she carried on like a reckless, hormone-crazed kid.

Thank heavens nothing had happened.

She had to look on that encounter as a warning, and to be forewarned was to be forearmed. Now that she knew she was susceptible to Jack she would be much more careful in future.

On the back veranda, Jack stared out into the black night, idly stroking the springy fur between Cobber's ears while his mind replayed the scene in the kitchen.

He'd been so close to kissing Lizzie. Her mouth had been mere inches from his. He'd been able to smell her skin and the hint of lemony shampoo in her hair. He'd been about to taste her.

You're invading my personal space.

Are you objecting?

Most definitely.

'What do you reckon?' Jack asked the dog softly. 'Was that a stinging rejection? Or a lucky escape?'

Lizzie dreamed she was a child again. Wearing a blue dress and sandals, legs brown and bare, she wandered along the familiar, cobbled streets of Monta Correnti where purple petunias spilled from sunny balconies and washing hung from lines strung between windows.

Wherever she went, she could hear the church bell ringing the angelus from the top of the mountain, and she felt wonderfully safe.

But then, in the haphazard way that dreams changed, Lizzie was in her uncle Luca's kitchen where dried red peppers hung in loops from the ceiling and an old timber dresser held glassware and thick, blue and white plates. The fragrant aroma of tomato sauce, rich with basil and oregano, drifted from a pot on the stove.

Her cousins, Luca's twin boys, Alessandro and Angelo, were there in the dream, too. The three of them were eating spaghetti from deep bowls, slurping happily.

The scene changed again to a hot summer's night, and Lizzie and the twins were lying on the terrazzo balcony of her uncle's house, hoping for a cool breeze, while they looked up through stone arched windows to the jasmine-scented moon.

Suddenly, Isabella burst into the scene, but she was an adult, crying to Lizzie that she didn't know about the boys, and demanding to know where they'd come from.

When Lizzie woke the dream still felt real, even though Alessandro and Angelo had left Italy so very long ago—so long ago that Isabella and Lizzie's sisters hadn't even known about them.

Most of Lizzie's memories of the little boys were vague, but she could clearly remember their shiny eyes and cheeky smiles. She could definitely remember being in trouble with her mother for visiting Uncle Luca's house, and she remembered later being given strict orders never to speak to the rest of the family about the boys. Lizzie had never understood where they'd gone and she'd almost forgotten about them until her recent visit home.

With a heavy sigh, she rolled over in bed, cringing as she thought again about the terrible row that had erupted during her visit to Monta Correnti.

She'd gone to Italy full of her exciting baby news and she'd been even more excited about Isabella's engagement to Max, but she'd left hurt and bewildered, struggling to understand why her mother had so suddenly and angrily exposed the long-held secret that Luca had kept from his children.

Lisa was full of her own news because she'd just come back from New York where she'd seen a photo in the paper of Angelo, one of the twins who was a baseball star now. But… But it seemed incomprehensible to Lizzie that her mother would choose Luca's birthday to reveal the dark secret he'd kept from his children. Of course, the sudden news of the twins' existence had blown the family apart, but Isabella had been hit hardest of all.

But now that she was fully awake, Lizzie tried to shake off the dream. Last night, she'd reminded herself that she'd come to Savannah for a break, to focus on her pregnancy and on the changes that lay ahead. And yet here she was, still finding something to worry about.

By the time Lizzie arrived in the kitchen Jack had already breakfasted and gone, so she ate quickly, and returned to her room, carrying her mug of tea, where she downloaded her emails and discovered a brief message from her mother.

I'm too busy as always, but the restaurant is doing very well, so can't complain. I hope you're looking after yourself, darling. Do remember to take your iron tablets.

Lizzie knew she shouldn't have been surprised by the message's brevity. She should be used to her mother's ways by now.

Still, Lizzie longed to hear news of peace between her mother and her uncle. Perhaps it was too much to expect the brother and sister to kiss and make up. Just the same, she was worried. And there was still no message from Isabella. She'd sent her cousin several emails now, but Isabella was yet to reply.

There was every chance, of course, that Isabella was extremely busy. She'd always worked harder than anyone else, taking care of her smaller brothers after their mother died. Even now, when she was engaged to a wealthy Italian prince, Isabella was still working hard in the family restaurant.

Given Isabella's devotion to her family, it was no wonder she'd been especially upset by the news of Alessandro and Angelo in America. And it was completely understandable that she'd resented the fact that Lizzie had known about her brothers all along.

Thinking about it now, Lizzie felt as if she were almost as guilty as her mother was, which was pretty silly. She'd been a child, after all, and she'd promised to keep the secret without understanding any of it.

A sudden knock on Lizzie's door interrupted her thoughts. She whirled around, saw Jack standing there, sunburned and smiling in his dusty work clothes, and she was overcome by another astonishing burst of pleasure, as if someone had lit a flame inside her.

'How are you?' he asked.

'Fine, thanks.' Was she grinning foolishly?

'I was wondering if you're madly busy.'

Normally she would have responded automatically that of course she was terribly busy, but this morning she recognised how much like her mother that sounded.

'Why do you ask?'

'I was hoping you could lend me a hand again. Another quick job. I need to get feed to the newly weaned calves, the ones not included in the muster.'

To Lizzie's dismay, his request had instant appeal. She told herself it was because she felt motherly towards the weaned calves. 'What does it involve?'

'I was hoping you could drive the truck. It's only a matter of driving slowly along a track, and I'd be on the back pushing off bales of stock feed.'

'I've never driven a truck.'

'It's a standard floor gear shift.' Jack grinned. 'And it's perfectly harmless now.'

Her first thought was for her baby's safety, but she was sure Jack wouldn't put her in a dangerous vehicle. Then she thought about how slow this job would be for him if he had to do it on his own—stopping the truck, leaping out and climbing onto the back to push off a bale or two, then jumping down and driving on to repeat the job, over and over. 'When do you want to do this?'

'Late this afternoon? Say, about four o'clock?'

She refused to smile. 'All right.'

For the rest of the day, an uncalled-for tingle of excitement zipped through Lizzie every time she thought about her late-afternoon assignment with Jack. *It's only work. It's perfectly harmless.*

She worked steadily, lunching on a sandwich at her desk, but promptly at four o'clock, dressed in blue jeans and a long-sleeved, blue and white striped cotton shirt, which she'd jokingly thought of as her country-woman shirt, she met Jack outside the machinery shed.

The sun was already slipping to the west and it sent a pretty, coppery-tinged light over the bales of hay on the back of the truck. Feeling only a little nervous, Lizzie climbed behind the driver's wheel for a practice drive, while Jack swung into the passenger seat beside her.

To her relief, the truck's motor started first go, and when she eased the vehicle forward there was only one kangaroo-hop and one teeth-clenching clash of gears before she got the hang of it and drove smoothly. Jack pointed the way via a dirt track that wound through paddocks of dry grass dotted with gum trees, and Lizzie drove on, appreciative of the quietness of the outback afternoon—the wide starch blue skies, the distant mauve hills and white-trunked gums, all bathed in soft, golden light.

It was such a very different world out here.

Having grown up in Italy, Lizzie still found herself marvelling at the sheer size of Australian properties. Savannah station was miles from Gidgee Springs, the nearest township, and it was a thousand miles from Brisbane, thousands more from Sydney, from Canberra and Melbourne.

Every so often they came to a gate, and this time it was Jack who got out to open them, and then close them behind her, but it wasn't too long before they reached the huge paddock with the weaned calves.

'OK. This is where I start dropping off the feed,' Jack said. 'All you have to do is drive on slowly and we'll drop a line of feed across a couple of kilometres.'

Using the rear-vision mirrors as guides, Lizzie watched him swing up onto the tray-back of the truck with his customary ease. She drove slowly, watching him framed in the mirror, with his shirtsleeves rolled back over muscled forearms, using his pocket knife to cut the twine on the big bales of hay, then tossing them to the ground, as if they weighed no more than sugar cubes.

Young cattle came from everywhere, head butting each other like schoolboys tussling in a tuck-shop queue in their eagerness to get at the fresh sweet hay.

Too soon all the hay was dispersed and Lizzie stopped

the truck, while Jack dismounted and got back in beside her. 'Well done,' he said with a smile. 'I'll make a country-woman of you before you're through.'

They exchanged smiling glances.

Jack said, 'You'll be riding a horse next.'

'Oh, no, I won't.' No way would she threaten her pregnancy on the back of a horse.

Again, she considered telling Jack about her baby. After all, he was very friendly, and he'd managed to thaw her frostiness despite her best efforts to remain remote.

Perhaps she might have told him if she was confident that he wanted no more than friendship, but she couldn't ignore last night's close call, and the inappropriate, two-way attraction that seemed to be getting stronger every minute. There was enough tension beween them already without adding her pregnancy to the mix.

When they reached the homestead and climbed down from the truck, Jack was surprised that Lizzie didn't seem in any hurry to go back inside. Instead, she walked to the timber fence of the stockyard and leaned her elbows on the top rail, looking out across the plains.

The sun was low in the west now, tingeing the sky with pink, and a cool breeze stirred the grasses. Lizzie, in her blue jeans and striped shirt, looked amazingly at home in that setting. Her profile, softened by loosened strands of dark hair, was pensive as she looked out at the land.

Jack couldn't resist going over to her. 'A penny for your thoughts.'

'I was thinking how very peaceful it is here.' She lifted her face to the rosy sky and took a deep breath. 'Especially now, at this time of day. The light's so soft and the land's all lovely and dappled by shadows.'

'If you can't relax here, you never will.'

She sent him a rueful smile. 'Is it living here that makes you so relaxed? Is everyone in the outback easy-going?'

'Not everyone. My father certainly wasn't.'

'I've been wondering about your family,' she said. 'Are they still on the land?'

'No.' Jack's shoulders slumped and he leaned heavily on the rail beside her. 'I'm an only child and my parents split up years ago. Mum went to Melbourne to live with her sister, and my father died of a heart attack about six months later.'

'I'm sorry.'

Jack gave a dismissive shrug. 'Mum's remarried now, and very happy.'

'And you stayed on the land, working for Kate?'

The breeze caught a strand of Lizzie's hair, blowing it towards Jack. He contemplated catching it, letting it slide through his fingers like a satin ribbon, then he came to his senses and erased the thought, answered her question instead.

'I ended up here eventually, but it wasn't what I'd planned for my life.' He dragged his gaze from Lizzie and watched a bird circling high above them. 'My parents used to own a cattle property almost as big as Savannah.'

Lizzie turned to him, her face soft with sympathy. 'Is it too nosy to ask what happened?'

'We lost it thanks to my pig-headed father.' Jack grimaced. 'My old man argued with everyone—the local council, auctioneers, neighbours, bank managers. He completely ignored his accountant's advice, made a stack of rash investments on the stock exchange, and lost all his money. The bank tried to foreclose on the property, and Dad had a whale of a time, arguing and resisting.'

'Did they take him to court?'

Jack nodded. 'The trial dragged on for ages, but the old

man wouldn't compromise and settle out of court. He wanted a fight. Stubborn as a broken bulldozer. In the end—' he gave a shrug '—we lost the lot.'

'Ouch,' Lizzie said softly. 'That must have been terribly hard for you and your mother.'

'It was the last straw. Ended their marriage.' Jack's mouth thinned. 'Dad died six months later, still furious with the world and everyone in it.'

It was a terrible story.

Lizzie almost wished she hadn't asked. Jack's eyes had completely lost their usual sparkle and they'd taken on a haunted look, as if he was seeing ghosts that still troubled him.

Surely it was a miracle he'd come through such an unhappy time without losing his cheerful and easy-going temperament. She wondered how much it had cost him to retain the 'Jack-factor' that she'd taken for granted.

'At least you know you're not anything like your father, Jack.'

'I should bloody well hope not. I've gone out of my way to make sure I'm not even remotely like him.'

'So you ended up working for Kate instead,' Lizzie said to change the subject.

'I got involved with Savannah after Kate's husband died, and she had all sorts of trouble. Corporate cowboys tried to frighten her into selling this place for a pittance.'

'But you were able to help her?'

'I had to,' he said with an offhand shrug. 'Kate might be a tough old cookie, but at that time she was a grieving widow and she couldn't stand up to those thugs on her own.'

So, Lizzie thought as darkness crept over Savannah and they left the stockyard and headed for the house, Jack had deliberately chosen to be different from his dad. Mr Nice

Guy. But although he was easy-going, he wasn't a push-over. He'd proved that when he'd stood up for Kate.

Even so, Jack had chosen well to stay here in the out-back where the only stress came from the weather and the seasons and the market fluctuations.

The lifestyle here suited him. He would hate her frantic pace, and for the thousandth time Lizzie told herself she was pleased she'd called a halt to last night's kiss.

The little niggle of regret that squirmed in her chest would disappear in time. Surely?

'You can cook a mean steak,' she declared at dinner.

Jack sent her one of his trademark smiles. 'Just as well you like it. I don't have a very wide repertoire.'

'Doesn't matter. This will do me.'

The steak was cooked to perfection, blackened and seared on the outside and rosy pink in the middle, and the accompanying lettuce, tomatoes and radishes were won-derfully crisp, straight from the garden.

They didn't talk a great deal as they ate. Lizzie wondered if Jack regretted having shared so much about his family. He didn't seem particularly upset, but perhaps he was good at hiding his feelings beneath his easy-going exterior.

Or perhaps she was thinking about him far too much.

'Would you like ice cream for dessert?' he asked as he cleared their dishes.

'Oh, no dessert for me.' Lizzie patted her stomach, aware of the bulge below her navel that seemed to be grow-ing exponentially.

'It's chocolate-fudge ripple.' Jack sent her a cheeky wink as he opened the freezer door.

Her taste buds leapt. 'No, I really shouldn't.'

He shrugged. 'Your loss.'

Didn't he worry about triglycerides? She supposed he could offset his eating habits with plenty of outdoor exercise.

Watching Jack fill a bowl with rich creamy scoops of vanilla and chocolate, she folded her arms and resisted the temptation to lick her lips. To her surprise, when he sat down again he handed her a spoon.

'In case you change your mind.' A slow smile unravelled, lighting his green eyes. 'I'm happy to share.'

Share?

Lizzie flashed back to her student days with Mitch and the way he'd so easily charmed and enslaved her. She'd made more mistakes over guys since then, especially with Toby. Hadn't she finally learned her lesson? Shouldn't she reject such easy familiarity from Jack?

But she was ridiculously relieved to see him looking happy again, and, after all, what was the harm in a spoonful of dessert? Lizzie lasted almost no time—perhaps, oh, all of twenty seconds—before she reached across the table and took a spoonful of ice cream from Jack's bowl.

It was cool and creamy against her tongue and it tasted sinfully luscious.

'Good, isn't it?' Jack said, pushing the bowl closer.

'Mmm.' She helped herself to a second spoonful.

'Not quite as good as Italian gelato, I guess.'

'Oh, I think this ice cream could hold its own.'

Jack grinned. 'So you don't feel compelled to stick up for everything Italian?'

'Why should I? I'm half Australian. My father's Australian.'

'I guessed with a surname like Green that he wasn't Italian. Does he live in Australia or Italy?'

'In Australia. In Sydney.'

Jack looked as if he wanted to ask another question, but was holding back.

It seemed only fair to expand her story, after he'd told her so much about his family. 'My mother was a fashion model,' she said. 'She travelled a lot when she was young, and she met my father when he was a dive master at a resort on the Great Barrier Reef.

'And no,' Lizzie added, guessing the direction of Jack's thoughts. 'My parents didn't marry. My father stayed here in Australia and my mother went back to Italy. I lived with her, mostly in Monta Correnti, until I started university. By then, my father had a boat-building business in Sydney, and I wanted to study English literature, so I decided to come out here to study, to be near him and to get to know his family and his country.'

'He must have been pleased about that.'

'Yes, he was. Very pleased.' Lizzie smiled, remembering their wonderful, emotion-filled meeting. It had been such a shock to discover how very deeply her father loved her, and how much he'd missed her.

Jack was watching her closely. 'And you've stayed on,' he said, 'so you must have liked it here.'

'Yes,' she said simply.

She helped herself to one last spoonful of ice cream, tipping her head back and holding the icy sweetness in her mouth until it began to melt, slipping slowly, languorously down her throat.

Out of the corner of her eye she caught Jack staring at her, and the unmistakable desire in his eyes sent flames shooting under her skin. Ribbons of heat formed knots in the pit of her stomach.

Caro Dio. She reached for her glass of mineral water

and took a deep swig, and then another, draining it. 'I—I'll do the dishes,' she muttered, jumping to her feet.

Slowly, Jack scooped the last of the ice cream from the bowl and then even more slowly he licked the spoon. When he stood, at last, and came lazily towards her, she realised she hadn't done a thing about the dishes. She was still standing there, watching him.

He set the bowl on the sink and his arm brushed hers. Another flash of heat engulfed her. He didn't move away.

It was a breathless age before he said in a low, lazy drawl, 'I'm invading your personal space.'

'Yes.'

It was no more than a whisper. Tonight she couldn't dredge up the right level of frostiness.

Jack placed a hand on the bench on either side of her, trapping her against the cupboards. 'I'd like to stay here, Lizzie.'

No. No. No. No. No. This was where she had to tell Jack, *again*, to step back, to stop saying such things.

She tried to speak. Couldn't summon the words. Heaven help her, she was too enchanted by the gathering storm inside her, and, already, she could feel the heat of his body surrounding her.

Already he was touching her. His hands slid lightly up her arms. She was shivering. Melting. His arms were closing around her…while his lips explored the curve of her neck.

She closed her eyes, savouring the astonishing, sweet pressure of Jack's mouth on her skin.

There was no way she could stop him. It had been so long since she'd experienced this gentle intimacy. Too long. She could feel her skin smiling wherever his lips touched her.

Her skin grew greedy and she arched her neck, seeking

more. Jack obliged beautifully, letting warm, lazy kisses trail over her neck to her jaw, while his hands traced the shape of her shoulders through the thin fabric of her T-shirt.

At any moment now their mouths would touch, and all chance of stopping him would fly out of the window.

It was already too late.

She was filled with a sweet, aching need that deadened all thoughts but her deepening yearning to be touched and kissed... She was desperate for the moment when Jack's mouth finally reached hers...

When it happened, her lips were already parted.

Breathlessly, he whispered her name. 'Lizzie.' Just once, brushing the soft syllables over her open lips. Then his tongue traced the rim of her parted mouth, and her knees turned to water.

Jack caught her, and she was instantly lost, drowning in the perfect taste and smell of him, in the hint of sun-drenched outdoors that clung to his skin.

Everything about his kiss was perfect—the texture of his mouth, and his grainy skin, and the muscly strength of his body pressing against her.

She felt rosy and warm and insanely happy.

When Jack broke the kiss, she was devastated. She'd wanted it to go on for ever.

Clearly, Jack had much more control than she had. With one last gentle kiss on her forehead, he released her.

He smiled. 'You taste delicious. Of ice cream.'

'So do you.'

She was smiling goofily when, without warning, common sense returned like a cold slap. What on earth was she doing? How could she have been such a fool? The kiss was a mistake, and the way she'd responded was an even bigger mistake.

Jack would think she was available for further seduction. She wasn't available. She was here for a brief stay. She was years older than he was, and she was pregnant, while he was young and fit and virile.

'We shouldn't have let that happen,' she said.

Jack smiled easily. 'Of course we should.'

'But—' Her mind skidded and slipped as she tried to think sensibly. She couldn't start a relationship with this cowboy. The press would have a field day.

With an air of desperation, she said, 'We hardly know each other.'

Jack stared at her for long, thoughtful seconds. 'I suppose I should have asked if there's a man in your life.'

'Yes, you should have.' Lizzie knew she had to take control. 'We need to talk about this, Jack. To set some ground rules.'

When he didn't object she was relieved that he was being reasonable. Now that they'd broken the spell, she couldn't believe she'd let things get so out of hand without asking all kinds of questions. The kinds of questions nearly every sane man or woman asked before leaping into each other's arms.

But the questions were also the sort that would lead to informing Jack that she was pregnant, and already she could picture him reeling back with shocked dismay, could feel the chill of isolation as he retreated from her.

She knew it was appallingly wrong of her, but in that moment she wished they'd both stayed crazy for just a little longer.

CHAPTER FIVE

THEY went through to the lounge room.

To talk.

Jack still couldn't believe he was doing this, couldn't believe he'd pulled back from the most sensational kiss he'd ever known. He'd been a lost man, on the very brink of taking an Australian federal senator. Right there. In the kitchen.

Unless he was terribly mistaken, she'd been as swept away as he was. In another five seconds they might have been too lost in passion to stop.

Now, it was hard to be grateful for the inner voice that had urged him to remember why Kate Burton had sent Lizzie Green to Savannah.

She'd wanted Lizzie to be safe. Safe. In his care. She was in some kind of trouble and she'd been placed under his protection. He knew zero about her private life. Which meant he had no choice but to cool his heels, and his ardour, until he'd extracted satisfactory answers.

So, yeah. He'd let Lizzie talk, and he'd listen, and *then* he'd kiss her senseless.

As Lizzie took a seat in Jack's lounge room, she was sure she'd never felt more shaken or self-conscious. She was, of course, grateful for this reprieve. If she hadn't stopped Jack, she would have broken every single one of her relationship rules. But she felt bereft now, rather than thankful.

She also felt terribly exposed.

From the moment she'd decided to be a single mum, she'd been so careful to hold men at bay. Relationships simply weren't worth the pain.

Tonight, Jack Lewis had ripped through her defences. From the very first touch of his lips she'd been shameless, and even though she'd stopped him, she was certain he knew *exactly* how needy she was. Even though she was sitting primly with her ankles crossed, he could probably guess that he only had to reach out and touch her and she'd be scrambling down the sofa and into his arms.

Oh, for heaven's sake, get rid of those thoughts. Get over it.

At least Jack didn't ply her with questions the minute they were seated. Lizzie didn't want to discuss the men or lack of men in her life and she was grateful for the chance to sit in the lamplight, nursing a mug of peppermint tea while she gathered her wits. She had to work out how to warn Jack off, and, as they were still going to be living together, it had to be done nicely.

A practised tactician, she took the roundabout route. 'The silence out here is really quite amazing,' she said. 'I found it strange at first. In my apartment in Brisbane there's constant background noise—traffic, building construction, roadwork. Sirens blaring day and night.'

'I suppose you get used to the noise and you don't even hear it after a while.'

'That's true.' Lizzie turned to Jack. 'Have you spent much time in the city?'

He answered with a shake of his head, then he smiled.

'But I do enjoy the big smoke, and when I get there I make the most of it.'

'I suppose you paint the town red?'

His smile took a wicked tilt. 'Wouldn't you like to know?'

Actually, yes, Lizzie thought, dismayed. She was unbearably curious about the fun Jack got up to in the city, but no way would she admit it.

Jack looked annoyingly at ease now, sprawled casually at his end of the sofa, long legs loose and relaxed, his body angled Lizzie's way.

He was even able to smile. 'OK. You were going to tell me about the men in your life. Where would you like to start?'

'Actually, I don't think we should even begin, Jack. We should just accept that the kiss was a mistake and—'

'That's rubbish, Lizzie, and you know it.'

'What do you mean?'

'The kiss was fantastic and we're going to do it again.' Jack's eyes flashed emerald fire. 'Unless you have a damn good reason why we shouldn't.'

Lizzie looked away, afraid that she might blush.

'For example,' Jack said, 'it would be helpful to know if there's a boyfriend back in Canberra, or Brisbane, or wherever.'

After too long, she admitted softly, 'There's no one.'

'You're sure?'

'Of course I'm sure. It's not the kind of thing I'd forget. I—I haven't been in a relationship for some time.'

Surely Jack didn't need to know about Mitch, the first man who'd broken her heart, or about Toby, her banker lover who'd leaked their story to the press and almost finished her career?

She shot Jack a sharp glance. 'The question works both ways, Jack. What about you? Do you have a girlfriend?'

She held her breath, realising that she was far too interested in his answer.

'There's no one with a claim on me,' he said quietly.

It wasn't quite the unambiguous answer she would have preferred.

After a small silence, he said, 'So if there's no man in your life, what's the problem, Lizzie?'

She hesitated. After kissing him into oblivion, it wasn't going to be easy to explain that she didn't want a relationship.

'You've come here to get away from something, haven't you?' he said.

'Well, yes,' she admitted, grateful for the lead. 'Mostly, I wanted to keep away from journalists.'

'Any special reason? I thought politicians thrived on publicity.'

Of course there was a special reason, but Lizzie still baulked at telling Jack about her baby. She tried to picture sharing her news, going through the involved explanation and her reasons for choosing the sperm-donor option.

She had no idea how Jack would react. For some people, the whole idea of a single woman choosing an anonymous donor was too new, too confronting. Telling anyone about her pregnancy was like letting a genie out of a bottle. She never knew what kind of reaction she would get, but once it was out, it was impossible to cram it back. The damage was done.

Instead, she said, 'Unfortunately, journalists always target female politicians.'

'Especially the photogenic ones,' Jack suggested dryly.

Lizzie nodded. 'I'm afraid I've been called a bimbo once too often. It's beyond annoying. It doesn't matter how hard, or how seriously I take my job, journalists take one look at me and decide my head's full of chiffon and sequins.'

He smiled in sympathy. 'So how did you get into politics

in the first place? Was it really like you said? Something you sort of fell into?'

'Well…yes. It was…more or less.'

'Like Alice down the rabbit hole?'

She couldn't help smiling. 'Some people do say the PM looks like the Cheshire cat, but my story isn't nearly as interesting as Alice's.'

'I'm interested.' Jack's eyes burned, as if challenging her.

Lizzie squirmed. Any explanation would involve talking about Mitch. Then again, if Jack understood more about her, he might keep his distance.

'I think it started when I was very young,' she said. 'Way back when I was at school in Monta Correnti. My best friend's father was the mayor, and I used to go and play at Gianna's house. Her father wasn't home very often, but when he was, he was always kind and so much fun. Never too busy to talk to us.'

Dipping her head, Lizzie breathed in the scent of her peppermint tea. 'And I'd always hear grown-ups saying how wonderful Gianna's father was because he fixed our town's water and sewers, and helped the old people. The whole town loved him. I think he was probably my first inspiration.'

'But you chose Australian politics,' Jack said.

'Yes. When I started at Sydney uni, I was excited to discover how certain movements and certain ways of thinking could positively affect the world. I was full of noble aims—wanting to help people, to make the world a better place, to represent neglected viewpoints.'

She gave a self-conscious laugh. 'Then I fell madly in love with a politician.'

The mild amusement in Jack's eyes vanished. 'Who was he?'

Lizzie took another sip of tea. 'Have you heard of Mitchell MacCallum?'

'Of course.' Jack looked distinctly shocked. 'Don't tell me he was the one?'

Lizzie nodded. Even now, after all this time, saying Mitch's name out loud sent a chill chasing down her spine.

An awkward silence fell over the room, and Jack sat very still, frowning. She could almost see his mind working, thinking back through everything he'd heard and read about Mitchell MacCullum.

'This was well before the scandal,' she said.

'I should hope so,' he replied grimly.

So Jack had a very low opinion of Mitch. Lizzie wasn't surprised. Five years ago, the media had left little room for sympathy when they had exposed Mitch. He'd been married for years by then, and he'd been caught using his ministerial expense account to keep a mistress in a penthouse on Sydney Harbour.

Jack said tightly, 'Tell me more about MacCallum.'

She hesitated, but now that she'd started she might as well get it over with, so she took a deep breath and dived in. 'Mitch and I were both at Sydney University. Actually, we were housemates. There were five of us, sharing a big, old, tumbledown house in Balmain. He was a couple of years ahead of me, studying political science and economics. He was brilliant and charismatic, and I suppose you could say I became a kind of disciple.'

'A disciple who slept with the prophet.'

'Eventually.' A hot blush burned her cheeks. 'At first I simply spent hours in the university refectory, or in coffee bars listening to Mitch talk. He was incredibly articulate about human rights and international relations, and he championed all kinds of student causes. He was head of the student union, and a wonderful debater, so he was very easy to listen to.'

Jack looked as if he was going to say something, but changed his mind. He simply offered a thoughtful nod, like a journalist in a TV interview, and waited for her to continue with her story.

'After that, I started going to political rallies with Mitch. It all seemed very intellectual and idealistic and exciting, and when he graduated and decided to stand for parliament, I joined his campaign team. I spent every spare moment painting banners and putting up posters, doing clerical work, and running errands.'

'I dare say MacCallum was incredibly appreciative of your efforts.'

The hard glitter in Jack's eyes surprised Lizzie. Clearly, he disliked Mitch intensely.

'So what happened after he was elected?'

'I was given a job on his staff,' she said quietly.

'I'm sure you'd earned it.'

Jack wasn't referring to her help with the campaign, but Lizzie ignored the dig. 'We were working on really interesting and worthwhile programmes, and Mitch was invited to all kinds of receptions and charity balls. I'd never had such a busy social life.'

'And I suppose you'd moved out of the student share house by this time.'

'Yes.' Lizzie took a sip of her cooling tea as she remembered the day she and Mitch had moved into their own apartment. She'd been so thrilled. It had felt like a public announcement that she was Mitchell MacCallum's girlfriend.

Of course, she'd been desperately in love, and she'd expected that Mitch would propose to her at any moment, but there was no way she would share that dream with Jack.

She said, simply, 'I lived with him for about three months, and then—' she straightened her shoulders, determined not to let Jack see that any of this bothered her after all this time '—Mitch's party leaders decided that he needed a more settled image. They wanted him to marry.'

Jack frowned. 'So? Why didn't *you* marry him?'

'I wasn't given the opportunity.' She forced an extra-bright smile. 'Mitch married Amanda Leigh, the daughter of a former state governor. She came from one of Melbourne's most influential families, you see, so she had fabulous links to the old-school-tie network.'

'So, MacCallum showed his true colours.' Again, Jack spoke with clear distaste.

But then all the hardness fell out of his face. 'Lizzie,' he said, watching her intently. 'I can't believe you let him treat you like that.'

'It wasn't a matter of letting him. He did it on the sly. I went home to Italy to spend Christmas with my family and by the time I got back it was a *fait accompli*. My supposed boyfriend was married. He laughed it off, said we both knew there wasn't a future for us. But, of course, I'd had this silly idea—'

She bit down hard on her lip to stop herself from giving way to self-pity. 'Anyway,' she said quickly. 'I've gone off track. I was supposed to be telling you how I ended up in the senate.'

Her tea was stone cold by now, but she downed the last of it and set the mug on the coffee table. 'I resigned from Mitch's staff. I couldn't stay there—it would have been too awkward. But the party hierarchy didn't want to lose a hard worker. There was a vacancy on the senate ticket and they wanted a youthful candidate, preferably female.'

Lizzie shrugged. 'It was time to stop feeling sorry for

myself, and I could see this was a chance to do something to help others, so I said I'd give it a go. And I found myself elected.'

'And you've been there ever since.'

'It becomes a way of life.'

Jack was frowning again. 'What does that mean? Are you planning to stay there for ever?'

'The voters may not want me there for ever.' She forced a laugh. 'I certainly don't want to be an old lady senator.'

Ever since he'd started talking about the future, a worried shadow had lingered in Jack's eyes. Lizzie wondered what was bothering him. She thought about his kiss, and could still feel the tummy-tingling pleasure of his lips on her skin, the tantalising intimacy of his tongue. His thrilling mix of fire and tenderness.

It was a shock to realise that in a matter of days he'd penetrated the tough outer armour she'd spent so long building. For a brief moment, he'd exposed her softer centre. But surely he understood their kiss couldn't lead to anything serious?

She should make that clear. Now.

Before she could speak, however, Jack rose. 'You're looking pale and tired.'

Lizzie wasn't surprised. She felt emotionally drained and physically exhausted.

'You'd better get to bed.' To her surprise, Jack came towards her, bent low and kissed her cheek, just as a brother might. 'Goodnight.'

Puzzled, she watched him leave the room.

When they'd started this conversation, Jack had shown every intention of taking up where their passionate kiss had left off, but she'd achieved her goal. Her story about Mitch had been enough to make him think twice.

She knew she should be pleased and relieved. By walking away from their situation, Jack had saved her the trouble of explaining about the baby.

To Lizzie's annoyance, she couldn't feel grateful. She felt confused. And just a little sad.

She went back to her room and tried to read, but thoughts of Jack kept intruding, shattering her concentration.

The kiss loomed large, of course, and each time she struggled to fight off the memories.

She was off men. She was only here for a short time, focusing on being a mum. The last thing she'd expected or needed was a potential boyfriend in the outback.

It was all rather distressing. To centre herself once more, she leafed through her favourite book about single pregnancy, about mothers who'd met and conquered the challenges of raising their babies on their own. She lingered over the beautiful photos—even the first startling photo of an attractive blonde lawyer giving birth.

Lizzie viewed childbirth with a mixture of fascination, incredulity and awe. Right now, it was still hard to believe that it was actually going to happen to her.

She moved quickly on to other, more reassuring pictures—a mother breastfeeding her baby, another woman laughing as she bathed a chubby baby boy. There was a mother sitting cross-legged on the lounge-room floor, playing with blocks with her curly-headed toddler. Another mother pushed a pram through a park strewn with autumn leaves.

The very last photo was of a single mum with twins.

Twins. Now that was a scary thought. Lizzie always skipped quickly past this page. There were twins in her family, but she couldn't possibly imagine being the mother of twins. It would be too difficult to juggle a career and two babies without the support of a partner.

She lay awake for hours trying not to worry about that.

* * *

Jack rose at dawn and went straight to the horse paddock. Within minutes, he was mounted on Archer, a long-legged grey, and together they took off at a thundering gallop across the mist-wreathed plains.

It was good to be outdoors at this early hour. Archer was sure-footed, the autumn morning was cool and crisp, and heavy dew had dampened the earth, so the dust was at a minimum.

From as far back as he could remember Jack had loved riding, and, with any luck, this morning's long, hard gallop would knock the tension out of his muscles, and provide him with the necessary space and distance to think with a clear head.

He had to decide how he was going to handle the crazy situation he found himself in now—infatuated, after just one kiss, with a woman who couldn't be more wrong for him.

When Lizzie arrived in the kitchen for breakfast, her first surprise was a cleared table. All the mess was gone and instead there was a second surprise. A note propped against the teapot.

> *I've gone for a ride, so don't wait for me. Help yourself to breakfast. I'll catch you later.*
> *Jack.*

Her first reaction was disappointment. She'd spent far too much time last night trying to stop thinking about him. She'd come to breakfast, not sure what to expect, but determined to put last night's kiss out of her thoughts and to carry on as if it hadn't happened. Nevertheless, she'd been filled with fluttery anticipation.

It was silly, but she'd actually been wondering if he

might have another job for her. She'd even practised asking super-casually...*I don't suppose you need a hand today, Jack? Sing out, if there's any odd job you need help with.*

The fact that Jack was probably avoiding her bothered her more than it should.

As she made herself a cup of tea, a boiled egg and toast she wondered if she'd totally annoyed him by responding to his kiss so eagerly and then claiming it was a mistake. It was the kind of nonsense you'd expect from a teenager. At forty, she was supposed to know better.

Problem was, when Jack was around, Lizzie felt closer to fourteen than forty.

At the edge of the plain, Jack reined Archer to a halt, and walked the grey closer to the overhang of the rugged red cliff. From there he could see the river in the gorge far below, snaking over its bed of sand.

Dismounting, he wrapped the reins around a gidgee sapling and hunkered on the red earth, watching the sunlight hit the river and turn it to silver...

He drank in the silence, let it seep into him. Then, like a dog digging up a favourite, well-gnawed bone, he let his mind tussle with his problem.

The lady senator.

Just thinking about her made his body tighten. Remembering the way she'd kissed and the way her curvy body had melted beneath his hands only made matters worse. He wanted her so badly.

And he knew she'd been turned on, too.

OK, she'd called a halt, and she'd spent half an hour telling him about that rat MacCallum who'd hurt her, but Jack had seen the flare of disappointment in her eyes when he'd left her last night.

They were both trying to fight their chemistry. The tension was crazy. Being in a room together was a new form of torture, but what was he going to do about it?

He tried to tick off all the reasons he should stay clear of Lizzie Green. The first was obvious—she was a city-based career woman, and a federal politician, a woman with plenty of power and very big goals, and why would he get involved with someone like that when he'd finally thrown off the shadow of his pushy, overreaching father?

His next reason for avoiding Lizzie was shakier. She was quite a bit older than him, but for the life of him Jack couldn't turn that into a problem. Lizzie's age made her earthier and more womanly than any of the sweet young things he'd dated in the last few years.

It wasn't as if he were planning to marry Lizzie or anything…

Damn. He'd ridden out here to gain clarity, but the ride wasn't much help.

He'd already run out of objections…

The lady senator was worth another try.

Lizzie was finishing her breakfast when it occurred to her that Jack's absence provided a golden opportunity to phone Kate Burton. She didn't want to pry behind Jack's back, but she could ask pertinent questions about him that she should have raised before she'd left for Savannah.

To her dismay, Kate laughed at her very first question. 'You'd like to know more about Jack? Lizzie, my dear girl, that's delightful news.'

'I should think it's only common sense,' Lizzie said defensively. 'After all, I'm living alone with him for weeks on end.'

'Of course.' Kate still sounded amused, but then she sobered. 'Jack hasn't given you any—how shall I put it?—any cause for concern, has he?'

'Oh, no, not at all. He's been a perfect gentleman—perfect *host*,' she amended quickly. 'He's rather younger than I expected.'

Kate laughed again. 'Oh, Jack's at least thirty, I'm sure.'

Ten years younger than me. Lizzie wished she didn't feel so disheartened by this news. Why was it relevant?

'You might have warned me that he would be the only other person here,' Lizzie said.

'Is he?' Kate sounded surprised. 'Where are the cook and the ringers?'

'Out on a cattle muster, apparently.'

'Oh, dear,' Kate said. 'So who's cooking?'

'Jack and I. But that's not a problem. We're taking it in turns.'

'Lovely.' Kate very quickly brightened again. 'I'm not sure about Jack's cooking ability, but at least he's good company, and he's as handsome as the devil. You must agree that's a definite plus, Lizzie.'

'Well—I—maybe.'

'Don't worry, Lizzie. Jack might look like a larrikin, but his heart's in the right place.'

'I imagine he's been quite helpful to you?'

'Absolutely. When my Arthur died, I had all sorts of trouble. People were trying to frighten me into selling Savannah for much less than it's worth. Jack stepped in and rescued me. It was just wonderful to see the way he stood up to those fellows.'

'Thank heavens he did.'

'Yes, Jack's a darling, and he's totally trustworthy. I wouldn't have sent you to Savannah if he wasn't.'

'Oh, I didn't doubt that.' The word *trustworthy* settled inside Lizzie. Given her disastrous history with men, it gave out a warm little glow. 'Thank you for reassuring me. I'm surprised Jack didn't—'

Lizzie broke off in mid-sentence, suddenly distracted by the sight, through the window, of a horse and rider galloping towards the homestead.

The rider had to be Jack, but he seemed to be approaching at a breakneck speed, heading straight for the stockyard fence, and it was a tall fence, made of solid timber rails.

Lizzie gasped. Surely the fence was too high. Jack couldn't possibly clear it.

'Lizzie, are you there?'

'Yes, Kate. I—um—just a moment.'

Another gasp broke from her as Jack and his horse thundered closer.

Why wasn't he slowing down? Lizzie was already flinching, sure there was going to be a horrible crash.

Horrified, she held her breath as Jack's figure crouched low in the saddle while the magnificent grey horse gathered its long legs beneath it.

'Lizzie!' Kate cried. 'Speak to me. What's going on there?'

In the next instant Jack's horse took off in a magnificent leap, sailing over the fence and clearing it easily, landing in the home paddock as neatly as a ballet dancer.

Lizzie let out a whoosh of breath, and realised she was shaking. 'I—I'm sorry, Kate. It's just that Jack took his horse over this terribly high fence and I didn't think he could possibly make it.'

'Not the stockyard gate?'

'Yes. How did you know?'

'Good heavens. Is he all right?'

'Yes,' Lizzie said again and she was grinning now. 'He's fine. Absolutely fine.'

Kate let out a surprising whoop of delight. 'Lizzie, that's amazing.'

'Is it?'

'Yes. Good heavens, dear, Jack's just done something quite extraordinary. Only four horsemen have jumped that gate in the last hundred years.'

'Really?'

'Their initials are carved in the gatepost.'

'Gosh. I thought it was high. That's quite a feat, then.'

'It is,' Kate agreed. 'Quite a feat. Jack's never tried it before and that's what surprises me.'

As Lizzie replaced the receiver she knew she should go straight to her room to start work. There were emails waiting for her, and hard work and efficiency had become a habit, a good habit she enjoyed.

And yet…this morning she felt a mysterious urge to abandon her desk and to wander outdoors… She wanted to breathe in the gentle autumn sunshine, to smell the roses, so to speak, although there probably weren't any roses in the neglected Savannah gardens.

She thought how soothing it would be to drink in the peaceful landscape, to admire the beautiful horses, and the never-ending plains and the wide open sky.

With the idea only half formed, Lizzie found herself on the veranda, and Cobber, Jack's elderly cattle dog, came bounding up the steps to greet her. He looked up at her with gentle, honey-brown eyes and she patted the soft fur on the top of his head.

She thought how comforting it must be to have a faithful dog as a constant companion. She'd never had a dog, but there'd always been cats and kittens in Monta Correnti and she'd spent many happy childhood hours with a warm, purring cat curled in her lap while she read, or day-dreamed.

Cobber followed her quietly as she went down the front steps and onto the grass. She caught an animal whiff from the horse paddock, but it was quite pleasant when it came mixed with the sweeter scent of hay.

A kookaburra on a fence post began to laugh and the comical, bubbling call brought a ready smile to her lips. She remembered the first time she'd ever heard a kookaburra, when she'd come to Australia at the age of eighteen. She'd been delighted. Still, all these years later, the sound never failed to make her smile.

She saw the silver threads of a spider's web hanging loosely between the branches of a neglected rose bush, and found one small, pretty pink rosebud. She was contemplating plucking it when Jack appeared around the corner of the shed.

His face broke into a smile, and a sweet pang speared her chest, spreading through her veins like a witch's potion. He looked more appealing than ever in his soft blue jeans and his faded shirt, and with a heavy, cumbersome saddle slung over his shoulder. As usual, he handled the saddle easily, as if it were as light as thistledown.

She thought—*He's like catnip for me. I can't stay away.*

But she spoke calmly as she said, 'Hello.' And her eyes wide with surprise as she tried to pretend he was the last person on the planet she expected to see.

'Good morning, Lizzie.'

'You look happy.'

'Actually, I'm feeling pretty damn good.'

'I—um—saw you take that gate. I was worried. I was sure you'd never make it. It looked too high.'

Jack nodded, smiling. 'Matter of fact, that gate is a challenge I've been avoiding for a long, long time.'

'But you took it this morning.'

'I did,' he said with a beaming smile. 'Piece of cake.'

Lizzie was so used to the chest-beating of politicians that she waited for Jack to brag about being one of only five riders who'd cleared the gate. But Jack wasn't like other men she'd known. No bragging for him.

No crowds to applaud his magnificent jump. No spraying champagne, or kisses from pretty girls.

He simply looked pleased and quietly happy, and, looking into his eyes, Lizzie couldn't help feeling pleased and happy, too.

In fact, happiness was fizzing through her like soda bubbles, and on a reckless impulse she took two steps towards him, grabbed a handful of his shirt, and kissed him on the mouth.

CHAPTER SIX

LIZZIE smiled into Jack's surprised eyes. 'There's no champagne, but you looked so pleased with yourself for clearing that jump, and I thought you ought to be congratulated.'

'Well, thank you, Senator.'

Before she could slip away, he reached around her, gripping her low on her behind, trapping her against his denim thighs, and next moment, he was answering her kiss with a kiss of his own.

And *his* kiss wasn't a mere smack on the lips.

His kiss was mesmerising, slow and thorough—a happy kiss, perfectly in tune with Lizzie's mood and with the beauty and brightness of the morning. He tasted of the clean, crisp outdoors, wild and untamed. He hadn't shaved, and his beard grazed her jaw, but she loved the maleness of it, just as she loved the faint hint of dust and saddle leather that clung to his clothing.

The saddle slid to the ground, landing with a thump and a clink of buckles. Jack pulled her closer and deepened the kiss, and she felt her desire blossom like a flower opening to the sun, while her good sense unravelled.

'Let's go inside,' he murmured, grazing kisses down the line of her jaw until her reasoning processes ceased to function.

In a warm and fuzzy daze, Lizzie allowed him to lead her, with a strong arm around her shoulders, to the steps. She knew he was planning to take her to his room, and she was struggling to remember why it wasn't wise. Why *should* she resist Jack?

How could she?

It wasn't till they turned down the hallway leading to Jack's room that she was finally stabbed by her reluctant guilty conscience. Of course, there were solid reasons why she shouldn't let this happen, and the main reason was becoming more evident every day.

Jack's kisses might feel wonderfully, perfectly right, and perhaps her feelings for him were more than a mere, mid-trimester spike in her hormones. But was her all-consuming need sufficient excuse to sleep with him?

In the doorway to his room, Lizzie's conscience began to shout. She stopped him with a hand on his arm. She had to be strong, had to be honest with him. It would be unconscionable to make love when Jack didn't know she was pregnant.

Bravely, she said, 'Jack, I'm sorry. This isn't a good idea.'

'Nonsense. It's the best idea you've had since you got here.'

She almost protested that it hadn't been her idea, but she knew that wasn't exactly honest. After all, she hadn't gone outside looking for fresh air and scenery. She'd been look-ing for Jack, hadn't she? And she'd more or less thrown herself into his arms.

'I'm sorry,' she said again, and with stronger emphasis. 'There's a reason we shouldn't do this, and I really should have told you.'

His forehead furrowed in a deep frown. 'What are you saying? What reason?'

Unable to meet the ferocity of his gaze, Lizzie looked through the doorway into his room. Which wasn't much help. She saw his king-size bed piled with pillows and a thick, comfy, black and grey striped duvet, and she fought off pictures of Jack lying there. With her. Kissing her all over.

She swallowed. 'Can we talk?'

He touched a thumb to the corner of her mouth. 'Sure. As soon as we've finished here.'

Lizzie wished her legs felt stronger. 'No, Jack. Can we go to the lounge room?'

'Not another talk in the lounge room.'

'Please.'

Jack gave a disbelieving shake of his head, but finally, tight-lipped, and without another word, he turned back down the hallway.

Shooting her a puzzled glance, he said, 'I suppose you're about to tell me exactly why you've come here.'

'Yes.' Lizzie had intended to sit down, to have a civilised conversation, just as they'd had last night, but she felt too agitated to sit still. 'I probably should have told you straight away.'

'I said I didn't need to know. It's none of my business why you're hiding.' Jack's throat rippled as he swallowed. 'Of course, that was before—' He stopped, clearly hesitating. His green eyes shimmered. 'Before I became attached to the idea of taking you to bed.'

Help. His words stirred all kinds of tremors inside her.

He said quietly, 'Is that what you're going to tell me? That there's a very good reason why I shouldn't take you to bed?'

Lizzie nodded. Her baby was the most important reason in the world for holding Jack at bay. Her longing for Jack might have temporarily got in the way, but her longing for her baby was much more important and meaningful than any physical yearning.

Her baby was everything. Her future. The sole focus of her love. The very best thing in her life.

Jack stood at the end of the sofa, hands thrust deep in his pockets, and she could feel his tension reaching across the room to her.

'There's something important I should have told you before this,' she said quietly.

'Speak up, Lizzie. I can't hear you.'

She turned, forcing herself to face him, knowing that what she had to say would for ever wipe the sexy sparkle from his eyes, but she didn't want him to think she was ashamed of the dear, precious baby growing inside her.

Lifting her chin, she said proudly and clearly, 'I'm pregnant.'

Pregnant?

Jack couldn't have been more surprised if Lizzie had announced she was a vampire. He felt as if the earth had slipped from beneath him.

'But—' He tried to speak, realised that he needed air, took a breath and tried again. 'But you told me last night there's no man in your life.'

'Well, yes, that's right.'

The anxious tremor in Lizzie's voice and her nervous pacing were *not* helping Jack's concentration.

'What's happened then? Has he left you?'

'No, Jack.'

Bewildered, he lifted a hand to scratch at his head. This was *not* making sense.

Lizzie stopped pacing and stood by the window, chewing her lip as she parted the curtain and looked out across the sun-drenched landscape. Despite his shocked bafflement, he could still taste her kiss, could smell the subtle fragrance of her hair, could remember the happy burst of longing he'd felt when she'd grabbed him and kissed him. As if the floodgates had opened.

He longed to haul her back into his arms and kiss the soft, sulky tilt of her mouth. Coax a smile.

She's not available.

She's pregnant.

The thought dug into him. *Pregnant.* His brain clamoured with questions. *Who had made her pregnant? Why? When?*

Just looking at her, he couldn't tell that she was expecting, but he wondered now if the lush fullness of her breasts and hips had been enhanced by the presence of her growing baby.

A baby. For crying out loud, her body was a haven for another man's child. How could she have told him there was no man in her life?

Jack challenged her. 'There has to be a father.'

Lizzie turned from the window and gave a faint shake of her head.

'Where is he?' Jack demanded.

'I don't know.'

'For God's sake, Lizzie, *who* is he, then?'

Her chin lifted a notch higher. 'I don't know his name. All I can tell you is he's six feet three, and thirty-six years old, and he's an engineer with an interest in classical music and long-distance running.'

Jack's jaw sagged.

What the hell? How could she rattle off the guy's vital statistics, yet claim that she didn't know his name?

'He's donor number 372,' she said tightly.

Donor?

Jack blinked. 'Your baby's father is a sperm donor?'

'Yes.'

Shock ripped through Jack. He was well acquainted with artificial insemination—it was a common practice in the cattle industry—but why would a hot-blooded, attractive woman like Lizzie need a clinical insemination? It didn't make sense.

He stared at her as she stood there, her flowing curves outlined against the rectangle of blue sky. He remembered her eagerness both this morning and last night.

Why would a beautiful, passionate woman like Lizzie Green reject a living, breathing lover and choose an anonymous donation in a syringe?

'Hell, Lizzie, if you wanted a baby, all you had to do was put the word out. Blokes would have been lining up.'

I would have been there at the head of the queue.

Jack grimaced, aware that after two kisses the possessiveness he felt for her was totally unjustified.

On the far side of the room, she leaned against the wall, looking down at her hands, twisting them anxiously. 'I hope I didn't sound flippant about the donor. The decision wasn't made lightly.'

'But it doesn't make sense.' Jack's voice rang loudly in the quiet room, echoing his confusion. 'How can an anonymous donor be the best option?'

A wistful smile tilted her mouth. 'That's not easy to explain. It's why I'm here at Savannah. Avoiding that very question, because I know that whatever I say, there'll be people who won't understand. I don't want journalists hounding me, asking stupid questions, blowing my story out of proportion and whipping up the public's emotions.'

'But you can't hide here for ever. You'll have to explain eventually.'

'Yes.' Arms crossed, Lizzie drew a deep breath, let it out slowly. 'I just wanted time to get used to being pregnant, and to make sure everything's OK with the baby before I face the music. Ideally, I'd keep this quiet until the baby's safely delivered.'

'Is there much chance of that?'

Lizzie shrugged. 'Unfortunately, I can't hide for ever. But I'm sure people will react differently when there's a real live baby to show them, but right now the focus will be on the whys and hows of the pregnancy, and most people can't understand why I chose to go solo.'

And who could blame most people? Jack thought grimly. 'I can't promise to understand, but I'd like to hear your explanation,' he said.

Her smile was doubtful. 'Of course.'

At least she came back to sit on the couch.

Jack sat, too. At the opposite end.

In a perfect world, Lizzie would have kicked off her shoes and tucked her legs beneath her, settling in for a cosy, heart-to-heart chat.

No, in a perfect world she would have been in his arms, continuing where their kiss left off.

Instead, she began to trace the leafy pattern of the upholstery with her forefinger. 'It's hard to know where to start. It's not as if I woke up one morning and thought I'd like to have a sperm-donor baby. The idea more or less evolved.'

She lifted a hand to rub her brow as if it would help to clarify her thoughts. 'I'd been so focused on my career, you see, and on other people's problems. Throw in a couple of unlucky love affairs, and I was nearing forty before I realised I was missing out on things that were really important to *me*.'

'Like a family?'

'Yes, a family.'

'But most women start with a partner.'

Lizzie nodded. 'That was my dream once, to find a partner first, then have a baby.'

'But?' Jack gestured for her to answer.

Lizzie hesitated.

'Don't tell me you've never found another man to step into MacCallum's shoes.'

'Oh, I found one, all right. Problem was, he fitted those shoes only too well.' Her eyes glinted with the threat of tears, but she managed a shaky smile. 'An upwardly mobile corporate banker. Head of a couple of investment companies. We were together twelve months and I thought he was serious.'

Her mouth opened as if she was about to say more, then changed her mind. 'Can I ask you a question, Jack?'

'Sure.'

'Why aren't you married?'

'I— I—' An uncomfortable sensation blocked his throat. He swallowed. 'I guess I haven't looked all that hard, but—' he shrugged '—I haven't found the right woman.'

'Exactly. And I haven't found anyone I was happy to marry, but I chose a donor because I'm fussy. Not because there were no men available.'

Her mouth twisted in an embarrassed smile. 'It's really hard to talk about this to a man, especially after—'

'After we've just kissed each other into tomorrow,' Jack supplied in a grating tone. 'What was that about, Lizzie? Don't tell me you were simply happy to see me.'

The colour in her cheeks deepened. 'You jumped the gate—and I got caught up in the moment—and then we got a bit carried away.'

Blushing, she stared at a spot on the carpet. 'I said I'm sorry, Jack.'

He shrugged. There was no point in carrying on like a whipped puppy. He had no doubt that Lizzie enjoyed a wide circle of friends and acquaintances, and it was sobering to know that she hadn't found one guy who measured up to her high standards. Damn it, how high were these standards anyway?

He was still mulling over this when she said, 'The thing is I simply wasn't prepared to marry some poor unsuspecting man just because I wanted a baby.' She met his gaze and her hazel eyes flashed. 'It's not a very honest reason to tie the knot, is it?'

What could Jack say? 'I—I guess not.'

'I gave it a lot of thought,' she added, finally kicking off her shoes, as if she could relax now that her confession was complete.

Unhappily, Jack watched as she curled into her corner of the sofa with the unconscious grace of a cat. He thought about the way he'd thundered back to the homestead this morning, confident that he should try again with her.

Arriving at that decision had felt good, *really* good, and he'd taken the stockyard gate in a burst of triumph, and then Lizzie had met him, her face glowing, full of smiles and kisses…

Now, she began to speak again, earnestly, as if she felt compelled to explain and justify every reason why their kiss had been a mistake.

'Single mothers can do a great job. My mother's a prime example. She gave my sisters and me a very happy childhood. Being raised by a good single mum has to be better than being raised in a bad marriage.'

Jack couldn't argue with that. His parents' marriage had

been desperately unhappy, and his childhood had been blighted by their endless fights and arguments. He could remember lying in bed at night, head beneath the pillow, fingers jammed in his ears, trying to shut out their bitter, angry voices.

'What about your father?' he said. 'Was he happy for your mother to keep you to herself?'

'Actually, no.' Lizzie dropped her gaze. 'Not that I knew much about my father when I was a child. It was only later when I came to live with him that I realised how hurt and excluded he'd felt. That's another reason I settled on a sperm donor. Knowing how Dad felt, I knew that an affair with someone just to create a baby would cause all sorts of emotional fallout.'

No question about that, Jack thought. Lots of guys took being a father pretty seriously.

After the rough time he'd had with his old man, he'd spent a lot of time thinking about the fatherhood role. He couldn't deny that some fathers were jerks, but all his married mates were nuts about their kids, and he'd always reckoned that he would be, too, when his turn came.

'So,' Lizzie said, watching him carefully. 'That's my story. I—I hope you understand.'

Jack swallowed. He hated the thought of Lizzie facing parenthood alone. It seemed such a waste. But, clearly, it was none of his business.

'You put up a fair case,' he said.

'That's good to know.'

'But this doesn't mean you're staying clear of men for ever, does it?'

Her eyes widened with surprise. 'I—ah—haven't made any plans past my baby's delivery.'

A pulse thundered in Jack's throat. Lizzie mightn't have

made plans, but he'd had plans. His plans had involved exploring every inch of her luscious skin. He'd planned to make love to her with finesse and passion.

Now his plans were toast, and this morning's notions were nothing but a bag of bulldust. Hell, there was no point in even thinking about getting closer. Lizzie was focused on her baby. She didn't need or want a man in her life. And why would he want to be there, anyway?

Why would he want to be involved with a woman who came with so much baggage—a headache career, and now a baby that wouldn't even know its own dad?

No, thank you.

Jack cleared his throat, eager to put an end to this conversation. 'If I sounded critical, I apologise. I spoke out of turn. You have every right to make your own decisions. It's your life, your baby.'

He stood quickly, forced a quick smile as he tried to ignore the tempting picture she made, curled on the sofa, tanned legs glowing, dark hair shining in a stream of sunlight. 'I'm sure you're busy.' Already, he was heading for the door. 'So I'll let you get on with your work.'

It was time to get out of here.

His previously hazy reasons for staying clear of Lizzie were multiplying madly and already he was telling himself he'd had a lucky escape. It was time to get out of there before he said or did something foolish. There was no point in turning a bad situation into a flaming disaster.

CHAPTER SEVEN

STANDING at the open doorway of her room, Lizzie looked at the sunburnt plains, while she applied herself to the extraordinarily difficult task of *not* missing Jack.

He'd headed off somewhere to work, and she'd come here to her room—to *work*—but it was proving impossible. Jack was front, back and centre of her thoughts.

No doubt he was puzzled and possibly upset after she'd rushed out to greet him with kisses, then retreated, and promptly delivered the news of her pregnancy.

How could she have been so irresponsible? She prided herself on her prudence. She'd never been reckless around men. Well…not after she'd learned two very difficult lessons. But now, to her shame, she couldn't stop thinking about Jack's kiss.

Even though she'd stopped it, and delivered a speech that ensured it would never be repeated, he'd ignited a craving in her.

Lizzie knew it was wrong. Regret was such a useless emotion.

She'd never been a thrill-seeker, had never been bothered by any kind of addiction, not even to chocolate, but now every cell in her body screamed for the return of

Jack's lips. She wanted his mouth, teasing and warm, on her skin. She longed for—

Enough.

Angry at her weakness, she whirled away from the doorway, sat down at her desk and clicked on her Internet connection. Listening to the internal whirring of her laptop, she watched a raft of emails download. Her heart leapt when she saw a different name sitting in the middle of the familiar addresses of work colleagues.

Isabella Casali. Her cousin. At last, a message from Monta Correnti.

Lizzie smiled with relief as she opened the message. She'd been worried.

The message was in English. Isabella was proud of her language skills and loved to use English whenever she could.

Dearest Lizzie,

I'm sorry I haven't answered your emails before now. Papa's not at all well, so I'm in charge of 'Rosa', and we've been really busy. I've been run off my feet.

I hope you and your baby are fine, and keeping well. Are you still holed up in that place in the outback? It must be fascinating. A totally different world.

Now, let me tell you about Max. Forgive me, Lizzie, while I have a small rave. Max is wonderful. I'm so happy. I can't believe how sweet he is to me. His love still feels like a miracle.

A miracle. Lizzie sensed a wealth of happiness in Isabella's word choice and she was really pleased for her cousin, but she also felt an inexplicable stab of jealousy.

I'm afraid I haven't seen your mother. I've been too busy.

And too upset with my mother, Lizzie thought. Fair enough, too.

So far, there has been no news of the twins. As you know, I really wanted to go to New York to find them, but Papa can't spare me. Actually, this message will have to be brief as I have so much to do, and there's a problem in the kitchen.
I'll try harder to keep in touch.
Ciao,
Isabella.

Lizzie let out a sigh of relief, pleased to finally have contact from someone at home. After all these years in Australia, she still thought of Monta Correnti as her home.

If only her family could be more harmonious.

She thought of her mother—stunningly beautiful, fiercely independent, still harbouring deep resentment towards her half-brother, Luca.

It was such a pity. Why was she still so angry, after all this time? Why couldn't she let go?

On an impulse, Lizzie dialled her mother's number, but she only got her answering machine. She left a brief message. 'Thinking of you, Mama. Love you. I'm well. Please get in touch when you're free. *Ciao*.'

Over the next few days, Lizzie saw very little of Jack. He seemed to be extra busy with station work and she kept busy, too, working at her desk, and taking short morning walks and even shorter afternoon rests. She told herself that she was pleased at last to be able to give her full attention to the books she'd brought.

Jack's busyness was a good thing. This distancing from

each other was highly desirable. It was exactly what she needed. Now she could focus on her work and her baby, the two things that mattered.

Everything else, including Jack, was a distraction. She only wished she didn't have to tell herself this so many times. Every day.

She saw Jack at mealtimes, of course, and they continued to share the cooking. But while they talked easily about their different worlds, and she felt they both enjoyed getting to know more and more about each other, Jack was careful to keep any inference of flirtation out of their conversation. There were no stolen kisses. No sparkling glances. No touching.

It was a shock to learn that, despite the endless lectures she'd given herself, she missed the sizzle that had simmered between them. It was hard, *really* hard to let it go. To her dismay, she still found Jack incredibly attractive.

Too often, way too often, she had wicked fantasies.

One afternoon, she was busy answering an email from Canberra when she heard Jack's footsteps on the veranda, and she froze, fingers poised above the keyboard, listening with her full attention.

He went past her room, and turned into his room, and she heard his shower taps turn on. She tried—honestly, she *did* try—to stop herself from imagining him standing there, naked. She tried not to picture the soap bubbles sliding over his shiny bronzed shoulders, slipping down his muscly chest. Then lower.

Heat flared like tiny bushfires inside her. The picture of Jack sprang into painfully clear focus. She could see the gleaming slickness of his wet skin stretched over bands of muscles. She thought how blissfully liberating it would be to run her hands over his bare back, then over his front.

It wasn't till the sound of the water stopped abruptly that her common sense slammed a door on her thoughts.

For heaven's sake, how could she have forgotten so much, so quickly? Why was it so hard to remember she was a forty-year-old, pregnant woman, who'd chosen, yes, *chosen* to be a single mother?

Three evenings later, after another carefully polite and unsatisfactory dinner conversation, she ran into Jack. Literally.

It happened in the hallway, when she was coming back from the bathroom, after a long and supposedly calming soak in the tub. She'd wrapped a towel around her wet hair and she was wearing her white towelling bathrobe—nothing else—and her skin was warm and flushed and smelling of rose and lavender bath oil.

She'd used up almost all of Kate's collection of bath oils, and she'd made a note to try to buy some more.

She'd been reading in the bath till her toes were frilly, and she was carrying the thick paperback novel back to her room, intending to continue reading in bed. She had her head down, checking that she'd marked her place, when she banged into Jack.

The book fell to the floor.

'Sorry!' they both cried at once, and simultaneously they both stooped to retrieve the book.

What happened then was quite strange, like something out of a movie. Lizzie was bending down, conscious that her bath robe was gaping, revealing quite a bit of her cleavage, pink and perfumed from her bath, but instead of feeling embarrassed, or coy, instead of modestly adjusting the robe, she was frozen, as still as a statue, mesmerised by Jack.

He was kneeling inches from her, and they were both holding her book, staring at each other, breathing unevenly as if they'd run a hard race.

She could feel his heat, enveloping her like a mysterious fog, and they rose in slow motion, still holding the book. In unison, Jack took a step towards her and she took a step back, and it was like dancing a slow waltz.

Lizzie found herself against the cool paintwork of the hallway, holding her book. Trapped by Jack. His hands were now on the wall, on either side of her head, and she had stopped breathing.

Stopped thinking, had become nothing but a mass of wanting.

He was close. So close. Touching close. Kissing close. She could see each individual pinprick of his beard, and the surprising softness of his lips.

Her body was hot and tight with wanting.

Through the open neck of her bathrobe, Jack's fingers traced her skin, burning a trail from her throat to between her breasts, making her gasp.

'Lizzie,' he whispered and he smiled directly into her eyes. 'You know you only have to ask.' His mouth brushed a nerve-tingling, fiery sweep over her lips.

Then he stepped away, turned down the hallway, and disappeared into the darkness.

Somehow, Lizzie made her way back to her room, where she fell in a trembling mess onto her bed. She was shocked by the strength of her desire for Jack, by the force of her aching, physical longing.

You only have to ask…

She wasn't going to ask. She couldn't possibly ask, could she? She was so much older than he was, and pregnant. How could he find her desirable?

You only have to ask…

His words wouldn't leave her alone. They danced in her head like haunting, beautiful music. Like tendrils of enchanted smoke, they curled around her heart.

Only have to ask...

The idea was so alluring. Jack was so disturbingly attractive, and she'd been alone for so long.

But it was a mistake for all kinds of reasons. It was, wasn't it?

Wasn't it?

With one touch, Jack had destroyed her certainty.

Jack couldn't quite believe he'd said that to Lizzie.

You only have to ask.

Fool. He needed his head read.

Except...he hadn't been thinking with his head.

Lizzie had been there, practically naked, fresh from the bath and smelling of every temptation known to man, her skin so soft and pink and warm, her mouth trembling in anticipation of his kiss.

Thank God he'd managed to resist.

There was now a long list of ways she was wrong for him. After a childhood locked in a rigid career pattern, he was finally happy with his life. Why spoil it by getting involved with Lizzie and the complications of her high profile career, her ambition, her lifestyle, her pregnancy with another man's baby?

Problem was, he knew all that, but he still wanted her like crazy.

You only have to ask.

As if she would ask. He might be a fool, but Lizzie had her head screwed on.

And yet...

He'd seen the flash of disappointment in her eyes when he'd backed away. If he were a gambling man, he'd bet that he still had a chance.

* * *

That evening there was an email from Isabella. Lizzie clicked on it eagerly, keen for more news of her family and relieved to be distracted from her latest dilemmas over Jack.

Hi Lizzie,

I have such good news and I'm so excited. I've managed to track down Alessandro and Angelo's contact details, and I'm going to send emails introducing myself as their sister.

Actually, there's some other news, but I'm not sure that I should tell you.

Lizzie's heart gave a sickening thud when she read this sentence. She closed her eyes, not wanting to read the rest of Isabella's message. In her everyday life, she never avoided bad news, but this was different, this was family, and she felt a flicker of fear like the darting of a snake's tongue.

She opened her eyes and kept reading.

My father told me something today, something very disturbing. I'm sorry, Lizzie. I'm afraid it concerns Lisa.

I guess you're bound to hear some time, so I wanted to warn you, but I think it would be better if you heard it from your mother.

I hope I'm not scaring you, Lizzie. It's not an emergency. Your mother isn't sick. But I think you should ask her to explain her behaviour when my father went to her for help. I'm sorry if that sounds terribly cryptic, but that's all I want to say at the moment.

Love,

Isabella.

Appalled, Lizzie read the message again, trying to make sense of it. Ask her to explain her behaviour when my father went to her for help.

What could her mother have done?

Acid rose, filling Lizzie's throat.

As a child, she'd idolised her mother. Lisa Firenzi was regally beautiful, strongly independent, and the successful owner of Monta Correnti's most sophisticated restaurant. Lizzie's ideal woman.

Even after Lizzie had come to Australia to be close to her father, she'd modelled herself on Lisa. Her mother's example of self-sufficiency and feminine triumph was the one thing that had saved Lizzie when Mitch MacCallum had so heartlessly thrown her aside. It had helped again years later when Toby the banker had caused so much grief.

There'd been many times during her political career when Lizzie had used Lisa's strength as inspiration.

Without her mother as a role model, she might never have embarked on this pregnancy…

But what have you done, Mama?

It was a question she hardly dared to ask, but, unhappily, she knew she had no choice. Lizzie knew she must ask it, even though she was positive she wouldn't like the answer.

Her hands were shaking as she picked up her phone and began to press the buttons.

CHAPTER EIGHT

JACK stopped outside Lizzie's bedroom door.

He thought he'd heard crying, but that was impossible. Lizzie was so strong. He'd seen that with his own eyes, and he'd been reading on the Internet about her reputation for being a particularly tough senator.

Apparently, Lizzie had rarely let the opposition break her down, and he couldn't imagine her collapsing into a fit of weeping, but when he leaned closer to the door there could be no mistake. Lizzie was definitely crying. No, it was worse than that. She was sobbing uncontrollably, as if her heart would break.

Alarmed, Jack tapped on her door, but she was crying so loudly she couldn't hear him. He gave the door a gentle push, and it swung forward to reveal Lizzie sprawled on her bed, abandoned in misery, her face red, tear-stained, twisted with despair, her body shaking.

The sight sliced into Jack. At first he was too shocked to think, but then he raced through possibilities.

Was there a problem with the baby? A miscarriage?

He felt a slug of fear, but almost immediately reasoned that if there were pregnancy complications Lizzie would have come to him for help. She was too smart to suffer in silence. She would have asked him to take her to a doctor.

No, this had to be something else. Worse? Jack couldn't bear to see her like this. His impulse was to sweep her into his arms, to hold her close, to soothe her, as if she were a child. But he was uncomfortably aware that she wouldn't welcome such intimacy from him.

Uncertain and anxious, he hovered near the end of her bed. His eyes hunted her room for clues. It was all very tidy. Nothing appeared to be amiss. Her laptop had been turned off, but there was a mobile phone lying on the bed beside her. He wondered if she'd heard bad news.

Abruptly, as if she'd sensed his presence, she lifted her head and saw him, and then she sat up quickly, her hands flying to swipe at her tears.

'I'm sorry to disturb you,' Jack said. 'But I couldn't help hearing how upset you were and I was worried. I was hoping I might be able to help somehow.'

She swiped again at her tear-streaked face. 'That's kind, but no. It's just—' Her face crumpled and she gestured frantically towards her desk in the corner. 'Could you pass me that box of tissues?'

Jack did so quickly, and she pulled out a great wad of tissues and mopped at her face and blew her nose. When she'd finished, she dumped the damp clump on the bedside table, and tried, unsuccessfully, to smile.

'I must look a fright.'

'I don't scare easily.' He was relieved. Things couldn't be too disastrous if Lizzie was worried about her appearance. 'Anyway, a red nose looks good on you.'

This time she did manage a faint, shaky smile.

'Are you sure there's nothing I can do, Lizzie?'

She shook her head. 'It's just—' Her hands flapped in

a gesture of helplessness. 'My crazy family in Italy. Sometimes I just want to—'

She stopped, and sat there looking lost, and Jack's heart went out to her. Everything about her sent a message of huge need—the deep emotion in her eyes, the vulnerable droop of her shoulders, the lingering tremor of her soft lips, her hands now twisting a tissue to shreds.

When she looked up directly into his eyes, he read a silent entreaty to take her in his arms, to kiss away her tears, to sweep her away from whatever was troubling her.

Or was he getting carried away?

Prudently, he remained still. It would be all too easy to take advantage of Lizzie's vulnerability—but right now he simply wanted to help her.

He cleared his throat. 'Can I get you something? A cup of tea?'

Inside, he winced. He sounded like a doddering aunt who believed all the world's problems could be solved by a cup of tea.

Lizzie looked surprised, too. She blinked at him. 'Tea would be lovely. Thank you, Jack.'

'Hang in there,' he said gently. 'I'll be back in two shakes.'

She gave him a bleak smile. 'I'll go wash my face.'

Lizzie hurried to the bathroom, filled the basin with warm water, and washed her face with liberal splashes.

Normally, she hated to cry, but tonight after her phone call to her mother, she'd felt so alone, she'd more or less collapsed. Now, with her face washed and patted dry, she was already better. Cleansed. Calmer.

She took a cautious glimpse in the mirror, saw that her eyes and nose were still red and swollen.

At least she felt more composed. Actually, she'd begun

to calm down when she'd discovered Jack standing at the end of her bed. He'd looked wonderful standing there, so tall and handsome and reliable in his old blue jeans and a faded brown countryman's shirt. A steadying anchor.

She was very grateful that he'd braved her closed door and come in. His strong, companionable presence had made her feel suddenly safe and she'd wanted to fall into his arms, to dry her tears on his shirtfront, to bury her face against his shoulder.

It would have been perfect. With Jack's arms about her, she would have felt comforted, safe again, rescued from that awful feeling that she'd lost her bearings.

But Jack had kept his distance. He'd been friendly and kind and concerned—and distant—and shame on her for expecting anything else. This was what she'd demanded of him—to be a friend, not her lover. She knew she should be grateful. She *was* enormously grateful.

Now she stared hard at her reflection. *Come on, Lizzie. Shoulders back. You're strong, remember.*

She still didn't feel particularly strong as she went back to her room, where Jack very soon joined her with two mugs of tea.

'You should make yourself comfy,' he told her, in a kindly tone.

So she sat on Kate Burton's comfortable bed, with the pillows plumped up, and her legs, in slim cream Capri pants, stretched out in front of her. Jack swung the chair out from her desk and sat there, on the far side of the room, with an ankle propped on a knee.

'That chair looks too small for you, Jack.'

He sent a cursory glance to her bed, the only other place in the room, apart from the floor, where he could sit. 'This chair's fine, thanks.'

Lizzie dropped her gaze, and took a sip of her tea. It was very hot and strong and sweet, exactly what she needed.

'You're looking better,' he said. 'Not so pale.'

'I'm feeling much better, thank you.' She drank more tea, then smiled at him. 'You're a really nice man. You know that, don't you?'

'I hear it from the stockmen every day.'

They shared a grin and as they sat there, drinking tea in the quiet house, Lizzie found herself wanting to tell him about her family and why she'd been so upset.

'Do you mind if I talk? Get it off my chest?'

'Of course not.'

'I suppose it's a female thing—needing to offload emotional baggage.'

'As long as you don't think of me as a girlfriend.'

'Fat chance.'

Settling against the pillows, she began to tell him about her family, about the two rivalling family restaurants, Rosa and Sorella, and the tensions that seemed to have existed for ever, and about her uncle Luca and the twins, and how Isabella had always worked so very hard.

'But tonight, it got so much worse,' she said. 'There was an email from Isabella, telling me to ring my mother. So I did.'

Tears threatened, and Lizzie took a deep breath. 'It seems Luca's first wife, Cindy, went back to America, leaving him with their twins. He was struggling financially, so he asked my mother for help, for money.'

She closed her eyes, remembering the coldness in her mother's voice as soon as Luca's name was mentioned. All the usual warmth had vanished. It was like turning off a switch.

'My mother refused to help him.' Lizzie's voice broke on a sob, and she reached for the tissues and blew her nose.

'Maybe she had good reasons for refusing,' Jack suggested gently.

Lizzie shook her head. 'Luca's her brother, Jack. What kind of sister would refuse to help her own brother? I know the two of them have always fought like cats and dogs, but this was inexcusable. She's always had plenty of money, and Luca was struggling. How could she turn him away empty-handed? He had two little mouths to feed. But my mother, their aunt, wouldn't help and—'

Tears chased each other down Lizzie's cheeks. 'He had to send Alessandro and Angelo away to America because he couldn't afford to feed them.' Her voice rose on a note of horror. 'And it was my mother's fault.'

She could still picture those bright, eager little boys with their shiny eyes and cheeky smiles. It would have broken Luca's heart to give them up, to willingly separate himself from his sons. And now they'd been gone for so long.

Her mother's lack of compassion shocked Lizzie to the core. She felt betrayed by the person she loved most.

Twice in her life she'd loved and admired someone so much that she'd allowed that person to shape her life. Those two people had been Mitch MacCallum and Lisa Firenzi.

First Mitch had let her down badly, and tonight Lizzie felt as if her mother had pulled her very foundations from beneath her feet.

Such a big part of her decision to have a sperm-donor pregnancy stemmed from her certainty that her mother would approve and applaud her. Now she wondered why Lisa's opinion had seemed so damned important.

Nothing made sense any more.

Setting aside her mug, Lizzie sent Jack a shaky smile. She felt drained by her confession. 'You probably think I'm making a mountain out of a molehill.'

'Not at all,' he said. 'It's never easy to accept flaws in someone you love.'

Jack understood. He really understood. She'd momentarily forgotten his problems with his father, but, of course, he probably understood a great deal. Knowing that, and sitting here with him now, in her bedroom, wrapped by the silent outback night, she felt astonishingly close to him.

They talked on, sharing stories about their childhood, about their parents, and the difficulties of accepting that idols too often had feet of clay. They even talked, eventually, about the possibility of forgiveness, and Lizzie found the idea extremely comforting.

She would have liked to go on talking for ages, but when she yawned Jack stood and collected their mugs.

'Thanks so much for the tea and the talk,' she said, hoping she didn't sound too disappointed.

He looked down at her, an ambiguous expression in his gorgeous green eyes. 'You'd better get some sleep.'

He was leaving and she felt suddenly, desperately lonely. Truly lonely. It made no sense. To be alone was what she wanted—to be single and solitary and strong.

Like her mother.

Oh, help.

Jack's voice whispered in her head. *You only have to ask.*

On impulse, she reached for his free hand. 'Do you have to go?'

He went very still. 'Are you asking me to stay?'

'Yes, I think I am.' She held her breath. She couldn't believe she was doing this. Jack had said that she only had to ask, but how could she be sure he really wanted her? He was so hunky and fit and ten years younger. She was pregnant.

Embarrassment flamed her cheeks as she remembered

the recent changes in her body. She'd always been full-breasted, but now her breasts were bigger than ever, and heavy. Her baby bulge was becoming noticeable, too.

Silently, Jack set the mugs down on the small bedside table, then sat on the edge of her bed. Her heart thudded as the mattress dipped beneath his weight. She caught the faint drift of soap on his skin, saw that his green eyes were clouded with a smoky mix of wariness and desire.

His throat rippled as he swallowed, and the air in the room seemed to tremble.

Nervous flutters danced in Lizzie's stomach. After the way she'd turned Jack away in the past, she couldn't really blame him if he got to his feet again and walked out the door.

'If I stay, I'll want to make love to you, Lizzie.'

Her throat was so full she couldn't speak, could only nod.

The caution in his eyes gave way to his trademark sparkle. He hadn't shaved and her fingertips touched the masculine roughness of his beard.

She smiled. 'You're so lovely and whiskery.'

His hand captured hers, and he kissed her fingers. 'You're so lovely and silky.' Leaning in, he kissed her lips. 'And you're so soft.' He kissed her again, gently at first, and then with open-mouthed thoroughness. 'Lizzie... I love the way you taste.'

'How do I taste?'

'Like moonlight. Perfect.'

'You taste of sunlight. Perfect too.'

He smiled. 'Night and day.'

Their kiss deepened and he gathered her in to him, nipping, tasting, delving. Happiness flowed through her. For too long she'd lived in a vacuum of touch, but now Jack's hands were making dreamy circles on her arms, on her back, over her throat, her shoulders, and his mouth was awakening a thousand forgotten pleasures.

When he began to undo the buttons on her blouse she was no longer nervous, but rosy and warm, edgy with excited anticipation.

Her blouse fell open, and the night air was cool on her skin, and she closed her eyes as he kissed a sweet line from her throat down her chest.

But when he removed her bra her eyes snapped open, and she felt compelled to explain. 'My breasts have changed. Because of the baby. I hope you don't mind.'

Gently, almost reverently, he tested their weight in his hands. 'You're beautiful, Lizzie. Amazing. More perfection.' He lowered his head, bestowing the softest of kisses. 'But I don't want to hurt you.'

'You won't.' Already, desire was sweeping her coyness aside. 'Don't worry. I'm fine and so is the baby.'

'More than fine.' Jack's voice was thick and choked, and when he kissed her again any lingering shreds of doubt were exploded by her gathering desire and excited certainty.

She needed this. Every touch, every kiss was vitally, crucially important, and so very right for her.

Jack was right for her, so good to her, and she needed his loving. So much. Too much.

Morning. Jack watched the gentle sunlight filter through the curtains as he lay beside Lizzie, and his heart seemed to spin with happiness. What a lovely sight she was, with her cheeks warm with sleep and her dark hair a messed-up tumble on the pillow.

He still found it hard to believe that last night had happened. He'd known at the outset that Lizzie was primarily seeking comfort, but to his surprise she'd responded with stunning sweetness and passion, and it had seemed to him that she'd given so much more than she'd taken. This morning he was floating.

Unable to resist, he dropped a kiss onto her soft, sexy lips. She opened her eyes and smiled.

'Hey there,' she said softly.

'Hey to you.'

She yawned and stretched and smiled again. 'Wow. I'm remembering last night. It was amazing, wasn't it?'

'It was,' he agreed, and he kissed her bare shoulder. 'So are you and your baby OK?' He had to ask. He felt incredibly protective now.

'We're fabulous, Jack.' Lizzie met his gaze shyly. 'Thank you.'

Smiling, she slid her hand down her body, her marvellous, lush body, and let it rest on the gentle swell of her abdomen and the secret miracle inside her. 'I dreamed about her last night.'

'About the baby?'

'Yes. I dreamed I could see right inside, and she was curled up like a sweet little fern frond. She had dark eyes and tiny, perfect arms and legs, and tiny fingers and toes, just like the pictures in the medical books.'

'Wow.'

'It was so reassuring.'

'A good dream, then.'

'The best.'

'Do you already know you're having a girl?'

The lips he'd kissed so thoroughly last night pouted. 'Actually, no I don't know the baby's sex yet, but in the dream she was definitely a girl and I was so pleased. I called her Madeline, and now I feel certain that I'm going to have a girl.'

'I can picture you with a daughter.'

'So can I.' Lizzie grinned. 'It feels right. I grew up with sisters and no brothers, so I think I'll feel much more comfortable with a little girl.'

To Jack's dismay he found that he was jealous of this little girl who was not and never would be his daughter. He pushed the thought aside. 'Madeline's a pretty name.'

'It's a very feminine name, isn't it?'

'I guess.' To cover his feeling of exclusion, he resorted to teasing. 'But I thought you'd consider names like Cleopatra, or Boadicea.'

'Why would I want to call my poor baby—?' Lizzie stopped and watched him closely, then laughed. 'Oh, right. Sure. I should follow my mother's example and name my daughter after a strong woman.'

'Italians like to follow family traditions, don't they?'

'Not this Italian.' She gave his arm a playful punch. 'Anyway, I'm half Australian.'

'So you are.' Possessively, Jack traced her silky smooth hip. 'I wonder which half of you is Italian and which half is Australian.'

When she began to laugh, he stopped her with a kiss. 'I'd be willing to bet that your lips are Italian.'

She groaned softly. 'Jack, no. Please don't start seducing me now.'

'Why not?'

'I can't spend all morning in bed.'

'Of course you can.'

'I can't. I have a mountain of work to get through today, and I can't undo the good habits of a lifetime in a single day.'

'Why not?' he asked again, and he began to kiss her. All over.

'Because—'

He touched her with his tongue and she let out a soft whimper.

'You're right,' she said in a breathless whisper. 'Why not?'

If she concentrated, Lizzie could get on with her work. Except…every so often she simply had to stop…to remember how happy she was…and how truly perfect Jack's loving had been.

She'd felt perfectly safe entrusting her body to him, and he'd taken her with just the right balance of tenderness and passion, so that she'd felt totally free and relaxed and uninhibited, and everything had been—in a word—

Blissful.

That evening the Savannah paddocks were bathed in a soft purple twilight that matched the gathering silence as, one by one, the bird calls stopped, and the sun slowly sank, bleeding streaks of crimson into the western sky.

In the kitchen, Lizzie was running late. Having worked too long after her late-morning start, she'd almost forgotten it was her turn to cook, and now she was busy throwing together a last-minute scratch meal. Curried chickpeas, a staple from her university days, was something she still served in rare emergencies. It involved little more than a diced onion and garlic thrown into a pan with a handful of spices, a can of chickpeas and another of tomatoes.

Normally, Lizzie served it with naan bread, but the Savannah pantry didn't run to packets of reheatable naan, so she steamed rice instead, and hoped Jack wouldn't mind a vegetarian meal.

She was listening to jazz on the radio, something she hadn't done for years. A blues tune, slow and moody with a saxophone crooning and a double bass deeply plucking the beat. The music soothed her, as did the aromatic fragrance of the spices, and she thought with a sense of wonder that she couldn't remember the last time she'd felt so calm and deeply happy.

'Something smells delicious.'

At the sound of Jack's voice she turned from the stove.

It was the first time she'd seen him since he'd left her bed and she felt a sweet pang, exactly as if an arrow had speared her heart. She also felt just a little bit coy, but Jack was, as always, completely at ease, and he flipped her a friendly grin.

'You say the food smells delicious every night I cook.'

'Because you always cook something delicious.'

'Or because you're always ravenous.'

'That too.' After a beat, he said, 'Cool music. That's Fox Bones, isn't it?'

'Who?'

'Fox Bones, on the sax.'

'Oh? I'm not sure.' She shot him a curious smile. 'Do you like jazz?'

'Sure. It's my favourite kind of music.'

'I had you pegged as a country and western fan.'

'I thought you'd be an opera buff. All those Italians. Pavarotti.'

Lizzie shrugged. 'He's good, but I prefer Fox Bones.'

They exchanged happy grins.

Jack came closer, shooting a curious glance at the contents of her frying pan. 'That's not Italian, is it?'

'I've pretty much exhausted my Italian repertoire.' She felt compelled to warn him. 'Tonight it's chickpeas.'

He nodded. 'Chickpeas and—?'

'And rice.'

'And what kind of meat?'

'No meat, Jack.'

He stared at her.

'It doesn't hurt to have an occasional meatless meal,' she said defensively.

'Says who?'

'The health experts.' Lizzie was about to expand on the theme of a balanced diet when she caught the cheeky gleam in Jack's eyes.

Was he teasing her again?

Apparently, yes. When she served the meal, he tucked into it with enthusiasm.

She thought, *I'm getting too used to this companionship sharing leisurely meals without being interrupted by a phone call or having to rush off to a meeting…having someone to talk to about everyday things that have nothing to do with work…looking forward to seeing him at the end of each day…*

As if he could read her thoughts, Jack said suddenly, 'I was wondering about your plans, Lizzie.'

'My plans?'

He smiled cautiously. 'You know—how long you'll be staying here, and what you're going to do when you leave.'

To her dismay she was suddenly flustered and stammering. 'I—I—well, you see—I have to be back in Canberra next month.'

'What happens then?'

'Senate will be in session. That's what I'm preparing for now. There's so much reading to get through, and all sorts of preliminary discussions by email.'

'But after the session?'

'After?'

'Yes,' he said with quiet insistence.

'I have a decision to make.'

Jack's eyes widened.

She knew she should explain. 'I won't be able to keep the pregnancy a secret, so I'll have to decide whether I'll carry on with my current responsibilities and face the barrage of questions from the press, or resign and slip quietly away to have my baby out of the limelight. In Italy perhaps.'

'If I were you, I'd be taking the second option.'

Lizzie fiddled with her water glass. 'That would certainly be the easy way out. But as a politician, I feel almost duty-bound to stay in the senate, to be a sort of advocate, I guess, for single women's rights.'

'They don't need you. It's too much to take on. Too much pressure can't be good for you when you're pregnant.'

'That's true.' Before she could say anything more, the phone rang in Jack's study, down the hall.

He let out a huff of irritation. 'I suppose I'd better go and answer that.' Already, he was on his feet. 'Excuse me.'

After he'd gone, Lizzie stared at his almost-empty plate thinking about the way his face had sobered as she'd talked about the future. She couldn't expect him to understand that her career had to come first.

She was proud of her fierce commitment to her electorate, and she couldn't let one night of blissful lovemaking cloud the truth. Nothing had changed. She and Jack had very little in common. They were as different as espresso coffee and beer. Heavens, if she'd been in Jack's shoes she wouldn't have dreamed of staying back at the homestead to play host to a stranger when she could have been taking charge of the cattle muster.

When it came to the big things in life, they would always make different choices, but man, oh, man, it was hard to remember that when Jack was kissing her.

There'd actually been dangerous moments last night

when she'd almost wished she'd never started her pregnancy quest. But she couldn't think like that. It was wrong, and she had to stay strong. She knew she'd made her decision carefully and for all the right reasons.

Jack wasn't on the phone for long. Lizzie was putting the kettle on, and when he came back into the kitchen the look on his face was rather puzzling. Lizzie couldn't tell if he was pleased or upset.

'That was Bill,' he said.

'Bill? The cook?'

'Yes.' With a wry smile, he came and stood beside her.

Lizzie caught a whiff of his aftershave and she had to fight an urge to lean in to him, to inhale the scent of the smooth, tanned skin above his shirt collar.

'So,' he said, standing so close that they were almost rubbing shoulders. 'Do you want the good news or the bad news?'

Bad news? Startled, she said, 'The good news, I guess.'

'You don't have to do any more cooking. Bill's coming back.'

She almost blurted out that she didn't mind cooking. She'd really been enjoying their meals, with just the two of them alone.

'Well,' she said, letting out a huff of surprise. 'I guess that'll give us both more time for our work.' Cautiously, she asked, 'So, what's the bad news?'

'I don't suppose it's actually bad news,' Jack said with an awkward smile. 'The men have finished the muster, and the team's coming back.'

'Back here?'

'Yes.'

'I see.' Lizzie was shocked by the slug of disappointment that hit her as she pictured Savannah teeming with cattlemen.

She'd become so used to being alone with Jack. Coming to Savannah had been like being shipwrecked on a desert island with a gorgeous man. Wasn't that every woman's fantasy? And wasn't it typical that she was only realising now how very much she'd enjoyed this time with him?

'The place will be swarming with people tomorrow,' Jack said, and he shot her a sharp glance. 'You know what this means, don't you?'

'I certainly wouldn't want to give any impression that we've been—um—close, Jack. I can't afford to have tongues wagging.'

He nodded and pulled a face. 'I thought you'd say that.'

'But you agree, don't you?' She felt a riff of panic. 'We don't want a scandal.'

Jack's mouth twisted as he grimaced. 'I'd hate to compromise you. Gossip spreads like wildfire in the bush. It's going to be bad enough when the men simply set eyes on you. They'll give me a ribbing, for sure, but, of course, I'll tell the Savannah ringers to pull their heads in.'

He let out an impatient sigh. 'Some of the team are contract workers. They'll be moving on from here, and who knows what they'll say? So, yeah, I agree we'll have to be careful.'

'Exactly,' Lizzie said sharply, but she was shocked to discover how miserable she was. Unreasonably so.

Jack reached for her hand, interlacing his fingers with hers, and, to her dismay, the simple contact made her feel warm and glowing, as if her insides were lit by something far deeper than lust.

'At least we have tonight,' he said in that easy, warmly persuasive way of his.

Oh, heavens. Was that wise? Minutes ago they'd been talking about her plans for the future. Jack wouldn't be a part of that future, but another night together would make their eventual break-up harder.

Perhaps the return of the ringers was a blessing in disguise. A wake-up call.

She looked down at Jack's hand, linked with hers. It was very workmanlike, broad and brown, and there was a pale, crescent-shaped, almost-healed scar on the knuckle of his thumb. This morning, this very hand had traced the letters of her name on the inside of her thighs.

The memory drugged Lizzie, making her hot and hollow, urging her to curl into Jack, to beg him to touch her again, there and everywhere, to cover her with kisses.

His thumb rubbed slowly along hers, silently seductive. When she looked up she could see the quiet certainty in his face, the barely contained desire.

When it came to longing, it seemed they were on the same page.

He slipped his arms around her shoulders, surrounding her with his strength, and the heat of his desire. Gently, he nuzzled her chin. 'We can't waste this one last night, Lizzie.'

With his arms around her and his lips roaming her throat, anything he said sounded perfectly reasonable.

The tide of longing rolled over her and she thought she might drown if she refused him. How could she spend this last night alone? What harm could there be in one more night with Jack?

One last, heavenly night, before her life went back to normal.

CHAPTER NINE

MIDNIGHT, and the moon shone so brightly it seemed to come right into bed with them. They were in Jack's bed, a symphony in grey, black and silver, and Lizzie lay on her side, so she could see him in the moonlight, amazed that she felt utterly at peace with herself and with the world.

Jack was a perfect lover and the loveliest man, and she didn't want to analyse this moment, or to try to justify in her head exactly why she was lying here with him. She just wanted to drink in the memory, to save it for the future…this feeling of perfect happiness and safety, of being in the right place, with the right man…at the right time…

Except…in the silver moonlight Jack's eyes were too shiny.

'Are you OK?' she whispered.

'Yes, of course.'

'You look sad.'

'Not sad, just thinking.'

'What about?'

He made a small sound of impatience, rolled onto his side, facing her, and lifted her fingers to his lips. He kissed them gently one by one. 'It's nothing,' he said. 'A bad memory. It's gone.'

Lizzie leaned closer, rubbed her lips over his jaw, loving the scratchiness of his beard. 'I hope you're feeling OK, because I'm feeling very OK. I might even be feeling a little bit smug.'

Jack smiled, and she was relieved to see that he looked more like his old self. 'So, I'm fine, and you're fine. How about Madeline?'

She laughed. 'Madeline's fine, too.' She settled her hand over the bump of her baby, which seemed to be growing incredibly fast. Almost immediately, to her utter astonishment, she felt a tiny flutter—a bumping motion under her hand.

'Jack!'

'What is it?'

Instantly he was up on one elbow, leaning over her, blocking the moonlight, so she couldn't see his face, but she thought she heard fear in his voice.

'It's OK. It's just the baby. I can feel her moving. She's kicking.'

'Yeah?' There was a shake in his voice, as if he was excited now. Or scared.

The little flutters inside her went on, making her think of the times she'd caught a moth in her hand and had felt its wings flapping against her palm.

'Here, you feel it.' Grabbing his hand, she pressed it against her. 'Can you feel that?'

'No,' he said. 'I can only feel you.' He let his hand slide over her skin. 'And you feel as silky and sexy as—'

He stopped, and then suddenly, ever so softly, 'Oh-h-h…'

'Can you feel it now?'

'Yes, I can…wow.'

'Isn't it the most amazing sensation?'

'She's certainly a cute little kicker. Better sign her up for the Moulin Rouge. Has she done this before?'

'I've never felt her before.'

'She's punching *and* kicking now,' Jack said.

'Is she? Let me have another feel.' Lizzie pushed her hand under Jack's and gasped when she felt two sets of tiny, bumping movements. 'She can't decide whether she wants to be a boxer or a soccer player,' she said.

'I wonder who she'll play for. Italy or Australia?'

Lizzie grinned happily into the moon-streaked darkness.

'I guess it depends on where you decide to live,' he said.

'Yes,' she agreed, aware that a sober note had crept into his voice.

After a bit, the baby quietened and Lizzie yawned and snuggled against him, not wanting to worry about the future.

It was lovely to lie here with Jack, just the two of them in the silent homestead, surrounded by the quiet outback night. Then she spoiled the peace by picturing Jack in the future, long after she was gone from here, sleeping in this house, in this bed perhaps, with his young, country bride.

'Oh, God, I wish—'

She cut off the words, horrified that she'd almost spoken her thoughts aloud.

'What?' Jack said. 'What do you wish?'

That I was ten years younger.

Lizzie shook her head, pressed her lips together to make sure the words couldn't escape.

'Come on, Lizzie. You tell me your wish, and I'll tell you mine.'

So he wished for something, too.

Lizzie remembered the shiny glitter in his eyes. Had they been tears?

This conversation was getting risky.

Sexual attraction was one thing. Sharing intimate wishes and dreams was another matter entirely. When physical intimacy included emotional intimacy, a casual affair became…

What?

What was the next step? Love?

Lizzie sat up abruptly, clutching the sheet over her breasts. 'The men might get back early. I should go back to my room now.'

'Don't. There's no need to go yet. They won't break camp until daybreak, and it'll take them half a day to travel back here.' Gently, Jack pulled her down beside him. 'Sleep here, Lizzie,' he said. 'No more talking. Just curl up and sleep.'

She was actually too tired to argue. Besides, sleeping was safe enough, and, when she considered the inviting curve of Jack's shoulder, Lizzie knew there was no nicer place to sleep.

Jack lay awake in the darkness with Lizzie's curves nestled against him. He could smell her hair, feel the gentle rise and fall of her breathing, and he wished this night might never end. When Lizzie was in his bed she was soft and womanly, and vulnerable and sweet. She was wild. She was his, and his alone.

In the morning she would retreat. Before the mustering team returned, she would tie her lovely hair into a tight knot and pull on her armour, like a crab shrinking back into its shell.

If he'd had his way, and if Lizzie had been any other woman, he would have spoken up tonight. He would have told her how he felt, how very much he wanted her, that he was pretty damn sure that he was falling in love with her. Then he would have told her. No, he would have *insisted* that there was no need to hide their feelings from outsiders.

Why should they give a damn what anyone else said or thought?

All very well for him, of course. He wasn't a federal senator. He'd never faced the press crying scandal because word of a liaison had leaked out. The only newspaper he'd been featured in was the Gidgee Springs freebie. Lizzie had come here in the first place to escape the press, so she had every right to call the tune.

No point in trying to change her mind…it would only ruin a perfect night.

Lizzie woke to the sound of a teacup rattling against a saucer. She opened her eyes to see Jack setting a cuppa on the table beside her.

'Good morning,' he said with a smile.

'Is that tea? How lovely. What time is it?'

'Half past seven.'

'Goodness, are the men here?'

'No, don't panic. I told you they won't be here for ages.'

She looked up at Jack shyly. He was already showered and dressed. 'Have you been up long?'

He shook his head.

'I slept very well.'

'I know.' Jack smiled and sat on the edge of the bed. 'I could hear you, all night long, snoring away.'

Lizzie stared at him, appalled. 'I don't snore.' Quickly she added, 'Do I?'

'Like a buzz saw.' Jack's right eyebrow hiked skywards. 'Hasn't anyone told you?'

'No.' Her voice was shrill with horror. 'It—it's been a while since I—' She bit her lip. 'Maybe it's the pregnancy.'

It was only then that she saw the mirth twinkling in his eyes.

'Hey,' she cried. 'You're pulling my leg again.'

'Only because you're so easy to tease.' He grinned as his hand fastened around her ankle through the bedclothes.

Lizzie rolled her eyes. Prim-mouthed, she reached for her cup of tea. 'Thanks for making this,' she said super-politely.

'Thank *you*, for last night,' Jack answered with soft emphasis.

'It was—' Lizzie discarded words like wonderful, and fabulous. She had to back off now. With the return of the stockmen, it was time to widen the emotional distance between them. She left the sentence dangling, and perhaps it was just as well, because suddenly her throat was choked with emotion.

Backing off and widening emotional gaps were all very well in theory, but they weren't very easy to put into practice. She liked Jack so much. Too much, and for all the right reasons.

Just sitting here, drinking a morning cuppa with him, felt like the nicest possible way to start the day.

I'm going to have to give him up, cold turkey, she thought, unhappily—*before I become hopelessly addicted*.

Jack broke into her thoughts. 'I should warn you—there'll be a slap-up dinner tonight for everyone. It's a tradition on Savannah. At the end of every big muster, we always put on a big dinner at the homestead for the whole team.'

'That's nice. Would it be best if I ate in my room?'

He looked surprised. 'No way. You're part of the household. You should be there. The guys will want to meet you.'

She managed a broken smile. It was the end of paradise. Setting down her teacup, she began to tidy her hair.

It was early afternoon when Jack heard the distant growl of a motor signalling that the mustering team was almost home. He went out onto the veranda, with Cobber at his heels. The dog's tail wagged and his nose twitched at the first scent of dust stirring on the horizon.

Together, man and dog watched the familiar cavalcade emerge out of the dust. First came the large mob of horses, then the truck with the gooseneck trailer carrying the stores and the kitchen. These were followed by the tray-back ute and a second trailer loaded with a trio of quad bikes.

This was the first time in years that Jack hadn't been part of the muster. For him, the big muster at the end of the wet season was one of the best things about his job. He always enjoyed being out there with the team, on the back of a sure-footed horse, dodging saplings and melon holes as he chased stragglers and cleanskins out of the thick scrub.

He loved camping out, too, yarning around the campfire at night with the men, sleeping under the stunning canopy of stars. This year, he'd fiercely resented Kate's request that he stay back at the homestead to play host to the lady senator.

It just showed that a man never knew the strange twists and turns his life might take. Now the appeal of the cattle muster was nothing compared with the hold Lizzie Green had on him.

Admittedly, Jack had never been one of those men, like many of his friends, who were totally wedded to the out-back life. He knew guys who'd swear that there was no place on earth as good as this wide brown land, but those fellows had never really considered doing anything else. They'd gone away to boarding school for six years or so, and then they'd headed straight back to the bush.

More than once Jack had thought that he might have been happier, if he'd been like them. Knowing exactly where you belonged in this crazy world had to be a huge bonus. But he'd had his heart set on the Air Force and, once he'd known it was out of his reach, he'd returned to the outback as a second-best option.

Now he was setting his sights on another goal that was beyond his reach. Was he mad to feel so far gone over a high-flying woman from a different world? He knew deep down that he had little chance of a future with Lizzie, but the crazy thing was—he no longer seemed to have a choice.

She'd struck fire in his veins, and his life would never be the same again.

More than that—Jack knew now that it wasn't only his own happiness at stake. Deep in his bones, he was pretty damn sure he could make Lizzie happy, too. And her baby. Those two mightn't know it yet, but they needed him, no doubt about it.

He just had to find the best way to prove it.

'What do you want?' barked a voice in response to Lizzie's knock on the kitchen door.

'I was wondering if you'd like a hand.'

The man at the sink whirled around, and when he saw Lizzie his eyebrows rose high above his spectacles, his jaw dropped, and for a moment he seemed unable to speak.

She took a step into the kitchen and smiled. 'You must be Bill,' she said.

He nodded, shoved his glasses up his nose with a hand covered in soapsuds, and gave her a shaky smile.

'I'm Lizzie Green. I'm staying here, and Jack said you were putting on a big dinner tonight. I know he's busy, helping the men with the horses and everything. But I thought, after all the travelling and unpacking you've had to do, that you could probably use a spare pair of hands in here.'

'Well, that's mighty kind of you, miss—er—ma'am.'

'Lizzie,' she corrected, noting the remnants of his English accent.

Bill smiled shyly, showing a flash of gold in his front tooth, and he cast an anxious glance at the kitchen table, which was now almost sagging beneath the weight of unloaded camping supplies—half-used sacks of flour and sugar, bags of potatoes, tins of golden syrup, and bottles of sauce.

'So, what can I do?' Lizzie asked. 'What are you planning for dinner? I'm a dab hand at peeling potatoes.'

The cook swallowed his surprise and beamed at her, and she could tell she'd made a new friend.

The dinner was roast beef with Yorkshire pudding and roast vegetables and it was eaten in the big dining room that was hardly ever used.

Lizzie found a large white damask tablecloth and napkins in the linen press. They hadn't been ironed so she attended to that, and she found the good china and cutlery in the sideboard and had fun setting the table. She even went outside into the garden and found a few straggling daisies that made rather a nice centrepiece when combined with sprigs of purple bougainvillea.

At half past six, the men turned up on the veranda for pre-dinner drinks. They had showered and changed into clean clothes. Their riding boots were polished, and their hair was damp and carefully slicked back. They were all lean, wiry, sunburnt fellows, used to hard, physical work and unpractised in small talk.

Even so, while at first glance they seemed shy, when Jack introduced Lizzie they weren't fazed by the fact that she was a senator, and it wasn't difficult in the least to put them at their ease.

If she hadn't been pregnant, she would have had a beer with them. Instead, she accepted a glass of tonic water, and leaned back against a veranda post, asking only a few questions, happy to let the ringers talk about the weather and cattle, and the muster.

She rather liked the quiet, laconic manner of these men of the bush, and she thought how pleased she was to be gaining this insight into another aspect of Australian life.

Of course, she couldn't help noticing how disturbingly attractive Jack was by comparison. In a dark blue, long-sleeved shirt and cream chinos, he was the handsomest man in the group by a country mile. Across the veranda, she caught his eye, and for one heartbeat their gazes held, and she felt her skin grow hot.

Quickly, she looked down, hoping no one else had noticed her reaction. But she was sure she'd read approval in Jack's quiet smile, and she felt inordinately happy.

Jack would never have said as much, but he'd been uncertain about the likely success of the dinner party. The reserved outback men were bound to be a little star-struck about having a lady senator in their midst, and he wasn't sure if Lizzie would fit in.

He quickly realised that he shouldn't have worried. Lizzie put the men at ease straight away. Her clothes were right to start with—slim blue jeans and a dark red sweater with a simple V-neck that showed off the tiny gold cross—and she seemed to know exactly the right questions to ask, showing an interest in the men without being nosy.

Bill's enthusiasm for her was an unexpected bonus. The cook told everyone about Lizzie's help in the kitchen—another surprise for Jack. It seemed that, not only had she taken care of all the vegetables, but she'd helped stow away the provisions from the muster, *and* she'd got the dining room ready.

As the wine flowed so did the compliments from the men, corny or otherwise.

'Best peeled spuds I've ever tasted.'

'Better watch out, Cookie. You might lose your job.'

Fortunately, the men were sensitive enough to leave Lizzie's politics out of the conversation, so all in all the meal was relaxing and enjoyable for everyone.

It was all smooth sailing until one of the travelling contract musterers, a guy nicknamed Goat, dropped a clanger, out of the blue.

'I've seen a story about you,' he said to Lizzie. 'Saw it in a magazine down at the ringers' barracks.'

'Really?' Lizzie sounded cool enough, but Jack detected a nervous tilt to her smile. 'Which story was that?'

'Something in an old *Blokes Only*. I thought it was you and I checked it out before dinner.'

Jack stiffened, sensing trouble, then he saw the colour drain from Lizzie's face.

He forced himself to sound casual. 'Anything in that old mag is bound to be a lie.'

'Nice photo though,' Goat said, grinning stupidly. 'Would you like me to go and get it?'

'No!' Lizzie looked as if she might cry. 'I can't believe there are still copies of that around. It was years ago.'

'That's the bush for you,' chimed in Bill, clearly unaware of the undercurrents. 'People out here hang onto magazines for years, especially *Blokes Only*.'

'Anyway, it was all good,' said Goat. 'That old boyfriend of yours was full of praise. Said you were twelve on a scale of ten. In the sack, that is.'

'Goat!' Even Jack was surprised by the steely command

in his voice. Too bad. He was furious with the idiot. 'Pull your head in.'

Every head at the table turned to Jack. No one spoke.

His hands were tight fists, ready to slam the next mouth that let rip with a stupid comment. 'Show more respect to our guest,' he said coldly.

The men looked sheepish. Goat mumbled apologies.

Lizzie managed a brave smile. 'Has Jack told you that he jumped the stockyard gate?'

Jack's ears burned as attention turned to him, but he had to admire the skilful way Lizzie had deflected everyone's interest.

'What's this, Jack? You didn't take the round yard gate, did you?'

'With miles to spare,' Lizzie announced.

This was greeted by exclamations and cheers and thumping on the table.

Old Archie, the ringer who'd served the longest on Savannah, was grinning from ear to ear. 'Jeez, mate, you're a dark horse. When were you going to tell us?'

It took a while for the excitement to die down, but then Lizzie excused herself, saying she had to make an international phone call.

The men didn't talk about her again, at least, not in Jack's hearing, but he was pretty damn sure they'd be gawking at her in *Blokes Only* just as soon as they got back to their quarters. He couldn't believe how angry the thought made him.

Much later, when the men had gone and the house was in darkness, there was still a light showing under Lizzie's door.

Jack tapped lightly.

'Who is it?' she called.

'Me,' he said simply.

She came and opened the door just a chink. Her hair was loose to her shoulders and she was wearing a deep rose dressing gown, buttoned to the throat. Blocking the doorway, she stood with her arms crossed, eyes narrowed warily. 'How can I help you, Jack?'

'I just wanted to apologise for the way that fool carried on at dinner.'

'Thanks, but why should you apologise? It was hardly your fault.' She looked tired, with smudges of shadow beneath her eyes.

'I feel responsible,' Jack said. 'I knew how upset you were.'

She gave an exaggerated shrug. 'I'm OK. I'm used to it. The Iron Maiden Senator, remember?' With a glance down the darkened hallway, she said, 'Have they all gone?'

'Yes.'

She looked as if she planned to close her door. Jack said, quickly, 'Who spilled that story? It wasn't Mitch, was it?'

'No.' Lizzie closed her eyes, leaned back against the doorjamb. 'Even Mitch was above that. This time it was Toby.'

'Another boyfriend?'

She sighed wearily, slowly opened her eyes. 'Yes, the one I dated after Mitch. The successful banker I thought was serious. We'd been going together for twelve months, and we were unofficially engaged. I'd even started planning our family.'

A steel band tightened around Jack's chest. He wished he hadn't asked. He couldn't believe how much he hated hearing this, hated to think of Lizzie loving other guys, hated to see the bleak resignation in her eyes. But now she'd started, it seemed she needed to tell him the whole story.

'There'd been warnings,' she said. 'Photos of Toby in the

press with his arms around lovely models. He laughed it off. Said he'd been set up by the media and, like a fool, I believed him. Then I hardly heard from him for a month. He wasn't answering my calls. Suddenly the article in *Blokes Only* turned up. "Behind Closed doors with Senator Green".'

'How could you bear it?'

She tried to smile but her mouth wobbled. 'Not very well, especially when Toby admitted later that he'd done it partly because he knew I'd drop him. He hadn't been brave enough to tell me he wanted to break up.'

A groan broke from Jack.

'I toughed it out as usual,' she said, 'but it didn't do my career any good. I was about to chair a senate committee for family services. The story put an end to that.'

This time, her mouth turned square, and she really looked in danger of crying. She took a deep breath. 'So that's the story of Toby the toad. I'm going to bed. Good-night, Jack.'

'Lizzie, I'm so sorry.'

He was talking to her closed door.

The next few days were particularly depressing for Lizzie. Not only because the whole business of Toby had been painful to relive, but because the recollections had made her see how very foolish she'd been to become romantically involved with Jack.

She'd sworn off men. She knew they always let her down, and yet once again she'd fallen.

But she wasn't only worried about her feelings; she was concerned about Jack too. When she remembered the genuine affection he'd shown to her, she felt a pang of guilt. She found herself thinking about her mother and father's affair.

Goodness, how could she have forgotten that salutary lesson?

Lisa Firenzi had enjoyed a holiday fling with Heath Green, a handsome, young Australian, and then she'd moved happily on without a backward glance. Not once had she stopped to consider that Heath might have been hurt by her love-him-and-leave-him attitude.

It wasn't until Lizzie had come to Australia many years later that she'd realised how deeply the affair had affected her father. He'd loved Lisa and he'd taken ages to get over losing her, and as a result he hadn't married until his late forties.

He was now very happily married to the widow of one of his best friends, and he was a very proud stepfather to her two sons…but he'd travelled through some very dark years.

Remembering again her father's pain, Lizzie left her desk and went to the doorway to look out at the long stretch of pale golden paddocks.

The more she thought about it, the more she knew she couldn't afford any more reckless moments with Jack. A casual affair rarely stayed casual, especially when the couple in question were living together, but there was no way she could expect her relationship with Jack to last beyond her stay at Savannah. It couldn't possibly work.

Jack belonged out here in the outback. How could she expect him to adapt to her lifestyle ruled by endless phone calls and meetings, interference from the media, cancelled holidays and interrupted meals? He would be much happier here, and he would make an amazingly fabulous husband for some lucky, *young* countrywoman.

He had all the right husbandly credentials. He might not be rolling in money, but he'd be a steady provider, good with children, caring and calm in an emergency. Throw in his good looks and his masterly bedding techniques and the man was a rare prize.

It couldn't be long at all before some smart girl snapped him up. And Jack would live happily ever after.

This, Lizzie told herself, was a very important reason why she must not mess up his life.

For heaven's sake, she'd chosen to have a sperm-donor baby so she could avoid awkward emotional entanglements. But from the moment she'd stepped from the plane on Savannah soil she'd been slipping under Jack's spell. The red outback dust had barely settled before the change had started.

But had she been terribly selfish?

CHAPTER TEN

Two mornings later, Jack gave up trying to stay away from Lizzie. He stuck his head through her doorway and found her sitting at her desk, concentrating as usual on her laptop screen, so he knocked.

Her eyes lit up with pleasure when she saw him, and his heart skipped like a day-old colt.

'How busy are you?' he asked.

'Why? Is something happening?'

'I thought you might like to get out of the office for a bit. We could go for a drive and I could show you the gorge.'

Her eyes widened. 'What gorge?'

'Porcupine Gorge. It's quite spectacular, and part of it runs through Savannah land.'

Frowning, she looked from him to her computer, then back to him again. The frown faded and colour rose in her cheeks. 'I must say this work on the Senate Appropriations Bill is very tedious. I'm very tempted to take a break.'

'Great,' Jack said, not giving her room for second thoughts. 'How long do you need to be ready?'

'Five minutes?'

He grinned, and Lizzie smiled back at him, her eyes

flashing with the glee of a schoolgirl released from a boring detention.

They set off, driving across the plains, and Jack was pleased that Lizzie seemed at ease and happy. She sat with the window down, not minding at all that her hair was being blown about.

He wished he felt as relaxed. He'd hated the silence between them and the subterfuge of this past week. He'd hated having to deny to every man and his dog that he was mad about Lizzie.

Pretending indifference was torture. Lizzie was in his thoughts first thing in the morning and last thing at night and most of the times in between. This whole charade was driving him insane.

And the men knew it, damn it.

Jack had sent Goat packing after one too many risqué suggestions, and he'd given the other men fleas in their ears over their nudge-nudge, wink-wink innuendoes.

But now he'd had enough of living the lie, which was why he needed to talk to Lizzie today. He'd always been a straight shooter, the kind of man who laid his cards on the table, then dealt with the consequences.

Today, however, the consequences were potentially huge. His relationship with Lizzie was at stake and he was sick with nerves.

Beside him, Lizzie had settled her hand on her belly, as if she was feeling the baby kick, and he had to ask, 'How's Madeline?'

She smiled shyly. 'She's turning into quite a gymnast. I'm amazed how active she is. I hate to think what she'll be like in a few months' time.'

He pictured Lizzie in the months ahead, wonderfully

ripe with pregnancy. She would be lovelier than ever, a beautiful, Madonna-like mother-to-be.

'I suppose all babies are active, whether they're girls or boys,' he said.

'I'm sure they must be.' Lizzie turned to him and frowned. 'Jack, you're not suggesting that Madeline might be a boy, are you?'

He grinned. 'I wouldn't dare.'

The frown lingered as she brooded over this. Eventually, she said, 'I can find out next week, if I want to.'

'What happens next week?'

'I have to go into Gidgee Springs for a check-up. There's a doctor who comes from Charters Towers once a month and he brings a portable ultrasound machine.'

'That's handy. I was wondering what you'd do about doctors.'

Lizzie patted her tummy. 'By next week, the baby should be big enough for the scan to pick up its sex, and I'll have to choose whether I want to know, or not.'

'Haven't you decided?'

She shook her head. 'I'm hopeless. One day, I'm absolutely positive I have to know straight away. The next, I don't want to know till it's born. I want to keep it as a surprise, the way it's always been for women all down the ages.'

'And for men,' Jack couldn't help adding.

Lizzie sent him a careful glance, as if she was trying to gauge his mood. 'I guess I'll make up my mind on the day of the ultrasound.'

'What day's that? I'll make sure I'm free to drive you into town.'

'Don't worry. I can just borrow a vehicle.'

'No, you won't, Lizzie. I'm not letting you drive all that way on your own.'

'Well…thank you,' she said quietly. 'My appointment's next Wednesday.'

As they continued on across the grassy plains, the sun climbed higher and the autumn mists melted, leaving the air as crisp and sparkling as champagne. Lizzie watched a pretty flock of galahs take off in front of them, filling the sky with a fluttering mass of soft grey wings and rosy pink breasts.

She thought how familiar the landscape seemed now after only a short time on Savannah. She doubted it could ever feel like home for her, but she was beginning to understand why people like Kate Burton and Jack could live here quite happily for most of their lives.

Jack parked the ute in the sparse shade of a gum tree, but Lizzie, peering through the windscreen, saw nothing but plains ahead.

'Where's the gorge?'

'We need to walk the last little bit.'

With Cobber following, tail wagging madly, they left the vehicle and strolled across red earth dotted with occasional trees and pale, biscuit-coloured clumps of grass. The ground gradually became stonier and eventually turned to rock.

And then, in front of them, the ground disappeared completely, dropping away into a deep, wide ravine.

Lizzie took a cautious step forward. 'Oh, dear.' A wave of dizziness washed over her, and she swayed precariously.

'Whoa.' Instantly, Jack pulled her back into the safety of his arms. 'Careful.'

'I'm afraid I don't have a very good head for heights.'

'Come away from the edge, then.' He drew her further back, keeping an arm about her.

'It's OK now. I want to see it, and I'm starting to feel better.' Especially now that Jack's arms were around her.

She allowed herself to sink back against the solid wall

of his chest, and she closed her eyes, savouring the wonderful sense of sanctuary he gave her.

Jack, lovely Jack.

Carefully, she opened her eyes again, and discovered that she could look down at the sheer fall of the red cliffs and the narrow ribbon of the river way down below without feeling faint. 'You're right,' she said. 'It's spectacular.'

As his strong arms encircled her he pressed a kiss to the side of her neck, and she could smell the special spiciness of his aftershave.

The warm pressure of his lips was unbearably sweet on her skin, and she very nearly made the mistake of leaning her head to one side, in an open invitation for Jack to kiss her neck and her throat.

Just in time she remembered that this shouldn't be happening.

Oh, good grief. Oh, help.

Damn. She'd promised herself she would be strong.

'Jack.'

His arms tightened around her and he murmured something dreamily incomprehensible against her neck.

'Jack, you mustn't…we shouldn't…'

'Of course we should.' His lips continued their mesmerising journey over her skin, and she loved it.

Oh, heavens, she adored it. But she'd spent a week telling herself that she mustn't let this happen. She was older than Jack and supposedly wiser. It was up to her to call a halt. She had to; she must.

'Jack, no!'

It came out too loudly, so loudly that he couldn't mistake her command. He let his hands drop and he stepped away.

Crossing her arms over her front, Lizzie felt cold shivers

chase each other over her skin. She'd wanted to be in his arms, wanted his kisses…wanted his touch…wanted everything…

But to let things continue could only be selfish. She took several deep breaths as she struggled to think calmly and clearly.

Jack was standing with his legs spread, hands hanging loosely at his sides, jaw clenched, green eyes unhappy. Wary.

Lizzie tried to smile and failed. Their morning was already spoiled and it was her fault. 'I'm sorry, Jack.'

After the longest time, he said, quietly, *too* quietly, 'I've brought picnic things. Why don't you sit on this log, while I fetch them?'

She was startled by the change in him. She'd expected sparks and anger laced with charm, not this quiet, contained politeness. Sinking onto the broad, silvery log of a fallen river gum, she watched Jack go without another word back to the ute, with Cobber following.

He brought a woven cane picnic basket, a tartan rug and a blackened billycan, which he set on one end of the log, before he scouted around for dried leaves, twigs and branches for a fire.

'Can't have a picnic in the bush without boiling a billy of tea,' he said, without smiling.

'No, I guess not.' She couldn't help admiring the picture Jack made, crouched beside the fire, feeding in sticks, then lighting the match and holding it for a moment between his cupped hands, letting the flame burn steadily before carefully setting it to the dry leaves.

She was trying very hard to push aside memories of those same strong, capable hands making love to her. She concentrated very hard on the first wisps of smoke, then the red flames appearing, flickering and crackling. She caught the unique eucalyptus scent of scorched gum leaves and very soon the kindling blackened, then turned to ash, while the larger wood burned.

Jack set the billy in the middle of the fire, and she was relieved to see that he was almost back to normal. He'd always been so very good-humoured; it was disconcerting to see him upset.

Just the same, they had to talk. They couldn't go on without settling things. It was important that they both agreed their romance didn't have a future. Friendship was a much saner option.

When the tea was ready, Jack spread the rug on shaded grass with a fabulous and less scary view of the gorge. Sprawled comfortably in the dappled shade of an ironbark, they drank from tin mugs and ate biscuits.

Lizzie broke a biscuit in half. 'Is Cobber allowed one?'
Jack shrugged. 'Sure.'

She tossed it, and Cobber caught it in mid-air, downing it in one blissful, doggy gulp. She laughed, then quickly sobered. She mustn't put this off any longer.

'Jack, I'm sorry about…what happened before. I overreacted.'

He looked away, fixing his attention on a windblown tree that clung precariously to the edge of the opposite cliff. 'I guess it was bad timing.'

'I'm afraid it's not as simple as timing.'

His gaze snapped back to her. 'What do you mean?'

When he looked at her with those beautiful, challenging green eyes, Lizzie wanted to give in, to admit that resistance was beyond her.

Heavens, she had to be stronger than this. 'I'm sure you understand that we can't continue…the way we were…'

A muscle in his jaw jerked hard, and he sat up, abruptly. 'We could if we were prepared to be honest. It's crazy to try to hide how we feel.' He shot her a sharp glance. 'The men have guessed anyhow.'

'But if we're honest, what exactly can we tell them, Jack? That we've had a fling?'

'*Had* a fling?' He stared at her for long, painful seconds. 'You're talking in the past tense.'

'I know. Because—' Lizzie swallowed painfully '—I don't see how it can be anything else.'

More silence, longer and more painful than the last. Jack's unhappy eyes searched her face. 'What are you going to tell me next, Lizzie? That we both knew our relationship was going nowhere?'

Yes, this was exactly what she needed to tell Jack, but they were the very words Mitch had used all those years ago. Had Jack remembered?

Pinching the bridge of her nose, she tried to hold back the tears that threatened, tried to think sensibly. 'You know we can't have a long-term relationship, Jack.'

'I don't know that at all. Why can't we? I'd be happy to go back to Canberra with you.'

'No.'

'Why not?'

'You'd hate it. I know you would. You don't understand what my life's like. All the meetings. The pressure. Living out here is a holiday by comparison.' Despairing, Lizzie shook her head. 'Jack, we have to get this into perspective.'

She blinked, took a breath. 'We're a man and a woman, who suddenly found each other, and we were totally alone, with complete privacy, and there was…an attraction.'

'There's still an attraction.'

'Well, yes,' she admitted. At least she owed him that much honesty. 'But we both knew from the start that we couldn't have a future together.'

'We both knew?' he repeated coldly.

'Yes! For heaven's sake, Jack. You're a thirty-year-old man. You knew that I'm ten years older than you. You knew that I'm pregnant with a child that's not yours. You knew about my career and that I'm only here for a short stay.'

Jack merely smiled into the distance. 'Is that list supposed to scare me off?'

'I would have thought so, yes.'

Slowly he brought his gaze back to her, and it was so hard, so unlike the Jack she knew, she began to tremble.

'What if I told you that not one of those things bothers me, Lizzie? I don't give a fig about your age. You're you.' His eyes shimmered, turning her skin to goose bumps. 'You're a beautiful and gutsy woman. I could give you a list of qualities that's as long as your arm. Your age doesn't come into it.'

Oh, Jack. Any minute now she was going to spoil everything by bursting into tears. 'Jack—'

He silenced her with a glare. 'No matter what you say, I'm damn sure that baby of yours could benefit from having a father around. As for going back to the city to continue your work—' His shoulders lifted in a sudden shrug. 'I'm not tied to the bush.'

'But you've lived here all your life.'

'So what? This place doesn't define me.' With a wave of his hand he dismissed the gorge, the grassy plains, the bright blue sky. 'I'm here by default. My plan, when I was growing up, was to join the RAAF, as a fighter pilot.'

'A fighter pilot?' She couldn't hide her astonishment.

'It was all I ever wanted. I had no plans to stay in the outback. I worked my butt off to escape, to get away from here, and I made sure I had all the qualifications, the skills.'

Shocked, she tried to picture this alternative version of Jack. 'What happened?'

His mouth twisted in a bitter smile. 'I failed the psych test. Didn't have the vital mix of aggression and cockiness. I'd seen too much of that in my old man, and I couldn't pump my ego to the level they needed.'

This made perfect sense to Lizzie. Of course, Jack didn't have a killer instinct. Even so, she could feel the pain of his youthful disappointment, and her heart ached for him.

'But if you went to the city now, what would you do?'

'I have a few ideas. Business plans.'

Lizzie found herself entranced by this idea. 'Bill told me you've a great head for business. He said you do amazing calculations in your head, and you have a nose for the stock market.'

Jack frowned. 'When were you talking to Bill?'

'While we were working together in the kitchen.'

He shrugged. 'I've looked after my finances and I've made some successful investments. I don't want to make the same mistakes my old man made.'

She almost allowed herself to be swept away by the thought of Jack in the city, by her side, running his own business, and helping her to bring up her child. It seemed perfect. Too good to be true.

It *was* too good to be true.

Too soon the bubble burst, and Lizzie could see the real picture—the inevitable journalists swarming around them. The headlines about Jack, the photos, the questions.

Are you the reason Senator Green went into hiding? How do you feel about her sperm-donor baby? How old are you, Jack? Who do you vote for? Why aren't you the baby's father? Are you sterile?

Oh, heavens. She couldn't put him through that. It would be horrendous. He'd hate it. It couldn't work. She couldn't believe he would be happy.

And how could she take such a risk with *her* own happiness?

Twice before she'd fallen deeply in love—and she'd promised herself that she wouldn't line up for an agonising third bout of heartache. Not now, not with her baby coming.

She had to break up with Jack. Now. Cleanly and quickly. Not like the cowards, Mitch and Toby, who'd been too scared to face her. Their spinelessness had hurt her even more than losing them.

Straightening her shoulders, Lizzie turned to Jack, and her heart hurt as if it held splinters of glass. 'You know it can't work for us, Jack. I've told you why I settled on a sperm-donor baby, why I plan to live as a single mother.'

A muscle twitched in his jaw. 'Because you won't risk getting involved again.'

'Yes, that's part of my reason.' If only he didn't look so unhappy. 'But this isn't just about me. I'm trying to think about your happiness, too. You're a fabulous catch for any woman—any *young* woman, that is—and there must be oodles of girls, closer to your age, who'd snap you up in a heartbeat.'

Her brave admission was greeted by silence and she was left to stare, through a blur of tears, at the long, never-ending stretch of flat plains and the cloudless blue dome of the sky overhead. She knew the age difference was a poor excuse. Jack had a natural maturity that set him head and shoulders above men much older than him.

Hoping Jack couldn't see, she lifted her hand to dash the tears away. Then she heard his voice.

'Just think about one thing, Lizzie. Ask yourself if you were making love.' He spoke quietly and coldly, so unlike himself. 'Or were you just having meaningless sex?'

Without waiting for her response, he stood and began to stamp out the embers of their fire.

As they drove back to the homestead their chilled silence filled the ute's cabin. Lizzie wished she could think of something helpful to say. She wondered if she should offer to leave Savannah immediately, and she was shocked by how wretched that possibility made her feel.

When at last they drove through Savannah's gates she turned to Jack. 'Thanks for showing me the gorge.'

'My pleasure,' he said in his driest tone.

'About next week, Jack, when I go to the doctor, I'd be happy to drive into—'

Her words were cut off as he slammed on the brakes.

'You're not going to drive into Gidgee Springs. I won't allow it.'

'But it's a sealed road.'

'Lizzie, for crying out loud.' His hand thumped the steering wheel. 'It's over a hundred kilometres of bush, and there are no shops, no garages. No nice policeman to come to your rescue if you have a flat tyre. You'll be stranded.'

She knew that his anger was fuelled as much by their break-up as his concern for her driving safety. It was scary to know she'd pushed easy-going, sanguine Jack to the limits of his self-control.

'I'll take you in,' he said stiffly.

'Thank you,' she said, suitably chastened. 'That's very kind.'

Outwardly as calm as the quiet, copper-tinted afternoon, Jack stood at the horse-paddock fence, elbows on the weathered timber rail, while he inwardly wrestled with Lizzie's low blow.

He'd been through the gamut of emotions today. First he'd been angry at the way he'd stuffed up, rushing everything—the kiss, the conversation, the whole catastrophe. Hell, Lizzie had gone to the gorge expecting a pleasant diversion from her work. Instead, he'd put the hard word on her.

He hadn't told her nearly enough of the things he'd meant to say, about how important she was to him, how she made him feel, how special she was, the hundred reasons he was mad about her.

He'd returned, sunk in disappointment and despair. But now, at last, he was beginning to feel calmer, and he knew he wasn't going to throw in the towel. Not yet. There was no point in simply giving up, the way he had when he was a kid after he'd lost his career dreams.

No doubt Lizzie was expecting him to take her rejection sweetly on the chin and walk away without a fight. Laid-back Jack, easy to like, easy to let go.

Not so, sweetheart.

The woman had no idea how much he wanted her. Or why.

Truth to tell, Jack had asked himself that question many times this afternoon, running again through the list of negatives Lizzie had rattled off.

Why her? Why a politician? Why a forty-year-old? Why a woman who was pregnant with another man's child?

The more he thought about it, the more he was certain of his answers. To start with, he knew for sure that the overwhelming feelings he had for Lizzie weren't merely about her superb good looks. Lizzie was different, unique. Special. If she were eighteen or fifty, she would still be the woman he wanted.

Little things made him wild about her. The way she could turn to look at him and smile, tilting the left-hand side of her mouth more than the right. And then there was the gliding way she walked, and the way she carried herself like a proud princess, with her head high, shoulders back.

Lizzie had presence. She was smart. He totally understood why her political party had grabbed her. She was one classy woman.

But the biggest thing, damn it, the overwhelming reason Jack couldn't let Lizzie go was the dazzling chemistry between them. He'd sooner lose an arm than let *that* die.

Not that he had a clue how to win her back.

Only one thing was certain. It wasn't going to happen until she realised that she needed him. She did need him. Jack was sure of that—and Lizzie was too clever to overlook the truth—but it meant he had no choice but to be patient.

Sadly, patience was not his strongest virtue.

Over the next few days, Lizzie found Jack to be polite and friendly and distant, a perfect gentleman who treated her like a visiting lady senator. He respected her privacy, he ensured she had every creature comfort, and, in response to her questions, he courteously provided any amount of general information about the running of a cattle property.

She hated every minute of it.

She wanted the old Jack, the cheeky, cheerful Jack. Most of all, she wanted to see that intriguing, devilish sparkle in his eyes.

It was very alarming to discover that she was utterly two-faced. She'd told Jack flatly that their affair was over, and then, immediately, she was dying for it to resume. Her integrity seemed to have deserted her.

The worst of it was that, instead of feeling calm and relieved, she was more distracted than ever, unable to concentrate on her work, or her reading. Most nights, she reached for her book about single mothers and their babies, in the hope that it might clear her mind of Jack.

By the light of her reading lamp, she looked again at the photographs of women who'd become single mothers by choice. Giving birth, bathing babies, breastfeeding, cheering their babies on as they learned to crawl, or to place one block precariously on top of another.

Each charming photo was glowing evidence that a mother and her baby could be perfectly happy and a complete unit. Alone. Just the two of them, the way she'd planned when she'd first embarked on her pregnancy project.

The photos were supposed to help, but each night when Lizzie turned out the light and tried to sleep the only picture in her head was Jack.

She was beginning to think she had no choice but to leave Savannah sooner than planned—thank Kate kindly, but admit that the experiment hadn't worked—then return south, to face the music.

Alone.

On the morning of the doctor's appointment, Lizzie woke up feeling quite butterflies-in-her-stomach nervous.

Jack was taking her to town in Savannah's best vehicle, an air-conditioned four-wheel drive, and he had it waiting at the bottom of the front steps, promptly as she'd requested, just before nine o'clock.

When she came down the steps he strode around the front of the car, opened the passenger door, and greeted her with a frown. 'First time I've seen you in a dress.'

'I thought I'd better make an effort seeing as I'm going to town.'

'Gidgee Springs is not exactly Queen Street.'

'I'm not overdressed, am I?'

The look in Jack's eyes brought a lump to her throat. 'You're perfect.'

They drove out along the track that wound across the paddocks, stopping to open and close gates—Lizzie was now an expert—then onto a long, flat blue ribbon of bitumen.

'By the way, I've decided I want to find out,' she said.

His eyebrows rose. 'Whether Madeline's a boy or a girl?'

'Yes. After all, I'm having a very twenty-first-century pregnancy, and it makes sense to take advantage of all available information.'

He nodded. 'It's a red-letter day, then.'

'Yes, I'm pretty excited.' *And nervous*. She wouldn't tell him that. 'What will you do while I'm at the doctor's?'

'Oh—' He shrugged elaborately. 'I'll be busy. There's always plenty of business to see to when I'm in town.' He shot her a sharp glance. 'Unless you'd like someone there. For support.'

Her heart did a weird little jig at the thought of Jack sharing such a momentous experience, but she couldn't use him like that. For days she'd been feeling ashamed that she'd been the one to initiate their lovemaking. Jack was right to have asked about her motives. Looking back, it seemed terribly selfish. She couldn't lean on him any more.

'Thanks,' she said. 'That's a very kind offer, but I'll be all right.'

The visiting doctor from Charters Towers smiled at Lizzie. 'Now, if you'll just hop up onto this table, we'll check your baby's progress with the ultrasound.'

So this was it. The moment of truth. As Lizzie tried to make herself comfortable on the hard narrow bench she felt flutters of panic, and she wished that Jack were there beside her.

He'd been doggedly cheerful and perfunctory when he'd dropped her off at the doctor's surgery, saying that he'd be back in half an hour. While she was here, having her scan, he would be dashing around Gidgee Springs on business—calling at the saddler's, at the hardware store, at the bank, and the stock and station agency.

Once Lizzie was finished with the doctor, she was to join Jack at the Currawong café to try their famous hamburgers before they headed back to Savannah.

Their plan had all sounded exceedingly straightforward and sensible. Until now.

Now, on the very brink of discovering her baby's sex, the moment felt suddenly too big to experience on her own. Which was pretty silly considering there'd been no one besides the doctor when she'd been artificially inseminated, or when she'd been told she was pregnant.

She tried to cheer herself up by imagining Jack's reaction when she told him about the baby at lunchtime.

'All set?' the doctor enquired.

Lizzie nodded, and concentrated on slow, calming breaths as he applied cold gel to her abdomen. She'd never liked medical procedures, and she could never make sense of the black and white shapes on the ultrasound screen, so she closed her eyes, letting the doctor do his job, while she tried to relax.

Think yoga. You're drifting on a cloud...

She felt the probe sliding over her skin, and she remembered the dream she'd had about her baby—a perfect tiny girl curled inside her. The dream had been so very reassuring. All was well. She clung to the memory now.

The probe moved on, stopping every so often while the machine made clicks and beeping sounds.

'Well, well,' said the doctor suddenly.

Lizzie's eyes flashed open. She saw the surprise in the doctor's eyes and her relaxation evaporated. 'What is it? Is something wrong?'

CHAPTER ELEVEN

JACK chose a booth near the window in the Currawong café, so that he had a clear view across the street to the doctor's surgery. He couldn't believe how nervous he was, how much he cared about Lizzie and this baby of hers.

When the surgery door opened and Lizzie appeared, his heart gave a painful thud.

She looked beautiful, dressed for town in a sleeveless, aqua-blue dress, bare-legged and wearing sandals of woven brown and gold leather. His eyes feasted on her as she crossed the street, hips swaying seductively. She'd left her hair down for once, and it flowed about her shoulders as she moved, shining in the sunlight, dark as a raven's wing.

She reached the footpath and looked towards the café, and that was when Jack saw that her face was too pale and her eyes were glazed with shock.

Instantly, he was on his feet, his chair scraping the tiles, his heart knocking against the wall of his chest.

The doctor had given her bad news. There could be no other explanation. A rock the size of a tennis ball lodged in his throat. His fists curled tightly as he steeled himself to be strong. For Lizzie's sake.

He loved her.

As he watched her come through the café doorway he could no longer avoid the truth. If Lizzie had bad news, it was his bad news. He would do anything for her, would go anywhere in the world, work at whatever he could find, take on whatever role she wanted.

To his eternal shame, he also felt a glimmer of hope. Surely now she must know that she needed him.

Lizzie's mind was still reeling as she entered the café. She saw Jack standing at the table by the window, saw him wave and smile, and he looked so handsome and familiar and dear she could have kissed him.

She might have kissed him if the group of countrywomen at a nearby table hadn't all stopped talking and turned to stare at her. Lizzie gave them a nod and a scant smile, and she could feel their eyes following her as she made her way to Jack.

'You look as if you need to sit down,' he said, solicitously pulling out a chair for her.

'Thank you.'

Her shoulder brushed his arm as she sat, and she caught a comforting whiff of his familiar scent and his laundered shirt. He resumed his seat and looked at her with a complicated expression of tenderness and concern.

Tears threatened. Lizzie took a deep breath and willed them away.

Jack had ordered a pot of tea but it sat, untouched, between them along with the requisite cups and saucers, small milk jug, sugar bowl and tea strainer.

'How did it go?' he asked. 'Are you OK?'

Was she? She felt strangely numb. It was the shock, she supposed. 'It didn't go quite as I expected.'

Jack swallowed. 'Is there something wrong?' He repeated his first question. 'Are you OK?'

'Yes. I'm fine. Fit as a healthy horse.'

Lizzie sent a hasty glance over her shoulder and caught several women at the other table watching her from behind their teacups.

Leaning across the table to Jack, she lowered her voice. 'But I'm afraid there's not going to be any Madeline.'

'What's happened?' he whispered, and he looked understandably worried. 'You're still pregnant, aren't you?'

'Oh, yes. I'm most definitely pregnant.' It was hard to talk about this in whispers.

After a puzzled moment, Jack said, 'Does that mean you're having a boy?'

Lizzie nodded. 'But not just one boy.'

For a moment he simply stared at her, and then his brow cleared and his face broke into an incredulous grin. 'Twins?'

A nervous laugh escaped her. 'Twin boys. Can you believe it?'

The café fell silent. Too silent, Lizzie realised. Had she raised her voice?

'That's fabulous, Lizzie.' Reaching across the table, Jack gripped her hand. 'But I think we should find somewhere else to have this conversation, don't you?'

'Yes, please.'

'I've ordered our hamburgers. I'll tell them we want to take them away and we can find somewhere for a picnic.'

'Good idea.'

Avoiding the curious glances of the other customers, Lizzie went to the counter with Jack, where he paid for their tea and burgers and bought two bottles of lemon mineral water. Then they left quickly, escaping into the dusty, almost empty main street of Gidgee Springs.

Outside, Jack turned to her, grinning madly, clearly excited. 'Twin boys. Wow! That's amazing. Congratulations.' He gave her a one-armed hug. 'Aren't you pleased?'

'I don't know.' It was all Lizzie could honestly say. She still couldn't quite believe she was having twin boys. Two big, bouncing boys, the doctor had said. She knew she should be pleased. In time she was sure she'd be pleased, but she'd had her heart set on one manageable little girl.

Balancing her career with one baby, whether it was a boy or a girl, had always seemed doable. But twins? Twin boys? Even with a nanny, how on earth would she cope with raising two boys on her own?

'Here's our car,' Jack was saying, and Lizzie dragged her mind back to the present. 'I suggest we drive to Emu Crossing.'

'Is it far?'

'Five kilometres. There's a nice spot on the creek bank for a picnic.' Jack smiled. 'You can get over your shock without half the town watching.'

'I'd appreciate that. Thank you.'

As they drove out of town Lizzie watched the passing scenery in a kind of daze. Dimly, she was aware that everything about her seemed normal—vivid blue skies, ochre-red earth, white-trunked gum trees and grass the colour of pale champagne—but her head was buzzing with the idea of twins. Twin boys.

Double the trouble.

What on earth did she know about boys?

She had friends with sons, of course. From what she'd observed, little boys played endless soccer and cricket, and one or two of them had kept frogs in their pockets. Others had spent hours in the backyard—*heavens, my apartment doesn't even have a backyard*—playing with their dogs until they were covered in mud and came inside smelling like puppies.

Their mothers adored them, of course, so Lizzie was sure she would adore her boys, too.

Just the same, the idea of having two of them was overwhelming. Two rowdy and messy boys instead of one tidy and quiet girl. Perhaps it was some kind of cosmic joke?

Out of the blue, a new question arrived. Would the boys look like their father?

For the first time, she wished she knew more about donor number 372. What would it be like for boys to grow up without knowing him?

Then she remembered, with a bigger shock, that history was repeating itself. Her family would have another set of twin boys to follow on from Alessandro and Angelo. Another generation.

It was a sobering thought on all kinds of levels, and now, thinking again about the whole sorry business between her mother and Luca, Lizzie made an instant decision. She wouldn't let her little boys down. Whether she stayed in politics or found another job, she would do everything in her power to give her sons the very best start in life.

Encouraged by this resolution, she sent Jack a smile. 'I think I'm slowly starting to adjust to the news.'

'Good for you.'

'I just have to wrap my head around the idea that I'll be bringing up two boys.'

'It'll be interesting.'

Jack slowed down, then turned off the main road, disrupting a flock of grazing budgerigars that took off in a wild fluttering of bright green and yellow.

Ahead of them now lay a perfect picnic spot—a grassy bank overlooking a creek lined with majestic paperbarks that leant out over the wide, still water, as if they were admiring their reflections. Close to sandy shallows a lone white heron waded silently, patiently.

Jack threw down the tartan rug, and when Lizzie was comfortable he handed her a hamburger. 'Better tuck into these before they get soggy.'

Fortunately, the burgers weren't the least bit soggy. Lizzie licked her lips. 'This is so good. I hadn't realised I was hungry.'

'You're eating for three,' Jack said, smiling, and then he raised his drink bottle. 'Anyway, here's to your news.'

'It is good news, isn't it?'

'Of course it is. The best.' Slowly his grin faded and his expression grew serious. 'Do you think two boys will bring the father into the equation?'

Lizzie felt her cheeks grow hot. 'How do you mean?'

Jack shrugged. 'I know it's a long way off, but I was thinking that your boys will eventually want to know who their father is.'

'Oh.' Her stomach churned uncomfortably. 'I suppose it's more than likely that they'll want to make contact with him when they're older. They can do that now, when they're eighteen.'

'So your six-feet-three engineer could be a busy man.'

'Why?'

'He could have fifty or more kids trying to track him down.'

Lizzie winced. 'I—I suppose that's possible.' She hadn't allowed herself to think too much about the other babies her donor might have fathered.

'Eighteen years is a long time, Lizzie. Your sons will be adults by then, and in the meantime they won't have a male role model.'

'I'm aware of that,' she said tightly. 'But I grew up without a father, and I wasn't harmed.'

'But as soon as you were old enough, you came to Australia to be with your dad. And I imagine he welcomed you with open arms.'

Too true. Would her boys be so lucky? A sudden, painful ache burned in Lizzie's throat. Her eyes stung, and her appetite was ruined.

She dropped the last of her hamburger back into the paper bag, and leaned forward, hugging her knees, remembering her tempestuous teens, and her growing need to come to Australia to get to know her father. She could still remember exactly how she'd felt when she'd hurried from the plane at Sydney airport.

She would never forget that spine-tingling moment when she'd seen her dad, and the way his eyes had glittered with tears, and how he'd hugged her, so tightly she couldn't breathe.

He'd taken her to his flat near Sydney Harbour and they'd sat on the balcony overlooking the water, arms linked, talking and talking for hours and hours and hours.

The next day he'd taken her sailing, teaching her the ropes with gentle patience, and she'd felt as if she'd truly come home.

The memories brought goose bumps out on her arms, which only grew worse when she projected forward, and imagined her boys in their teens. Teenage boys were always a worry. More often than not they were angry about something, no matter how carefully they were raised. How would her boys feel about the unusual circumstances of their birth?

Had she made a terrible mistake, trying to do this alone? For so long she'd put her career first, but then she'd wanted a baby so much, and she'd planned to be both mother and father, but it wasn't possible, was it?

She stole a glance at Jack. He was, of course, perfect father material—warm and loving and full of fun, manly and athletic, tough without being rough. Her little boys would adore him.

She would adore him.

A hot tear fell onto her hand. Aghast, she tried to dash it away without Jack noticing.

Jack noticed.

He saw the way Lizzie's hands tightened around her knees, and he watched her chin tremble. Then, oh, God, a silver tear slid down her cheek.

It was too much. He couldn't stay away a second longer.

'Hey.' Leaning forward, he drew her gently into his arms. 'Hey, Lizzie… Lizzie.'

He couldn't bear to see her crying, but, if she needed to cry, this was how it had to happen. On his shoulder. In his arms. She might not have worked it out yet, but this was where she belonged. He loved her, and she needed him. The certainty of that was not fading.

'I'm sorry,' she sobbed, pressing her hot face against his neck.

'It's OK.' Jack stroked her silky, fragrant hair. 'You've been under too much pressure.'

For sweet seconds, she clung to him with a kind of desperation, but then, abruptly, she lifted her head, and took several deep breaths. 'I don't want to cry. I'm not really sad.'

'Just stressed,' he suggested.

'Yes.' Offering a watery smile, she touched her fingertips to his jaw. 'Thank you.'

He captured her hand in his. 'Lizzie, you've got to let me help you.'

'You have helped me, Jack. You've been…perfect. I'm really grateful.'

'I want to go on helping you.' His heart began a fretful pounding. 'If you give me a chance, Lizzie, I won't let you down.'

'It's too much to ask of you. I'm leaving here, Jack. And I'm forty, and I'm about to get huge and give birth to two babies and—'

'And I don't care. Honestly, Lizzie, none of those things bother me. Can't you believe that?'

Lizzie shook her head, as Jack knew she would, but he could no more remain silent than fly to the moon. 'I love you, Lizzie, and I want the whole package. To be a part of your life. I mean it. I love you.'

Her hazel eyes filled with tears and Jack felt his heart drop from a great height.

'Don't say that,' she whispered. 'You mustn't.'

'But it's the truth. I've been falling in love with you from the moment you stepped down from that plane. I'm mad about you, Lizzie. There's so much I want to do for you. Your life is so hard and it's going to get harder and you're trying to do it all on your own. I know you need me. And your boys are going to need me.'

'Oh, Jack.' Her face twisted miserably as she pulled her hands from his. She scrambled to her feet. Jack followed.

'Can't you understand?' she cried. 'I can't turn to you now, simply because my life's getting difficult. I've already worried myself sick because it looks as if I've simply used you. I don't want to make it worse by asking you to help me now, because I'm expecting twin boys. I'd really feel I was exploiting you.'

'Exploiting me? Are you crazy? You're the best thing that's ever happened to me.'

With a frantic shake of her head, she looked away, down the creek. 'I've been thinking for days now that I've imposed on you for too long. I know you feel sorry for me now, but it's time I left Savannah. I want you to get your life back to normal.'

'Back to normal. Hell, Lizzie!' He gave a wild laugh. 'Back to normal would be taking you back to my bed.'

Her response was a soft, sad little cry, half groan, half sob, and she seemed to sway on her feet as she closed her eyes.

Jack stared at her lowered lashes, at her quivering mouth, so lush and sexy, even though it was distorted by her effort not to cry. Without the slightest hesitation he stepped forward, wrapped her in his arms and kissed her.

And he delivered a message Lizzie couldn't miss.

Oh, heavens. Lizzie was full of great intentions. From the first, she tried to resist Jack's kiss. She stiffened the moment his lips touched hers, but then his arms tightened around her, and she was enveloped by the smell of sunlight on his skin…and then his tongue touched hers, and she was clinging to him, and she couldn't remember how to resist. Or why it was necessary.

Her protests were swept away by whispers in her head that Jack loved her, loved her, loved her…and by blissful sensations…and soaring happiness…

Until he finally released her.

Only then did she hear the ripple of wind on the water and in the trees. She felt its coolness on her skin, and she came, panting and breathless, to her senses.

Quickly, she regathered her wits, and her armour. 'That kiss wasn't very helpful, Jack.'

His eyes glittered with a knowing green light. 'Now that's where you're wrong, Lizzie.'

'Why? What do you think you've proved?'

'That you do want me.'

Unfortunately, it was true. Lizzie only had to hear Jack say the words—*you want me*—and coils of longing tightened inside her again.

She straightened her shoulders. 'We've been through all the reasons why we can't have a future. Why are you trying to make it hard for me to leave?'

'Because you're being stubborn. You won't admit how you feel.'

She couldn't meet his gaze. If she looked into Jack's eyes again, she'd weaken. 'I have to go, Jack.'

For his sake, she had to be strong. Why couldn't he see he should be with some pretty-eyed, horse-riding country girl? 'This should have been a straightforward holiday romance, and I'm sorry if I let it get out of hand.'

For the longest time Jack didn't speak.

Then Lizzie heard the snap of a twig. Her head jerked up and she saw him toss broken sticks into the water.

The pain in his face made her want to weep.

He wouldn't look at her.

'I have to do this on my own, Jack.' Oh, God. She felt as if she'd volunteered to have surgery without anaesthetic, but she forced the tremors out of her voice. 'I have responsibilities, but they're my responsibilities. Not yours.'

The journey back to Savannah was strained and silent.

'Unless you change your mind, I'd rather you didn't talk,' Jack ordered through tight lips, and he stared straight ahead, knuckles white as he gripped the steering wheel, never once looking Lizzie's way.

The tension was awful—suffocating—and Lizzie sat in an agony of despair. Over and over, she reassured herself that she was doing the right thing. Leaving Savannah was her only option, and she had to make her departure as quick and clean as possible.

It might have been different if she was sure she could make Jack happy, but how could she? He was such an easy-going, and likeable and genuinely warm guy, and if she transplanted him into her world, if he became her life partner, dealing with the pressures of her job, her babies, and her family, he would be forced to change.

How could he be happy then?

Her only solution could be to give up politics, but should she give it up for a man, when she'd stopped trusting men years ago? Where men were concerned she'd totally lost faith in her own judgement, and now, when she'd just had a shock, was the worst possible moment to ditch the wisdom she'd garnered over so many years.

Loving Jack might feel wonderful and right, but with her track record she couldn't trust something as intangible as feelings. Her only sensible option was to stick with her original plan, which meant she had to leave.

Each day she stayed here only messed up Jack's life more, and she cared about him too much to go on hurting him.

By ten o'clock that evening, Lizzie's matching pale green leather suitcases sat, packed and ready, on the floor beside the wardrobe. Her reading material was packed into the green leather holdall, her laptop was stowed away, and she'd organised her charter flight for first thing the next morning.

She had no idea where Jack was. She hadn't seen him at dinner.

Bill told her he'd joined the ringers for a meal and to discuss a problem they had with one of the bores, so she'd eaten alone, and she'd had to leave a note for Jack, explaining her arrangements. Now she was alone again in her room, miserably searching her soul for the five thousandth time.

The problem with soul-searching was that it dug up answers she didn't want to find. Like her feelings for Jack…the way her heart lifted whenever he walked into a room…the way being with him made the simplest things special…the way his skin was warm and smooth beneath her fingers…

She tried to force the thoughts out of her head and to concentrate on the amazing fact that in a little over five months she would have two babies. Two cuddly, snugly, warm and cosy baby boys.

They would be everything Lizzie needed, the perfect, sweet companions. They had to be. Lizzie was pinning her faith on it.

No maternal pressure or anything.

Oh, gosh. Jack had said that on the day she'd arrived at Savannah, when he'd learned that she'd been named after Queen Elizabeth. Now she pressed a hand to her mouth as painful questions clamoured.

Was she asking too much of her little boys? Before the poor darlings had even been born, was she expecting them to fill the Jack-sized gaps in her life?

CHAPTER TWELVE

THE small plane was due to arrive at nine-fifteen.

Jack rose early, skipping breakfast to clear the horses and flatten the anthills on the airstrip. Then he returned to the homestead to find Lizzie's luggage at the bottom of the steps, waiting to be packed into the back of the ute.

He'd been trying to stay numb ever since he'd read her note, and he loaded the suitcases like an automaton. It was the only way he would get through this.

Lizzie had been in the kitchen saying goodbye to Bill, but now she appeared, dressed in Jack's favourite soft blue jeans and the pale green top with the ruffles down the front.

Last week, she'd joked that she wouldn't be able to wear these clothes much longer, and they'd talked about ordering maternity clothes over the Internet. Now she was leaving, and Jack was stunned that it was all happening so fast.

He'd failed. Again.

If he'd been smarter, he would have found a sure-fire way to convince Lizzie that he loved her, that she belonged with him, and he with her. Maybe he should have told her earlier, later, with flowers, on bended knee. Anyway he looked at it, he'd stuffed up.

And Lizzie had morphed back into Senator Green, organising her return to the city and the plane that would fetch her with one efficient touch of a button on her mobile phone.

Now it was too late.

In the skies above Savannah, the plane was already circling like a silver toy, glinting in the sunlight. Even Cobber knew what that meant, and the dog leapt lightly into the back of the ute.

It was time to go.

Apart from a polite hello and a nodded thank-you when Jack opened the door for Lizzie, neither of them could find anything to say on the way to the airstrip. They reached it at the same time the plane landed, amidst its usual cloud of red dust.

Lizzie was pale as she got out of the ute.

Jack had to ask. 'Should you be flying? You don't look well.'

'I'm OK. I didn't sleep much, that's all.' She looked across to the plane. 'Jack, I really do want to thank you for—for everything.'

He was dying inside, but he forced himself to speak. 'Look at me, Lizzie.'

She gave the tiniest shake of her head.

'Lizzie.'

Slowly, she turned, and he saw the sheen of her tears. Her chin trembled.

'I love you,' Jack said, and to his horror his eyes filled with tears, too. 'I love you so much. I'd do anything.'

'Jack, please.' Her tears spilled onto her cheeks. 'Don't make it worse.'

'It can't be any worse.' In despair, he said, 'You know you're going to take a long time to get over this, don't you?'

Her face crumpled, but abruptly she turned and, stumbling a little, she began to walk towards the plane.

Jack didn't follow her. He couldn't bring himself to meekly step forward, carrying her suitcases, when all he wanted to do was to throw her over his shoulder, and stop this insanity.

How could he let her go?

He thought of wild schemes to stop the plane—ripping its propeller out, tearing off its wings.

Already, Lizzie was halfway across the stretch of red dirt that took her to the plane's metal steps.

It was happening. Heaven help him, she was determined to walk out of his life, but it was like watching a loved one die, or walk the green mile. How could she do this to herself?

How would he live without her?

Ahead of him, Lizzie stopped and looked back at him as he stood there with a suitcase in each hand.

She looked at the plane, then to Jack again.

She was clearly hesitating and Jack stood his ground and his heart began to hammer. Blood pounded in his ears.

Only a few more steps.

Eyes wide in a bid to stem the tears, Lizzie stared at the little plane as if, somehow, staring could help. But all she could see was a figure, ridiculously dressed in white, stepping down from that cabin, and seeing Jack for the first time. That had been the beginning...

She looked back at Jack again. He hadn't moved.

Was he going to make her go back to fetch her own bags?

He was standing there, and she knew from the set in his shoulders and the stiff way he held himself that he was hurting. So much.

What am I doing?
Going back to face my responsibilities.
Why?
Good question.

For so long she'd put her career first. Even now, she was turning away from Jack because he wouldn't fit in with her career.

Like someone drowning, Lizzie saw her life at Savannah flash before her—saw the morning she'd worked on the truck's brakes with Jack. Saw herself driving the truck to feed the weaner calves. The over-the-top ossobucco meal. Jack jumping the stockyard gate. Tearing outside to kiss him. Making love. Talking with him long into the night about families.

Families.

Oh, help.

Jack wanted to join her and her boys to create a little family. He loved her. He wanted to love her sons, yet here she was, walking away from him, just as Angelo and Alessandro's mother had walked away from her uncle Luca. Just as her mother had walked from her father...

What-am-I-doing-what-am-I-doing-what-am-I-doing?

How could she do this? To herself? To her boys? Most of all how could she do it to Jack?

How could she pretend that Jack would be happier without her? How many times did he have to tell her that he loved her before she believed him?

As her heart began to break Lizzie turned.

She began to run.

Jack saw Lizzie running.

Tears were streaming down her cheeks, but she was smiling. Laughing.

The bags fell from his hands, tumbling to the ground, and Lizzie, smiling through her tears, ran into his arms.

'I couldn't do it,' she sobbed. 'I love you.'

'Of course you do.'

'I thought I could leave you, but I can't. I couldn't take another step. I was leaving for all the wrong reasons. I wanted you to be happy, but it's not going to work, is it? If I leave we'll both be unhappy for the rest of our lives.'

'Darling girl.'

'This is not a plea for help with the babies, Jack.' She touched her fingers to his lips. 'This is just about you, and how I feel about you.'

He kissed her fingers, her nose, her eyelids.

'We can make it work. I can leave politics.'

'Not on my account, Senator. Only if you want to.'

'I've done enough. I want to leave. I want you, Jack. I want us to be a family. I promise I'll make you happy.'

'You've already made me happy.' He would have swung her around and around, if he weren't worried about making her dizzy. Instead, he kissed her again, on the chin, on the ear, then said, 'There's only one thing that could make me any happier.'

'I'll do anything. I love you. What is it?'

'Marry me.'

A sudden voice called from behind them, 'Is everything all right, Senator Green?'

The pilot, clearly puzzled, had climbed down from the cockpit.

'Everything's fine,' Lizzie called back to him. 'Jack's asked me to marry him and I'm about to give him my answer.'

Turning her back on the plane, she looked joyously

into Jack's eyes. 'And the answer's yes. A thousand times yes. I promise we're going to have the happiest marriage of all time.'

Although the Italian summer was just around the corner, it was cool on Sorella's terrace when Lizzie took Jack outside to show him her favourite Monta Correnti view.

'Come here,' he said, noticing that she'd shivered, and putting his arms around her. 'Let me keep you warm.'

Lizzie laughed. 'Any time.'

Snuggling against him, she looked out over the sea of pale terracotta rooftops to the sloping green rows of the vineyards and the neat olive groves, and further on across the valley to the distant purple hills. 'What do you think of my home town?'

'Amazing. It's so beautiful here. I don't know how you ever left.'

'Beautiful landscapes can only go so far,' she said. 'They can't actually make you happy.'

Jack kissed her cheek. 'I won't argue with that.'

Turning in his arms, Lizzie smiled at him and held out her left hand to admire, yet again, her beautiful green sapphire engagement ring. 'These last few days have been the happiest days of my life.'

'And the busiest.'

'Yes.' She remembered all the meetings, the press conferences…especially the one with Jack at her side helping to explain about her pregnancy and her choices for the future. It was all behind them now. 'I'm so glad I've resigned. Such bliss. I still haven't got used to the freedom.'

'I don't think you'll regret it.'

'I won't, Jack. I know I won't. I promise. I just love

knowing that we're both free to make whatever plans we want for our marriage, and our own little family.'

She was rewarded by a warm hug and another kiss, on the lips this time.

When they drew apart, she said, 'What do you think of my mother's offer to hold our wedding reception in Romano's palazzo?'

'It's a very generous offer.'

'She's trying to make up for all the trouble she's caused.'

'A palazzo sounds very grand.'

'It is rather grand.'

'Would you like a reception there?'

'I have to admit it's a fairy-tale setting. On Lake Adrina.' Lizzie slipped her arms around Jack. 'Don't be alarmed, but I'm thinking it would be wonderful if we had a really big wedding and invited everyone in the family—even my long-lost cousins from New York.'

Jack grinned. 'I'll go along with anything as long as we tie the knot.'

'And I'll invite my sisters, of course.' Lizzie was pensive for a moment. 'There's been a silly problem between Scarlett and my cousin Isabella ever since they were children. Actually, Scarlett doesn't get on too well with Jackie either, for that matter. Our wedding can be the perfect excuse to bring the family back together.'

'Then there's no question,' Jack said. 'Let's invite the lot.'

'I'll ring everyone tonight to warn them to start making plans.' With a tender smile, Lizzie traced the line of his jaw. 'Have you noticed, my darling, that you've been a huge hit with every member of my family that you've met so far?'

'They've been very kind to me.'

'Kind?' Lizzie laughed. 'They're smitten. They adore you,

Jack. You've charmed them to pieces. Especially my mother. Even Isabella, and she's madly in love with her Max.'

Isabella, however, wasn't quite so charmed when Lizzie rang her later that evening to tell her the latest wedding plans.

'Romano's palazzo?' Isabella was clearly agitated. 'Why would you want a reception there?'

'Why not? It's a gorgeous setting on Lake Adrina. I thought it would be perfect.'

'Yes, it's beautiful, but—'

'But *what*, Isabella?' It was hard not to sound annoyed. 'You're as bad as Scarlett.'

There was a distinct gasp on the other end of the line. 'Have you been talking to Scarlett?'

'Of course. She's my sister, after all.'

'Well, yes.' Isabella's voice was thin and decidedly anxious. 'What did Scarlett say when you told her about the palazzo?'

'Her reaction was almost the same as yours. She wasn't happy, but when I pressed her she couldn't give me any proper reason. It didn't make sense.'

'I suppose it is silly to be worked up about a venue.' Isabella sounded distinctly calmer now.

'It is if neither of you can give me a solid reason why I shouldn't have the reception there.'

Later, in bed in the best guest room in Lisa's villa, complete with marble floors and views through arched windows to the diamond-studded sky, Lizzie confided in Jack. 'I'm beginning to think this wedding of ours will either make or break my family.'

'You worry too much. It'll work out fine.'

'How can you be sure?'

He nuzzled her neck, drawing her in. 'We're so in love it's going to rub off on the others.'

Lizzie wrapped her arms around him. 'Wouldn't it be wonderful if you were right?'

'I am.' Jack's lips met hers, the first kiss of the night. 'You wait and see.'

THE MATCHMAKING
TWINS

CHRISTY JEFFRIES

To my great-aunt, Mary Jane Templeton. Thank you for providing me with so much characterization for this story and thank you for providing me with so much love and acceptance as a child. I miss our shopping trips, our beauty parlor visits, and our lunches out. I'm sure Heaven has a lot more gold painted pine cones, Pepsi-Cola, and Grand Ole Opry episodes now that you're there.

Chapter One

Officer Maria Carmen Delgado had once come under heavy fire while guarding some of the most remote military encampments in the world before leaving the Marine Corps to become a cop, patrolling the roughest gang neighborhoods in Las Vegas. But eight-year-old twins Aiden and Caden Gregson of Sugar Falls, Idaho, were certainly going to be the death of her.

"Boys," she said as she unlocked the driver's-side door to her squad car. "I told you that if you were going to ride along with me, you had to promise to stay in the backseat of the Explorer."

"Sorry, Officer Carmen," Aiden said, looking anything but remorseful. "Chief Cooper was calling you on the radio, and we had to tell him that you were ten-seven 'cause you were taking a leak. We couldn't figure out the secret code for the leak part."

When she'd volunteered for the after-school mentorship program at Sugar Falls Elementary, she'd expected to get assigned as a quasi-big-sister to some disadvantaged young girl. She hadn't expected the director to pair her up with a couple of identical little boys with a penchant for mischief and a knack for speaking their overly bright minds.

Normally she only hung out with the Gregson twins when she was off duty. But the officer scheduled to relieve her had come down with the flu and the small-town police department was still new and slightly understaffed, so she'd volunteered to stay late and cover his shift. Since Carmen didn't like letting anyone down, she'd gotten special permission to pick the boys up from school in her patrol vehicle and bring them back to the station. It would only be for an hour, she'd told herself. What trouble could they possibly get into in that amount of time?

She should've known better.

So far, they'd already locked themselves inside a jail holding cell, lost a week's worth of their allowance money by betting the dispatcher she couldn't finish their math homework and got kicked out of the local Gas N' Mart.

And now they'd just told her boss that she'd been taking a leak. Actually, Carmen wished it was just that simple to use the restroom while wearing all her tactical gear along with her police uniform—especially since she went more frequently following her surgery.

Because she couldn't very well take the boys inside the ladies' room with her, she'd told them to stay put inside her cruiser and asked Scooter Deets, one of the older volunteer firefighters who was parked nearby, to keep an eye on the twins. Apparently, ol' Scooter was no better at maintaining control than she was.

Carmen shook her head, thankful the bobby pins securing her coiled bun prevented her hair from being as frazzled as her nerves.

"I knew I never should have let you guys learn our radio codes. You two are in violation of ten-thirty and about to become ten-fifteens," she said, referring to their unauthorized use of police equipment.

"Wait." Caden pulled out the little notepad he'd started carrying in his pocket lately. "What's a ten-fifteen again?"

"It's a prisoner in custody," his twin brother answered before flashing his cheeky smile, minus two recently lost incisors.

"Hey, Officer Carmen, will you teach us Spanish, too?"

"Vámanos, mi liositos," she said before shooing them out of the front and using the handheld radio mic to respond to her boss.

"Sorry about that, Chief," she said after his voice crackled on the other end. "The Gregson twins are officially on administrative suspension for disobeying a direct order to stay put in the *backseat.*"

"Roger that," her boss said. "Tell them that their dad came by the station to pick them up, but since you all were still out, I told Luke that you'd meet him at the Little League fields. You can drop them off there."

Her belly twisted and she resisted the urge to throw the mic out the window. Captain Luke Gregson, the twins' father, was the last person she wanted to see today. Or, really, any day for the matter. But she couldn't say that to Chief Cooper.

"Ten-four," she replied instead, before clicking off. Then she turned to her two mischievous passengers. "Buckle up, kiddos."

"Can we go Code Three with the lights and sirens and everything?" Caden asked as she pulled the vehicle back onto the main highway and headed toward the small park on the other side of town. "Dad's gonna make us do extra laps if we're late to practice."

She should've just taken the boys to the ball fields after school and let them run wild. Maybe if they got more of their energy out, they wouldn't be prone to getting into so much trouble. Not that anyone ever really disciplined the adorable rascals.

And speaking of their lack of discipline, by having to take them directly to baseball practice, she'd be forced to shoot the breeze with their father, the hunky and obviously heartbroken Captain Gregson. It wasn't that there was anything wrong with the handsome and widowed Navy SEAL turned recruiter. Or that Carmen didn't know how to talk to men. It was just that the man had this extremely frustrating habit of treating Carmen like she was one of the guys.

Of course, she couldn't really blame him, or the rest of the males in the small touristy town of Sugar Falls. With her long black hair always pulled into a tight no-nonsense bun and a complete lack of makeup, Carmen was used to working in a male-dominated environment and having to fit in with the good ol' boys.

It was difficult for people to see that beneath the Kevlar vest and the blue polyester unisex uniform, she was still one-hundred-percent female. Keeping one hand on the steering wheel, she rested the other one underneath her sturdy leather duty belt and rubbed along her longest scar. Well, she was *mostly* female.

She took a deep breath, squared her shoulders and tried to focus on the innocent chatter of the eight-year-olds behind her. In her brain, she knew that she was a strong woman and her ability to have children, or lack thereof, should not define her.

But there was always that niggling sense of what she'd lost.

"Hey, Officer Carmen," Caden said, breaking her negative reverie. "Are you gonna be at our game this Saturday? Dad and Coach Alex said I could be lead batter."

Carmen sagged against her seat, wishing she could go to all the twins' games. But no matter how much the two charming troublemakers were growing on her, she'd rather relive her emergency surgery than be faced with spending more time near their father, Captain Dimples.

Luke had returned to town only a month after she'd taken the position with the Sugar Falls Police Department. When she'd been in the Marine Corps, she'd heard about his elite Special Ops team who'd carried out some of the deadliest missions in Afghanistan. Of course, she hadn't thought that one of its members would eventually end up living in the same small city. Or that said member would have such adorable kids, who needed more supervision than the single dad could provide.

She especially didn't know that he'd be so damn good-looking.

"I'm not sure about this weekend," Carmen said. "We'll see what my schedule looks like."

"Aw, c'mon, Officer Carmen," Aiden chimed in. "Ever since Aunt Kylie had her babies, we're the only kids on the team who don't have someone in the stands cheering for us."

Her chest grew heavy with guilt and she tugged on her weighted vest as if she could physically relieve the pressure. Here she'd been feeling sorry for herself and the fact that she'd never have a family of her own, yet these poor young children had to grow up without a mom. As much as she'd bonded with the two wild and wonderful boys, was she doing them all a disservice by allowing herself to get too close to them when what they really needed was a mother figure?

She was usually much more empathetic than this, which was why she'd been a good MP and an even better cop in Vegas. It was why she'd made the big move to a small town like Sugar Falls in the first place. She needed to find herself again.

And she needed to get her emotions in check.

She pulled into the dirt lot behind the bleachers and was saved from making any additional commitments by the sudden appearance of the tall, muscular, blond male walking toward them and waving.

Her stomach grew uncomfortable and she almost undid her seat belt, thinking the baton attached to her duty belt had shifted and was digging into her flesh. But she knew the feeling well enough to realize it wasn't from anything she was wearing. She got that same tightening of her insides every time she saw Captain Luke Gregson.

"Hey, monkeys," he said to his children as he leaned into the open driver's-side window. "Did you guys catch any crooks today?" His face was close enough that she could see where he'd cut himself shaving this morning. And she could smell the lemon and oak moss scent of his aftershave.

Button it up, Delgado, she told herself.

"Well, we almost stopped a robbery at the Gas N' Mart," one of the kids said from the backseat. But Carmen was so focused on not attaching her nose to the tanned and fragrant skin on Luke's neck that she couldn't tell which of the boys was talking. "We were getting our slushies and a man walked in with his hat pulled down past his eyebrows and he was reaching into his back pocket, like he was gonna pull out a gun."

Luke raised one brow, clearly aware of his children's fondness for exaggeration. Carmen should interject here, but she was too busy commanding her tummy to relax to get any words out.

"So, me and Caden made a run for him, 'cause we were gonna karate chop him up before he could start shooting down the place."

"Oh, crap," Luke muttered, and she finally got her hormones under control so she could explain.

"Don't worry." She put her hand up as though she could physically stop his thoughts. Then she returned it to the wheel when she realized how close it was to touching his face. "It was only Scooter Deets, and he was reaching for his wallet, not a gun."

"Yeah, but we didn't recognize him 'cause he wasn't wearing his normal Boise State cap. His new goat chewed a hole clean through it, and now he has to wear a diff'rent one until he goes into the big city next month."

The big city was Boise. It was only an hour's drive

down the mountain, but it was probably a yearly excursion for a local like Scooter.

"So nobody actually got hurt?" Luke asked. Was it her imagination or was his sudden release of air a little too warm and minty? "There wasn't any damage?"

"Well, Scooter didn't really get hurt 'cause we landed on all those chips when we jumped at him. But Mrs. Marconi told Officer Carmen that someone was gonna hafta pay for a new display stand since hers is all bent up now."

Luke drew his fingers through his short military-cut hair. Carmen had seen the exasperated mannerism several times just this past month and knew the poor dad was once again frustrated at his children's antics. "Okay, boys. Hop out and go warm up for practice. I already put your gear in the dugout."

"Do we hafta do extra laps?" Aiden wanted to know as they exited her car.

"You will if you don't mind your manners and thank Officer Delgado for putting up with you two this afternoon."

"Thanks, Officer Carmen," Aiden said. Ever since she'd taken the job with the police department, the twins were the only people in town who called her by her first name. Well, actually her middle name, since Maria Carmen was a mouthful even to her.

"Yeah, thanks," Caden added. "We'll see you next Tuesday again. And maybe Saturday for the game, remember?"

After this afternoon, she was looking forward to a little peace and quiet. But would it really be almost a whole week before she'd get to see them again?

"I'll see you next Tuesday, but I don't know about

Saturday, yet." Unfortunately, her last sentence wasn't even heard by the two boys who were now running toward their teammates.

"So, do I really have to pay for a new chip display at the Gas N' Mart?" Luke asked.

Uh-oh. He was still there. And her little towheaded buffers had made a beeline for the field. She shifted her hips to the right, but because of her holster knocking into the seat belt buckle, she couldn't scoot any farther away from him.

"It really didn't look too busted to me," she said, thankful she was wearing her mirrored aviator sunglasses. Hopefully Luke couldn't tell that she was barely able to make eye contact with him. "I set it back up and the boys put all the bags that didn't burst open back on the shelves. I was going to have them clean up the broken chips, but I think Elaine Marconi just wanted us to get out of there at that point. She was annoyed, but she has kids of her own so she didn't seem too put out. I'll have the chief let you know if she files a claim for damages."

There. She'd directed any future conversation through her boss, who also happened to be Luke's friend. While she loved spending time with his funny and impulsive children, being around the man himself caused the butterflies fluttering around in her stomach to migrate straight to her brain.

"Those boys are going to be the death of me," he said, voicing aloud the exact thought she'd had forty minutes ago. His forearms now rested on her windowsill, as though he wasn't planning to shove off anytime soon.

"Anyway, I'm sorry we're late. It was my fault," she

said quickly, hoping he'd take the hint that she was in a hurry to finish the conversation.

"Don't worry about it. Listen, I really appreciate you spending time with them after school. I'm sure you have much more important things to do around town than play big sister to a couple of little monkeys." The way he smiled showed his dimples to advantage and indicated that he used the nickname for his kids out of affection.

But she wasn't particularly fond of the way he classified her into his sons' peer age range, as if she wasn't just a few years younger than Luke, himself. At least he'd said *sister*, though, and not *brother*. That was something, right?

As much as she wanted to get far, far away from his sexy grin, politeness dictated she respond. "Actually," she said, "you may find this hard to believe, but the Sugar Falls PD doesn't see too much action on the weekdays. Foiling a nonrobbery at the Gas N' Mart has been the most exciting thing to happen on one of my shifts since last January when those tourists didn't check out of the Snow Creek Lodge by eleven o'clock."

She clamped her lips tightly together after she spoke. Why did she do that? Why did she always downplay the importance of her job—the value of her abilities? Shrinks would probably say it was some type of residual defense mechanism from growing up in her oversize machismo family or trying not to stand out in a male-dominated profession.

"Still, I know they're in good hands with you." Did the man ever stop smiling? "Coop said you outwrestled half his force in defensive tactics training last week."

"That's not saying much considering we only have

four other officers on staff." There she went again. She should be proud that she was an expert in martial arts. But she didn't want Luke to think of her as some juiced-up, studly gladiator. She wanted him to see her as...

Stop. It was this kind of foolish thinking that would seriously undermine all the work she'd put into getting her mind right and her head back in the game since she'd broken up with Mark and moved here. Man, she needed to get away from Luke and her AWOL thoughts.

Thinking quickly, she reached beneath the dashboard and double clicked on the mic of her bandwidth radio, causing the volunteer dispatcher to respond. Carmen clicked on the mic again, then leaned down toward the radio as though she was listening to something Luke couldn't hear.

The resulting static probably wouldn't fool a former SEAL, but she went through the pretense of answering a phony call out. "Ten-four. I'm en route."

She looked back at him as she put the vehicle in gear. "Gotta run," she said, barely waiting for him to move his arms off the window before tearing out of the dirt lot.

That was the worst fake radio call out Luke had ever seen. And he should know. He'd trained as a communications specialist before going through Basic Underwater Demolition/SEAL training.

He watched Officer Delgado drive off, gravel crunching and dust flying. Why had she been in such a hurry to get away from him? Was he giving off that lonely "I need to talk to someone who understands kids" vibe again? He rubbed his forehead, then dragged his fingers through his hair before shoving his hands in his jeans pockets.

His twin brother, Drew, said it was obvious whenever Luke was missing the guys from his unit—or worse, when he'd been in the cabin all weekend with his squirrelly sons and he needed adult conversation—because it was the only time Luke uttered more than a few sentences.

But moving to Sugar Falls to become a full-time dad, changing assignments from team leader of an elite Special Forces unit to pushing paper at the naval recruiting office outside of Boise…well, it was all proving to be more challenging than he'd anticipated.

Luke poked his athletic shoe at some tiny rocks that had been kicked up from Carmen's patrol car as she'd blasted out of the lot. The action was instinctive, as though his feet needed the physical reminder that he was actually standing on solid ground.

He thought back to the night before Samantha's accident several years ago. Luke had been in a training exercise where the team was being hoisted from the ocean and into a hovering Osprey helicopter. It was dark and the water was choppy, with waves crashing over his head. When it had been his turn, part of his safety harness ripped and he'd had to hold on to the cable with his bare hands to keep from dropping. He'd dangled like that, with the chopper blades stirring up more wind force than the actual storm, for at least a minute before being pulled up to safety.

Ever since his wife had died, he hadn't been able to shake that feeling of being suspended in the air, swinging above a raging dark sea and holding on as if his life depended on it.

"Hey, Dad," Aiden yelled from the outfield. "Are ya comin' or what?"

He waved at the boy and started to jog toward the dugout. He needed a good run tonight. Something that would clear his thoughts or at least make his mind too tired to think.

"How's Officer Delgado today?" Alex Russell, the team coach, asked Luke when he finally made it back to the dugout. He liked Alex, whose family owned the local sporting goods store, but he didn't like the sly half smile the man was now wearing.

"What's that supposed to mean?" Even Luke heard the unfamiliar agitation in his voice.

"I've just noticed that she's been dropping the boys off at practice a few weeks in a row."

"Yeah, that mentorship program at the school finally found someone who was willing to take them on. Once a week, I have to stay at the recruiting office later and can't pick the boys up, so I think Delgado must've taken pity on them—the people who work at the after-school program, that is."

"Some kids have all the luck."

His kids? Lucky? No way. They'd already lost their mom before they could really remember her and they'd been bounced around with various relatives while Luke had played Captain Save-the-World. Now it was taking a whole ski resort village to raise the lovable little hellions. "What do you mean?"

"Not only do they get to hang out with a cop, which would be any boy's dream, but they get to ride around with the hottest one on the force."

"Officer Delgado?" Okay, so Luke was faking the surprise in his voice. The woman was naturally beautiful with those classic high cheekbones and full lips, but he'd quickly gotten the impression from the woman herself, as well as most of the other men in town, that she definitely was not on the market—not that *he* was, either. So then why was Alex bringing up her hotness?

"C'mon. Like you haven't noticed the way she fills out that uniform."

Sure he had, and he wanted to take the aluminum bat leaning against the fence and swing it at the head coach for even suggesting that he'd noticed, too.

Whoa. *Shake it off, Gregson.* What was up with the irrational jealousy?

"I try not to," Luke said, his jaw locking around each word. And that was true. He felt guilty sometimes just for looking at her.

"Hell, we all *try* not to, Luke. She obviously isn't the type to flaunt anything and probably wouldn't appreciate it if we were noticing. She's all business, that one." Alex picked up a glove and patted his shoulder before walking out of the dugout. "Let's get started, boys!"

Maybe Luke wasn't the only guy in town who Officer Delgado wasn't warming up to. He should be somewhat relieved that it wasn't just him. Still, the woman turned into a block of ice whenever he spoke to her, and he didn't know what to make of that. Luke wasn't usually so chatty, but he'd tried to talk to her about things they could possibly have in common—like the military or martial arts. Once, he even asked her what she bench-pressed because, clearly, the shapely woman worked out. Yet, unless they were talking about the twins, she shut down completely every time.

She'd made it plain that she was indifferent to him, but for some damn reason, anytime he was within a few feet of her, he couldn't get his mouth to stop yapping.

Not that he was actually interested in Carmen like that. Or in any woman, for that matter. When he'd been active on the team and going to bars with his single buddies, he'd had no problem charming the ladies. But those days were over soon after he'd met Samantha.

After his wife died, it had taken him a while to get his head back on straight, and he wasn't entirely convinced he'd succeeded yet. He used to think that volunteering for the most dangerous missions and staring his fears in the face would make him feel more in control. Then, after a near-death experience last summer, he realized he couldn't be so selfish as to put Aiden and Caden at risk of becoming total orphans. So he'd settled down and aimed for the safety net of Sugar Falls.

Now all his charm was exclusively used for smoothing over the trouble his children unintentionally caused. So far, neither his charm nor his commitment to his children had diminished that dangling, out-of-control feeling he still got. To make matters worse, when Carmen Delgado was around, his safety net seemed further away than ever—and he wasn't sure he could survive another free-fall.

Chapter Two

Carmen had just finished lunch at the Cowgirl Up Café on Snowflake Boulevard and was walking back to the station to do some paperwork before her shift was over when a very pregnant Mia McCormick waved her over from across the street.

"Hey, Officer Delgado, you're just the person I wanted to talk to," Mia said as she held open the door to the Sugar Falls Cookie Company to allow Kylie Gregson, the twins' aunt, to maneuver her double stroller inside. "Do you have a second?"

"Sure." Carmen followed the women into the little shop that brought so much business to Sugar Falls. She inhaled the scent of vanilla and looked around at the cute displays to see what the flavor of the month was. She'd always been a sucker for fresh baked goods, and even though the turkey sandwich and potato salad she'd finished a few minutes ago threatened to pop open the button on her uniform pants, she might order a couple of cookies and save them for later.

She tried to look anywhere but at the other custom- ers who cooed and made googly eyes at the twin baby girls, talking to Kylie and Mia about feedings and dia- pers and all the things Carmen would never get to ex- perience.

Carmen had never felt like such an outsider, which was saying something considering she'd been the only female in her MP unit and had had to hoof it clear across the base to take a shower in the women's head while all of her coworkers got to use the communal locker room.

At least as a Marine and a cop, she had the job in common with her male counterparts. But there was absolutely nothing she could say at that second that would make her fit in with this duo of mommies. And she never would.

When the customers finally left, Mia said, "I'm so behind schedule. I should've taken Maxine up on her offer to deliver the cookies to the old Remington Theater for tonight's dance recital."

Maxine owned the Sugar Falls Cookie Company and was married to Carmen's boss. Since Carmen knew Chief Cooper was off duty this afternoon to ac- company his wife to an obstetrician appointment, she doubted the pregnant dance teacher would get much help running errands. Maybe that's what Mia wanted to talk to her about. But before Carmen could remind the woman she was on duty, the other mom spoke up.

"Thank goodness you got the city council to okay you using the old theater for performances," Kylie said to Mia as she rocked her stroller back and forth. She directed her next comment at Carmen. "Sometimes I worry about my girls growing up in a small city with a limited access to culture, so having a legitimate venue for school plays and band concerts is a total win. Last year, when the community center got double booked, we had to watch the fifth grade's talent show while the bingo club was shouting out B-39 and O-14 the whole time."

Carmen smiled politely as the women laughed. She hadn't been in Sugar Falls very long, so she didn't share the same memories, but she appreciated these ladies including her in the conversation and not making her feel so out of the loop. Although she was still waiting for them to clue her in on why they wanted to talk to her.

"You're from Vegas originally, right?" Kylie asked before reaching into the stroller and unstrapping the infant who'd started fussing. Carmen nodded but averted her eyes quickly for fear that if she watched the tender maternal moment too long, she wouldn't be able to look away. In which case, they'd probably see the hunger and the desperation in her eyes. She planned to avoid that scenario. Sympathy was never easy for her to handle.

"Hey, I thought I saw my nieces being wheeled in here," a masculine voice said from the doorway. Carmen didn't have to turn around to recognize the speaker. Her stomach's telltale reaction to his voice already alerted her.

She told herself it was due to the big lunch she'd just consumed, not his unexpected arrival. Just like it was the sudden crisp spring air rushing in from the open door that caused the shiver to race from inside her starched collar all the way down her spine—not Luke Gregson, himself.

Maybe if she repeated that lame excuse eight more times, she might actually believe it.

The tall man was dressed in his blue battle dress uniform, looking like he'd spent all morning modeling in a photo shoot for some Navy recruitment poster. She would think that seeing him in his military uniform would trick her mind into believing that he was just like every other guy she'd worked with over the past ten years.

But judging from the second shiver making its way down her back, it wasn't her mind doing the thinking.

A sudden wail jerked Carmen's attention from the muscular male legs tucked into shiny black boots and toward the small bundle of pink still strapped in the stroller.

"Oh, no." The pitch in Luke's normally deep voice raised a few octaves as he reached for his other niece, talking to her. "Did your mean ol' mama pick up your sister and leave you behind all alone in this big contraption?"

"Luke Gregson." Kylie stood up even taller than her five-foot-ten height as she faced her brother-in-law. "If you call me or my fashionable stroller 'old' one more time, I will drive straight to the school and tell your sons that you promised to take them and five of their best friends camping this weekend."

"Aw, come on, Kylie." Luke's voice sounded just like his sons last week when Carmen had told them they had to practice their spelling words before she took them to Noodie's Ice Cream Shoppe. "That's not cool. It's supposed to rain this weekend, and you know what happened last time I let them invite a friend—one friend—for a sleepover at the cabin. I still have mustard and toilet paper stuck to the living room ceiling."

Carmen laughed. It didn't take much to imagine how Aiden and Caden had managed that.

"Hey, Officer Delgado." Luke finally turned his warm gaze to her. Seeing him holding that precious baby made her stomach drop to her knees, which was the only explanation for why her legs felt so unsteady. "I didn't expect to see you in here chitchatting the afternoon away with these two."

Didn't he? If he saw his sister-in-law and nieces enter the cookie shop, then he had to have seen Carmen come in right behind them. More than likely, he was probably surprised to see her socializing with other women. Not that she wasn't a little surprised herself.

"First, you call me old and now you suggest we're all just wasting our time talking about important town business?" Kylie tried to sound stern. "Give me my daughter, Luke. She can't wait to surprise her cousins at school with the news of their fun-filled weekend."

Luke maneuvered himself and the pink bundle nestled on his shoulder behind Carmen, as though she were the barrier that would protect him from his brother's wife, who was clearly only feigning her annoyance. His dimpled smile struck again.

"Now, now, Kylie. You couldn't ever get mad at me. That's just the hormones talking." When his sister-in-law chuckled, Luke finally moved back into the line of fire. "I remember when Samantha had just given birth to the boys and she called my commanding officer in the middle of the night, reading him the riot act because I was still on deployment and she was out of baby wipes and didn't have any clothes not covered in spit-up that she could wear to the store."

"Your wife was a saint for putting up with you gone on all that secret assignment mumbo jumbo. I couldn't even imagine what I'd do if Drew got deployed before the girls go off to graduate school."

Luke rocked back on his heels but didn't say a word. He didn't have to. The sadness in his blue eyes and the steeliness of his jaw did the talking for him.

"Oh, my gosh, Luke." Kylie must've seen the same hurt expression cross his face because she tenderly stroked his arm. "I am so sorry. I didn't mean it like that."

"It's okay, Kylie. I know what you meant. And you're right. Samantha *did* put up with a lot."

If Carmen had felt mildly awkward before, she was downright uncomfortable at being a witness to his heartache. What was she doing here, anyway? Should she even be listening to them reminisce about his deceased wife, a woman who obviously deserved the pedestal they'd all placed her on?

"So, Mia," Carmen said, trying to verbally tiptoe her way out of the emotional land mine. "What was it you wanted to talk to me about?"

"Oh, that's right. Sorry, I have pregnancy brain and can barely hold on to a passing thought."

Carmen, knowing she would never be able to personally relate to such a symptom, had no response to that statement. Instead, she forced a smile toward the sweet woman.

"You know how we do group exercise classes at the dance studio?" Mia asked but didn't wait for a response. "Well, I normally teach a yoga class on Monday mornings, but with the baby due soon, I'm trying to find some substitute instructors while I'm on leave."

"But I've never taught yoga."

"Delgado's a Marine," Luke said, apparently listening in on their conversation. Kylie must've decided to distract him from his grief because now he was holding both babies, one nestled against each thick bicep. *Whoa.*

"She's a devil dog," he continued. "They don't do sissy yoga. Right, Delgado?"

She cringed slightly at the Marine nickname and his inaccurate assessment of her.

"Easy there, skipper," Carmen said, throwing a naval moniker right back at him. His use of her last name was all the proof she needed that she'd been placed in the Friendzone. It was also a good reminder that she shouldn't be lusting over him. "You just got out of trouble with Kylie and now you're trying to pick a fight with Mia, as well? I think you're underestimating your battle odds."

Mia's hand shot between them like a white flag of surrender. "That's not what I meant. I was actually moving yoga to a different day, which leaves Mondays open. So, I was thinking that maybe you could lead some sort of kickboxing type class or teach self-defense. You know, that type of thing?"

"Oh," Carmen said, at a loss for words. She hadn't been expecting the request. She was flattered that the dance instructor thought her capable of teaching, and a little pleased that the small community was beginning to welcome her into their folds. But still. Would other ladies in town even be interested in such a class?

"Give it some thought." Mia, probably sensing her hesitation, quickly added, "I have the recital tonight, and then the girls and I normally get together on Thursdays for dinner. Why don't you meet with us tomorrow and we can discuss things more?"

"And by discuss things," Kylie added, "she means maybe we can help her talk you into it."

"Uh-oh, Delgado." Luke smiled showing a single dimple. "These women are trying to get you to come over to the dark side with them. I'm sure you'd rather hang out with us tomorrow at poker night."

And there she had it. She knew he was part of the group of men who got together with Chief Cooper once a week to play cards. Which meant Luke Gregson definitely thought of her as one of the guys.

It should feel good that both groups wanted her presence at their Thursday night rituals. But there was still the underlying reminder that the man she couldn't stop thinking about didn't reciprocate her feelings—and probably never would, considering the loving way he spoke of his late wife. It was enough to dash all hope of her ever finding a man who would accept a damaged woman.

In the past ten years, Carmen had had her share of poker nights and locker-room jokes and testosterone-fueled bragging. A night out with the girls actually sounded like a nice change of pace.

So she looked at the two women and, for the first

time, stepped over the invisible line she believed had been drawn in the sand. "What time should I be there, ladies?"

Could Officer Delgado try any harder to avoid him?

As Luke stood outside the bakery, he had to wonder what he'd done to annoy the beautiful cop. Sure, he enjoyed his sassy sister-in-law and her group of friends. But Carmen didn't seem like the type of woman to hang out with a bunch of former cheerleaders turned moms.

She had way more in common with him, and he'd simply been trying to point that out. Okay, so maybe he sounded like an arrogant tool with all that ooh rah Marine business. He wasn't trying to be a chauvinist or imply that she wasn't capable of teaching yoga. From what he'd seen of her with the twins, and from what he'd heard of her reputation with the MPs, she was one tough cookie.

So then why did she always act like he was a melted chocolate chip stuck to the bottom of her black utility boot?

He would've asked Kylie if he'd done anything to offend Carmen, but she'd sat down to nurse one of the girls and Luke had gotten the heck out of Dodge. Not that he was uncomfortable with seeing a woman breast-feed. At least, he doubted he would be. He'd been on a classified mission when his own boys were born, and by the time he'd come home, Samantha had decided that formula was much easier for her. And who was he to object? He couldn't be there all the time and he still felt immeasurable guilt that his wife had had to do everything on her own.

Not that she'd totally been on her own, he'd found out after the fact. Still, it had been a hell of a lot more than he'd done.

When Aiden and Caden were babies and toddlers, Luke was usually only home for a couple of months at a time. He and his late wife didn't necessarily share the same parenting philosophy, but they also didn't share the same workload when it came to the kids, so he took a backseat to her softer approach. Then, after her accident, he'd stayed home long enough to help the boys get through the initial grief before his parents convinced him they could help out. Luke had told himself that the three-year-olds needed a mother figure more than they needed him—after all, it was Samantha who had done most of the work so far.

So when Aiden and Caden were staying with different family members and babysitters and he was still out of the country half the time, the boys lost even more structure.

His cell phone rang, and when he saw the number for the elementary school on the display screen, Luke wished for the thousandth time that he'd been more on top of their discipline. He loved his children more than anything, but man, were they magnets for trouble.

"Captain Gregson, here," he answered.

"Hello, Captain. This is Mrs. Dunn, the nurse over here at Sugar Falls Elementary."

Thank God, it was the nurse this time, and not the principal. Wow, *that* was a really bad thought. "Are my sons okay?" he asked.

"Yes, everyone is fine. Now. Caden had a little incident on the tetherball court and Aiden tried to help him get untangled and, well, the rope got caught. Anyway, I think it's just a bad sprain, but you should probably get some X-rays just in case."

"Which one?"

"The left one."

"I mean, which of my children got injured."

"Aiden has the actual sprain, but from the way Caden is carrying on, you'd think he was the one hurt."

It was a twin thing. Luke and Drew had experienced the similar phenomenon growing up. And even as adults.

"I'm coming right now. Is his arm in a sling?"

"Uh, no. Why would it be?"

Luke only had basic medic training to assist in emergencies until a corpsmen got to the scene, but it would seem to him like the nurse would at least want to take pressure off the injured body part. "I just thought that maybe it would help stabilize his arm."

"Oh, sorry, Captain Gregson. I should've been clearer. The sprain is to Aiden's ankle."

"How in the world did he sprain his ankle with a tetherball rope?"

"That's a great question, Captain. And as soon as he gets his brother to relax, maybe Aiden can tell us. I had to snatch some pudding cups out of the school cafeteria to help in the calming-down process."

"I'll be right there."

Luke disconnected the call, got into his nana's brown Oldsmobile and drove less than a mile from downtown to the school. He'd grown up in Boise, but his parents owned a cabin here and he had spent most of his summers in Sugar Falls before joining the Navy.

While the town setting was familiar, he was still getting used to the slower pace of life.

He would've preferred to drive around in the yellow Jeep his family kept at the cabin, but when his brother, Drew, had stepped in to care for the boys last summer during Luke's last deployment, his overly cautious and analytical brother had insisted that the thirty-year-old sedan was safer for shuttling children than the fun and masculine four-by-four.

At least the Oldsmobile was in good shape. Before she'd passed away ten years ago, his grandmother had only driven the thing three times a week—to the grocery store, to the beauty shop and to the casino out on the reservation—so it had low mileage and only some minor dings in the right front fender. Nana never could make the tight turn into her carport at the mobile home park.

He kept meaning to buy a more functional and fuel-efficient car, especially since he was making the hour-long commute into Boise four times a week. But, contrary to what Drew and their sister, Hannah, thought, he'd always been Nana's favorite grandkid and he missed the old gal.

Growing up, Luke had been the naughty twin—the proverbial pastor's son who drove his mother to distraction. Nana would come pick him up to give his mom a break, calling him her wild child and having him light her menthol cigarettes for her so she could keep both hands on the steering wheel.

He took a deep breath, still able to smell the Benson & Hedges along with the lingering scent of her Shalimar perfume. His parents were fair and loved him, but Nana had been his island—his place to escape. Driving this brown beast made him feel closer to her.

When he pulled into the school lot, he gunned the eight-cylinder engine, just like she used to do, before pulling into a parking spot. He also overestimated his turn radius and the right bumper knocked into the custom sign that read Principal Parking Only.

Yep, just like Nana.

He walked inside and waved at the school secretary, who, after the third week of school, had programmed Luke's cell number into her phone's speed dial.

He let out a little sigh of relief when he turned left to go to the nurse's office instead of heading straight down the hall toward the principal's. He'd spent plenty of time sitting outside doors just like that one when he was growing up. And, since history seemed to be repeating itself, his children had a tendency to do the same.

Karma was definitely on the upswing with his genetics. Luke's parents often referred to it as God's sense of humor.

When he entered the room, he saw Aiden, the injured twin, sitting behind Mrs. Dunn's desk and showing her how to play a computer game. Caden, the uninjured one, was propped on the cot and eating a chocolate pudding cup. His left foot was elevated on several pillows with an ice pack balanced precariously on top.

Even Luke's brother, Drew, a well-respected Navy psychologist, couldn't explain twin telepathy. But both he and Luke had experienced it firsthand and he didn't doubt for a second that Caden could legitimately feel his brother's pain.

Although, from the way Aiden was swinging around in the nurse's chair and yelling commands at the woman on how to fight the Creepers on her computer, it seemed nobody was really the worse for wear.

"Dad? Oh, good. You're finally here," Caden said as he sat up and reached for his backpack. "We need to get Aiden to the hospital for some X-rays. Let me see your phone."

Luke patted his pocket, ensuring his cell was far out of reach from his dramatic and impulsive son. "Who were you planning to call?"

"Officer Carmen. I'm gonna tell her we need a police escort with lights and sirens and the works."

Luke raised his blond eyebrow at Aiden, who had just high-fived Mrs. Dunn for reaching the next level on his favorite game. "I think your brother will be fine on the way there. We can forgo the Code Three routine."

Besides, he was pretty sure Carmen was off duty by now. Wait. How had he known that? Had she mentioned her schedule to him when he'd seen her at the cookie shop earlier?

Considering she hadn't said more than two words to him, he doubted it. So why did he know what her shift was? Because today was Wednesday. And she always worked the afternoon shift on Sundays and Mondays, then the morning shifts on Tuesdays and Wednesdays.

He tapped his toe against the linoleum. Yep, the ground was still solid. So then maybe he could stomp out some of this useless information he was carrying around about a woman who would just as soon do fifty pull-ups than say hello to him.

Of course he would know her schedule because Tuesdays were the days she always picked up the boys after school, right after putting in a ten-hour day. He had to give the woman credit for that. She was an absolute sweetheart with the twins and had the patience of Job. Aiden and Caden couldn't stop talking about her or singing her praises, which was probably why she kept popping up in Luke's head so often—just like his renewed knowledge of *Star Wars* sequels, now that he'd shown the DVDs to the boys.

"Sorry to have to bother you at work, Captain," Mrs. Dunn, the fiftysomething-year-old former Ski Potato Queen, said. He knew she had been on the homecoming court and had earned her crown at the annual ski festival the same decade his grandmother had bought her Oldsmobile because the woman kept the framed pictures and newspaper articles displayed on a shelf right above the bandages and antiseptic wipes.

"Actually, we had a presentation at one of the high schools this morning so I was off early today."

"Being a recruiter must be so exciting. Helping all those young people find their careers." When the nurse smiled at him, he noticed some of her coral lipstick had smeared onto her front two teeth, but he didn't have the heart to point it out to the former beauty queen. When it came to those holding any sort of authority position over his children, he found it best to keep them locked in as allies.

"That's sweet of you to say. It really makes me appreciate all you school employees do to help shape the minds of our next generation." Which was true. Luke loved his own boys, but he didn't think he could deal with so many students and their high-energy personalities on a daily basis. He gave the woman his best get-out-of-trouble smile.

Her mascara-clumped eyelashes fluttered as best they could and he knew he'd hit his mark. She smiled back and said, "I bet the high schoolers just adore having a hotshot hero like you come speak to them."

In Luke's mind, being a SEAL wasn't such a big deal. He had just been doing what he loved. Still, maybe he could ask Nurse Dunn to share her flattering insight with Officer Delgado. Not that he cared what the female cop thought of him.

"Dad?" Aiden tapped him with a one of the crutches he must have borrowed from the school nurse. "You ready?"

"Oh. Um, yeah." After hearing the nurse explain to Caden that she only had one set of crutches, Luke carried Aiden's backpack and watched as his injured eight-year-old hobbled in front of him on one foot. His other son trailed behind with only a slight limp.

Anytime he had a slow day at the recruiting office and thought he missed the excitement of Spec Ops, all he had to do was drive home to his children. No amount of skilled warfare training could have prepared him for the adventure that was fatherhood.

Of course, it was times like these when he wished he'd pursued sniper school. Maybe then he'd be better equipped to work without a teammate. Without a partner. Sure, he had his family for backup, but sometimes he felt so alone.

The kids climbed into the back of Nana's Oldsmobile and then immediately turned the crutches into dueling lightsabers.

It was going to be a very long night.

Chapter Three

"Hey, Officer Carmen, you wanna sign my cast?" Luke heard Aiden say to the long-legged curly-haired brunette wearing tight jeans and high-heeled boots. Caden rushed inside Patrelli's Italian Restaurant to join his brother before Luke could stop them.

Crap. It was bad enough that the boys talked about their cop friend all the time, but now they were so eager to see her, they were mistaking her for random ladies in town. Albeit, a very curvaceous and sexy random lady. Luke let go of the heavy oak door and hurried over to the hostess stand to prevent his son from creating an embarrassing situation.

"Monkey, that's not... Oh." Luke stopped when the woman turned around.

Wow. He'd never seen Carmen wear anything besides her police uniform—something that clearly hadn't been tailored with such a womanly form in mind—or track pants and long-sleeved T-shirts when he'd caught glimpses of her out running.

"It's just a stupid ACE bandage," he heard Caden say, yet the pending argument barely registered in Luke's ears.

Double wow. The woman really had some nice legs.

"Yeah, but I'm pretending it's a cast," Aiden said. "Casts are cooler and way tougher."

"I would love to sign your pretend cast." Carmen reached for a pen off the hostess stand and bent down to write.

Luke had once been skilled at utilizing all five of his senses in any given situation, but try as he might, his eyes were the only thing functioning at that moment. And they were shamelessly staring at Carmen's, ah, assets. She had on some type of loose, flowing, purple top, and from this angle, he could see down to where the rounded curves of her breasts met the V-shaped neckline.

He almost grabbed one of Aiden's crutches to steady himself as a sudden wave of lust nearly knocked him sideways. Where had *that* come from?

When Carmen finally straightened up, Caden asked, "How can you drive your police car with those girl shoes on?"

"I promise, the next children I sire are going to have better manners," Luke joked as he forced his eyes up to meet her face. But she must have been purposely ignoring him, because she wasn't looking his way at all. Instead, she was completely focused on his children and smiling. Was she wearing lip gloss? And where in the world had she been hiding all those inky black curls?

"I'm not working tonight. I'm having dinner with some fr—some ladies…with some lady friends." She waved at Maxine Cooper and Mia, who were already seated at one of the red vinyl booths. "What about you boys? I thought tonight was poker night?"

Had she remembered the invitation he'd awkwardly delivered yesterday? Probably not, since she still wasn't making eye contact with him. Maybe she was one of those females who related better to kids.

"It is. But it's Dad's turn to bring the food. Hey, you should come with us. It'll be more fun than sitting here and talking about lame girl stuff."

See. He wasn't the only one who'd just assumed she'd be more comfortable hanging out with the guys. But before he could say as much, his sister-in-law breezed into the restaurant.

"Aunt Kylie," both of the boys squealed before throwing their arms around her.

"Oh, you guys are getting so big!" Kylie said. "I've missed you two."

Luke felt a twinge of remorse. The boys had lived with her and Drew for several weeks and often stayed with them when Luke had to go out of town for trainings and recruitment seminars. But now that the couple had two newborns, Luke had tried to keep the boys away so they wouldn't become too much of a burden.

"Hey, Officer Carmen, in those boots, you're almost as tall as Aunt Kylie."

Luke had never really noticed the cop's height before, but in heels, she came to his chin. At least he guessed she would, if she ever got close enough to him to allow for an accurate measurement.

"My dad and Uncle Drew are both six foot four,"

Aiden volunteered. "But we might not grow as big as them because Grammie said our mom was only—how tall was Mom, again?"

It took a second to realize his son was asking him a question. Then it took another second to figure out what that question was. But after half a minute, Luke realized that he didn't have an answer.

How tall *had* Samantha been? She was on the shorter side, but he couldn't recall an exact height. He could remember the way she'd cried and threatened to leave the day he'd gotten his orders to go on a three-month overseas mission. He could even remember the defeated look in her eyes when she'd gone off that night to "have a few drinks with the girls." But lately it was getting more and more difficult to focus on the rest. No wonder Samantha used to accuse him of being emotionally unavailable.

Think, Gregson! Five foot four maybe? She was definitely shorter than the beautiful woman in front of him. He shook his head. What kind of man compared his dead wife to another woman? And what kind of father couldn't keep his thoughts in check when his children asked him such a simple fact about their mother?

"She was five foot four," he finally said while silently appealing for forgiveness in the event he was wrong. As well as forgiveness for the way he'd been too focused on Carmen's long legs.

His career and dangerous deployments had not only taken its toll on his family, it had also driven a wedge so deeply between him and Samantha that she'd turned to a bottle of vodka to ease her burdens. Just because he hadn't been the one behind the wheel on the night she'd died didn't mean he wasn't to blame.

Yet here he was, staring at Carmen, shamelessly taking in every glorious detail about her. The boys barely remembered their mother, and it was up to him to keep her memory alive for them—not get all hot and bothered about some incredible-looking female cop who had a soft spot for his kids. A flood of shame weighed him down, making him feel like he was closer to two feet tall.

Officer Delgado had her hands shoved into her jeans pockets and appeared to be reading the specials on the menu board several feet away. She obviously couldn't even bring herself to look at him. His toes flexed inside of his hiking boots and he clenched his jaw in disgrace.

"Well, you boys have fun at poker night," Kylie said, probably trying to lessen the awkwardness. "I figure I have about sixty-three minutes to get a bit of sustenance before Drew is gonna need me to head back over and feed the girls. So if I don't get some garlic knots and fettuccine Alfredo in me before then, there will be *three* very unhappy Gregson ladies."

Just then, a waitress walked up balancing four large pizza boxes and a couple of white paper sacks filled with Italian subs, and Luke had never been so glad for an excuse to get away. Even though he didn't think he'd be able to stomach a single bite.

"C'mon, monkeys," he said, peeling some bills out of his wallet and putting them on the hostess stand before taking the food from the server.

He maneuvered himself and the boxes out the door while the twins said their goodbyes and gave Kylie her usual three hugs, a ritual they'd started when she and Drew had been looking after the boys last year.

The cool air felt great on his overheated face, so he decided they would walk the few short blocks to Maxine and Cooper's apartment above the Sugar Falls Cookie Company.

He liked his cabin out in the woods, but Luke couldn't deny that the Victorian buildings lining downtown held their own appeal. If the boys didn't need so much space to run around, he'd gladly move in to one and try his hand at renovation. It might also shorten his commute. But then he'd have to interact more with the townspeople.

And, as he'd just displayed, he sometimes ended up looking like a complete ass when he did.

His life certainly hadn't turned out the way he'd expected. His training had conditioned him to always be ready to adapt and overcome—to put the mission goal first. However, just because he was ready to move on didn't mean he knew the direction in which he was headed. Maybe he should focus on figuring out a new mission instead of standing there like a tongue-tied fool who had no business lusting after his children's volunteer mentor.

They climbed the stairs and Cooper let them inside before grabbing the pizza boxes, carrying them to the white kitchen and opening them up on the counter. "Okay, kids, grab a slice and head on back to Hunter's room." Their host handed them each a paper plate then pointed to his stepson's bedroom down the hall.

Setting the rest of the food down, Luke said hello to Drew, who was pushing his sleeping daughters' double stroller back and forth, and to Alex Russell.

Luke was still somewhat new to the group, but Drew and Cooper had been stationed in Afghanistan together, and Alex coached both Hunter's baseball team, as well as Aiden and Caden's.

A knock sounded, and Coop grabbed a slice for himself as he walked to the door to let in the newcomer. Garrett McCormick had been Cooper's knee surgeon at the nearby Shadowview Military Hospital before opening up an orthopedic clinic in Sugar Falls after his discharge. Garrett had married Mia a few months ago—or had it been longer than that? Hell, Luke could barely manage to remember details from his own marriage, let alone all these dudes in Sugar Falls who seemed to be drinking from the same Kool-Aid cup.

"Sorry I'm late," the doctor said. "I had to drop off Mia's coat at Patrelli's. Her hormones are all kind of whacked out and she's been forgetting everything."

Alex, the only other single male present, covered his ears. "This is an estrogen-free zone, gentlemen. I do *not* want to talk about anything but baseball, beer and Clint Eastwood movies."

"Speaking of Clint Eastwood movies," Drew said as he piled food high on his plate. "Kylie and I were watching *Bridges of Madison County* the other day on TV and..."

A collective round of "No" and "C'mon" and "Yuck" went around the room. Someone threw a plastic pouch of red peppers at Luke's twin, who made the catch and then sprinkled some on his pizza.

"Actually, speaking of estrogen..." Garrett paused when he saw several packets of parmesan cheese aimed his way. "Wait, let me rephrase that. I was gonna say that when I stopped by Patrelli's, I saw Officer Delgado sitting with the ladies, and I hardly recognized her out of her uniform."

Luke's ears buzzed as the rest of the guys settled back into their seats. This was his chance to find out more about her without bringing too much attention to himself.

"Hey, Coop." Alex took a swig of beer. "I was meaning to ask what her deal was."

If anyone knew Carmen, it would be Chief Cooper, who was the woman's boss and had previously worked with her before as an MP when they were both stationed stateside. Luke held every muscle still, not wanting to miss the scoop and not wanting to grab the coach by the shoulder and tell him to back off.

There was that weird jealousy feeling again. What was up with that?

"What do you mean?" The police chief arched a brow. Yeah, what exactly *did* Alex mean? Was he interested in the female cop?

"I mean, does she do anything outside of work for fun? We have that intramural softball team we're trying to put together for the Western Idaho League and, well, I don't want to stereotype, but I've seen her out running and she looks like she'd be pretty athletic."

Luke let out the breath he hadn't realized he'd been holding.

"Oh." Cooper got up and brought a foot-long Italian sub sandwich over to the table. "I thought you were asking about personal stuff, which you know I can't give out."

"I'm not looking for a date, man," Alex said, and laughed. "I'm just looking for a shortstop."

"Why wouldn't you want to date her?" Luke felt

the words coming out of his mouth before his brain could process them. Just a second ago, he'd felt like shoving Alex's face into his pizza for even inquiring about Carmen. Now he was accusing the man of not finding her worthy enough of his interest. *Get back on solid ground, Gregson.*

"I didn't say I wouldn't date her. I said I wasn't looking for a date. Any date. At least not with anyone locally. Don't get me wrong, I know love and babies and rainbow-colored unicorns are running rampant in this town—" Alex looked pointedly at Drew, Cooper and Garrett "—but that pile of marriage crap you guys stepped in isn't for me."

"Amen." The word was out of Luke's mouth before he could stop himself. He tilted his beer toward Alex's and they clinked their bottles.

"Wait." Drew held up his hand. "Luke, I can't believe you just said that. Hello? You were married once, too."

"That was a one-time deal and it turned out I wasn't cut out for it, either." He didn't want to talk about Samantha or the shame-inducing lapse of forgetfulness he'd just had at the restaurant in front of witnesses. He didn't want to think about his marriage at all. He tried to keep all thoughts of that disaster hidden away in that footlocker in his mind and wasn't sure why everyone else on this planet suddenly wanted to bring it up.

"Don't you think you could be happy with someone again?" Garrett asked him.

A vision of Carmen's long hair framing her face, her glossed lips smiling at his sons, was the first thing that ran through his mind. But an occasional smile wouldn't be worth the inevitable heartache that would result from getting seriously involved with a woman again. Even if he could be happy, it wouldn't be long before whoever he married wouldn't be.

"Nope, I'm good." He realized he'd responded a little too loudly when he saw four pairs of doubting eyes staring at him intently. "Look, the boys and I are just settling into a routine and I'm still getting used to the new job. My plate's pretty full right now. Besides, every time I see her, she pretty much shuts down, so I'm guessing she's in the same boat."

"Who?"

Luke looked up at Drew. "Uh, Officer Delgado? Wasn't that who we were talking about originally when Alex and Garrett brought her up?"

"Actually," Cooper said. "That was the conversation *before* it got segued into you not looking for a relationship and Carmen not being interested in you."

"Did she tell you she wasn't interested?" Luke raised his eyes like a hungry puppy looking for confirmation that there were no more pieces of pepperoni being thrown his way. "I mean, not in *me* per se, but… Stop staring at me like that, you guys. I thought we were talking about relationships and people not looking for them."

"Oh, boy." Cooper retrieved a wooden game box off the television stand. "We better deal the cards while Gregson is still struggling to maintain his poker face."

"I don't have a poker face because I don't *need* one for this stupid conversation that you idiots steered me into."

"Well, to answer your question," Cooper said, not trying to hide his smirk. "Carmen hasn't said whether or not she was interested in you or in any other man at this particular moment. But I *do* know that she's getting over some serious garbage she had to deal with in Las Vegas."

Luke remembered his sons telling him she had worked as a cop with the Las Vegas Metro PD before moving here, and he wondered what might've happened to cause her to leave such a large department, which probably had a lot more options for upward mobility than the tiny Sugar Falls Police Department. Maybe a cheating boyfriend on the force?

"Apparently she's taking out whatever the last guy did to her on men in general." Luke took another drink, holding himself back from asking for more information. "She treats us like we're all IEDs she needs to go out of her way to avoid."

"Hmm." His brother adjusted his gold-framed glasses. "She doesn't act like that around me."

"I've never gotten that impression from her, either," Garrett said, grabbing more pizza.

"Okay, so it's just me she can't stand to be around. Anyway, I'm not trying to get Carmen to like me." Oops. Had they heard Luke slip and use her first name?

"You could do worse," Drew said, and the other men chuckled. "In fact I've seen you do way worse back in the day. Maybe that's why you're so attracted to *Officer Delgado*. Because she isn't throwing herself at you."

Yep. They'd caught the slip.

"Don't try to psychoanalyze me, bro. Why can't I just be attracted to her since she's a beautiful woman who looks absolutely amazing in jeans and... Oh, shut up," Luke finally said when he realized Alex and Garrett were giggling behind their beer bottles like a couple of teenagers.

An infant let out a wail, and Luke wanted to kiss his sweet niece for coming to his rescue.

"I will say this for Carmen Delgado," Drew said. "She sure can put up with those adorable nephews of mine, so your battle to win her is halfway fought."

"Just a word of advice," Cooper said as he picked up plates to clear off the table. "You might want to take it slowly once you decide to finally bite the bullet and pursue her."

"Who says I want to pursue anything with her?" Luke would've kept arguing, but he saw all the men double over in laughter.

What he didn't see were his two blond curly-haired twins, standing on the other side of the door and giving each other a thumbs-up.

The following Saturday afternoon, Carmen pulled into the long driveway of the small riverside cottage she'd rented when she first moved to town. Her new home was on the southern border of Sugar Falls, and a little far from downtown, but she liked her privacy.

It was her third day off in a row, and she'd driven to the mall in Boise to stock up on makeup at her favorite department store. And to buy another pair of the jeans she'd been wearing Thursday night. It might've been just her imagination, but she could've sworn that Luke Gregson had been staring at her legs. At least until she'd knelt down to sign Aiden's pretend cast and he'd leaned over to stare at something else.

He was probably just curious as to how she signed her name or what kind of message she'd written. Still.

She'd experienced the heady rush of flattery for a split second. And, during that moment, she'd remembered that even though she'd had an emergency hysterectomy a year ago, the rest of her lady parts were still alive and well.

Then his words about his future children had turned her butterflies into blocks of concrete and her stomach had felt like lead when she'd tried to stand up.

She also recalled how pensive and eerily quiet Luke had gotten when Caden had brought up the boys' mother, the love of Luke's life. The man had completely shut down. His grief must be immeasurable to keep that kind of pain bottled up so tightly. A man that stuck on his dead wife was most likely *not* checking out Carmen in her civvies.

That was why she didn't do butterflies anymore. It was also why she shouldn't have wasted so much money at the mall earlier today.

As she parked her compact SUV next to her cottage, she caught sight of an empty canoe floating down the river behind her house. Uh-oh. That wasn't good. She hopped out and ran toward the bank to see if she could spot the riders who'd possibly fallen out of their boat. The river was fairly gentle here because of the bend a few hundred yards ahead, which tended to slow its current.

If the rowers had lost their craft farther up north, and closer to town, where the rapids were stronger, she might not see them for a while. But if they'd somehow tipped over near here, then they were obviously novices—most likely tourists—who would be in way over their heads when the flow picked up speed half a mile down.

Running up to her back porch, she grabbed a long rope, then raced to the water's edge. She didn't have to keep her eyes peeled for long when she counted three people in bright yellow-and-blue life jackets coming her way. She tied off the rope to a sturdy tree trunk along the river's edge and threw it across the water just as the trio floated by.

Her stomach tightened again when she saw who she'd just thrown a line to.

"Hey, Officer Carmen," a little towheaded boy called out as the more than capable Captain Gregson grabbed hold of the rope. Aiden and Caden were both holding on to their father, who was pulling them toward the shore.

"We lost our boat!" The other eight-year-old smiled in excitement, as though he'd lost another tooth, not a hand-carved, custom teak watercraft.

"How'd that happen?" she asked, trying not to stare at the sinewy muscles moving in Luke's biceps as he steadily alternated his grip, working his way up the rope.

Oh, to have those strong hands on her body, his arms flexing as he moved up her legs and...

Yep. Her lady parts were definitely still alive.

"You know, Delgado," Luke called out, sounding frustrated but not the least bit winded, "we might get to the shore faster if you helped pull a little bit. Boys, stop wiggling."

Duh. She'd been standing there salivating at the poor guy, as if he was a participant in a Navy SEAL wet T-shirt contest.

She grabbed on to the other end and put her own muscle into it. Lord, the man was as heavy as a tree trunk. Granted, he had the extra weight of his giggling and squirming sons to deal with, plus the river's current was starting to pick up speed, creating more resistance.

It took a few more heaves and the boys jumped off their dad and scampered up the bank, their interest diverted by some sort of amphibious creature in the shallow water. Luke took off his life vest and his wet shirt, and Carmen almost dropped to the damp pine-needle-covered earth below her.

Don't look, don't look, don't look.

She looked.

How could she not? The man had a torso that could've been sculpted from marble. He had muscles in places she'd didn't know humans were capable of having them.

"Do you have an extra towel by any chance?" he finally asked. Carmen jerked her head up, meeting his steady gaze, which she normally tried to avoid. She wished she'd tried harder this time. He was grinning at her, that little dimple winking in amusement, and she knew she'd been busted checking out the goods. But, man, were they some goods.

"I thought you Special Forces boys were used to getting things wet." Her hand almost flew up to cover her mouth. "I meant *getting* wet. In the water."

She had tried to be snarky, thinking that if she insulted his macho pride it would cover up the fact that she'd been eyeing him the way a barefoot woman would eye the shoe rack at a Nordstrom half-yearly sale. The resulting comment only made her seem even more like a sex-starved pervert.

"Yeah, well it's been a while since I've been exposed to anything that cold," he said. "Besides, with this unexpected heat wave, we wore shorts because

I didn't actually expect to end up in the river with the boys."

"Oh, my gosh! The boys." She turned to Aiden and Caden, who were standing ankle deep in the water, trying to catch bullfrogs and smiling through chattering blue lips. "Come on, kiddos. Let's go inside and get you in a hot bath to warm you up."

She jogged over to where the boys were and helped them get out of their soaking wet life jackets before steering them toward her cabin. She noticed Aiden's ACE bandage was gone and probably long forgotten. He didn't have so much as a limp.

"Uh, what about me?" Luke asked, still standing there, droplets of water trickling off the ridged planes of his abdomen. "Aren't you going to warm me up, too?"

She'd worked alongside men with oversize egos and the predispositions to flirt with a rock. But judging by the torch he was still carrying for his late wife, he was probably only making a dig at her for staring at him so blatantly. Even if he had been flirting, she knew better than to engage in any sort of banter that could lead to him thinking she was the type of woman who would welcome some tired line like that one.

"Simmer down, skipper. There's a stack of towels on the dryer in the mudroom. Help yourself while I get the boys in the tub."

"Maybe the water isn't the coldest thing I've been exposed to lately." He'd mumbled the words, but she'd heard the remark and shot him the withering look she'd perfected back when she was a Lance Corporal and the lone female in a platoon full of horny, young twentysomething-year-olds thousands of miles away from their wives and girlfriends.

She left him standing on her back porch and, after making sure the twins were in a warm bath and had something dry to put on afterward, she went into her room to change out of the jeans she'd been wearing when she'd stepped into the water to get the kids out of their vests. Come to think of it, her blouse was a little damp, too.

A few minutes later, when she padded out of her bedroom wearing cropped turquoise yoga pants and a plain white tank top, she found Luke in her living room, the towel he'd wrapped around his hips cinched low and tight. He was leaning against the back of her pink toile sofa; the only thing between his golden skin and the terry cloth material was the damp fabric of his shorts.

She sucked in her breath and felt her nipples tightening into hard buds.

"Nice, uh, outfit," he said. But his steel-blue eyes weren't looking her up and down. They were staring at the two points barely concealed by the thin white fabric of her tank top.

"You know what?" She crossed her arms over her chest, knowing the gesture was made to cover herself, as well as hold herself back from him. "I think I have a shirt around here somewhere for you to use."

She made an about-face and hustled to her bedroom where she stared at a pile of oversize T-shirts she'd accumulated over the years. Although many of the tees were gender neutral and came from a variety of tactical units and trainings she'd participated in, she was hard-pressed to find any sized double extra large, let alone double extra sexy. She finally settled on a dark green one at the bottom of the pile.

She'd been in such a hurry to get Luke covered up, it wasn't until she was standing in front of him with the shirt that she realized she should've grabbed one for herself instead of practically exposing herself in her skimpy tank top. Again.

"Hey, Officer Carmen," one of the boys said from behind her. She jumped away from Luke, as though her skin was completely on fire. "Where should we put our wet bathing suits?"

She blushed, thankful her back had been toward the bathroom door so the twins hadn't caught her reacting so physically to their father. She needed to get them out of there. All of them.

"Let's put them in the dryer so you can get them back on as soon as possible."

"That's okay," Aiden said. "I like wearing your stuff. It's soft and smells good."

Luke groaned when he saw his son in one of her oversize shirts. Apparently, he didn't like his son wearing a shirt that read "My Heroes Have Always Been Marines."

Well, it wasn't like she had kid-sized clothing just lying around her house. And the boys didn't seem to mind. In fact, Caden was still pumped from winning the round of rock-paper-scissors and getting dibs on the red one with a bulldog wearing a drill instructor hat.

"Do you guys need a ride home?" She handed over another T-shirt to Luke and walked toward the kitchen, trying to put as much distance between them as possible.

"No, but can I use your phone?" Luke asked. "Mine was in the boat when we tipped over and Cooper was supposed to meet us at the pickup point. I don't want him worrying if he sees the canoe floating by. He can probably swing by here and give us a lift."

"I'll just go make some hot cocoa," she said, then handed him her cell before walking to the kitchen. Normally, she found comfort in the sunny room with its blush colored walls, dark-stained wood cabinets and oversize white farmhouse sink. But today, the ninety square-foot space was closing in on her.

The boys followed her, and she could hear Luke making his call to Cooper and explaining where they were. She was just filling up four mugs when he walked into the kitchen, still wearing that damn towel. Too bad she didn't have any shorts big enough to fit him. Or a cabinet big enough to hide in.

He'd tried to squeeze into the shirt she'd given him, but it wasn't leaving much to the imagination. "Coop said he's still thirty minutes or so out. I hate to impose, but would you mind if I used your shower, too?"

"No." Was that husky voice hers? Maybe she was coming down with a cold. "Go ahead."

But before he could leave, Aiden spoke up.

"Hey, Dad. Officer Carmen kinda saved us, huh?"

"Well, she threw us the rope, but your old man could've done fine all on his own."

Macho jerk. Didn't they teach those SEALs how to be team players? She settled her fists on her hips and lifted her brow at him, as if to challenge otherwise.

"What? It's not like we were in any real danger. Just past your house is that old boat dock. We could've pulled ourselves out there and then walked back here."

"You know what?" Caden took a sip of his hot cocoa. "Choogie Nguyen told us there's this old Native American legend about a young girl who risked her life to save a brave warrior from the waterfall—you know that big one up the river? The one the town is named after?"

Luke's borrowed shirt was so snug Carmen saw his shoulders tense up underneath. He probably didn't like his children thinking he needed to be rescued by anyone.

"I'm sure lots of young girls had to risk their lives to save their tribe members," she said before sticking her head into her pantry, pretending to look for marsh-mallows. Couldn't the dryer go any faster?

"Your friend Choogie is a know-it-all," Luke told the twins. "People have been talking about that old wives' tale since I came up here as a boy. You guys know you shouldn't believe everything you hear."

Was big, tough Luke Gregson opposed to believing that a woman was capable of saving a man? Carmen was now intrigued. "What legend?"

"Oh, it's just some stupid nonsense that if a person rescues you from the Sugar Falls River, then you're going to fall in love and marry them." Luke waved his hand dismissively.

"Ew, gross!" Aiden cried, wrapping his arms across his face.

"You couldn't pay me enough money to get rescued by a girl and then hafta *marry* her." Caden flapped his loose red sleeves back and forth as if he could ward off the idea by making the international sign for stay back.

"No offense," Luke whispered to her. "The boys

are still in the stage where they think girls are yucky. Don't worry, kids. It's probably a big hoax some lonely woman made up to trick a guy into marrying her."

"Humph." Carmen looked at the ragtag trio standing in her kitchen, wearing her clothes. "More likely, it was the other way around."

Luke walked off to her bathroom and she leaned against the counter, drinking her hot chocolate and listening to the boys ramble on about other Native American stories and folklore. Oh, to be a kid again and to believe in all those glorious, adventurous tales. It was too bad people had to grow up and learn about the harsh realities of life.

Like the reality that no matter what some old legend might say, nothing could ever become of her and Captain Luke Gregson. Her brain knew it. And if she could just stop thinking about him lathering up his rock-hard torso in her shower, maybe the rest of her might realize it, too.

Chapter Four

Luke hadn't failed to notice that the shirt Delgado loaned him had the Marine Corps emblem on it. Or that it must've been made to fit someone much smaller than his six-foot-four frame. It wasn't his fault he'd ripped it when he took it off the moment he'd closed the bathroom door. Hell, he hadn't wanted to put the damn thing on in the first place.

Especially not after the way he'd seen her staring at him, first outside by the river, and then inside when he'd come in wearing that towel. Officer Delgado was finally looking at him as though he was a man and not a stain on her perfectly pressed uniform. And don't even get him started on how amazing she looked *out* of her uniform.

Seeing her flushed expression, his initial desire was to lift his arms up in victory. But his next desire had been to pull her into those same arms and show her exactly how much of a man he was.

Thankfully, his children had walked in on them and Luke was reminded of his commitment to being a better father. The boys had a special relationship with the female cop and they didn't need him interfering and messing things up.

So he'd grudgingly pulled the tight cotton material over his body and sat in that cozy, dainty kitchen, making small talk about old legends and trying to pretend that he was totally capable of being in the same room with a woman who'd surprised him by looking so damn...womanly.

Seeing her with her hair down at Patrelli's last week had been shocking enough, but then seeing her wearing that skimpy tank top in such an intimate, homey setting had melted his insides quicker than his hot cocoa melted the tiny marshmallows she'd sprinkled on top.

He picked the ripped shirt off the wooden floor and tried to fold it before placing it on the towel rack. Carmen Delgado seemed like the type of woman who took things seriously—her T-shirts, her job, her relationships. And Samantha's death had proved that Luke wasn't the ideal candidate for a serious relationship.

A chill reverberated through Luke's body and he stepped under the hot spray of the Roman shower, a luxury he hadn't expected her tiny cottage to have. Actually, there was a lot about Carmen Delgado he hadn't expected.

He stared at the array of bath products and specialty body washes before reaching for the turquoise—the most manly color option of all the bottles lining the tile shelf—shampoo and flipping open the cap to sniff it.

Hmm. Moroccan oil sure didn't smell too bad. As he squirted a large dollop in his palm, he caught sight of the price tag on the underside. Thirty-three dollars? For a twelve-ounce bottle of shampoo?

That seemed like a pretty big splurge for someone living on a small-town cop's salary. As he massaged the overpriced suds through his own short hair, Luke realized he'd used too much and worried that he might be depriving Carmen's long, thick hair of its expensive shampoo. Those dark silky curls were definitely worth the cost.

Luke turned the knob to lower the temperature of the spray. Fifteen minutes ago, he'd been a human Popsicle floating down the river and worried about developing frostbite on his appendages. But judging by the way his body was responding to the mere thought of Carmen in this shower washing her hair, he was getting way too heated.

And since he didn't want to go back out there and discuss girls rescuing warriors—or the fact that he'd needed rescuing in the first place—he took his time in the now-cool shower.

Let's see. What other interesting beauty products did she have in here? Coconut-mango sea salt scrub. He looked at the purpose and directions on the back of the glass jar, then rubbed the grainy texture between his fingertips. He'd spent enough time doing surf torture during trainings and maneuvers that he couldn't imagine why anyone would want to purposely cover their bodies in something most SEAL team members learned to despise.

Between the apricot mud facial exfoliant and the rose satin shave cream, Luke was hard pressed to find something he could wash his body with that wouldn't leave him smelling like a home garden show being held in a cotton candy factory.

He settled on something called Glacial Retreat Shower Mousse. Even the woman's bath gel was distant and aloof.

He shut off the water and didn't hear the boys yelling or otherwise causing any problems, so it was safe to say Officer High-And-Mighty had them well under control.

After he dried off, he wrapped a towel around his waist and took an inventory of all the small bottles of girlie potions organized neatly on the counter. He knew he should get back out there and check on the twins. Cooper would be here soon to give them a ride back to the cabin. But, besides the occasional family dinners at his mom's house in Boise, he hadn't been in a feminine domain since Samantha passed.

The familiar pang of guilt started low in his gut and he took a deep breath to try to tamp it down. Drew had told him plenty of times that he needed to stop feeling so responsible for his wife's death. That getting in a vehicle and attempting to drive when her blood-alcohol content was twice the legal limit was Samantha's mistake.

Yet, the reason she'd gone out drinking was *his* fault.

He looked at his reflection in the mirror over the sink and ran a hand through his wet hair, trying to pat down the cowlick that had always frustrated his mother, as well as any ship's barber whose chair he'd

sat in. Drew would say that he needed to see a coun-
selor, but Nana—if she were alive—would tell him
to stop dwelling on the past and get right back into
living for the now.

Speaking of the old gal, Nana would certainly have
loved the assortment of beauty products on display in
Delgado's bathroom. Luke saw a bottle labeled clari-
fying tonic and looked at the list of ingredients. He
wondered how much it would cost to ship a case of
this stuff to the guys on his team. It would be perfect
for cleaning off that camouflage face paint they used
during missions.

But it was no longer his team. Or his mission. His
new team was the two eight-year-olds out there and
his new mission was to be present. To provide them
with a solid upbringing and unwavering love.

A lump formed in his throat and he shook it away.
It was getting late and he needed to get the boys home
and cook up some chow. He looked at the torn T-shirt
and decided it probably wouldn't be very appropriate
to go back out there in just a towel. His clothes were
still drying, so that only left the short, silk robe hanging on the hook behind the door. Thank God it was
yellow. Everything else in her damn house was fifty
shades of pink. For such a tough Marine and cop,
Carmen Delgado sure had a frilly girlie-girl side she
seemed to keep hidden. The realization made Luke
want to ruffle her feathers just a little. After all, what
kind of self-respecting soldier surrounded themselves
with all this fancy goop? It wasn't like she needed any
of this junk, anyway.

As he stepped out of the bathroom, he called out,
"Hey, Delgado, are you supposed to use the tea-tree-

and-avocado polishing mask before or after the cocoa shea-butter eye-firming cream? Oh, hey, Coop."

The chief of police and Delgado's boss was leaning against the back of the pink-and-white sofa. He was midsip from a mug of hot cocoa when he choked and then pinched the bridge of his nose, probably in an attempt to keep the liquid from shooting out of his nostrils because he was laughing so hard.

It took a lot more to embarrass Luke, though. "My clothes were wet. So it was either this robe or one of the eight hundred T-shirts Delgado keeps in her Marine Corps shrine collection. As a Navy man, I felt yellow and satin were better options." A little friendly rivalry between military service members was expected, so he didn't worry about Cooper taking offense.

"Nah, Gregson, I wasn't laughing at the robe. I was laughing at the fact that Delgado has something called cocoa shea-butter eye-firming cream."

"Why's that so funny?" Carmen crossed her arms over her chest, which she'd thankfully covered up with a bright pink hoodie. Luke didn't want anyone to witness his reaction to seeing her firm, round breasts on display again.

"Because, Delgado," Cooper said, still chuckling. "When I knew you in the Corps, you were one of the toughest MPs in our unit. And at the station, you're all business and no-frills. You don't even take creamer in your coffee. Therefore, I wasn't expecting your cottage to secretly house a day spa."

"Well, guess what. I like spas. I also like shopping and watching *Dancing with the Stars*."

"Wait, those are all girl things," Caden said before

looking at his brother and pretending to stick his finger down his throat.

Carmen rolled her eyes. "Well, I *am* a girl."

Luke tilted his head slightly to get a better view of her back curves in those yoga pants. He didn't think anyone would ever doubt that. Or that he'd ever be able to forget it.

Carmen would've laughed at the boy's skepticism if she wasn't already so annoyed with Luke's and Cooper's teasing. It wasn't her fault that nobody else in this town could see her softer side. Actually, that was fine as far as Cooper was concerned. She didn't want her boss to see her as anything other than a capable officer.

"Obviously, you're all female," Luke said, but she wondered if it really was all that obvious to him. "You just didn't strike me as a girlie-girl."

"Come on, boys," Cooper announced to the twins, who were all too pleased to borrow her shirts for an indefinite length of time. "Let's go wait in my truck while your dad thanks Officer Carmen for her hospitality."

"Aw, man. Why didn't you bring the patrol car?" Aiden asked.

"Because I'm off duty," Cooper replied as the twins followed him to the front door. "Besides, last time I let you ride in my squad car, I couldn't get my red-and-blue flashers off for a week.

Wait. Why was Cooper leaving her to deal with Luke by herself? What about the motto Leave No Man Behind? Did that suddenly no longer apply to her because she liked quality bath products and the color pink?

Maybe the chief sensed the uncomfortable attraction between her and Luke and wanted to distance himself from the fact that nothing positive could come from her lusting over one of his poker buddies.

At least the buddy in question was slightly more clothed than he had been twenty minutes ago—even if he did look absolutely ridiculous in her favorite yellow robe.

"Listen, Delgado. Coop's right. I should be thanking you for helping us out of the river and for letting us bombard your house like this."

Oh, Lord. That apologetic dimple of his should be illegal. When Luke smiled at her like that, she wanted to melt into a puddle at his feet. The man was probably used to women falling all over themselves just to get a chance to help him out. Which made her wonder how many females' houses he'd bombarded in the past, strutting around in nothing but a towel and steaming up their bathrooms with all his sexy masculinity.

She'd never be able to use her shower again without thinking of him in it. And she really loved her shower, damn him.

"It was no problem." She tried to sound casual. As if what she'd done for him was nothing out of the ordinary. "You and the boys needed help. I'd do the same for anyone else."

His grin shifted downward and he stood a little straighter. Nope, he definitely didn't like hearing that he wasn't special. Well, good. She couldn't have him thinking that he had any sort of impact on her.

"Of course you would, Officer Delgado. You're a regular Girl Scout."

She didn't know him very well, but she recognized sarcasm when she heard it. Why was he acting like the aggrieved party? She was the one who'd just had her whole world turned upside down when he and the boys capsized upstream from her house. Seeing them floating down the cold river had scared her, but then seeing Luke wet and in all his muscular glory had been a shock to her system. So then why was *he* so offended?

And why was he still standing in her living room?

A loud horn interrupted their standoff and he glanced at the open door before looking back at her. Why wasn't he leaving? "Sounds like the Chief is waiting for you, Captain Gregson."

"That's not Cooper honking." Luke rolled his eyes. "That's Caden. He always does three short blasts." Next, a long steady horn sounded. "*That* would be Aiden's honk. I better get there before Coop comes to his senses and kicks them out of the truck and we have to walk back to my cabin."

But he didn't make a move for the door. And then it dawned on her.

"Oh. Your clothes." She hustled over to the mudroom and opened the dryer midcycle. He was standing in her kitchen when she turned back to him. "The board shorts aren't bad, but the shirts are still pretty damp."

"Well, I can't exactly wear your robe home. I mean, I *can*, but I'd look pretty silly."

"Here." She handed him his bathing suit. "Put these

on and I'll go get you another shirt. Wait? What happened to the one I already gave you?"

"It was a little tight. I…uh…kinda tore it when I took it off in the bathroom. I'll get you another one to replace it."

"Don't worry about it," she called out over her shoulder as she headed back toward her room. "I have plenty more."

In fact, he could have his pick, as long as he got himself covered and out of her house. She searched her stack of T-shirts again, this time trying harder to find the biggest one. She started leave her room and then paused. She needed to allow him plenty of time to slip his shorts back on.

Normally, she was trained to run toward physical danger. It's what she was paid to do. But putting her emotions in the line of fire was a tactical mistake. Lord knew that if she walked in and saw him completely undressed, she'd be a goner. Or at least, more of a goner than she was now.

"Hey," he said, walking toward her bedroom doorway. She sucked in her breath and tried to focus her eyes on the yellow robe he was holding in his hand and not his bare torso. "The natives are getting restless out there."

"Right," she said, totally embarrassed to be caught standing there like a statue. It'd been a long time since she'd had a man in her bedroom and it had been even longer since she'd been near one that made her heart flutter this quickly. *Settle down, you traitorous butterflies.*

She threw him the T-shirt she'd been hugging to her chest. Her aim was a bit too high and he had to reach up to catch it. Big mistake. The muscles in his arm rippled into a well-defined bulge and stayed like that for way longer than necessary.

It took several blinks and an infinite amount of willpower to drag her eyes toward his face.

Whether his taunting smile was meant to mock her bad throw or to tease her for checking him out, Carmen didn't know. But she certainly didn't like it. Or her body's reaction to him. She needed to get him out of the house.

Instead, she let her eyes slide to the light pink puckered scar along his rib cage. "What happened there?" she asked.

He shrugged, absently touching the scar. "I was on a mission and our plane took a couple of rounds before we could jump. I was knocked back into the cargo door and…well, let's just say I was lucky enough that the surgeon who had to dig out the shrapnel was on board an ally ship and not working inside a POW camp."

"It looks fresh."

"It happened a few months ago. Right before I moved back to Sugar Falls. But you know what it's like to be a soldier. We all carry our battle wounds around with us."

Carmen tried not to move her hands to the scar below her abdomen. Her wound hadn't come from being a Marine, but she knew exactly what he meant.

"What's that right above it?" she asked. "A tattoo?"

"Yeah. After I left my SEAL team, I decided a scar wasn't enough. I needed a reminder of the most important moments in my life."

Carmen stepped closer and, while he kept his arm raised, allowing her to fully view his sculpted torso, she still had to stop herself from reaching out and tracing her fingers over the numbers. "Are they dates?"

"Yes. The first one is the day the twins were born. The second one is the day I started acting like a father."

Her head shot up to meet his eyes, but before he could explain the cryptic response, another honk sounded. He slowly brought his arm down, all the while staring directly at her face—which was mere inches from his. She could feel the warmth of his breath and she wondered if he could see her pulse thumping along her neck.

"I meant what I said, Carmen. I really appreciate you helping us out today." He backed away, pulling on the gray T-shirt as he went. She didn't respond, didn't say a word, until she heard the front door closing behind him.

At the sound of Cooper's truck roaring out of her dirt driveway, she finally allowed herself to move. She sat on the bed, then fell backward, laying her arm across her forehead. She could barely hear her own whisper above her pounding heartbeat.

"He didn't call me Delgado."

On a Thursday morning in late March, Carmen stood in the Snowflake Dance Academy, still surprised that there were so many women in this town who'd signed up for her cardio self-defense class. Most of them were sweaty—just like her—and a few looked zealously empowered after repeating the kickboxing moves she'd just shown them.

Mia had been right about offering a class like this, and Carmen was learning not to be so quick to make assumptions about the locals. Unfortunately, the mental preparation it'd taken for her to organize it hadn't been enough to steer her mind clear of its annoying habit of dwelling on Luke Gregson and his smug dimples.

It had been almost two weeks since she'd gone all googly-eyed on him while he stood there, shirtless in her bedroom. And it wasn't like she'd never seen a bare-chested man before. Hell, she grew up in a hot desert city with two brothers and a mess of boy cousins before joining the Marine Corps, where she was outnumbered by men four to one. But no man made her tingle like Luke did. Not even Mark, her ex-boyfriend and almost fiancé.

Carmen felt that tightening pang where her uterus should be. She'd heard of soldiers in the war who'd lost a limb and later experienced a sort of phantom pain, and she decided the expression was just as applicable to her.

Yesterday, she had talked to her mom, who'd delivered the not-so-surprising news that Mark and Carmen's cousin, Maria Rosa, were expecting their first baby. But the feeling of loss wasn't from missing her ex or from the awkwardness of her cousin being engaged to the man Carmen had once expected to marry. Her phantom pain came from knowing that she would never carry her own baby, that she was unable to give the gift of life to a child. That she'd never share the joy of parenthood with a husband.

"Okay, ladies." Carmen redirected her energy toward the thirteen women awaiting her next instructions. "Let's finish with some stretches and get you out of here."

She grabbed a mat, wanting to focus more on her tight muscles and less on her high-strung nerves, trying to remember one of her grandmother's favorite phrases about strength and character and being a woman. How did that old saying go? Maybe after this class she would call Abuela.

"That's it for today," she called out to the group, who gave her a polite round of applause. Carmen had recognized most of the local women, like Freckles, the older and sassy owner of the Cowgirl Up Café, and Elaine Marconi, who had told everyone about the twins knocking over Scooter Deets and the chips display. At least she hadn't completely banished them from getting slushies at the Gas N' Mart. Probably because the woman was always hoping for any juicy bit of gossip that came into her store.

Keep your friends close, and your enemies closer. No, that wasn't one of Abuela's sayings. Why couldn't she think of it?

Just then, Kylie Gregson handed her a cold bottle of water. "I thought I was a strong woman, Carmen, but you take strength to a whole new level."

"Se necesita un hombre fuerte para manejar a una mujer fuerte." Carmen's palm shot to cover her mouth. But the Spanish proverb was already out there. "Sorry, I'd been trying to recall something my grandmother always says and it just came to me out of the blue like that."

"I took Spanish in high school," Elaine Marconi volunteered. "And it does take a strong man to handle a strong woman."

Carmen wanted to grab the nosy woman's workout towel and cover the pink flush she felt climbing up her cheeks. Who'd asked for Elaine Marconi's translation, anyway?

"What strong man are we talking about?" Freckles wiggled the eyebrows she'd painted on to match her fire-engine-red-dyed hair. Carmen loved beauty products as much as the next woman, but she vowed to limit herself to face cream and lipstick by the time she reached the older waitress's age.

"I wasn't talking about a man," Carmen protested. "Kylie and I were just talking about being strong."

"Oh. Well, if anyone decides they want to talk about strong men, come on over to the café," Freckles said. "Post-workout smoothies and love advice are on the house."

Several other women laughed as they followed the self-proclaimed relationship guru and gathered their bags and water bottles. Carmen had heard that Freckles had been married at least four times, and rumor had it that she'd been driving up to Helena every other weekend to spend time with a former rodeo cowboy.

Unfortunately, before the crew of ladies could make it outside, Kylie added, "Oh, Carmen. Before I forget, Drew and I have been talking about doing a remodel of our bathroom and I need some construction advice. Luke told Drew about the shower he took at your place—"

"Hold the smoothies." Elaine Marconi was the first one to whip back around. "I wanna hear about Captain Gregson in Officer Delgado's shower."

"Luke Gregson could definitely be classified as a strong man," Freckles said to a chorus of feminine nods and sighs.

"No, it wasn't...he wasn't—" Carmen started, but Kylie jumped in.

"Officer Delgado was brave enough to rescue my brother-in-law and his sons a couple of weeks ago when their boat capsized on the Sugar Falls River." Kylie winked at her and whispered, "I got this," before hustling the busybodies toward the door.

But no matter how Kylie managed to spin the rescue story into a heroic tale of valor, there was at least one woman whose lips remained in an insolent smirk. On second thought, instead of using a workout towel to cover her blush, maybe Carmen could shove it in Elaine Marconi's gossipy mouth. Preferably before the woman spread rumors about her misadventures with the sexy SEAL all over town.

Chapter Five

"Thank God you're finally here, Captain Gregson," the school secretary said when Luke yanked open the front doors to Sugar Falls Elementary School. "Everyone's in the cafeteria with Caden right now, trying to talk him down."

Luke didn't bother with pleasantries or even a briefing of the situation at hand. Forty-five minutes ago, he'd been in the middle of a speech to several potential recruits at his office when he'd gotten the phone call from the school. He wasn't sure what had set his child off, but what he'd deduced over the phone from the frantic principal was that Caden had gotten upset during the weekly assembly and, instead of returning to his class afterward, had somehow barricaded himself above where most of the children would be arriving soon to eat their school lunch.

His heartbeat raced a mile a minute as Nana's Oldsmobile had labored just as quickly back up the mountain. But when Luke saw Officer Delgado's patrol unit—he knew it was hers by the "394" stenciled on the rear bumper—parked diagonally at the curb alongside a ladder truck from the Sugar Falls Volunteer Fire Department, he slowed himself to a light jog. At least there were professionals on the scene.

Hopefully.

When he entered the cafeteria, he saw the principal and a couple of lunch ladies wringing their hands and staring up at the ceiling. Luke followed their eyes and saw Caden, sitting on an exposed beam, tears in his eyes and his small arms wrapped tightly around the truss.

Officer Carmen Delgado, in her full gear and uniform, was calmly sitting beside an obviously distressed Caden, eating something that looked an awful lot like a chocolate pudding cup.

Luke's first instinct was to yell, but he didn't want to startle anyone when their balance looked precarious enough as it was. He saw a curly blond head sitting at a table with Scooter and Jonesy, the two old coots who ran the volunteer fire department. An aluminum ladder was propped up beside them, but instead of being on it, or actively trying to rescue his son, they were all sitting below it, eating pudding cups, as well.

What the hell was this? Some sort of pudding party?

"Aiden," Luke said when he made his way over to the trio. Make that a foursome, since his view of Nurse Dunn had been blocked by Scooter. "How'd your brother get up there?"

"I think he climbed up." Aiden pointed to where

some folding chairs had been stacked up high on a table. "But I didn't see him on account of our teacher made us sit separate from each other during the morning assembly because we were trying to teach some of the girls in our class how to make armpit fart sounds. But the girls aren't very good at it. Officer Carmen is, though. She can do a real good armpit fart when she isn't wearing her bulletproof vest."

Luke didn't exactly know what to do with that little bit of knowledge. "Aiden, do you know *why* Caden is up there?"

"I'm not sure, but I think he's pretty upset about something. He's been crying for a while and when the principal and teacher told him to come down, he wouldn't budge. I tried to go up and get him, but Nurse Dunn wouldn't let me."

The former Ski Potato Queen smiled at him, a dab of chocolate stuck to the corner of her purplish painted lips, and gave him a thumbs-up while keeping a tight grip on her plastic spoon.

"Anyway," Aiden continued, "they threatened to call you and the police but instead of making him scared, he seemed to relax a little bit and said he'd just wait up there for you and Officer Carmen to get here. All the other kids had to go back to class, but they let me stay and watch because Caden hollered real bad when they tried to make me leave."

"Okay." Luke ruffled his son's hair, thankful one of his children was safe and somewhat sane at this moment. "You stay down here. I'm going up."

Scooter stood to hold the ladder steady and Jonesy handed him a pudding cup. "You might want to take one of these with you."

Luke waved it off. "I'm not rewarding my son for this little stunt."

"Nah, that's for you," the man said, shifting a wad of pudding—or possibly tobacco—to his other cheek. "You might be up there for a while."

Great. Luke tucked the plastic container into the front pocket of his uniform and began climbing. When he got to the top, Caden turned his teary eyes toward Luke. "Hi, Dad."

"Hey, monkey," Luke said as he threw a leg over and straddled the beam. Just a few inches from Carmen's holstered gun. This wasn't exactly the way he'd imagined their next intimate meeting would take place. And ever since she'd stared at him so intensely in her bedroom, he'd been envisioning those a lot more frequently. "Care to explain to me why we're all hoisting ourselves up the rigging and there's no sail in sight?"

His son simply shook his curly head and stared straight ahead. Carmen looked at him and shrugged her shoulders, as though to tell him she had no idea what any of them were doing up here, either.

Her voice was soft and steady as she debriefed him. "We got the call and I offered to respond. I've been sitting up here with him for the past thirty minutes or so, but he hasn't said a word so far."

At least she was calm. Or giving one hell of a performance.

Maybe the guys below were right and they would be here for a while. He cracked open his pudding cup, then realized he'd forgotten his spoon. Carmen handed hers to him and he had to remind himself that this was about the least appropriate time to be thinking about the fact that the utensil had just been in her mouth, pressed against her tongue.

Hell. Luke rolled his ankles in circles—he hadn't been this high off the ground since the accident that had ended his SEAL career. He was officially horrible at this fatherhood gig. He could easily rescue a prisoner of war from a terrorist holding cell, and he could disarm almost any improvised explosive device, as well as manufacture and set one himself. Underwater. But he couldn't get his son to tell him what had upset him so much and he couldn't keep from having impure thoughts about the female cop trying to assist them both.

Drew was the psychologist and knew how to talk to people. His brother was the rational twin—the thinker. Luke was all about action. Act first and talk later.

"Caden, your daddy and I both want to help you," Carmen said. "But we can't do that until you tell us what's wrong."

"I don't want to talk about it." The boy sniffed.

"Okay, so why don't we talk about the assembly this morning, instead." Was this some sort of interview tactic? Because Luke didn't want to spend the rest of the day sitting on this rafter and shooting the breeze about routine school happenings. But he let the cop do her job. "Did you guys say the Pledge of Allegiance?"

"Yes," the boy mumbled.

"What about awards? Did the teachers give out any awards?"

"Not today. They just made a bunch of dumb, stupid announcements that nobody cares about anyway because they're so boring and lame and nobody will want to go anyway and you guys can't make me go."

Luke saw Carmen close her eyes and nod. Okay, so she was getting somewhere. Maybe.

"What kind of boring stuff will nobody want to go to?"

"That stupid dance. It's the worstest idea this school has ever had."

"But, Aiden," Luke started, "you love to dance. Remember when you took that hip-hop class at Mia's dance studio? She said you were a natural."

"But that's a different kind of dancing. One that we don't have to bring our moms to."

The realization cut through Luke's heart. He'd passed a flier on the office bulletin board but hadn't thought much about it. He should've been better prepared for something like this to happen.

"I'm not trying to add any pressure, Captain Gregson," the school principal called out, interrupting them just as they'd made some progress in figuring out what had the boy so upset. "But it's almost lunchtime and pretty soon we're going to have a bunch of hungry students headed in this direction."

"I'm not coming down until you cancel that stupid Mother-Son Dance," Caden yelled. Luke held up his index finger, trying to silently ask the principal to give them another minute.

"Aw, sweetheart," Carmen said, her soothing voice calm and understanding. "Now we get it."

"How are me and Aiden supposed to go when we don't even have a mother? We'll look stupid and everyone will make fun of us."

A tear floated on the tip of Luke's eyelid and he

looked up, trying to command it back into place. Even though they'd only been three when it happened, he'd known that Samantha's passing would leave his children with a huge void that he couldn't fill, and he was still learning how to be there for them as a dad. He had no idea how to be a mother to them, as well.

"You know, Caden, when I was a little girl, my school had a father-daughter chess tournament one year. But it was during the day and my dad couldn't take the time off work. So my mom made my oldest brother, Hector, take me."

"My dad used to not be able to take time off work, either," Caden said, adding to Luke's cup of guilt, which was in danger of overflowing. "But now he's around all the time and we get to be with him every single day. See? He's even here right now when he's probably supposed to be at work."

His son almost seemed proud of that fact, and since Nana had always taught him to focus on the positive rather than dwell on every mistake he'd ever made, Luke held on to that one tiny point in his favor.

"You're right, kiddo." Carmen nodded. "He *is* here right now. And he's doing such a great job of taking care of you and your brother, even though your mom's not here to help him."

"So you're saying I should have my dad take me to the Mother-Son Dance?"

That's not what she was saying at all. At least Luke hoped not, knowing full well he'd do whatever it took to make things easier on his children. Even if it meant dancing in a room full of boys and their moms. "Actually, I think Officer Delgado means you could ask one of your female relatives to take you. Like Aunt Kylie."

"Oh, yeah. Aunt Kylie'd probably go, right, Dad? She likes to dance."

"I bet she'd be honored if you asked her, monkey."

"Your dad will even let you use his cell phone to call her." Carmen's pointed tone was clearly not just a suggestion. "Let's climb down, so that you can do that."

His son now seemed eager to return to solid ground. Thank God.

"I'll go first," Luke said, since his foot was closest to the ladder rungs. "Then Officer Carmen can hand you to me."

"You don't want to just go down the way I came up?" Caden asked.

"No!" Luke's and Carmen's voices were in unison.

He motioned to Scooter and Jonesy and then waited for the older men to steady the ladder before holding out his arms for his son. Carmen easily picked the boy up and passed him over. Man, the woman was sexy and strong and a great voice of reason.

Luke squinted, catching a quick glimpse of the pattern between the top of her boots and the hem of her pants. Were those purple hearts dotting her socks? Yep, the woman definitely tried to keep her feminine side hidden when she was on the job. He held Caden in one arm and made his way down, trying not to look up and stare at her polyester-covered rear end above him.

Just then, several students entered through the doors, forming a line at the lunch counter.

"What's going on with your brother?" a kid asked Aiden. Luke recognized the boy as the twins' friend, Choogie Nguyen.

"He was mad that we don't have a mom to take us

to the Mother-Son Dance," Aiden explained, relishing in his role as information provider.

"Wait!" Caden, who was now standing on the linoleum floor, yelled loud enough to make everyone in the cafeteria freeze. "But that just solves *my* problem. What about Aiden? He doesn't have a mom to take him, either. We can't just share Aunt Kylie. We each need our own."

"I have two moms," Choogie said. "You can borrow one of mine."

"But your moms aren't my relatives." Caden shook his head. "I think we need someone who is a mom and a relative."

"You don't need a relative," Scooter said, throwing away the empty pudding cups as his partner Jonesy lowered the ladder. "Any gal will do."

"But what about a mom?" Aiden asked Choogie and the volunteer firefighters. "Does it have to be a mom?"

"Hey, Officer Carmen," Caden yelled, even though she was right beside him. "Are you a mom?"

"No," came her quiet reply. Luke could barely hear the woman, probably because his guilt was still pounding in his ears.

"Why not?" Choogie asked, like it was any of his— or anyone else's—business.

Her face paled and she looked at Luke before her eyes darted around, probably looking for an answer. But he was just as curious as the rest of the third-graders staring at them. She adjusted her leather duty belt. "Because I'm not married."

"Our dad's not married and he's still a dad."

"Listen, kiddos," Carmen finally said. "I think the

bottom line is that you can take any woman to the Mother-Son Dance. She doesn't need to be a relative and she doesn't need to be a mom."

"Oh, cool." Aiden pumped his fist in the air. "I call dibs on taking Officer Carmen to the dance, then."

By the time Carmen steered her patrol car into the parking lot near the Little League fields on Saturday afternoon, the baseball game was half over. But she was covering the afternoon shift for Officer Washington and she'd gotten a call to help a stranded motorist who, along with three college buddies, had attempted to do some off-roading in his Honda Civic. Luke Gregson was no longer the only man she'd rescued this month, but he was definitely the only one who'd made her nerve endings feel like someone had put a Taser to them.

It had been over a week since she'd been called to the school to help talk Caden down from the cafeteria rafters and almost three weeks since she'd pulled him and the boys out of the river. In the meantime, Kylie had tried to squelch the shower rumors, but Sugar Falls was a small town and just the hint of a potential scandal could turn her reputation and her relationship with the twins into a shredded paper target at the gun range.

Which was why she had no business getting any romantic ideas about Luke Gregson. Or promising Aiden and Caden that she'd come to their baseball game if they behaved and didn't get their names written on the whiteboard at school all week.

Really, after the cafeteria stunt, she'd thought winning that bet had been a sure thing. She'd never been more wrong.

She slammed her car door shut as if she'd just put all of her emotions under arrest and loaded them into the backseat to transport them to a faraway jail—out of her life and out of her mind. As she made her way toward the bleachers, she recognized the boy wearing the green jersey walking up to the plate, his blond curls peeking out from beneath his batting helmet.

"Hey, Officer Carmen," Aiden yelled out, making everyone in the stands turn to watch her approach. "Watch this."

She gave the boy a thumbs-up and stood near the bleachers instead of taking a seat among the moms and dads who actually belonged there. She told herself she didn't want to cause a distraction to the players or to the parents who were there to watch their children play ball. But, really, she didn't want to draw any more attention to herself. Or to the fact that she was on duty and taking her lunch break at the ball field because she'd been conned into it by a couple of precocious twin boys.

Last week, worried about their upset over the Mother-Son Dance, she'd shown up at their game after the first inning started and then hastily made a beeline for her car as soon as the teams began chanting their two-four-six-eight cheer signaling the end of the game. But it'd been easier to blend in last Saturday because she'd been off that day and didn't stand out like a sore thumb in her blue polyester uniform.

And at least she hadn't had Luke Gregson staring at her like he was now. She shoved her sunglasses into place, not wanting to make eye contact with the man.

Shouldn't he be watching his son? Aiden already had two strikes and Carmen was sure he'd get a third, but then he stepped into the pitch and swung with all his might.

Crack.

The ball flew toward center field. The kid on the opposing team was positioned under the fly ball, but ended up dropping the catch, causing Caden, the runner on second base, to make a mad dash toward third. Carmen glanced at Luke, who was acting as the third-base coach, and she had a brief flashback to that moment in her bedroom when he was holding his arm up and she was reading the inscription of the tattoo across his rib cage.

But this time, Luke's hands were waving in an attempt to convince Caden to stop running and remain on base.

Yet, Caden continued running and Carmen's heart froze when she saw the catcher, a sturdy girl who probably outweighed him by twenty pounds, holding the ball at home plate.

His brother had made it safely to second and was hollering out words of encouragement to Caden. Carmen's knees locked when she realized what the little daredevil was going to do. "No," she heard herself yelling.

Caden paused, and took a couple steps back. Thank God, he wasn't going to risk it. Then she caught the tilt of his small pink lips and as soon as the catcher threw the ball to third, the boy made a break for home plate. He slid in before the baseman could throw the ball back.

Which caused a domino effect as Aiden, who had

been perfectly content on second came rounding his way to third. Coaches from the red team began shouting instructions and kids from the green team began cheering while Aiden took advantage of the confusion and sprinted toward home, his slide not quite as graceful as his brother's.

"Safe!" the umpire, who looked suspiciously like Kylie's brother, Kane Chatterson, beneath that headgear and mask, called out.

Carmen let out the breath she'd been holding, relieved that both kids were uninjured. When the Comets won, the twins ran straight out of the dugout and toward her before they could even shake hands with the opposing team. Maybe it was unsportsmanlike conduct, but she couldn't help but be flattered.

"Did you see us, Officer Carmen?" Caden asked as he hurled his dirt-stained body at her. She caught him up in her arms and barely had time to brace herself before Aiden followed suit.

"Did you see us?" he questioned, as well.

"I did. You guys almost gave me a heart attack with that play." She set Caden down so she could give Aiden his hug. Then she said, "I think your coaches are waiting for you back in the dugout, though."

"Promise you won't leave," Caden said, and Carmen's heart felt like it had just slid into home, as well. But when she saw Luke motioning the boys over, she had to wonder if her heart was as overworked and tattered as the twin's white baseball pants.

"Well, I'm on duty and might get called out," she said.

"Then just don't leave without telling us goodbye." She fixed the crooked brim of Aiden's hat, knowing that the kid was busting her for sneaking away after last week's game.

But, really, what was she supposed to do? Stand there and make small talk with the rest of Sugar Falls, including their father? With the exception of that day in the school cafeteria, she'd been pretty successful at avoiding any conversation with Luke these past couple of weeks and, even though she knew it couldn't last forever, she was hoping to buy herself a little more time.

"I promise," she said, finally caving in. Was it even physically possible to tell these two boys no?

"We'll be right back," they shouted together before running to rejoin their team.

She smiled and said hello to a few of the parents trickling down the bleachers and toward the parking lot. After all, it was a small town and she was the only female officer in Sugar Falls, so many of them knew her, or at least knew of her.

Carmen wondered how many people really knew her at all.

But before she could ponder that lonely thought, Kylie Gregson, Luke's sister-in-law, made her way over, pushing the extrawide double stroller in front of her.

"Hey, Officer Carmen." Kylie, wearing a green team jersey, smiled at her. Even in a man's baseball shirt, the woman looked like a cover model. Some women gave off the feminine vibe without even trying. "The twins are so excited you made the game today."

Carmen's own smile was tentative, hoping the Gregson family didn't think it was strange that some Marine turned cop from Las Vegas was forming quite the bond with the two blond boys. "Are they always so reckless when they play?"

"When aren't they reckless? If it weren't for the strong family resemblance, I'd question whether any of the Gregson males were even related to my calm, good-natured husband. Especially this one."

Carmen hadn't seen Luke approaching behind her. His ability to show up unexpectedly and throw her off course was something she wasn't proud of, considering her career. She preferred to remain in control and unflustered at all times. Which was another reason she hadn't stayed after last week's game.

"Beautiful day for a ball game." Luke shot his dimpled grin at her before lifting up the sunshade on the stroller to peek in at his nieces. "Did they sleep through the whole game?"

"Yep." Kylie smiled proudly. "The Chatterson gene must've skipped a generation, because they've shown absolutely zero interest in baseball."

Luke laughed. "Don't let Kane or your father hear you say that."

Carmen had only found out recently that Kylie's dad was a famous major league coach. And everyone in town knew her brother, Kane, was on hiatus from his pitching career. In fact, he was hiding out from the mainstream sports media for reasons Carmen couldn't figure out, but she knew Kane's secrecy had something to do with the ball cap he sported at all times and the beard he'd recently shaved off. But Kylie and Luke both smiled at her as if she was in on the joke.

"We're back, Officer Carmen," Aiden said as the twins approached them. The strap of his bat bag was looped over his wrist, allowing him to drag his gear behind him while his hands were busy trying to open the plastic bottle of fruit-punch-flavored Gatorade. "Me and Caden decided you're our good luck charm."

"Yeah," Caden said around a slice of orange from his after-game snack bag. "Every time you show up at our game, we play better."

Her? She was nobody's lucky charm. And being from Vegas, she was well versed in what constituted good luck. "I don't know about that."

"No, it's true. Remember two weeks ago when I was pitching and the other team got three walks in one inning?"

"Yes." Carmen nodded. "I was here for that, which means maybe I was bad luck."

"Nah. You had to run over to the playground area to help get Choogie's little sister unstuck from the monkey bars. So you weren't really watching. But after you came back, I threw five strikeouts that game."

She raised an eyebrow at Kylie, as if to say *help me out here.* Carmen didn't want the boys thinking she had anything to do with how they played the game. But the redhead shrugged her shoulders. "Don't ask me. The girls both had colds so I wasn't here."

"Well, what about when Aiden hit that foul ball in the sixth inning last week?" Carmen asked. "The one that hit Marcia Duncan's new Smart car and cracked her windshield? That wasn't very lucky." Pointing out an innocent kid's mistake left a bitter taste in her mouth. But she couldn't very well have the twins thinking she had supernatural powers. They needed to realize that they played well all on their own.

"You saw that?" Luke winced. "But you were off getting some nachos when that happened."

"How'd you know where I was?" she asked, then tried to erase the surprised look from her face. "Besides, I was watching them from the snack bar area. Anyway, even if I hadn't seen it, I had to take the accident report on it so Mrs. Duncan could file a claim with her insurance company."

"But we couldn't see you 'cause you weren't near the bleachers," Aiden said. "So it doesn't count."

"Did you tell Mrs. Duncan that she looks funny driving around such a teeny tiny car?" Caden added. "Remember those clowns we saw one time at that rodeo in Grangeville, Dad? We probably did her a favor by wrecking that thing for her. So maybe you're good luck for us *and* for big ol' Mrs. Duncan."

"Boys," Luke finally interrupted his sons. "I think you're making Officer Delgado uncomfortable with all this good-luck talk."

So they were back to Officer Delgado again. Almost four weeks and she was still trying to forget the way her first name sounded on his lips. She should've been relieved. Instead, she felt her own lips turn down and her blood heat up in annoyance.

"Oh, look," Kylie said, and pointed out a white van in the parking lot. Recorded organ music was coming out the speaker mounted to its roof. "There's an ice-cream truck. C'mon, boys. I'll buy you guys a Popsicle to celebrate your win."

The woman winked at Carmen before pushing the stroller away, her nephews trailing behind her. Which left Carmen in the exact position she'd successfully avoided for the past twenty-three days and twenty-two hours.

Alone with Luke Gregson.

Luke had seen her the moment her patrol car pulled into the parking lot. Hell, if he was being honest with himself, he'd been trying to catch glimpses of her in town all week. Or at least since he'd seen her sneaking away from the stands at the bottom of the ninth inning last Saturday.

In the school cafeteria, she'd been all business. And even though his sons saw her every Tuesday afternoon and they'd shared a rafter and a pudding spoon, he hadn't made any attempt to talk to Officer Delgado alone since that heated moment in her bedroom.

Had he been inappropriate in any way? After Samantha died, Luke had lost all interest in the rules of attraction. Still, he'd gone over the bedroom conversation and the sequence of events in his mind several times since then. But the only thing that remained the same was the way she looked, standing there by her bed in her tight athletic pants and body-skimming pink hoodie. Or the way she'd stared at his bare torso, her full lower lip caught between her straight white teeth.

Of course, it didn't help that he couldn't forget the smell of her, probably because the scent from her shampoo had lingered in his own hair for several days—despite the fact that he'd washed it repeatedly.

"It's funny what they get into their heads," she finally said, drawing his eyes away from her tight no-nonsense bun.

"What who gets in their heads?"

"The boys. Thinking that I'm some sort of good luck."

"Oh, that," he said, then used the toe of his sneaker to push on the dirt beneath his feet. *Get back on solid ground, Gregson.* "The twins mentioned it last week, too. Not that I believe in any of that, but they'd both struck out before you got here today and Caden missed an easy catch at first base earlier in the game. I don't know if it's self-fulfilling prophecy or what, but they're more convinced than ever that unless you're at their games, they won't play well."

"But that's silly," she said.

"Try explaining that to a couple of eight-year-olds. Actually, nine-year-olds as of this Friday."

"Oh, that's right. The boys mentioned you were throwing them a big birthday party since it's a half-day at school."

"Did they invite you?"

"I'm pretty sure they invited half the town, Luke."

He smiled when she said his name, even if she had ducked her head as soon as she'd said it. Was Officer Always-in-Control embarrassed?

"Well, they didn't invite Marcia Duncan," he said, trying to make a joke to keep her talking.

"I'm pretty sure that after the windshield incident and what happened last week in the meat department, Mrs. Duncan is all too happy to *not* be attending their party."

Luke felt the familiar sensation in his gut. "Oh, no. What happened?"

Carmen sighed. "I took them to Duncan's Market to get some fruit after school since things are still a little tense over at the Gas N' Mart after, well...you know. We started out in the produce section, but then I turned to talk to Mayor Johnston and next thing I knew, I found them by the beef display case pretending that the ground round on sale was actually some sort of brain science experiment and... Well, my freezer at home now contains quite a few packages of hamburger with finger indentations poked through them."

Luke would've groaned at his children's antics if she hadn't just reminded him of her home, and her freezer, which was in her kitchen. Where she had stood in that skimpy little top that outlined the shape of her—

"Hey, Dad." Caden's voice interrupted his train of thought just in time. "We got you a choco-freeze bar."

"And we got a strawberry shortcake one for Officer Carmen," Aiden added.

"Where's your aunt Kylie?" Luke asked.

"One of the babies started cryin' so she said she had to leave. But not before she agreed with us about Officer Carmen being our good luck charm." Here they went again.

"Yeah, she even paid for yours, Officer Carmen, and said there's more where that came from if you keep showing up for our games. Maybe she'll even buy you some nachos at the snack bar next time so that you don't miss a thing."

"That's awfully nice of your aunt." Carmen unwrapped the melting treat. How long had they been hanging out by the ice-cream truck? "But nobody needs to buy me food to keep me around."

"Oh, good, then you'll be at our next game. And we

don't need to buy that dulkie de—what's that flavor called again?" Caden looked at Carmen.

"Dulce de leche," she said, her accented pronunciation making Luke think of other things her tongue might be capable of.

"Yeah. *Dulce de leche* cake for our birthday party. That's Carmen's favorite kind," Caden told his dad. "We can just have regular chocolate with chocolate frosting and you'll still come."

Was she really coming to the birthday party? The one he planned to throw at his cabin? The one he'd had to promise five nights of niece babysitting if Drew and Kylie would help him organize the thing? In the back of his mind, he knew that it would just be a simple event for kids—a little cake, maybe a piñata—but he still was dreading his first foray into hosting anything more than a family cookout. Surely, she had better things to do on Friday night then hang out with some kids, their clueless dad and a store-bought chocolate sheet cake.

He wanted to ask her all those things, while not giving away any indication that a small part of him was hoping she'd be there. But the boys were too busy describing all the toys they'd written on their gift wish lists.

While she nodded along with them, indicating she was listening to their rambling chatter, Luke had the feeling she was staring right at him, those damn sunglasses preventing him from reading her full expression. Did she not want to come to the party? Was she looking to him for an out?

It was bad enough that his children had already guilted her into showing up for their next baseball game. She wouldn't be the first woman who needed a break from the twins. And if he wanted her to stick around—strictly as a mentor to the boys, nothing else—he needed to tell her she was off the hook, but she spoke before he could.

"I'm sure you guys don't want some boring girl like me at your party. You'll be so busy with all of your friends, it won't matter that I'm not there."

"But, Officer Carmen, you're one of our bestest friends. Of course you have to be there." The sad, Popsicle-stained faces stared up at her from beneath the brims of their green caps.

If he wasn't used to the twins making that same expression every time they wanted to stay up past their bedtime or eat pancakes for dinner, he almost would've felt sorry for the little rascals. Almost. But he'd invented that helpless look when he'd been their age and needed to get out of trouble—which was almost every day.

He told himself that the only reason he didn't tell the boys to knock it off was because she was such a good influence on his children and he wanted them happy. Then, when he heard her exhale a deep breath and saw her shoulders relax, he knew she was close to giving in.

Which meant he was getting closer to doing something about this growing attraction to her. Something that they would both surely regret.

Chapter Six

"I know I said I'd help you with the party, Luke." His sister-in-law raised her voice to be heard over the two fussing babies on her end of the line. "But the twins are teething and I'm in the middle of tax season."

Luke looked down at his cell phone, wishing he'd sent the call to voice mail and kept on making dinner. But then he remembered that he was no longer hiding behind his former job title. He was now a full-time a dad. An impulsive one who didn't always make the best decisions, but a dad nonetheless. If he could parachute into enemy territory on covert operations, he could tackle the simplest of domestic duties without fear.

In his defense, though, he wasn't dealing with the simplest of domestic duties. He didn't know how to throw a birthday party for nine-year-olds. He'd missed their last two birthdays and wanted to make sure that this year was beyond memorable for Aiden and Caden.

"But don't worry," Kylie continued. "I'll email you the lists and Drew and I will be there on Friday to help set up. And I already recruited…to go get…with you."

"Kylie, I can't hear you." His nieces were getting louder on the other end of the line and the timer on his stove was going off. "What lists?"

"Oh, you know. The guest list and the food lists and the games and prizes list."

"Games and prizes? We need a list for that?"

"Only if you don't want the kids to get bored and stage a piñata mutiny. Carmen said that happened at one of her cousin's birthdays and it's not pretty when you get that much sugar into forty children half an hour after their parents drop them off."

"Carmen? Did you say Carmen?" He pushed a button above the stove and finally got the timer to stop beeping. "And what was that last part about forty kids? That's not what's on the guest list, is it?"

"Luke, focus. I ran in to Officer Carmen today when I was downtown, and she said she was off work and could help you shop for supplies on Thursday after her kickboxing class. She has a huge family back in Vegas and said they average three birthday parties a month. I'm leaving you in good hands."

In good hands? As in Carmen Delgado's good hands? While Luke had to admit that the cop certainly had nice, capable hands—probably scented with some sort of fragrant specialty lotion—Luke didn't know if that would be asking too much. After all, she already helped him out with the boys through that mentor program, and if they worked on the party together, their sudden closeness might give the wrong impression.

Not that he wouldn't welcome the help, but did he really want the rest of the townspeople getting the idea that she was some sort of surrogate mother?

And was she? He was pretty sure that even if she wanted to play mom or big sister or whatever to a couple of boys, she wasn't particularly eager to step into the wife role.

Whoa. Where had that idea come from?

"Why would Carmen agree to help me?" Luke asked instead.

"Because she loves the twins and wants them to have a fantastic party. And because I bribed her with an all-expenses-paid trip to the Cove Spa in Mc-Call." Another burst of crying interrupted them and he barely heard Kylie's voice say that Carmen would be by tomorrow morning with the lists before the call was disconnected.

There was no way he could spend the whole day with Carmen Delgado. She would be all uptight and he'd be on edge trying to get her to loosen up, and then she'd probably throw those so-called good hands up in the air in frustration and never want anything to do with him or the twins again.

Maybe his mom would drive up from Boise and help… But she'd already been responsible for the birthdays he'd missed and had hosted her share of kid-themed parties in the past. Nope, he didn't want to trouble her with something he should be able to handle.

After all, he was a captain in the Navy, the head of recruiting for the entire West Idaho region. He was handling everything else in his life just fine. For the most part.

Luke looked down at the pan of ground beef he'd been browning for dinner. Why was it smoking? Damn. He'd forgotten to turn off the flame after the timer went off. He slammed the skillet on the back burner and opened the window over the sink.

Just when he thought he'd been doing pretty well in the dad department, another setback came his way. He stared at the bits of charred meat, hesitating to call the twins over to the table.

A flashback from his boyhood hit him and he remembered his nana cooking one time when he'd spent the night at her house. She'd put a frozen pizza in the oven and then turned on the Country Music Television channel, calling an eleven-year-old Luke into the living room to do the "Boot Scootin' Boogie" with her. He'd thought dancing was for girls, but the cowboys on TV didn't look all that girlie. Plus, Pioneer Days was on the calendar at school soon and his teacher had warned the students that they'd all have to learn to square-dance as part of the festivities. So after a small amount of convincing, he'd line danced with Nana, learning the Cowboy Cha Cha and the Eighteen Step. By the time they'd mastered the Watermelon Crawl, Nana's smoke alarm was shrieking at full blast.

She'd tossed the burned pizza in the trash and told Luke, "It's not the food we eat, it's the company we keep that makes a good meal." Then they'd made root beer floats for dinner and watched reruns of *Hee Haw* until he'd fallen asleep on her sofa.

Sure, the cheesy beef and macaroni he'd made tonight was a bit on the overdone side. But he'd had way worse meals in bunkers and tents around the world. What mattered was that he was here with his children and that he was providing for them. They were a family—and they were together.

And he was about to throw them the best damn birthday party Sugar Falls had ever seen.

Carmen couldn't believe she'd agreed to help with this birthday party. Actually, she pretty much would've agreed to anything that made Aiden and Caden Gregson happy, but it was their aunt who'd convinced her.

When Kylie ran in to her outside of Domino's Deli yesterday, the woman had been panicked that the birthday party would be a complete failure since she was too busy to take care of the last minute details herself. And it hadn't taken much begging on Kylie's part to convince Carmen to step up to the plate.

Truly, Carmen would've done it for free. But now, as she navigated her SUV over the ruts in the dirt road leading up to the Gregson cabin, she decided that working side by side with Luke today was enough of an emotional chore to earn a relaxing trip to a day spa.

She put the car in Park and turned down the radio station she'd been listening to. Her appreciation for George Strait and Garth Brooks rather than Jenni Rivera and Intocable should've been her first clue that she didn't fit in well with her own family. She loved them and knew they loved her, but she'd always been destined for different things.

However, today wasn't a day to be thinking about her past and all the things she couldn't change.

She gathered the lists she'd printed off earlier this morning and exited her car. As much as she had wanted to wear a dress or something more feminine to remind Luke that she was more than just a cop, she also wanted to be comfortable with all the shopping and hauling that they were going to be doing today. So she'd settled on the low-waisted jeans she'd been wearing that night at Patrelli's—the night he'd said he wanted more children—and a black V-necked sweater. Although she did add her metallic purple ballet flats at the last minute, just to soften things up.

She ran her fingers through her loose curls, debating whether she should've pulled her hair into a ponytail, then wondered what she was even doing on his front porch in the first place. Before she could second-guess herself, she knocked on the door, taking a slight step back when Luke flung it open.

"Hi," he said, somewhat winded and twisting a dishcloth in his hands. The sleeves of his blue thermal shirt were pushed up to his elbows, his forearms slightly wet with soap suds. "I was just trying to get the dishes done and a load of laundry going before you could see what a wreck this place is."

He and his dimples stood back, allowing her to step into the cabin. It wasn't dirty, but she could definitely tell that a couple of creative and high-energy boys lived here—along with their high-energy dad, who could charm the socks off most of the ladies in Carmen's growing kickboxing class.

"It's not a wreck," she said, thinking back to some of the meth houses and condemned buildings she'd made arrests in when she'd worked in Vegas. "It just looks...lived in."

"That's one way to put it." His smile deepened and she found herself a little disappointed to see him pull down his sleeves. The guy's forearms really were amazing, as was the rest of his upper body. "So what's on the party planning agenda?"

She jumped at the opportunity to launch into professional mode. Controlling mode. "I figured we could pick up the decorations and most of the groceries today. The rental company will be by tomorrow to set up the chairs and tables and I can pick up the cakes in the morning on my way over here to help prep the food." She saw his eyes glance down toward her breasts but then realized he was probably looking at the papers she was holding against her chest. "Oh, and Kylie emailed me these."

She thrust the papers at him, and his fingers brushed hers as he took them out of her hands. She felt that zappy feeling again and tried to remember her stun-gun training. One small tingle of current wouldn't hurt, but a full force of electrical shock could do some serious damage. She made a mental note to avoid any more accidental physical contact with him.

"Why do we need to rent tables and chairs?" he asked before flipping to the page with the guest list. "What the...? Is this all the people invited?"

She wanted to laugh at the surprised look on his face and felt just the slightest twinge of guilt for her growing desire to overwhelm him a bit more. "No, those are only the people who can make it."

"But there's gotta be over a hundred people on this list!"

"Actually, there's one hundred and fifty-two if you don't count the girls from the Junior Jazzette dance troupe. Since school gets out early, they have a late matinee performance at the Remington Theater tomorrow and Mia doesn't know if they'll be done in time for the party."

Carmen caught a movement on the hardwood floors and saw Luke's bare toes do an odd flexing thing. Man, even the guy's feet were muscular and sexy.

"Are there even one hundred and fifty-two people living in Sugar Falls?" he asked sarcastically.

"Oh, come on, Captain Gregson. Don't tell me that a big, tough Navy SEAL is afraid of a simple gathering."

He looked up. "It's not the large group I mind. It's the being responsible for entertaining them all that I wasn't expecting. I told the boys last Monday that they could invite a few friends, but this is ridiculous. How did they even get the chance to talk to so many people in such a short amount of time?"

She showed him the printout of the online invitation. "I was under the impression you'd sent this to everyone since it came from your email address. But, knowing the twins, I probably shouldn't have assumed anything."

"'Come one, come all?'" He read aloud. "Did they really put that on the e-vite?"

"Luke, I'm starting to see where Caden gets his flair for drama. It's really not that big of a guest list. In my family, anything less than two hundred people isn't even considered a party. We call it Sunday night dinner. My cousin Maria Rosa had three times that many to her *quinceañera*." Of course, Maria Rosa, being younger by six months, had always tried to go out of her way to outdo her older cousin.

"You mean this is going to get worse every year that they get older?" Luke's face paled.

She finally laughed out loud. "Relax. Just think that with twins, you're getting two birthdays for the price of one."

"What a bargain. So where do we get enough food to feed all these people? I've been too nervous to step foot in Duncan's Market since you told me about the boys getting eighty-sixed from there."

"There's a big party-supply store in Boise, so I figured we'd go there first. Then we can swing by Costco after that."

"Swing by Costco?" He lifted one eyebrow. "I haven't been to a bulk warehouse like that since the twins were in diapers. Samantha used to say that we should've bought stock in that place. And in baby wipes."

The butterflies in her tummy had just turned into hornets. She wished she didn't feel so stung by the sudden mention of the twins' mom. Carmen had absolutely no claim to Luke and shouldn't be even the slightest bit jealous of his love for his late wife. Yet, some of her humor was lost by the reminder that not only would she never be buying diapers with a husband, the one man she was attracted to was in love with someone else and, therefore, on the shelf.

"Well, then, get your wallet ready, Captain." She retreated into her default professional mode. "Judging by Kylie's list, you're going to be spending a lot of money today."

He grabbed on to his back pocket dramatically, as if he could protect his billfold, and she tried not to think of what it would feel like to cup her own hand against that perfect curve of his jeans.

"Okay, sailor." She yanked the lists out of his hand and turned toward the door. "This ship needs to sail if we're going to get all this done before the boys get out of school."

"All right. As long as I can steer the ship." She heard the jangling sound of his keys.

"No way," she said. "We have a lot to buy and my car's bigger."

"I'm starting to think you have control issues, Officer Delgado."

"I'm a woman in a male-dominated field. I'm supposed to have control issues," she said.

"Not with me, you're not."

"Listen, Gregson. There's something I've learned about the two types of men out there. There are the ones who don't like a woman being in a power position. And the ones who think they like a woman in a power position, but when they end up finding out what that entails, they can't handle it."

"Well, allow me to introduce you to the third type of man," Luke said, pointing to his chest. "The one who's a team player. Gender doesn't matter to me as long as the mission gets accomplished. And this mission requires a roomy Oldsmobile."

"I'm sure Nana's car is a real beaut and that the ladies are all lining up for their turn to be squired around in it. But my car has way more space. If we fold down the seats, you could even lay down back there. It'll make for a better ride."

His gaze dropped to her waist and there was no mistaking the way the warm color rose along his neck. Or the fact that gender *did* matter to him when he'd misconstrued her suggestive words.

"I meant since you're so big and... Oh, never mind,"

she muttered, turning away before he saw her matching blush. "You can drive."

"I don't know why we had to get two piñatas," Luke
said as he tried to shove the papier-mâché-covered
cartoon character into the backseat of Nana's Oldsmobile. He sure hoped his children enjoyed this birthday,
because after filling two shopping carts full of decorations and favors at the party-supply store, this was
the last one he was willing to throw.

"We got two piñatas because you have two children," Carmen explained as though Luke didn't know
exactly what it was like to have twins. Hell, he'd
grown up as one himself. But his parents had been
on a budget and they'd been smart enough to make
sure their children didn't invite that many people to
their parties. Plus, Luke hadn't had access to online
invitations back then.

"Aiden wanted a superhero theme," Carmen continued as she piled bags onto the seat. "And Caden
wanted ninjas. So we're getting two of everything."

"But we haven't even made it to Costco yet. How
are we going to fit everything in here?"

"You're the one who wanted to bring the Nanamobile." He looked up just in time to see her roll her eyes.
"I offered to drive, remember?"

Luke remembered all right. The minute she'd suggested putting the seats down in her car so he could
lie back there and have a more comfortable ride, he'd
made the mistake of looking down at her athletic body
and envisioning the exact type of ride he'd prefer to
enjoy with her.

Then she'd made an about-face and headed straight

for the driveway, her coolness serving as a reminder that Luke had no business getting involved with another woman, let alone the controlled female cop. The drive to Boise had been awkwardly silent until they'd finally passed the Shadowview Military Hospital and Luke couldn't stand the quiet any longer. He'd turned on the radio, the old dial stuck on a country music station. By the time they'd made it to the party-supply store, Carmen didn't seem as tense and had naturally fallen into her element by taking over the list of what they'd need for the party.

Now he watched her yank her arm out of the way just in time to slam the car door closed against the tumbling bags. He doubted they really needed paper napkins in five different colors, but every time he'd expressed an opinion about buying so much stuff, she would point out the item on Kylie's never-ending list of things to make sure this was the biggest kids' birthday party the town of Sugar Falls had ever seen. Carmen Delgado must've been one hell of a Marine with the way she followed orders.

He got into the driver's seat and glanced at the sushi restaurant across the street. Was it too early for lunch? His stomach was telling him it wasn't, but his no-nonsense passenger's professional demeanor was telling him that going out to lunch—just the two of them—might seem a little too date-like. And he didn't want her thinking he was trying to come on to her. Instead, he put the car in Drive without saying a word.

They were on their way to get groceries when he saw the sign for the giant toy store and a little light inside his head clicked.

"Man, I totally forgot," he said as he hit his turn signal. "I haven't even gotten the boys their presents."

Carmen looked at her watch since the display clock in the Oldsmobile was stuck indefinitely on 8:56. "It's already eleven hundred hours and you need to be back in Sugar Falls in time to pick up the twins from school."

"I'm their dad. I can't *not* get them something for their birthday. Besides, I'm sure they'd rather have new toys than—" he picked up the grocery list sitting on the bench seat beside him "—two pounds of hummus. Who's going to eat all that, anyway?"

"Oh, fine," Carmen responded with a sigh. "But let's try to get in and out in under twelve minutes."

Twelve minutes? Did the woman think they were running some sort of covert op here? Maybe they needed to synchronize their watches or wear radio headsets to communicate throughout the assignment. But instead of making a sarcastic comment to Officer Controlling, he revved the engine of the Oldsmobile and pulled into a parking space in front of Toy Town, barely missing the curb. Nana would've been proud.

Carmen grabbed her purse, a purple leather satchel that matched her dainty shoes, and Luke followed her to the entrance, thinking he still wasn't used to seeing her with so many feminine accessories. She even had large gold hoop earrings on and several delicate bracelets tinkling against her wrist.

Not that he was paying attention.

"I used to love this place when I was a little girl," she said, slowing her stride as they walked inside. Her chocolate-brown eyes were enormous, taking in all the colorful displays of the latest toy crazes. Luke couldn't imagine someone as proper and as stiff as Carmen ever being a child.

"Really? I didn't know they had a bossy-pants section here."

"Actually, I preferred the rocket-blaster section. It was right by the sarcastic-tough-guy section, making it easy to shoot at targets." But her smile caused him to chuckle, and seconds later, she joined him. He liked the sound of her laughter. It was sweet but throaty at the same time. A complete contradiction in terms, much like the woman herself.

"C'mon, partner," he said, placing a hand above the curve of her hip and guiding her toward the Lego area. "According to my calculations, we've got less than nine minutes to accomplish this mission."

Her face turned to his in surprise, but she didn't make an effort to remove his hand or to step away from him.

"Besides," he added. "The manager here knows me by name, and even without the twins with us to wreak havoc, he'll probably still be watching me like a hawk."

"So it's not just Mrs. Duncan who doesn't appreciate your family's patronage in their stores?" She held her body rigid yet shot him a teasing smile. Even though the polished floor was smooth, Luke lost his footing and almost stumbled, causing him to pull her in closer to him.

"I know it's hard to imagine," he said, trying to resume his pace. "But not everyone is as charmed by the Gregson twins as you are."

Carmen stopped and put her hand on his shoulder. Since he had yet to pull his own arm away from her waist, they were standing face-to-face in somewhat of an embrace.

"Luke, your boys are wonderful and you're so lucky to have them. Don't let anyone else's misguided judgments make you think otherwise. Sure, they're a handful and they have a lot of energy. But they also have a lot of compassion. They're smart and sweet and extremely happy. That means you're doing something right."

His throat threatened to close and he sucked in a deep breath, not wanting to get emotional in the walkway between the Matchbox cars and the Nerf guns.

"Thank you for saying that," he said. Then he lifted his eyes to the ceiling and away from her gentle and caring gaze before speaking again. "When their mom died, I felt like I wasn't worthy of being a dad to them. I was gone a lot on deployment, both before and especially after. Some people thought I was running from my responsibilities when I would leave them with my family and go out on dangerous assignments. But I figured it would benefit them more to be raised by people who knew what they were doing. I'd already let Samantha down and I didn't want to let the boys down by not being the father they deserved. It took a…"

The front of Luke's jeans suddenly vibrated, causing Carmen to quickly jump back. He hadn't realized they'd been standing close enough for her to feel it. He fumbled in his pocket before pulling his cell phone out.

Seeing the school's number on the display brought a familiar moment of panic to his chest and he cleared his throat before answering, expecting the worst. Again.

"Hi, Dad." The voice on the other end sounded perfectly healthy and not the least bit in trouble.

"Hi, Aiden," Luke said, noting the worried look in Carmen's eyes. "Is anything wrong?"

"No. We just told the school secretary that you didn't pack us our lunch and she let us call you."

"Hi, Dad," Caden yelled in the background.

"But I gave you both money to eat at the cafeteria today," Luke said, and then mouthed to Carmen that everything was okay.

"I know," Aiden said. "Which means we didn't really tell a lie because technically you didn't pack us one."

"Well, *technically*, you better have a good reason for calling me during school time."

"We do. Are you still shopping with Officer Carmen for our party?" Aiden asked, having apparently overheard Luke's conversation with Kylie last night.

"Yes, I am, but I doubt we're going to have enough time to buy you two any presents if you keep interrupting us."

"Well, Hunter said Mrs. Cooper was inviting us over for dinner tonight because the poker game got canceled. So we just wanted to let you know that you don't need to be back until dinnertime…"

Luke heard some mumbling on the other end of the line before Caden's voice replaced his brother's. "What Aiden meant was that there might not be enough dinner for you guys. So you and Officer Carmen should just stay in Boise and have dinner by yourselves…"

There was more mumbling followed by a scuffling sound, which probably meant Aiden had snatched the receiver back. "Anyway, Mrs. Cooper is gonna pick us up after school so you guys can take your time buying us presents and getting the rest of the stuff for our party. Especially the buying-us-presents part."

"Yeah," Caden's voice called out. "Don't forget that I want the rebel ice fortress. And Aiden wants the pink dream palace! Hey, here comes Nurse Dunn."

"We gotta go, Dad. Tell Officer Carmen hi."

"Bye, you two. Get back to class." Luke disconnected the call.

"What was that all about?" Carmen asked.

He hesitated to tell her because he knew that his children shouldn't be calling him in the middle of the day from school for no good reason. Luke was used to their random antics and didn't want Carmen to read anything into it.

He explained that the boys were going over to Maxine and Cooper's after school, so they could take their time shopping. "Which is a good thing," he said as they stepped into the Lego aisle. "My wallet doesn't want me going grocery shopping on an empty stomach. Let's finish up here and go grab some lunch."

"Lunch, huh?" She grinned again. "We've got a million things to get done today and all you can think about is your stomach?"

"I'm a man. What else am I supposed to think about?"

Certainly, he wasn't supposed to be thinking about how he was going to have Carmen all to himself for the rest of the afternoon.

Chapter Seven

Carmen used the excuse that she was concerned Luke's wallet couldn't handle much more withdrawals today. But the real reason she'd suggested they drive through and pick up fast food was because she didn't think she could handle sitting across the table from him at lunch. Even the strongest of women knew their limitations.

Hey, maybe Abuela should add that to her list of quotes.

Even if Carmen tried to tell herself that going out to eat with Luke was no different than grabbing a sandwich with Cooper on break, or having breakfast with Scooter and Jonesy at the Cowgirl Up Café, Carmen knew her heart shouldn't be tested.

It was tempting enough to pretend that this little shopping trip was like a quasi date, but as soon as she let her mind meander in that direction, it would be too difficult to reverse course. She and Luke were barely friends. More like acquaintances.

"Plus," she argued her point as he steered the Nanamobile out of the Toy Town parking lot, "even with the twins being picked up from school, we still should try and get back to Sugar Falls as soon as we can. Maxine and Cooper are familiar with how long it takes to drive into Boise and stop at a few stores. If we don't get back by dinner, they're going to think something's up."

"Like we got lost or something?" he asked, draping one arm along the back of the plush bench seat as he pulled into traffic.

Her eyes darted back at his hand resting mere inches from her shoulder. "I was thinking more like you and I were up to…" She pinched her lips together and raised her eyebrows, but he was checking out the review mirror instead of her.

"What could we possibly be up to?" He made a smooth right turn at the intersection and Carmen had to wonder how much practice Luke Gregson had at driving one-handed with a female in his passenger seat.

Did she really have to spell it out for him? "That maybe we're enjoying spending time together. You know, *without* the kids."

"Well, why wouldn't we? I mean, I love those little monkeys, but unless I'm at work, I don't get a lot of one-on-one time alone with other adults."

"But this is kind of different than just playing poker with the guys on Thursday nights." She looked back at his relaxed hand again.

His eyes followed hers and he pulled his arm away

so quickly the sudden movement caused him to swerve into the next lane. Another driver blasted their horn and Luke lifted his fingers out the window in an apologetic wave.

"What? Nah. I don't think anyone would think that," he said, then coughed. "But if you'd prefer to grab something to go, there's a Sonic burger place up ahead."

If he was using a burger joint as an attempt to divert her attention away from the subject of them being romantically involved, then maybe he wasn't as smooth as she'd first suspected. Or maybe he wasn't diverting anything. Maybe it was simply too ridiculous for him to contemplate the possibility that other people might think they were on a secret date.

But she'd already put the suggestion out there and now she was kicking herself for bringing it up, since he was clearly not of the same mind-set. How did they go back to normal—or at least, normal for them—after that?

"Burgers sound good," she said, leaning her body closer to the door. She wanted to put as much distance between herself and the awkwardness she'd just created.

Luke chose one of the larger parking spots behind the restaurant and maneuvered the car much too close to the menu sign before asking her what she wanted to eat. Because of his huge, muscular, perfect manly body, she had to lean forward to see around him, bringing her into closer contact. The smell of his aftershave was tickling her nose, tickling her nerves, tickling her ability to think rationally altogether. So she just ordered the first item on the menu that she could read. "I'll take the Coney dog combo with the cheese tots."

"What do you want to drink?" he asked.

Crap. She had to lean forward again and when she did so, he chose that particular second to look her way. His eyes drifted toward the V in her top and she whipped back against the seat quickly. "Cherry lime-ade," she said louder than she intended.

Luke ordered but didn't look at her again, even after the carhop skated out to deliver their food to them. He handed Carmen the bright red drink and she tried to delicately take the foam cup from his hand without touching his fingers. They might as well be tiptoeing around a crime scene; they were both deter-mined to avoid contact with each other.

So maybe he *was* worried that someone else—particularly she—might think their excursion into Boise was a date.

Carmen had done the whole avoidance song and dance with Mark after her surgery and found that it was just better to be direct, cut to the chase and pull the pin out of the conversational grenade once and for all. Then run for cover.

"You know what, Luke," she finally said. "Let's just pretend I never said anything about people getting the wrong idea about us. Obviously neither one of us thinks of this as a date or anything. Besides, even if we *were* attracted to each other, it's not like anything could ever come of it. We're not even friends. So let's just agree that we're both here for the kids' sake and try to work together to make sure their birthday party goes well."

"That's fine," he said, pulling her chili dog out of the paper sack, then holding it out of reach as she tried to take it. "Except for one part. I really do want to be friends, Delgado. You're an important part of Aiden's and Caden's lives and I think it's kind of weird that we can't act more friendly around each other."

She didn't appreciate him holding her lunch hostage, but she did agree with what he was saying. "Fair enough. Friends?"

She held out her hand and he shook it before turning over the chili dog, replacing his warmth with the wrapped gooey mess she'd mistakenly ordered.

"Now that that's settled," she said, "next stop, Costco."

"Actually," he said, snapping open a plastic container, "I can't drive and eat my food."

"What is that? Who orders a chicken salad from a burger joint?"

"The guy who normally lives on a steady diet of Honey Smacks for breakfast and macaroni-based casseroles for dinner. Unless I take the time to cook multiple meals, lunch is the only healthy time of the day for me." He took his time ripping open his ranch dressing, and his tan fingers made an elaborate work out of stroking and squeezing every last drop from the packet. She was too mesmerized to look away. "But now that we decided we're just friends, and that there's nothing more going on, you're not still in a hurry, are you?"

"No," she said, settling back with her cherry limeade. "I'm in no hurry." The only thing she was in was a heap of trouble if she kept looking at him.

Yuck. She hated these sweet artificially flavored drinks, but she'd panicked and ordered the first thing she could think of. But after taking the initiative to confront him on their awkwardness and her attempt to make things seem more normal, she wasn't going to admit she'd much rather be eating the salad, as well.

"Speaking of food," he said, after finishing a few bites. "What exactly does my sister-in-law have planned for the birthday dinner?"

Carmen licked some cheese sauce off her finger before consulting the list. "It looks like grilled chicken, hot dogs, potato salad, baked beans, spinach salad, fresh fruit, that kind of thing."

"That kind of thing? You make it sound so easy."

"You have a grill, don't you?"

"Yeah. The hot dogs are no problem and the chicken might be doable if we buy enough barbecue sauce to cover up the fact that I tend to overcook meat. But I've never made a potato salad or any of that other stuff before."

"That's why I'm here to help you." Carmen almost called him *friend* but didn't want to patronize him or remind him of the reason for their newly formed relationship.

"Do you know how to cook?" He was lifting an eyebrow at her and she wanted to throw a tater tot at him for doubting her.

"Of course I know how to cook."

"Well, it's just that you never really struck me as that type of woman." Was he making another crack about her just being one of the guys? Before she could respond, he added, "You always seem like you'd be way more comfortable on the shooting range than in the kitchen. But then again, after seeing all those froufrou beauty products in your bathroom, maybe I should've known better."

"Whose products are you calling froufrou?" She

threw a tater tot at him, then laughed when he caught it in his mouth.

"Okay, soldier," he said, shoving his empty salad container into the paper bag. "Break's over. Time to get back to work."

She wadded up her napkin and added her half-eaten lunch to the bag before getting out and throwing it all away in the trash bin two spots down from theirs. When she got back in the car, she saw that he'd maneuvered the drinks in the cardboard holder so that his diet soda was now on her side.

He must've detected her observation because he put the car in Drive, then commented, "I needed a taste of something sweet, so I switched them. Besides, you weren't going to drink yours, anyway."

He was right, but she hated the fact that he'd noticed. She also hated the fact that no matter how quickly he'd been willing to agree to their truce, she was dying to give him a taste of something sweet.

They were halfway through Costco and Luke was still replaying her words in his mind.

It's not like anything could ever come of it.

So was she admitting to a mutual attraction between them? Because it kind of sounded like she was. Not that he could be sure. Despite Samantha's accusations to the contrary, Luke was no expert on women or whether they wanted him. Sure, some of his buddies from his former SEAL team used to tease him about his pretty-boy looks, but he'd never been all that interested in what women were thinking when they looked at him.

He only knew that he wasn't capable of giving them what they wanted.

"Do you want breasts or thighs?" he heard her ask, and he almost crashed the shopping cart into the refrigerator case.

"What?" he asked, trying to keep his eyes focused straight ahead so they wouldn't stray below her neck again. As much as he'd appreciated the view when she'd leaned over him to order off the lunch menu, they were in a public place now and his blood pressure didn't need to be spiking like a launched projectile missile.

She lifted the chicken packages higher and repeated her question. "Oh. Both," he said, wishing he could make an inappropriate joke. But she'd made it clear that flirtatious teasing wasn't even an option. Hadn't she?

He clenched his jaw as he pushed the oversize cart down the wide aisles, following her as she added items to it and then made notes on that damn list of Kylie's. He could read GPS coordinates in the dark, but he sure as hell couldn't read the sexy brunette who was walking through the warehouse store like a rear admiral inspecting her crew.

If he didn't have Carmen's perfectly curved butt as the charming view in front of him, Luke would've been tempted to call his sister-in-law and tell her to forget her stupid list. He could just order a bunch of pizzas from Patrelli's instead.

But no matter what Carmen had said earlier, the fact of the matter was he *did* enjoy spending time with her. Especially when she wasn't in her tough-cop mode.

She stopped by a sample display and took a tiny paper cup filled with part of a beef chimichanga, handing it to him before snagging one for herself and taking a bite. "They're not as good as Abuela's, but not too bad for frozen."

"*Abuela* means grandma in Spanish, right?" he asked.

"Yes. She's my dad's mom and the best cook I know. It drives my mom crazy that any time we had a family party, everyone would always ask Abuela to make most of the food. Luckily for you, I emailed her and asked for her potato salad recipe."

"You said *had.*" He took the empty sample cup from her and tossed it in the trash.

"Had what?" She must not have noticed the telling slip.

"Any time you *had* a family party. Does that mean you don't have family parties anymore?"

She shrugged, then grabbed a fifty-count package of hot dogs from the case. "I'm sure they still have them. I just haven't attended one in a long time."

"Why not?"

"Because most of my family lives in Las Vegas and I'm up here."

"Don't you miss them?"

"Sure. Sometimes." She tugged on the front end of the cart, but he wasn't going to follow along any more. She'd said they were friends and, as friends, he wanted to learn more about her. He stood still, keeping the cart locked in place until she looked back at him.

"Fine," she said. "I should probably go visit more often but things are kind of awkward right now. Besides, it's not like my family isn't used to the distance.

I joined the Marine Corps straight out of high school and was stationed all over, including two deployments to the Middle East."

He nodded. "I get that. My own parents live in Boise, and after Drew and I joined up, we all just got accustomed to going for long periods without seeing each other."

"So there you have it," she said, then walked around the corner to the next aisle without waiting for him to follow.

"But here's what I don't understand," he said, catching up to her. Man, this cart was getting heavier to push by the minute. "You moved back to Vegas after you got out of the military and you became a police officer there, right?"

"Right…" Her tense shoulders suggested she wanted to roll her eyes, but instead she kept her head down, staring at the list. He was getting closer to uncovering something. He could feel it.

"Now, I'm just speaking from personal experience, so bear with me. But now that I've moved back to Idaho to be close to my family and my hometown, I can't imagine ever packing up and leaving again."

"Is there supposed to be a question in there?"

Whoa. She'd gone from annoyed to defensive in a snap. *Reel it back in, Gregson.* Luke shifted from one foot to the other.

"Listen." He shot her a grin and tried to make his voice sound more teasing. "Not all of us can be trained cops and interrogators. Anyway, you said things were awkward with your family now. Plus, out of the blue you recently moved to some nowhere town in Idaho to take a job on a tiny police force even though you don't know anyone in Sugar Falls. So I'm just wondering if those things go hand in hand."

"You're wrong about the part that I didn't know anyone in Sugar Falls. I was stationed at Camp Lejeune with Cooper, and when he said he was building up a new department out here it seemed like a good time to change course. But there *is* one thing you're right about. You're not a trained interrogator."

She'd felt the need to change course. He'd keep that little nugget of information stored for future use.

"So train me," he said, moving next to her so he could help her load cases of soda. They were going to need a forklift soon. "If you wanted to know all about someone's past, how would you go about asking them?"

"Well, I wouldn't do it in the beverage aisle of Costco." Her controlled smile was appealing and gave a hint of sauciness. But Luke wasn't satisfied yet.

"Should I have asked once we got to the checkout line?" he asked, deciding to banter with her while he bided his time.

"Nah. If it were me, I'd wait until my subject was frustrated with the impossible task of cramming all these groceries into the trunk of the Nanamobile and then spring my questions on them when they were too overwhelmed and distracted to gauge their answers."

"Fine," he said, taking a cup of green juice from the next sampling station and handing it to her. "I'll hold all my personal questions until then. I knew there was a good reason for bringing my car."

There went her pretty blush again. And, despite the shot of organic kale smoothie he'd just swallowed, his mouth went dry.

"Hmm," she said, and smirked. "Maybe the question you should be asking is how many ice chests are you going to need to borrow to hold all these drinks? We haven't even gotten to the beer section yet."

He laughed, not so much at her attempt to scare him back into birthday-party-planning action, but at her feeble attempt to thwart his curiosity. Her refusal to talk about this only made him more determined to breach her heavily guarded walls.

Apparently Officer Delgado didn't realize that once a SEAL took on a mission, he didn't give up until he got the job done.

Sure enough, the blasted man took Carmen's tongue-in-cheek advice to heart and decided that the best time to bring up her family history was while she was trying to figure out how to shove the hot dog buns into his trunk without risking the bag of potatoes crushing against them the moment he made the turn onto the highway back toward Sugar Falls.

"Luke, I wasn't serious about you interrogating me out here in the parking lot."

"Hey, if you're going to be calling me Luke all the time, I'm making the executive decision that it's only fair if I call you Carmen."

She didn't want to point out that he'd already called her that before, and that when he did her heart expanded and her resistance began slipping. So, instead, she blew a stray curl out of her eyes and tried to be as nonchalant as possible. "I don't care what you call me."

There. That sounded believable.

"I think some of this stuff is going to have to be squished up front with us," he said when it became obvious there was nowhere else to put the huge bags of chips and the new plastic oars she'd decided to buy the boys. After all, they'd recovered the canoe, but their paddles had been washed away when they'd lost control of their craft in the river behind her house about a month ago.

But the extra stuff in front was just fine with her. Maybe the additional barrier between them would prevent him from asking any more questions.

Nope, she realized as soon as they turned onto the highway and he said, "Okay, we have an hour back to Sugar Falls. That should be plenty of time to tell me about why things are awkward in your family."

"Oh, come on, Luke. You don't really want to know all this, do you? Hey, listen." She turned up Blake Shelton's voice on the radio. "This is one of my favorite songs."

"No way, *Carmen*." He reached over and switched the knob into the off position. Maybe they should've stuck to using last names. "I need to know what kind of person is going to be making the potato salad for my party tomorrow."

"The kind of person who can pass multiple departmental background checks, as well the person who you entrust your children to every Tuesday afternoon for the Sugar Falls Elementary mentorship program."

"Background checks and fingerprints are all fine and good, but I take my side dishes seriously. So spill it."

"Fine." She leaned her head against the velvet upholstered headrest and looked at the sun sinking lower, just like her resolve. "What do you want to know?"

"Why did you leave Vegas PD?"

"I wanted a change of pace."

"That's a vague answer."

"It's the only one I'm willing to give."

"So then when's the last time you saw your family?"

"About nine months ago. My dad and brothers helped me move into the cottage where I live now."

"So you haven't been back to visit since you relocated to Sugar Falls?"

"No." But before he could fire off another question, she said, "My turn to ask something."

"Shoot," he said. "My life's an open book." She took that as an implication that hers wasn't.

"When I saw the scar on your rib cage, you said that the tattoo was the date you became a father. But it's different than the date the twins were born."

"Is there a question in there somewhere?" he asked, throwing her own line back at her.

"What's the significance of that?" she continued.

"The significance is that after the boys' mom died, I spent a lot of time running from my responsibilities. Hell, Samantha would say that I was running from them way before she died. But, like I said earlier today, I thought the twins were better off without me as their primary caregiver."

"Why would they be better off without you?"

"Uh-uh, Officer. My turn. Why haven't you been to Las Vegas since you moved here? You said you come from a large family and you're used to large parties. I find it hard to believe that they haven't had some sort of big celebration since you left. And your hometown isn't all that far. So why haven't you been back?"

"Because the last big family celebration was my

cousin Maria Rosa's wedding and I didn't feel like going. Why would the twins be better off without you?"

"Actually, this back-and-forth questioning is too confusing," Luke said. "I'll make you a deal. Five questions at a time. Let me get to the bottom of this one thing, and then you can ask me whatever else you want."

Carmen didn't think that was particularly fair, but the man had a point. It was getting tricky to keep track of whose personal story they were following and she wanted him focused if she hoped to get real answers out of him about his relationship with his kids. And, if she were honest with herself, about his late wife. "All right. Go ahead."

"Why wouldn't you want to go to your own cousin's wedding?"

She stole a glance at Luke over the five-pound bag of Ruffles, but he was keeping his eyes on the highway. Everyone in her family knew, but nobody actually brought it up to her—probably to protect her feelings. This would be the first time she'd said it out loud or talked about it to anyone, so at least he wasn't looking at her.

She took a calm breath and then forced the words out. "Because she was marrying my ex-boyfriend."

Carmen had to give Luke credit for not completely skidding off the road when she'd made that announcement. Instead, he'd only swerved a little and then overcorrected his steering, causing the rear tires to fishtail briefly before straightening out.

"Did you just say that your cousin married your ex-boyfriend?"

"Yep."

"Did she know he was your ex?"

"Yep."

"Did this jerk know she was your cousin?"

"Mark isn't really a jerk," she admitted. Just a man who wanted what Carmen couldn't give him.

"How can you defend him?"

"Well, I didn't say I was *happy* about the wedding. I just said he wasn't a jerk. I was the one who broke things off with him." More like she'd been the one to let him off the hook and he'd eagerly jumped at the chance. Either way, Carmen was the one responsible for it all. Putting herself at risk was one of the downfalls to having a dangerous job.

"But still," he said. She couldn't see his expression, but his tone was incredulous. "Your own cousin? There wasn't anyone else he could've married?"

"My Tia Lupe offered, but she's seventy-eight, so my cousin was probably the better match."

"You seem so calm and unaffected by the whole situation," he said.

Unaffected? Hardly. Yet, what could she do but try to remain calm? And try to justify her reality as something completely ordinary.

"You know how I mentioned that my big family loves to get together for dinners?" she asked, but didn't wait for his response. "Well, Mark attended plenty of those dinners and got to know all of them pretty well."

"But you'd think that once you broke up with the jerk—I mean the *guy*, and I use that term loosely— their loyalty would stick with you."

"Well, now their loyalty is with Maria Rosa. Besides, my family all understood why we broke up and nobody could really blame Mark."

"So they blamed you? I don't get it. What'd you do

that was so bad you deserved to have your ex run off and marry your cousin?"

Carmen shook her head, not wanting to admit to him or anyone the responsibility she felt for her injury—for her wounds that would never heal. But, with the sun sinking behind the mountain, she doubted he could see her in the darkened interior of the car. Plus, if he didn't keep his eyes on the road, he would miss the turn for his cabin. But he skillfully maneuvered the bulky Oldsmobile over the ruts along his dirt driveway while curiously glancing her way, which meant that she needed to get herself in check right now. She ran a hand through her curly hair, wishing she could reach a ponytail holder in her purse and pull it under control, pull herself under control.

"Unfortunately, your five questions are up, Captain Gregson." She tried to make her voice sound cheery. "And we need to get this car unloaded before the ice cream melts all over the cheese tray."

Chapter Eight

Luckily for her, Luke couldn't do much talking as they carried in load after load of party supplies and groceries.

"We should've picked up something to eat on the way home," he said after Carmen finished transferring several items to her own car so she could prepare some of the side dishes at home. "That salad didn't last long and I'm starved."

"Luke, you have so much food in your fridge, we could barely get it closed. I'm sure you can find something."

"Yeah, but the only thing already made is the hummus and the veggie tray." He looked at his watch. "Hey, maybe if we hurry, we can make it to Cooper and Maxine's before they put dinner away."

Not a chance. There was no way Carmen was going

to show up at his friend's house with him for a family meal. That was just way too…couple-like.

"You go on ahead," she said. "I'm going to take some of this stuff to my house and get a head start on the cooking tonight."

"Hmm, maybe I should just come over to your house and test out the menu before I serve it to my guests."

"*Your* guests? You mean the hundred and fifty or so people you had no idea were coming tomorrow?"

"Yeah." He revealed that dimple and the butterfly wings inside her started flapping again. "Those."

"It'll take too long. I think you may have better luck at Cooper and Maxine's. Besides, the kids are probably waiting for you."

"You're right," he said, the divot in his cheek disappearing. Was he disappointed she wasn't inviting him over for uncooked potato salad?

"Oh, before I forget," he said, the dimple returning. "I have something for you."

He ran into his bedroom and she tried not to let her imagination run right back there with him. Luckily, he returned a second later and she no longer had to force herself to not contemplate following him.

"Here." He threw a wadded-up ball of blue fabric at her.

"What's this?" She held it up.

"I figured I owed you a T-shirt since I ripped yours the other week."

She looked at the white vinyl USN logo and the words below that read Tough Girls Wear Anchors and then burst into laughter.

"I like seeing you laugh, Carmen." If he liked that,

then he'd probably love seeing the way her heart danced around inside her chest whenever he smiled at her.

"Thanks for giving me a reason to." She'd needed it. Especially after such an unlaughable conversation in the car. "And don't forget to wrap those presents before you pick up the twins. You know they're going to be a couple of live wires tonight and all kinds of excited for their party tomorrow."

"They're a couple of live wires even when they *don't* have a birthday party to look forward to."

She smiled again, finding the urge more natural the longer she stood in front of him.

"And thanks for all your help shopping," he said. Was it her imagination or was he closer? "You really didn't have to do all that."

"Really, Luke, it was no problem. I was off anyway today and I can be here first thing tomorrow to help with the rest of the setup."

Yep, he was definitely moving in closer to her. Maybe he was just in a hurry to get out the door and was trying to maneuver her into leaving.

She made a move to grab her purse off the small entry table just as he was reaching for his keys. At least, she *thought* he'd been reaching for his keys. But the moment their fingers brushed, it felt so natural, as though it was what they'd both been intending all along.

His hand clamped down over hers, leaving her purse and all her good judgment out of reach. His grip was firm but not forceful. She was a martial arts expert and could break his hold if she really wanted to. But at this exact second, she didn't.

"I have just one more question, Carmen." Her name on his lips was its own sentence. Its own question.

And her answer was yes. Hell, yes. But she couldn't let him see that. So she held herself perfectly still, her eyes under strict orders from her brain to not meet his. If her pupils went AWOL, then she was in big trouble.

"Since you broke up with that Mark guy who isn't a jerk, do you have any current jerk boyfriends that I should know about?"

Her heartbeat was throbbing so loudly in her ears she wondered if she'd misheard the question. When she didn't answer, Luke used his free hand to lift her chin up so her traitorous eyes were forced to look directly into his. "What do you mean?"

"I was asking if you currently have a boyfriend."

"No." She barely managed to breathe out the word.

"Good. Then nobody will mind when I do this." Luke kept his grip on her hand as he wrapped his arm around her waist, using her own limb as a willing accomplice in anchoring her body to his. The tilt of his head left no question as to what he was going to do next.

After securing her against his body, Luke lowered his lips to hers. He'd already been waiting too damn long to kiss her. And oh, man, were her full, sweet lips worth the wait.

Carmen's fingers twined with his and squeezed his hand. But judging by the fervent pressure of her mouth, she had no intention of backing away.

He angled her jaw so that he could deepen the kiss, but as soon as he opened his lips to begin his assault, her tongue made the first move. She delved deeply inside his mouth, exploring him before he could do the same to her.

He felt her free arm sweep against his shoulder before curving along the back of his neck as she rose up on her toes to meet him. Her cool fingers dipped below the cotton neckline of his shirt and he returned the gesture by skimming his own hand along the waistband of her jeans. He released her other arm and she quickly brought it up and wrapped herself around him, the movement lifting the edge of her sweater and allowing him a strip of access to the smooth, warm skin below.

She made a little mewling sound, which allowed him the chance to overpower her tongue and gain entrance to plunder her depths, to make the same explorations she'd already made. His hands splayed wider, resting just under her rib cage, and he wished he could touch all of her at once.

He wanted to move his hands toward her breasts, to feel the taut nipples that had teased him so badly that day at her house. But her body was pressed up so close against his own he couldn't bring himself to move away from her long enough to do so.

Instead, he slid his hands lower, cupping her bottom as he pulled her against his erection. Her hips moved slightly, as though she was seeking to fit herself over him, and he groaned, moving his lips along her jawline and down her neck.

He wanted to taste more of her. But before he could make it to her collarbone, he heard a musical-like wailing sound in the distance. Carmen took a step back and, though she seemed to be panting just as deeply as he was, she moved to open the door.

"It's just another ice-cream truck," he said, reaching for her waist to pull her back.

"No." She shook her head, as though she could shake off the passion they'd just shared. "That's a police siren. Luke, I've got to go."

"I thought you were off duty today."

"I'm never off duty," she said, grabbing her purse and jogging toward her SUV, still parked in the driveway. Her cell phone was at her ear before she'd even started the engine.

He had to lean on the doorjamb to prop his still-reeling body up, his feet feeling wobbly as they tried to arch over the uneven threshold. At least, he told himself it was because of where he was standing. He wasn't ready to admit that their kiss had practically knocked his legs out from under him.

And judging by her response, she'd been just as affected as him. He'd tried to relax and let her lead in the kiss, but there was something about the normally in-control Carmen Delgado that made Luke want to be in charge. It was probably his sense that he had absolutely no control when it came to her.

Of course, she'd apparently been able to shake it off better—literally—and spring right back into tough-cop mode.

As he watched her taillights disappear down his driveway, he had a flashback to a time when the boys were still crawling. Samantha was taking a video of them on her phone when Luke got a call from his commander and had rushed out of their Coronado apartment.

I'm never off duty.

He'd said those exact same words to Samantha,

who'd yelled back that, just once, he should think about his duty to his family. It had taken a family disaster and a near-death experience, but that duty was now clearer than ever. Just as his desire for Officer Maria Carmen Delgado was now clearer than ever.

Luke stood there in his doorway feeling a lot less guilty than he probably had a right to be. Carmen's abrupt departure was a reminder of all the times he'd done the exact same thing for the exact same reason. He couldn't say he was experiencing a feeling of empathy, because, unlike his wife, he didn't resent Carmen's dangerous job. In fact, a small part of him—that impulsive part he tried to keep locked away—was actually envious of it. That was enough to add to his already burdened complex about all the mistakes he'd made in the past.

Yet, as ashamed as he was to admit it, none of his guilt was because he'd just kissed another woman and felt more grounded than he ever had.

Luke was standing in front of the borrowed grill, a cold bottle of Samuel Adams in his hand, as he talked to his twin brother, Drew.

"You remember any of our birthday parties being this big?" Drew asked.

Luke looked around at all the Sugar Falls residents who had come to celebrate his children turning nine. His yard was a madhouse, but at least with Kylie and Carmen running things, it had the appearance of controlled chaos.

"Nope." Luke shook his head. "Not even the party we had in fourth grade where Mrs. Giddles told us we had to invite everyone in our class. Including the girls."

"That's right. I seem to recall Mom and Dad throwing in the towel after that one. Every year after that, we got to pick one friend to bring with us to play miniature golf."

"Our parents were saints."

"Still are," Drew said before taking a sip of his own beer. "Too bad they couldn't make it today."

Donna and Jerry Gregson were enjoying their well-earned retirement, crisscrossing the United States in their Fleetwood Bounder. "Mom called the other day," Luke said. "I told her about the boys making the Little League all-star team and their first tournament in Rexburg. They said they'll try and make it back in time for that."

"Good. Maybe Kylie and I will make the trip with the girls. It'll give the folks a chance to see all their grandchildren at once."

Luke flipped over the chicken. "Speaking of parents, the boys seem to be adjusting pretty well to having just me around."

"They really have," his brother agreed. And Drew should know. He and Kylie had kept the twins for part of the summer when Luke had been on that last life-changing mission. "I know Kylie wishes she could spend more time with them. Maybe once we get the girls on a better sleep schedule, we can plan to have them over for a night."

"That would be nice. You know I worry about them not having a mother figure in their life."

Drew squeezed his shoulder. "I know. But they have you and you shouldn't be selling yourself short."

"Carmen has been spending a lot of time with them, and that seems to help." Luke felt like he was testing the temperature of something other than the meat on the grill.

"Carmen's great," Drew agreed. "Kylie told me she really helped you pull off this party."

"Party? More like a three-ring circus. But I think Kylie was well aware of what she was doing."

Luke was adding hot dogs to the upper rack and didn't see the quick look of culpability flash across Drew's face. "What do you mean?"

"I mean, your wife rented all these tables and bounce houses and hired that goofy guy in the superhero costume without even telling me because she knew I'd say no. And don't even get me started on that petting zoo in the driveway so that the younger kids would have something to do, too."

Drew let out a breath and Luke, knowing his twin, immediately picked up on his normally relaxed brother's release of tension. Why should he be relieved? Did he think Luke was actually annoyed with his sweet but over-the-top wife?

"Don't get me wrong," Luke defended. "I really do appreciate all her work and how much she loves the boys. I was just saying it was a godsend that she talked Carmen into pinch-hitting for her because I wouldn't have been able to pull this off by myself."

"It's Carmen now, huh?"

"Well, we spent the whole day together yesterday and it's kind of hard not to become friends when you're debating what kind of candy to stuff in the piñatas and how many sets of plastic silverware to buy."

"So you're *just* friends?" Drew arched one golden eyebrow above the rim of his wire-framed glasses.

Dammit. Luke should've known that his psychologist twin knew him better than that. Of course, wasn't that exactly what he'd been counting on when he'd brought up this conversation in the first place? He needed to talk to someone about what had happened between him and the woman who'd set his body into high alert before racing away from his house last night in hot pursuit of justice.

"Okay, here's the deal," Luke said, then leaned in toward his brother. "I sort of…kissed her."

"You *what*?"

Quickly, Luke confided a few of the details that had taken place less than twenty-four hours ago. He kept his voice low, because even though all the other adults seemed to be either gorging themselves on onion dip or chasing the children around the makeshift laser tag zone, this was a small town and he didn't want anyone overhearing him.

"So how'd you feel afterward?" Drew asked when Luke finished speaking.

"How do you think I felt?"

"Not physically, moron. I mean emotionally."

"I felt fine. I guess."

"Come on, Luke. You can do better than that. You have a shrink for a brother. If you want me to psychoanalyze this relationship, you need to give me more than that to go on."

"Who says I want you to psychoanalyze anything, Dr. Annoying?" Luke looked up just in time to see Carmen refilling a huge bowl of chips on one of the food tables. "And who says we're in a relationship?"

A small fire leaped up between the grate and Drew shoved him aside, taking the barbecue tongs from him. "Here, hotshot. Let me get things under control for you. As usual." His brother was used to Luke's impulsive nature and his tendency to fly by the seat of his pants. And he was used to bailing Luke out of trouble when the need arose. So it was a habit to stand by and watch his brother quickly move the meat out of the way of the flames, waiting for Drew to help him make sense of the scorching situation he'd caused last night when he'd kissed Carmen.

"I hate to point out the obvious, Luke," his twin finally said once the heat of the grill returned to normal. "But you're a single man and, as far as I know, Carmen is a single woman. Why can't you guys enter into a mature, consenting relationship like two normal adults?"

"But what about my kids?"

"What about them? I thought it was pretty common knowledge that they're crazy about Carmen and they like having her around."

"Sure they do. But what about when I can't be the kind of man Carmen deserves and we inevitably break up? The twins would be devastated."

"Listen, Luke. I bit my tongue for almost six years because I knew you needed time to grieve for your wife and come to terms with your perceived guilt over her death."

"My guilt isn't perceived." He crossed his arms over his chest and kicked at a pinecone near his foot. "It's very real and very justified. I was never the kind of husband Samantha deserved. I don't want to make that mistake again."

"What do you mean you weren't the kind of husband she deserved? You were you, Luke."

"What kind of psychobabble is that?" Luke asked, then made the mistake of watching Carmen grab an open bottle of wine from the temporary bar set up near the back porch. He really wanted to ask Kylie who had a bar at a children's birthday party, but frankly he needed another beer himself. Besides, if they were going to have a mobile petting zoo, they might as well have some booze to keep all the parents more relaxed.

"It means that you did the best you could," Drew said gently. "Samantha knew you were a SEAL when she met you at that bar in Coronado. She knew you were a SEAL when she got pregnant with the twins and you talked her into marrying you. Anyone who has spent more than five minutes in your company knows where your heart is. You love your boys and you love your family, but up until that point, the Navy and your team were your life. I don't want to speak ill of the dead, but Samantha was well aware of what she was getting into."

"That doesn't mean it was fair that I abandoned her and the boys every time I got called out on an assignment."

"I agree," Drew said. "Being a Navy spouse is a tough life. That's why my department offers classes and workshops and support groups for people in the same position she'd been in. She was fully aware that there was help out there. Hell, I called her once a week to check in and to give her recommendations of places where she could go for assistance. But she chose to deal with your absence and her stress in her own way. It ended up being an unhealthy and fateful way, but that was *her* choice. Luke, being a SEAL did *not* make you a bad husband or a bad father. It made you *you*. When are you going to be done serving your penance for Samantha's death?"

Luke was quiet for a moment. "I don't know. Maybe never. Or maybe I was done last night. Who the hell knows?"

"What do you mean maybe you were done last night?"

"I mean, after I kissed Carmen, I didn't really have any of that guilt I should've felt. It would have been easier if I had."

"So, circling back to my original question, what did you feel after you kissed her?"

"Great," he said. "Happy. Aroused."

"Don't need to hear the last part," his proper brother said, probably wishing his hands were free so he could cover his saintly ears. "What about after she left to go chase bad guys?"

Luke had found out today from Cooper that chasing bad guys actually meant assisting on a call to rescue a group of drunk tourists who'd lost their car in the Snow Creek Lodge parking lot and had no business being behind the wheel, anyway. But he knew that her job was dangerous and someday she might get called out to deal with some pretty dicey situations. He was actually fine with it. No—more than fine. He was pretty impressed.

"I had this weird sense of reverse déjà vu," Luke admitted. "Like I was used to being the one being called out on duty, but now I was experiencing what Samantha must've felt anytime I'd left unexpectedly like that."

"How did you respond to being in that situation for the first time?"

"I didn't respond. How could I? I was proud of Carmen for her dedication to her job and I wasn't about to stand in her way. Maybe a little worried for her, but I wasn't jealous or feeling abandoned. More than anything, I was confused and wanted some reassurance that what had just happened between us wasn't a colossal mistake. But she left without giving me any clue and I can't trust my own instincts when it comes to stuff like this. Then I was too busy thinking about what would happen when I saw her again."

"And now you've seen her again. So how are you feeling about it today?"

"Like I can't wait to kiss her again."

"Then what's stopping you?"

"The fact that she might not want me to. How am I supposed to know what she's thinking?"

"Have you thought about asking her?"

Drew made it sound so simple. Yet, Luke had learned that just because a woman said she was fine with something, didn't mean she was happy about it.

He shrugged. "We haven't had a second alone. She's been pretty good at avoiding me."

Drew grinned. "Well, she isn't avoiding you now. Look alive, brother. She's coming this way."

Chapter Nine

"How much longer do you think the chicken is going to be?" Carmen tried to sound as businesslike as possible when she asked Luke the question.

See. They were just a couple of *friends*. She might argue that today they were coworkers, partnering up together to work on this birthday task force. She'd even responded to his call for backup when Caden had led one of the goats from the petting zoo into the bounce house. "The younger guests are getting restless and their parents need something to soak up all the wine and beer. I was wondering when we should start bringing out some of the side dishes."

She'd been careful to make sure that the only time she'd spoken to him—or gotten within a twelve-foot radius of him—was when there were plenty of witnesses around to stop her from leaping into his arms and picking up right where they'd left off last night. And what better witness than his straight-laced brother, Dr. Gregson, also nicknamed Saint Drew.

"The hot dogs are done now. By the time you get stuff set out, I should have the first batch of chicken ready to go." Luke smiled at her and she searched his expression and his words for any sign of what he was feeling. But he was too used to masking his emotions.

So if he was knee-deep in regret, he'd be extra careful not to give off any sign or show any weakness. Just like her.

"Here, Luke," Drew said, piling the last of the grilled hot dogs onto a tray. "You help Carmen get the food out and I'll bring the chicken over when it's ready. Besides, you should be enjoying the festivities."

Carmen wasn't sure, but she'd thought the doctor had possibly winked at Luke. Her stomach dropped at the implications of what that could mean. Had Luke told his brother what they'd done inside the family cabin last night? That she'd made a fool of herself in his arms, then run off at the first wail of a siren?

Hopefully, Dr. Gregson just had smoke tickling his bespectacled eye, because she would be mortified if anyone from this town suspected she'd been so weak to fall for a couple of harmless kisses. And some arousing caresses. And the feel of his hands on her... Ugh.

She turned to go into the kitchen in order to carry out the bowls and platters of food she'd worked on last night after getting home. The police call she hadn't needed to respond to ended up being a couple of drunk tourists that one of the other officers had easily been able to handle on his own. Her cop instinct had been to rush into the fray. It just so happened that timing wise, her woman-in-over-her-head instinct had been to look for any excuse to get the hell out of Luke's too-intoxicating embrace.

She'd tossed and turned all night thinking about his kiss and the many ways it was going to affect her rapport with the twins once she told Luke that it was best if she didn't spend any more time directly with him. After the way she'd behaved last night, she didn't think she could trust herself around him. A relationship with her was a dead end for any man looking for something permanent. And a man like Luke, who was committed to his family and was hoping for more children, would eventually be relieved in the long run.

By oh two hundred, she'd decided that she'd get through today, focusing on giving Aiden and Caden a memorable birthday party. Then she'd wean herself from their lives. By oh six hundred, she'd given up on any more sleep and had gone into her kitchen to keep herself busy prepping food until it was time to go over to the Gregson cabin.

Luckily, getting the yard decorated and the party set up had kept her and Luke out of each other's way until all the guests arrived. Now she just needed to get through dinner and then she could officially end her shift and save her soul.

Carmen was pulling a pan of baked beans from the oven when she heard the hinges creak on the back screen door. She turned to see Luke standing there in his cargo shorts and polo shirt, looking twice as good as he'd looked last night. Abuela always said, *La fruta prohibida es siempre la mas dulce.* Unfortunately, that woman was usually spot on about recipes and forbidden fruit always being sweeter.

"What can I do to help?" he asked.

"We need to get this and the rest of the side dishes outside." She nodded her head toward the counter loaded down with bowls of potato, macaroni and spinach salads. "Kylie made some sort of coleslaw thing with raisins and marshmallows, but I think she used butter lettuce instead of cabbage so we might want to accidentally forget that in the fridge."

"My sister-in-law isn't exactly known for her skills in the kitchen." Luke grabbed a dish towel and took the hot dish from her hands. She expected him to take it outside, but instead he set it directly down on the kitchen table.

"Actually," she said, not wanting to sound too bossy but needing to get this situation and her battling emotions under control. "I was thinking we should put all the food on the *outside* tables so that people aren't coming in and out of your house."

"I know the food is going outside, Carmen. But right now, I have you *inside*. Alone." Her body, which was in good physical shape for responding to emergency situations, went limp and tense all at once.

"But we need to get people fed," she said, wanting to deter him. When he moved in front of her, she held up her hands as though she could stop him from what she'd secretly been hoping he'd start again.

He looked at the rooster-shaped potholders on her hands before grinning and sliding them off. "Luke," she whispered, even though she doubted anyone else was in the house. "What are you doing?"

"What do you think I'm doing?"

But before his playful lips could get any closer, the back door screeched open. Carmen jumped away from him, backing into the open oven, which was probably less likely to leave a lasting burn than his heated embrace. At least mentally.

"Do you need anything in here?" Kylie said as she walked into the kitchen. "Oh, hey, Luke. I didn't know you were giving Carmen a hand."

He was actually about to give her a lot more than a hand, but Carmen turned to gather the basket full of condiments before the other woman noticed anything was off between the two of them.

"I'd love some help," Carmen said, seizing on the opportunity to put more distance, or at least more obstacles, between her and the man she shouldn't be left alone with. "Luke was just about to start carrying out some of the food, so if you could take a bowl or two outside, that'd be great."

Nobody said a word about the fact that this party and its organization had been Kylie's idea in the first place. After all, this was Kylie's family and, by default, this kitchen should've been her domain. Yet, Luke's sister-in-law seemed willing—actually, eager—to turn over her planning and hostessing role to someone who was a little more than a glorified babysitter.

"Perfect," Kylie said, turning her back to them and opening the refrigerator. "Let me just get my Waldorf coleslaw out of the—oh, no. Why does it look so wilted already?"

Carmen used the distraction to make a fast break toward the back porch.

"We'll finish our conversation later." Luke's whispered words caught Carmen by surprise and she fumbled her grip on the screen door.

She turned to whisper back and her head nearly

collided with Luke's since he was so close behind her. "But we weren't really having a conversation."

"I know." His lips grazed the side of her neck and she almost dropped the ketchup and mustard she'd been balancing in the crook of her arm. She could actually feel the vibration of his laughter against her collarbone. "Here, let me get that for you."

His hand skimmed her waist as he reached in front of her and closed his fingers over hers, helping her release the door latch. A crowd of hungry guests looked up toward them and Carmen walked outside, her legs feeling about as firm as the hot dog buns she was trying to carry in her shaky grip.

"Food's on," Luke announced jovially from behind her.

She deposited the condiments and buns and retreated to the kitchen for more dishes. And maybe that plastic cup of wine she'd poured earlier. She passed Kylie, who was carrying more food and didn't mention the wilted green-and-purple mess Carmen spied dumped into the trash can.

It took several minutes to get her breathing back to normal. By the time the guests had lined up for the buffet-style meal, Alex Russell had taken over on the grill. She wasn't sure where Luke was, but Carmen was glad he was getting a reprieve to enjoy his sons' party since he'd been working so hard on it the past two days.

Freckles, defying both gravity and age, balanced three plates of chicken in one hand as she strutted by wearing bright orange cowboy boots and a halter top to match. "Great party, you two."

You two? Who was...? Carmen felt Luke's palm against her lower back.

"Thanks, Freckles," Luke said, his fingers making a slow small circle before he walked away to tell the children to go wash their hands.

The rest of the evening, Luke made a habit of sneaking up behind Carmen when she was least expecting it, touching her ever so subtly, then taking off seconds later. She prayed that Elaine Marconi, who was holding court near the makeshift bar, hadn't noticed.

But Luke was a master at the hit-and-run displays of affection. A quick caress here, a soft smile there—he'd even refilled her wine cup when she finally took a break to sit and talk with Maxine and Cooper and Mia and Garrett McCormick.

"This is going to be a tough birthday party to top," Maxine said when Luke eventually stayed still long enough to pull out the chair next to Carmen's and take a seat. "I saw one of Mia's dance moms over by the mobile video game trailer asking the face painter if he was available for her daughter's princess party next month.

"You can thank my charming sister-in-law for that," Luke replied, then lifted a cold bottle of beer to his lips. *Stop staring at his lips*, Carmen had to command herself. "I had no idea she was orchestrating all this."

The group of friends all turned to look at the pseudo-carnival that had magically sprung up on Luke's property. He took the opportunity to slide his hand onto Carmen's knee beneath the table.

"Just be thankful my wife told the party-rental people there were only three acres of land here," Drew said. "Do you know that company rents snow-cone booths, inflatable waterslides and human-sized hamster balls?"

Carmen was more thankful that the woman had had the foresight to rent these long green linen tablecloths instead of going with the short plastic ones Luke wanted to buy at the supply store yesterday. Otherwise, everyone would be able to see Luke's hand slowly inching its way up the leg she was praying wouldn't tremble.

"Don't worry, babe," Kylie said to her husband as she fed one of her daughters. "I'm getting plenty of practice for the girls' first birthday."

Drew paled slightly, then recovered and said, "Too bad we don't have the space for all that at our condo. Maybe we'll just have a nice intimate family dinner."

"Don't be silly," Luke chimed in, still not removing his hand from under the table. "This is still Gregson land. You can have the party here. Carmen and I would be happy to help."

Everyone laughed and Carmen tried not to shift in the white plastic folding chair. He made it seem like they were a pair, that they were partners. Even if he'd been sly in the way he'd been touching her all evening, people might already be lumping the two of them together, assuming she would be around for future Gregson family events.

She really needed to get Luke alone to tell him that this birthday party, as well as that kiss last night, was a onetime thing. She needed to convince him that he and the twins were probably better off not getting too close to her. The problem was getting him alone. And then not falling victim to those damn dimples.

* * *

"But, Dad, we don't want to help clean up," Caden told Luke. "Now that everyone's gone, we want to open our presents."

"And have another piece of cake," Aiden whined before shoving a blue lollipop from his piñata treat bag into his mouth.

Luke stood in his almost-empty yard. The party rental company had loaded up and left his property looking like less of a carnival and more an abandoned battlefield. Most of the guests had gone home, with the exception of a few friends who were either collecting remnants of streamers and empty plastic cups or putting his house back to rights.

"See Officer Carmen in the kitchen?" Luke pointed to the window framing her as she washed dishes at the sink and laughed at something one of the other women must've said.

For the first time, Luke realized that his feet hadn't been restless at all today. Sure, they were tired and aching as he'd been standing since seven that morning, but they felt grounded. Seeing Carmen in his home, having her work beside him for a common goal, feeling her eyes on him when she thought no one was looking, felt grounded.

"What about her, Dad?" Aiden interrupted his trailing thoughts.

"Oh, look," Caden yelled before dropping his plastic garbage bag and running toward the driveway. "Uncle Kane's here."

Kane Chatterson pulled up in his old SUV. While the famous baseball pitcher wasn't Luke's brother-in-law exactly, he was Drew's—which made him family and somewhat of an uncle figure to the boys.

The late arrival turned his engine off and grabbed a couple of oversize gift bags from the backseat, causing the boys to shriek and jump up and down over the idea of more presents. Great. At this rate, he'd never get his children to settle down.

Oh, well. They'd probably get more done with the boys out of the way and occupied.

"Good timing." Luke walked up and shook the man's hand. "Did Kylie assign you cleanup duty tonight?"

"Yep. She knows how I feel about avoiding big crowds. Got any beer left?"

"You bet. Come on into the kitchen and we'll get you a plate of food, too. Your sister had me buy enough to feed the crew of an aircraft carrier." What Luke didn't say was thank God Carmen had been there to help him prepare everything, or he'd have been at a complete loss.

Carmen's feet were probably just as tired as his. He thought of the one time he'd seen them bare, her dainty toes with their bright pink polish nervously hustling around on her cottage floor as she brought him and the boys T-shirts to borrow. He would love to send the rest of the cleanup squad home and sit on the sofa with her pretty feet in his lap. He didn't even need her pricey peppermint tree-bark foot cream.

If it were just them, the kids would be in bed and he'd start a fire in the big stone hearth. Maybe put on some of the country music that she enjoyed. His mind started to get lost in the fantasy, but was cut short when he heard the boys let out a whoop at the brand-new bow-and-arrow sets their uncle Kane had just bought for them.

"Can we try them out, Dad? Huh? Can we?"

He shot Kane a look that promised retribution for the irresponsible gift. Even if it did say "beginner" on the packaging.

"Maybe tomorrow. We should probably get inside and open the rest of your presents," Luke said, trying to distract them. "We'll have some more cake while we're at it."

"But I thought you said we had to clean up first, Dad?"

"No bows and arrows tonight, guys." Luke ignored their groans. "Besides, it would hurt everyone else's feelings if you played with Uncle Kane's...uh...gift before you even opened theirs."

"Oh, right. Come on, Caden. Let's go."

He watched them race into the house, Kane helping them carry the arrows that hopefully had somewhat blunted tips. Luke took one last look at his kitchen window just in time to see Carmen step away. The arches of his feet tingled and he had a moment of panic before she came back into view, carrying the empty pan of beans.

Yep. She felt like home.

Maybe Drew was right and he could try again. Maybe he could be the kind of man someone like her would deserve. He heard several raised voices, the zinging sound of a released bowstring and then Kane yelled, "Ow. That was my *good* shoulder."

Man, Luke could barely control his own children. Calling him adequate at being a father would be generous. So who was he to say that he'd be any better at a romantic relationship? He remembered his brother's advice and decided there was only one way to find out. Hopefully, he could do so before his wild little monkeys made up Carmen's mind for her.

Carmen hugged herself, unsure of what to do now that most of the cleanup was finished. The boys sat on the floor, tearing into packages as their uncle Drew tried to keep some semblance of order and Mia Mc-Cormick took notes on which person had brought which gift. Cooper and Maxine were drying dishes, and Kylie had just put the girls down to sleep in their portable crib. Luke was sitting on the sofa, having a beer with Alex Russell, while Kane and Hunter worked on a Lego set that was deemed appropriate for ages fourteen and up. The whole scene was too warm, too intimate, too family for Carmen.

She needed to get out of there.

"Hey, kiddos," she finally said, stepping over bows and strewn pieces of torn wrapping paper. "I'm on duty first thing in the morning, so I've got to get home and get some rest. Happy birthday."

She bent down to place a light kiss on each curly blond head.

"Bye, Officer Carmen. Thanks for helping with our party," Aiden said. Then both boys rose up and gave her three hugs, a gesture she'd recently found out Kylie had established with them to help ease their separation anxiety.

"Yeah, thanks, Officer Carmen. It was our bestest birthday ever." Her heart squeezed at Caden's sweet words. Then it dropped at what he said next. "And don't forget to book your room for the tournament next weekend. Choogie said the team hotel in Rexburg will be sold out and if you don't make your reservation, you'll have to stay at the Big Horse Motel down the street. And that one's haunted."

"It's not haunted," Alex said, and all the other adults agreed. "I told you not to listen to Choogie Nguyen. There's no such thing as ghost horses."

"Still, I wouldn't want to stay there and find out," Caden said, sitting back down with his brother and tearing into a gift bag.

"If you can't get a room at the not-haunted hotel, then you could just stay in our room with us," Aiden suggested.

No. She was not staying in a hotel room with them and their father. She rolled her eyes. She wasn't even going to Rexburg in the first place. "Sorry, boys, but I won't be able to make it next weekend."

"But, Officer Carmen, the big tournament starts on Saturday and you've *gotta* go with us. You're our good luck charm. The whole team needs you."

"You guys are great players and you'll try your hardest," Carmen explained. "You don't need me or any luck for that."

The room grew quiet and several Legos fell on the hardwood floor. Actually, Carmen wasn't entirely sure which happened first. But everyone in the room stopped talking, stopped what they were doing and stared at her. Even the twins paused their unwrapping midpresent. "What's wrong? Why's everyone staring at me as if I'm standing on a buried land mine?"

Her answer came from the notoriously quiet Kane Chatterson, who apparently was the only one willing to explain. "You know, Officer Delgado, baseball players are very superstitious. We don't take luck lightly."

They couldn't be serious. She looked around the room. "So you all believe in a person as a good luck charm, but you don't believe in ghost horses?"

Why were they looking at her as though she were the crazy one?

"I can't rightly attest to the goings-on at the Big Horse Motel," Kane continued, speaking for the group. "But I do know baseball. And if the boys and the team think you're good luck, then you are."

"But I'm on duty next weekend," she argued, and saw Luke flinch. What was that about? He couldn't possibly believe his children wouldn't win their game if she wasn't there. Could he?

"Actually," Cooper called out from the kitchen. "You're off on Saturday, and Washington can probably cover your shift on Sunday. Plus, Hunter's team doesn't play until the following weekend, so I'll be on duty while you're gone. The department's got things handled."

Now her boss was assuming she'd just up and leave town for some Little League all-star game? This was utter nonsense. The more she tried to protest, the more everyone insisted she be there. If she argued any more, it would look suspicious. But it wasn't like she could state the real reason she should stay in Sugar Falls.

In fact, she looked straight at that reason, whose eager, smiling expression matched his children's. She really needed to learn how to say no to that ridiculous Gregson dimple.

"Fine. I'll go." The boys cheered while the rest of the room seemed to let out a collective breath. "But I'm getting my own room."

Chapter Ten

Carmen cut off Tim McGraw midchorus as she lowered the volume of her satellite radio and exited the highway. She'd been raised a big-city girl and, being a cop, she had a pretty good sense of direction. Still, she'd never ventured too far from Sugar Falls and Boise since moving to Idaho and she wanted to concentrate on where she was driving.

God forbid the good luck charm get lost on her way to the baseball tournament.

Several times this week, the twins had tried to talk her into riding with them and their father to Rexburg. But there was no way, no how, Carmen was allowing herself to be at the mercy of those Gregson males for nearly four hours.

In fact, she'd purposely waited to book a room and was checking last minute prices online for the so-called haunted motel, when Kylie had texted her last night to say she and Drew had to cancel at the last minute because one of the girls had come down with an ear infection. Kylie said the team hotel was booked up, but she could transfer over their reservation. In fact, Kylie had already taken the liberty of calling the hotel and giving them Carmen's name.

She thought some people were going a little overboard in the name of luck for a kids' recreational sports team. But at least Carmen didn't have to share a room with a horse's ghost. Or Luke Gregson. She honestly didn't know which option was less scary.

Probably the former.

After leaving her house at oh six hundred and making two rest stops along the way—damn her weak bladder—Carmen stepped up to the check-in desk at the Springhill Suites with only a few minutes to spare before heading to the ball fields for the first game of a doubleheader.

The lobby was overcrowded with kids wearing ball caps and assorted team jerseys along with the haggard-looking parents who were their chauffeurs, chaperones and cheering sections all in one. Which must've been why she'd had a difficult time hearing the desk clerk explain that there was a notation on her reservation.

"Yoo-hoo, Officer Delgado." Elaine Marconi waved from the other end of the counter. "I barely recognized you in regular clothes. What are you doing here in Rexburg?"

"Just taking in some baseball." Carmen smiled tightly at the woman, not wanting to explain anything else to the town gossip. Then she looked at the clerk, trying to convey her sense of urgency with her eyes as she slid her credit card across the counter. "I'll just take my room key, please."

"Of course, Ms. Delgado. But, as I was explaining, it seems Mr. Gregson has already checked in for you and prepaid for the room. So we won't be needing this." He slid her credit card back toward her.

"Oh, you're here with Luke Gregson." Elaine's magenta-painted lips smirked in a knowing smile.

Had that smug busybody just winked at her? "Oh, no. It's not like that," Carmen tried to explain, but Elaine was busy tapping something into her phone.

"You're in room two-oh-four." The desk clerk handed her a key card. "Your room is adjoining Mr. Gregson's."

Of course, Mrs. Marconi would look up just in time to hear *that* juicy bit of information.

Ugh. Carmen didn't owe this woman or anyone else an explanation. Her head was already pounding and she had a difficult enough time justifying to herself what she was doing at some youth baseball tournament miles away from home.

Besides, she barely had enough time to drop off her suitcase and drive over to the fields if she didn't want all twelve players on the Sugar Falls Comets to blame her for costing them the win.

Her brain hurt, but she managed a pleasant smile as she took the room key and wheeled her small bag toward the elevator as quickly as she could.

By the time she found a parking spot at the crowded park, the boys' team was already taking the field. She scoped out the bleachers and saw the only spot open was next to a woman wearing a pink straw cowboy hat sitting next to an older, shorter version of Luke and Drew Gregson.

No. This couldn't be happening.

"Excuse me." Mrs. Pink Hat waved her fingers to get Carmen's attention. "By any chance are you Officer Carmen?"

With the stands full of fans and parents there to cheer on the team from Sugar Falls, it would've been hard for Carmen to deny it. So she forced herself to smile and nod.

"Here." The woman Carmen suspected was Mrs. Gregson gave her husband a friendly push to make more room. "We've been saving you a seat."

"Hey, Officer Carmen," the shortstop yelled across the field, causing all the players, coaches and spectators to look her way. "My Grammie saved you a seat right next to her and Pop Pop."

If Elaine Marconi hadn't effectively spread the word by now, Aiden or Caden—she couldn't tell which from this distance—had just announced to everyone that Carmen was, in fact, there with the Gregsons.

Like one big happy family.

Coach Alex had repeatedly told the entire team to stay focused on the game. But apparently, Luke wasn't taking those instructions to heart, because he kept peeking over at Carmen when he should have been signaling runners from third base.

He'd seen her several times around town this week, but she'd been working and he hadn't wanted to bother her when she was on duty. Plus, he liked standing back and watching her in her police uniform, all stiff blue polyester and black gear and duty belt. He liked knowing that underneath the bulletproof vest and mirrored sunglasses was a sexy, passionate woman whose skin smelled like gardenias and whose hair smelled like Moroccan oil—whatever that was.

Thanks to the twins, he had her cell phone number programmed in his phone and he could've texted her after the birthday party. But he didn't want to scare her off by coming on too strong. He'd been well aware of her stiff control every time he'd touched her that evening, but he hadn't been able to have her so close and not put his hands on her. He could understand that she probably didn't want everyone to know that their relationship had accelerated directly past the friendship zone and was careening straight toward the romantic expressway.

Luke had been honest with her the other day. His life really was an open book and maybe it was his impulsive and reckless nature, but he didn't like hiding the fact that he was more than attracted to Carmen. The problem was that he couldn't risk a potentially bad outcome, especially publicly.

Again.

At least the twins had been too young to understand what had happened in their parent's marriage or the fact that their father's lack of insight drove their mother into another man's arms. Now, though, the boys were older and would be smart enough to blame him if—or probably when—he messed things up for them.

Even if he'd been willing to listen to Drew's tough-love campaign about him not being the only one at fault, Luke had been lost and racked with guilt for so long, it was instinctive for him to question his judgment about any decision that had to do with his children. And acting on his attraction to Carmen was definitely something that would affect his kids. If he was wrong about where things were heading with her, his selfishness might cause the boys to lose another important woman in their lives.

Which was why it would be easier to avoid any thoughts of a future with Carmen altogether. Unfortunately, judging by the way his mom and dad were yapping in her ear up there in the bleachers, other people were definitely taking an interest in the direction of their relationship, as well.

The team won and the boys had a forty-five minute break to grab a bite to eat before the second game started. Luke was pleased to see that his children ran straight to greet Carmen instead of following the rest of the team to the snack bar. Given the choice between her warm smile and welcoming hug or the standard baseball fare of hot dogs and nachos, he couldn't blame them.

"Did you see the home run I hit, Officer Carmen?" Aiden asked, bouncing up and down on his cleats.

"How about when I got that guy out at third base?" Caden said around a wad of chewing gum. "Did you see *that*?"

"I saw it all, kiddos," Carmen said, then tweaked both their hats. "I was sitting right by Donna and Jerry the whole time."

"You mean Grammie and Pop Pop?" Aiden took both of his grandparents' hands, pulling them toward the snack bar. "They don't like it when we call them Donna and Jerry."

"No, young man," Luke's mom said. "We don't like it when eight—I mean, nine-year-old boys call us by our first names. But Officer Carmen can call us whatever she likes as long as she keeps being your good luck charm."

"No pressure there," Luke thought he heard Carmen mumble.

"See, Officer Carmen." Caden stepped between Luke and Carmen and took them by the hand so they could follow the others. "Everyone knows about your good luckiness. But speaking of nine-year-old boys, Grammie, did you guys maybe remember our birthday just happened last week?"

Luke smiled at Carmen as his parents explained to the children that their birthday presents were still inside the RV, which was parked back at the hotel.

A familiar organ song sounded from the parking lot behind them and Caden squeezed their fingers. "Can we go get something from the ice-cream truck?"

"Sure," Luke said. "But, first, you need to eat something healthy for lunch." Although Luke wasn't seeing many healthy options displayed on the menu board outside the snack bar.

"Okay then, you guys stay here and order us something healthy." Caden put Carmen's hand, which he'd still been holding, into Luke's palm. "Me and Aiden will go get our ice creams before the truck leaves."

With that, the twins took off, leaving Luke and Carmen standing there, linked together.

"Oh, look." Donna Gregson pointed to a food truck that had been set up in the parking lot. "They're selling street tacos. Let's go get those, instead. Jerry and I haven't had any good Mexican food since we left Arizona."

Luke kept Carmen's hand in his own as they followed his parents toward the taco vendor. He'd just spent almost two hours in a dugout with a bunch of rowdy preadolescent boys telling knock-knock jokes and staging a belching contest between innings. If he had to listen to his parents talk about all the roadside diners they'd hit along their travels, then at least Carmen could provide him with a physical distraction.

"So, what's the plan for the rest of the day," Jerry Gregson asked from his spot in line in front of them.

Carmen tried to pull her hand away, but Luke kept his grip firm. "It's a single elimination tournament, so they play again this afternoon. If they win that one, they play again tomorrow morning. The championship game is that same afternoon, but I don't think our team will make it that far. The kids from Sun Valley are pretty good this year."

Luke's mom ordered, then turned back to Carmen. "What are you having, dear?"

"Oh, you don't have to order for me, Mrs. Gregson." At his mom's frown, Carmen corrected herself. "I mean Donna. I can get my own lunch."

"Nonsense. You drove all this way and, from what I understand, you've been great with our grandchildren these past few months. The least Jerry and I can do is buy lunch for—" his mom looked down at their linked hands "—Luke's special friend."

She tried to pull her hand away again, but Luke wasn't having any of it. So, instead, she used his own hand to add momentum as she shoved against his hip.

But Luke didn't budge. "Carmen will have the carnitas, Mom. Extra salsa."

Carmen shoved at him again and twitched her head in the direction of his parents, who were now talking to the woman behind the cash register. He could mentally give himself orders all day long about the inappropriateness of his attraction to her, but it was another thing to make his body obey.

"What?" Luke flashed her a smile, trying to look innocent. "You like things spicy."

"I'm not talking about the salsa, Luke. I'm talking about you paying for my hotel room and now your mom and Elaine Marconi and everyone else back home thinking that we're *special friends*."

He had a feeling that if her fingers hadn't been wedged tightly between his, she would've used air quotes on that last part. "But I thought we *were* friends. And what does Elaine Marconi have to do with anything?"

"She saw me at the hotel and overheard the desk clerk say that you'd already paid for my room."

"I didn't pay for your room. Up until last night, I didn't even know where you were staying. You've been avoiding me all week, remember?"

"I haven't been avoiding you, I've been working. And what do you mean you didn't pay for my room? He clearly said 'Mr. Gregson.' If you don't believe me, ask Elaine. I'm sure she's already telling everyone back in Sugar Falls about it."

"Um, did you ever consider that the *other* Mr. Gregson paid for your room?" Luke asked.

"Your dad?" She squinted her eyes at his father, who was doing a remarkable job of butchering the Spanish language while placing his order. "Why would he pay for it?"

"No, not my dad. My brother, Drew. It was his and Kylie's room originally, remember? He called me last night to say that they couldn't come and were giving you their reservation."

"Oh." Some of the heat left her eyes. "I didn't even think of that."

"Really? And here I thought you were some elite cop with your sexy sunglasses, your tight bun and those fancy interrogation techniques you've been trying to teach me. By the way, I like your hair like this much better."

He reached out his finger and stroked one of the glossy black curls. She jerked her head away, but not before he saw the pink blush streak across her cheeks.

"I know you're teasing me, and normally my investigation skills really are top-notch. But you make it hard for me to think with all your dimpling and high-handedness and...oof." She cut off as he pulled her in closer and wrapped his hand around her waist.

He brought his head down to hers, wanting to show her exactly how high and how low his handedness could reach.

"Two carnitas tacos. Extra salsa," his mother interrupted loudly. Then she lowered her voice and winked before saying, "Save the mushy stuff for later, you two. We're at a family event here."

"This one," his dad said to Carmen, while pointing at Luke, "gets his moves from his old man." Jerry Gregson then spun his wife toward him and dipped her into his arms, extra salsa and all, before planting a big kiss on her laughing lips.

That was what Luke had grown up with. That was the kind of easy, lighthearted relationship he'd always wanted for himself. But seeing Carmen's forced smile, feeling her suddenly tense up against him... It was beginning to occur to him that his instincts had been wrong again. And that maybe she didn't want the same things. Or at least, not with someone like him.

That evening, Carmen sat next to Luke on the wooden bench in the pizza parlor, her appetite slowly returning to compete with her building frustration at the man for being so damn sexy and funny. The team had stopped for dinner on the way back to the hotel and there was no sense in her going hungry all alone in her prepaid hotel room.

She'd finally convinced herself to just have a slice of the sausage-and-mushroom pie, maybe even loosen up enough to allow herself to relax and enjoy Luke's playfulness and close proximity.

Temporarily.

Yet, now that she'd ordered herself not to fight it, she could sense that something was off. Luke's arm was touching hers, but he hadn't been as blatantly affectionate since that stunt he'd pulled earlier today.

Maybe the fun for him was in sneaking the touches and kisses and whatnot—like he was getting away with something or trying to get her rattled. If he was anything like his offspring—and she was quickly realizing that he was—the man had a penchant for getting himself into borderline mischievous situations. But now that the nonsecret was out of the bag, perhaps the game for him was over.

Carmen had known plenty of men who were only interested in the chase. While Luke seemed comfortable flirting with her, the fact remained that he was still not over his late wife. Maybe he was having some guilt over this make-believe one-big-happy-family situation he'd gotten himself into.

"Dad, did you pack our swimsuits?" Caden yelled, popping his curly blond head out of the arcade room.

"I sure did, Caden." Luke smiled at his son and Carmen forgot about relaxing. Who could relax when seeing the man's dimples felt like the carbonation from her soda was bubbling around in her chest? "Remember, you reminded me about eight times?

"The kids have been talking about the hotel's indoor pool all day," Luke said, finally breaking the awkward silence between them. Was he trying to make small talk?

"I know," she replied, remembering the message she'd gotten from Luke's cell phone, which turned out not to be from Luke at all. "Aiden texted me on Wednesday telling me to pack my own bathing suit." And she had, because, sure, she liked a good swim. And up until now, she'd done whatever the sweet boys had asked. But that was before everyone suspected that she and Luke were involved.

"I really need to figure out a way to keep those boys away from other people's phones."

Was he annoyed that his kids were talking to her more regularly and had invited her on this trip? She sat up straighter. Or maybe he just wanted her opinion on how to establish better boundaries. If so, he was talking to the wrong person.

She watched the other parents round up their children to leave the restaurant and go back to the hotel for the night. Despite working in a male-dominated occupation for years, she'd never felt so out of place as she did now. She was used to being the one in charge, the one making the commands, yet seeing the moms wiping pizza-smeared faces and herding kids wired on soda and video games, Maria Carmen Delgado was at a complete loss.

She felt like a fraud. She wasn't a mom, and she never would be. She shouldn't be playing up some happy little family role or pretending that things could continue on like this.

In fact, at some point this weekend, she needed a one-on-one with Luke to explain to him that *nothing* was happening between them. Well, technically, something had already happened, but it needed to stop there. They weren't in a relationship; nor was she planning to enter into one with him.

No matter how stinking adorable he was when he lifted up his sons, one in each muscular arm, and carried their giggling little bodies out of the restaurant and toward the parking lot.

"Can we ride back to the hotel with you, Officer Carmen?" the boys begged in unison, and all her tough resolve melted like the mozzarella cheese they'd all just consumed.

"If it's okay with your father," she said, wanting to make the point that she wasn't their parent. She didn't get to make these kinds of decisions about them, no matter how much she might want to.

"Make sure you wear your seat belts," Luke said. And don't ask her to stop at that ice-cream parlor we passed on the way here."

Carmen loaded the boys into her SUV and, as she pulled onto the main road, she saw that Luke followed in the Nanamobile with his parents. Which made it impossible to give in to the twin's requests for ice cream without getting busted.

After their failed attempts, Caden switched tactics. "So, when we get to our rooms, Officer Carmen, you go get your swimsuit on and we'll give you the secret knock to let you know we're ready."

The secret knock? "What secret knock?"

"Like this." Aiden demonstrated four quick raps on the window, followed by two bangs, then a tapping of fingers.

"Oh, of course. *That* secret knock. Actually, boys, I'm pretty tired from the long drive today. I think I'm going to skip the pool and just go to bed."

"But how can you be tired, Officer Carmen?" Aiden asked. "You didn't even hafta play baseball today. You just got to sit there and watch us do all the work."

"I'll have you both know that being a good luck charm requires a lot of focus and concentration." And nerves of steel to be questioned so thoroughly by Donna Gregson during the second ball game. The woman could teach a training class at the Military Police School. "I wasn't able to use the restroom or get up and walk around at all for fear you guys might lose the lead. That's a lot of work, you know."

The boys conferred in the backseat. "Maybe you're right. In that case, you should come with us to the pool and sit in the hot tub. Choogie Nguyen said we have to be fourteen to go in the hot tub because it's for adults only who want to relax."

"Oh, you guys. I think my room will be more relaxing than the pool."

More nine-year-old whispers.

"All right then, Officer Carmen. We'll just skip the

pool and come hang out with you in your room so we can *all* relax. Together. We have a big game tomorrow and need to be ready for it."

"We found the pay-per-view channel and Dad said we couldn't get the new space robots movie because it would give him nightmares. But maybe if we open that door between our rooms, we can come watch it in yours. If Dad hears it and gets scared, we'll tell him you're there to protect us. It'll be like having a sleepover. But with a gun. You *did* bring your gun, didn't you, Officer Carmen?"

Suddenly, her evening plans were sounding about as relaxing as a nighttime airstrike in the Afghani desert.

She steered her car into the hotel parking lot and saw—or rather heard—Luke pull into the space alongside her. He really needed to get that muffler checked—it was roaring so loud she needed earplugs. "You know what, kiddos. Let's just go to the pool, after all. I think your friend Choogie is right about the hot tub being more relaxing."

She wasn't sure, but the smacking sound she heard coming from her backseat sounded suspiciously like a high five. But before she could chastise the two little manipulators, they swung her door open, banging it into the side of the Nanamobile. She cringed, but figured the sturdy vehicle wouldn't be affected much.

"Easy there, monkey," Luke said to his son, who was already running with his brother toward the hotel entrance. He examined Carmen's back passenger door for dings. "I don't think there's any dents. You want to come over here and have a look?"

No. No, she absolutely did not want to stand that

close to Luke and have a look at anything. Especially not the way the dim orange glow from the parking lot lighting made him look even more golden, if that was possible—like a damn sexy golden angel, when she knew her thoughts about him were anything but angelic.

"I'm sure it's fine," she said, then coughed to clear the raspiness from her throat. "Besides, the twins are over there pushing a couple of their teammates into the lobby on the luggage cart. You better go after them."

She watched Luke sprint and dodge several cars to catch up with his sons. It would've been comical if she hadn't been transfixed by the muscular definition in his legs as he ran.

Instead of teaching a kickboxing class, she should've specialized in yoga; maybe that way she would've learned how to take more calming breaths. As it was, Carmen took her time walking and breathing and trying not to think of the man who set her pulse racing one minute and her brain skidding to a stop the next.

She made it to her room just in time to overhear Luke chastising the twins from next door. His firm voice promised that if there were any more shenanigans, they wouldn't be going swimming tonight. Not that she wanted the boys to be in trouble, but she'd honestly been hoping for a slight reprieve.

This was fast becoming the uncomfortable day that would never end. Even in her most depressed days of painful recuperation from her hysterectomy, she hadn't been this emotionally miserable, knowing her life was changing for the worse.

She massaged the scar tissue below her belly button. Hey. Maybe that was what she should do. Carmen looked at the two-piece bathing suit she'd thrown into her suitcase at the last minute. When she'd packed early this morning, her tired brain had instructed her hand to just grab the first thing available. She'd recalled Aiden's text to pack a swimsuit and she'd grabbed both of hers, not planning to participate in any group activities besides attending the games.

Yet, now she needed to decide. Should she wear the functional one-piece and cover up her scars? Or should she put it all out there and let Luke—and everyone else—see what she'd been hiding for far too long?

Carmen knew when to retreat—and when to draw her battle lines.

Hearing the anxious chatter next door, she realized the clock was ticking. She wiggled into the suit and paused to look at herself in the bathroom mirror. At least she'd been somewhat modest when she'd originally purchased the two-piece, back when she and Mark had been planning their first vacation together. The bottoms provided plenty of coverage and the halter top kept the girls firmly in place. The only thing the bathing suit actually revealed was her abdomen.

Rap, rap, rap, rap. Bang, bang. Tap, tap, tap, tap.

The designated knock sounded on the adjoining door, but she refused to open it. That thin plywood barrier was her last line of defense from the intimacy of the Gregson family, and she wasn't about to give it up.

"I'll meet you guys in the hallway," she called out before grabbing a cotton sundress she'd packed as an impromptu cover-up.

When Carmen walked out of her room, she tried

not to stare at Luke's board shorts, the same ones he'd been wearing when she'd helped pull them out of the river by her cottage. Instead, she and Luke followed the two boys as they bounced off the hallway walls all the way downstairs to the indoor pool.

She looked at the clock on the wall. It was almost eight o'clock and the small pool was filled to near capacity with shouting children doing cannonballs, shooting water guns and splashing each other silly.

She offered to get them towels and was setting all their belongings on an empty chaise longue when the boys made a mad dash into the overcrowded pool. Deliberately turning her back to Luke, she took off her dress, though she could feel his eyes on her when she finally, slowly turned around.

This was it. The moment of truth.

Chapter Eleven

Thankfully, the whirlpool was nearly empty, hosting only a pair of goggles, a few toddler toys and an abandoned water wing. Luke whistled through his teeth as he dipped a toe into the heated water. No wonder the kids were avoiding this particular location. Well, that and the big sign posted on the wall that read Adults Only.

He had already stripped off his shirt and was soaking in the hot tub when he saw Carmen pull her dress over her head. Thankfully, he was halfway submerged under water because he couldn't control his body's reaction to her curves.

He'd known plenty of beautiful women, including his wife. But there was something different about Carmen. She was strong, athletic and capable of probably anything. Was there anything more alluring than that?

She walked toward Luke, her gaze locked straight

on his, and it felt like she was moving just for him, just to gauge his reaction to her perfectly proportioned and very female shape. Luke was so overwhelmed with desire he couldn't even manage to smile.

Boing. A wet plastic football hit him right in the temple.

"Sorry, Captain Gregson," Choogie Nguyen, the know-it-all teammate, said as he ran over to retrieve the ball. The twins were right behind him.

"Wow, Officer Carmen, you got a lot of lines on your tummy," Caden said when he plopped his little wet body on the cement by them.

Prompted by his son's comment, Luke allowed his eyes to roam across Carmen's body. He spotted a few scars on her lower abdomen. Those were probably nasty wounds at one point. Still, that didn't make his son's rude observation okay.

Luke touched the boy's shoulder in gentle reproach. "Caden, you're being very impolite."

"No, that's okay," Carmen said. "He's just being observant. You're right, kiddo. I *do* have a lot of lines on my tummy. They're scars."

"Lemme see," Aiden said, jostling in beside his brother.

Carmen stood on the second step of the hot tub, allowing his brashly curious children to look at her.

"How'd you get them?"

"When I was a police officer in Las Vegas, a very bad man didn't want me to arrest him. So he stabbed me."

"Oh, cool," Choogie said.

"Actually, it wasn't cool at the time. It hurt very badly."

"Did you shoot the bad guy dead?" Caden wanted to know.

"No," Carmen said patiently. She was clearly uncomfortable talking about this, yet she wore a brave face for his children. Luke should've stopped the questions, but, like his boys, he was just as curious. "I wrestled his knife away."

"While you were bleeding?" All three pairs of nine-year-old eyes were wide open, starstruck.

Carmen nodded. "That's my job."

"You're pretty tough for a girl," Choogie said.

"She's pretty tough for anyone," Luke corrected. "Okay, you guys. Give Officer Carmen some space and let her relax."

He waved the kids off, laughing as they tried to outdo each other's belly flops into the pool. Luke turned back to Carmen, who had put on her Officer Controlling mask again as she sank into the jet bubbles. He noticed she did it whenever she didn't want to be asked any personal questions.

Or maybe she did it because she wanted to express to him in no uncertain terms that she was off-limits. He'd been out of practice too long so it was possible he'd misread her patience for attraction. It could also be that she'd spent enough time with the wild monkeys he called children and decided she wanted nothing to do with the three-for-one package deal.

Before, he'd thought her aloofness was simply because she was reserved, and he'd been careful but playful with his displays of affection. Yet, this afternoon, he'd taken a step back, like Drew always cautioned him to do, and tried to see things more rationally.

Up until recently, Luke had doubted that he'd ever get over his perceived role in Samantha's death. But in the dark recesses of his mind—where he'd pushed back the possibility of finding someone to share his life with—he knew that he couldn't be with a woman who didn't love his children as much as he did. He was pretty sure Carmen loved the boys. After all, nobody could fake that kind of patience and tolerance for their antics.

Which brought him back full circle. If it wasn't the twins, it must be him.

He hated to give up so easily, to abandon a mission once he'd taken it on. But he wasn't going to force Carmen into a relationship or anything else she so clearly wasn't comfortable with.

So it looked like he needed to tamp down his impulsiveness. Get used to this whole friends idea she'd suggested that day they went shopping. Being friends was better than nothing.

Not wanting to stare at her, he tried to focus on his surroundings. The room housing this indoor pool was packed and had acoustics that must be echoing the shrieking and splashing kids throughout the rest of the hotel. Yet, the silence between the two of them was deafening.

"It's been a long day," Luke said, wanting to make small talk. Or any kind of talk.

"It really has," she answered. But instead of looking relaxed, she looked more keyed up than she had all day. In fact, she looked like she was on high alert.

"You look as if you're waiting for a criminal to burst in and burglarize the swimming area."

"I think a burglar would take one peek inside this

madhouse and start running." She nodded toward a group of kids staging a chicken fight of UFC proportions.

"Boys," Luke yelled when he saw what was going on in the shallow end. "No wrestling in the pool. It's dangerous."

When they leaped out of the water to chase one of their teammates, Carmen added, "And no running."

He watched the boys slow down to a speed walk, not surprised that they were quick to obey her directions. "They respond really well to you."

"They're good kids. They have good hearts."

He wanted to tell her that he had a good heart, too. But so what? Other than that, he didn't have much to offer a woman.

"They've gotten really close to you," he said.

"I know." She sighed. Was that a good sigh or a bad sigh? Luke couldn't tell. "I worry that maybe we've gotten too attached to each other."

"We? You mean you and me?"

"Actually, I was talking about me and the kids," she said, making his chest sink like the toy anchor at the bottom of the hot tub. "Listen, Luke. I really need to tell you something. To explain why—"

"Hold that thought," Luke interrupted, seeing his mom waving at him from the doorway. Carmen whipped her head around, the black curls piled on top of her head threatening to spill into the water. "The boys are sleeping in the RV with my parents tonight and I need to get them out and dried off before Mom and Dad change their minds."

She held her mouth in a tiny O of surprise. And if he wasn't sure where her conversation had been headed, he would've been tempted to kiss the surprise right off her lips. But he really did need to get his kids out of here before Carmen delivered her big thanks-but-no-thanks speech, which would end up breaking more than one Gregson heart.

"Give me two minutes," he said, rising out of the water. "Then we can finish talking about this."

Carmen followed Luke to where they'd left their dry stuff, trying not to stare at the way the droplets of water trailed down to the back of his narrow waist.

Not that she wanted to have this conversation in front of the children, but she'd liked the idea of having them nearby as sort of an added buffer in case they needed a quick change of topic. Or in case Luke smiled at her and made her rethink this whole exit strategy.

She grabbed a towel, unable to stave off the chill that had entered her well before she'd exited the hot tub.

"You know what," she said, pulling her cotton dress on over her wet bathing suit. "We can talk tomorrow. I'm just going to head back to my room now, anyway."

"Chicken," Luke whispered as the boys came running over to get their towels.

"See you tomorrow morning, Dad," they said, giving him three hugs. Then they turned to Carmen, pressing their wet bodies against her and counted out three hugs for her, as well.

Aiden and Caden were all the way to the door and walking out with their grandmother before Carmen could ask Luke to repeat what he'd just said.

"I called you a chicken," he said. The childish flapping of his pretend wings only served to draw her attention to the rest of his very adult and very real body.

"You think I'm scared of something, Gregson?" She shoved her toes into her flip-flops, the force of one foot causing the sandal to flip over. So much for a smooth exit strategy.

"I think that when you use my last name, you're scared. Or pissed. Or maybe both."

She looked around at the other parents and children still frolicking in the pool well past closing time. She was not about to do this right here.

"Fine. You want to talk, let's go talk." She finally got her shoe on and strode to the glass doors, not waiting to see if he'd follow. Or looking down at the damp towel directly in her path. She stumbled and was somewhat surprised that he was close enough to wrap his arm around her and pull her up against him.

Dammit. Why was he always doing that? The only secure thing she liked around her waist was her gun belt.

"Your room or mine?" Luke asked when they got into the hotel hallway leading toward the elevator.

"What?" She pulled back and jerked her head in his direction. The guy couldn't be serious. Did he really think she was about to jump into bed with him?

"You know that conversation you started and then changed your mind about when you got scared?" he asked. "I'm guessing that you don't want to give me the brush-off in front of a lobby full of witnesses. So whose room do you want to talk in? Mine or yours?"

She couldn't really see how he could call it a brush-off when nothing had really started between them in the first place. At least not yet. But the fact that he was thinking about them in terms of a potential relationship made her more determined to put an end to things before he got his expectations up.

"I guess we should go back to your room," she said, right as the elevator door opened to reveal Elaine Marconi carrying an ice bucket and a smile of delight at what she'd just overheard.

"No kids?" Elaine asked, then giggled. "Have a fun night, you two."

Luke smiled at the smug woman before she did a knowing finger wave and toddled off toward where a few of the other moms were sitting in the lobby with a couple of open bottles of wine.

Ugh. Carmen stepped into the elevator and tried to push the door-close button before Luke was even inside.

"Why'd you dimple her?" she asked, hating the accusing tone in her voice.

"Why did I *what* her?"

"Dimple. You dimpled her."

"What in the heck does that mean?"

"You smile with those cute, sneaky dimples anytime you're trying to get out of trouble or act all innocent. I saw you do it with Nurse Dunn a couple of weeks ago when Caden faked sick to get out of his spelling test and she told you he'd need a doctor's note saying he didn't have poison oak before he would be allowed to return to class. And you do it to me every chance you get."

"I can't help it," Luke said. "It's reflexive. Probably because I get into trouble a lot." His eyes looked down at the two wet triangle shapes outlined on her dress. "Does it work?"

"Only on women who don't know any better." The elevator doors dinged open and she walked out.

"And you know better?" he said, catching up to her and pulling his room key out of the hidden pocket in his board shorts.

She really needed to stop looking at him and the way the thin, damp material rode so low on his hips. *You're a cop, Delgado. Toughen up.* "It's my job to know trouble when I see it."

He slid his key in the electronic lock and she glanced next door, thinking it wasn't too late to avoid this whole thing and go straight to her own room.

But, like she'd told herself earlier, she wasn't a coward. Still, this was scarier than serving an arrest warrant at a gun show. She was trained in tactical procedures, but no amount of training could keep her heart from being blasted apart.

She followed him into his suite, only to be hit with an icy blast of air-conditioning. "Man, I told those boys not to mess with the A/C unit this morning," Luke said as he walked over and fiddled with the small control panel on the wall. "They think anything with a display screen is as much fun as an arcade game. I guess I should've reset the timer when we came back to get changed for the pool."

When he turned back to her, she could see that his bare torso was covered in gooseflesh, his dark pink nipples as tight as her own. And, apparently, despite the layers of wet fabric she was wearing, he could see the same thing.

Luke took a step toward her. Then another. She recognized the desire in his eyes because it probably mirrored her own. Carmen's back was now pressed against the wall, literally and figuratively.

"I can't have kids." Carmen heard the words but had no idea why she'd blurted them out. It must've been the safest thing she could think to say.

"What?" Luke froze, then shook his head, as though he could shake off her poorly timed admission. She would almost have laughed at the expression on his face if the whole situation hadn't been so sadly disappointing. He sure wasn't dimpling her now.

She decided to take advantage of his confusion and gain the upper hand. "I said I can't have kids."

"I know what you said." Even though his ears had apparently heard it, his eyes were asking *why* she'd said it in the first place.

"You know my scars?" she asked, trying to start over.

"What scars?"

"The ones I just showed you by the pool?" She waited for some sort of acknowledgment, but he just stood there, looking baffled.

Although, in his defense, she'd just blindsided him with an unexpected revelation. She'd been in the surgical recovery room when Mark had first found out, but she imagined her ex must have had the same reaction.

She yanked her damp dress off over her head, causing the knot of curls to come loose. She pushed several loose strands of hair out of her face and pointed to her bared midriff.

He glanced at her abdomen quickly before blatantly staring at every other part of her body. Was he too disgusted to look at that them?

"What about your scars?" he said, once his eyes

had made their way back down. "We all have them. You aren't self-conscious about them, are you?"

"No. I can't have children because of them." She heard the catch in her voice and realized it was the first time she'd ever said it out loud. Well, not counting the first two times just a minute ago when Luke obviously hadn't understood her. Now, she needed to make him understand. "I was stabbed multiple times. My armored vest protected me from any fatal injuries, but the guy got me right here." She held one hand under her belly button and the other right above the top of her swimsuit bottom. "The knife punctured my uterus. During my emergency surgery, they had to do a complete hysterectomy."

But Luke must've heard, because his confused face relaxed into tenderness and he angled his head and walked toward her. "Aw, sweetheart, I'm sorry."

His thumb skimmed against the biggest, ugliest ridge of flesh before he spread his hands along her waist and pulled her toward him. He kissed her temple and wrapped an arm around her.

She smelled the slight tang of chlorine on his shoulder as she buried her face in his neck. She felt his hand move from her waist up to stroke her back, and a sob she'd thought was nonexistent rose up through her chest and slipped out her throat before she could reel it back in.

Maria Carmen Delgado was not a crier. Especially not in front of good-looking macho men who might mistake her tears for a sign of weakness.

And she'd never felt more weak in her life. She stood in Luke's arms, in his warm and safe embrace, and cried for every time she'd been told that she couldn't do something because she was a woman, for every time that she'd had to sacrifice a small piece of herself—of her femininity—for a career that she loved. But, mostly, she cried for the unfulfilled dream of motherhood that she'd never get to experience.

If her body was shaking with sobs, she couldn't feel them. Luke held her in a cocoon of strength, allowing her outside to be safely protected while the inside of her raged with frustration and sadness.

But as her eyes dried up and his tender reassuring strokes became more sensual, more arousing, she forced herself to push him away.

"Are you okay?" he asked, his face still way too close to hers.

She nodded. "Sorry about that. I don't usually get so emotional."

"It's okay to have feelings, Carmen. You don't have to be a cop all the time."

"I know, but it's a safe role for me. Anyway, thanks for... Well, thanks for whatever that was." She couldn't bring herself to express gratitude for holding her up when she was completely breaking down. She'd already suffered the indignity of admitting her deepest injury, her biggest regret, and then crying about it while he patted her back and told her everything would be okay.

But it wasn't okay. And it never would be. She'd officially hammered in the final nail to the "just friends" coffin. This is when most men would give her the brush-off. But because she'd put herself into the power position, she could walk away with at least some of her pride intact.

Not much. But some.

She wiped her cheek with the back of her hand, making sure any traces of her tearful breakdown were gone. She couldn't help the small sniffle as she turned her head to the side, looking at the door.

"So I'm going to go pack up my things. Tell the boys that I had to get back to Sugar Falls, but I'm sure they'll play great even if I'm not there."

She didn't bother picking up her cotton dress as she made her way toward the door. She was walking out of all of their lives and it was best not to look back.

Chapter Twelve

"Wait? You're leaving?" Luke was incredulous. "In your bikini?"

"I'm just wearing it next door. I'll get dressed before I go."

"But why are you suddenly taking off?" Was he asking the wrong questions? He wanted to stamp his feet in frustration because he'd just held the woman and told her everything would be okay. So why wasn't she listening to him?

She held the door open but turned back to look at him. "Luke, didn't you just hear me? Were you not paying attention?"

"Oh, I was paying attention all right. How can a man not pay attention when you're standing there in that—" he gestured at the two-piece bathing suit "—with your hair all…?" He used both hands to motion at the sexy, tousled mess of curls.

"Then what part aren't you getting?"

"The part where you're *leaving*."

"I just told you why." She folded her arms across her chest, a stance he'd seen her take when she was reprimanding the twins or busy explaining to Scooter and Jonesy why they couldn't ride their horses down Snowflake Boulevard and through the center of town.

"No, you didn't. You showed me some scars and said some ass stabbed you." Luke drew in a deep breath and let it out slowly. "I said I was sorry. And then I held you while you cried. Did I do something wrong?"

"No, Luke. You did everything right," she accused, looking like she was about to cry again. "That's the problem."

Dammit. Where was Drew's analytical and rational thinking when Luke needed it the most? "Okay." He finally latched on to an idea. "Remember when you talked Caden down off the cafeteria rafters? I'm going to need you to talk me down here, because I'm still not getting it."

"I can't have children. And you want more children. Which means that I can't have you. I'm trying to do the honorable thing here and walk away."

"When did I say that I wanted to have more children? Have you met the ones I already have? They're a handful."

"You said it that night at Patrelli's, when you and the twins were picking up pizza for poker night. You told me the next children you had would have better manners."

"Carmen, I also said that it was okay for my son to pretend his ACE bandage was a real cast. I was trying to be funny and lighten the mood. It was the first time

I'd seen you out of uniform and I was too busy staring down your shirt to think about what I was saying."

A bubble of laughter escaped her lips. "I *knew* you were staring down my shirt, but you flashed those damn dimples and I thought it was just wishful thinking on my part."

He tried smiling at her again. "Sweetheart, I'll stare down your shirt whenever you want if you'll just come back inside."

"Oh, my." Luke heard a woman's voice down the hall, followed by a chorus of giggles. He saw Elaine Marconi and Choogie Nguyen's moms enjoying the drama unfolding in the hotel hallway.

"Come on," he said as he pulled a bikini-clad Carmen into his room.

He allowed the door to slam closed before chancing a look at the pink blush staining her cheeks. He needed to understand this woman. He needed to have a rational and logical conversation with her without his hormones getting in the way.

"So, to clarify, you're telling me you don't want to date me because you can't have children?"

"It's not that I don't want to, Luke. It's that it'd be unfair to you."

Did she just say unfair? He'd been beating himself up over whether he should tell this woman how he felt about her, but now that she'd initiated the conversation, he was going to use his SEAL logic and get comfortable being uncomfortable. To hell with rational thinking and common sense. He was going back to impulsive and reckless.

"You know what's unfair?" he asked. "It's unfair that you look at me with all that heat and passion and then put up emotional barricades every time I try to get close to you. It's unfair that your bathroom full of soaps and lotions and beauty products has officially ruined me from ever enjoying a shower again because all I can think about is the smell of your hair and the softness of your skin. It's unfair that you were right about taking your bigger car to Costco and how much potato salad to make for a birthday party, because you know how to do these things and I don't. It's unfair that you were the one who could talk Caden down from the cafeteria rafters and I just sat there eating a pudding cup because I never know what to say. It's unfair for you to come into my children's lives and love them as much as any mother could while I burn dinners and accidentally wave them on to home plate because I'm too busy staring at you in the stands to be a decent third-base coach." He stared at her, hot, angry—desperate. "And it's unfair for you to let me hold you while you're wearing that incredibly sexy bathing suit and then walk away without at least a goodbye kiss."

Before she could look down to confirm what she was wearing, he dipped his head to hers and kissed her with all the reckless disregard of a hopeless man hanging by a snapped cable out of a helicopter over the ocean. She was his harness, his lifeline, and he needed to hold on to her and scramble to save himself.

He paused for only a second, just long enough for her to push him away if she still wanted out of this. Instead, he felt her fingers course over his scalp and then to the back of his neck as she pulled his head in closer, his kiss in deeper.

Luke moaned and allowed his hands to roam freely

across her skin, which was smoother and warmer than it'd been ten minutes ago. He reached the clasp at the back of her bathing suit top and unhooked it, sliding his thumbs under the elastic strap as it released its hold on her.

He followed the lines of the loosened fabric around to the front, where he was able to cup her breasts. Her perfect, round breasts that he'd been thinking about ever since that night at Patrelli's. As she moved her tongue in and out of his mouth, taking advantage of everything he was offering, he used his thumbs and forefingers to massage her nipples into tighter peaks.

Carmen gasped and pressed against him more, causing him to take a step back. She didn't release his mouth as she brought her arms down and gripped his hips. At first, Luke relished in the pleasure of her pushing against him, but soon he realized that Carmen was actually walking him backward.

Toward the bed.

They were both used to being in control, but Luke had been waiting for this for so long he didn't want to give her the upper hand. He bent his head lower, kissing a trail down her neck and toward her chest. By the time he had his tongue on her nipple, he also had rotated their positions and maneuvered her against the down-filled comforter.

But she was quicker and hooked one of her legs around the back of his knee, then leveraged herself so that when she pushed against his shoulders, he turned to his left before collapsing on the bed.

"Nice takedown maneuver," Luke said, before reaching for her waist and pulling her down on top of him.

"I prefer being in the power position," Carmen said as she straddled her long legs on either side of him.

"So do I," he replied before flipping her onto her back, then fitting himself perfectly between her open legs.

He kissed her again and she lifted her body to meet his demand.

"Tell me you want this," he said, pressing the ridge of his erection against the thin fabric of her bikini bottoms.

"I want this," she admitted, wrapping her legs around his hips.

"Do we need protection?" he asked. Then he realized his mistake as he felt her grow not just still, but cold in his arms.

His words felt as though he'd just dumped that stupid ice bucket on her. "I thought I made it pretty clear that I couldn't get pregnant."

"You did. And I'm not worried about that," he said before pulling back and dropping to the bed beside her, his arm covering his eyes. "Man, there's no good way to talk about this."

The air-conditioning vent kicked back on, making Carmen aware that she was almost naked and lying in bed with a man she should've said goodbye to a month ago. She tried to tug at the sheets, but the six-foot-four man was planted firmly in the middle of the bed. She was tempted to at least grab a pillow and use it to shield herself. But that would only cover her nudity. Not her shame.

"We don't need to talk about anything," she said as she sat up and looked around for her bathing suit top.

"Where are you going?"

Carmen was surprised he'd had to ask. "Back to my room. Home."

"But I thought you said you wanted this."

"I *do* want this. But I know I can't have it."

"Are we back to that whole you-can't-have-children thing? Because that's not what I meant about using protection."

"Then what did you mean?"

"Look, I know this is going to make me sound unmanly and way out of practice, but I haven't been with a woman since Samantha died."

Oh, no. He wasn't over his wife. She hoped that the room was too dark for him to see the way her lungs trembled with her indrawn breath.

"I understand," she said, before standing up.

"Wait. You're trying to leave again?" His reflexes were quicker than she'd expected and he hauled her back toward the bed and had his arm wrapped around her waist before she'd even taken a step.

"Luke, even if you claim you're fine not having any more kids, it's pretty obvious you still love your wife. I could never compete against the mother of your children." She felt ridiculous, admitting this while he was practically spooning her. Could she have allowed herself to be put in any weaker a position? Both physically and emotionally?

"There's no competition," he said. But even with the assertive tone of his voice, Carmen still had her doubts. She tried to wedge an elbow behind her as leverage for getting back up.

"Why do you do that?" he asked, pulling her in tighter.

"Do what?" She stiffened, even though she knew she should be relaxing her body in order to get away.

"Try to tell me what I'm saying and then make a break for it and run off before I can even correct you."

"I'm not trying to run off." She couldn't see his face, but she was pretty sure his eyebrows were raised in doubt.

"Yes, you are. It's like you retreat before the battle can be fought."

"What battle?"

"This battle." His arm pulled her in tighter. "The one between the two of us." But instead of feeling locked in, she actually felt safe. Like she wasn't fighting this alone.

"It's called self-preservation."

"What do you need to protect yourself from?"

"From getting hurt," she admitted. Even saying as much made her weaker.

"I'm not going to hurt you, Carmen. I'm trying to love you. But you have to clue me in on the rules of engagement."

His words made her feel lighter, but slightly more vulnerable—as if she'd stripped off her Kevlar vest before her duty shift had ended. "I didn't ask you to try and love me."

"I know. I stupidly undertook that risky operation all on my own."

Hearing him refer to himself as *stupid* caused her feeling of being weak to fall by the wayside. Suddenly, his words were clicking into place. "Are you saying that you love me?"

"Yes, woman. What the hell do you think I've been trying to show you for the past hour?"

Her rib cage tightened and her spine tingled, and it felt like all the fluttering butterflies inside her body had just declared mutiny and were demanding their freedom. She held still, only allowing her head to tilt slightly back so she could see the earnestness on his face.

"Listen, Carmen, I get that you've been hurt and that your life plans probably got all kinds of jacked up by that knife attack. But how could you think any of that would matter to a man who loves you?"

"Mark loved me, but it mattered to him. He was relieved when I broke up with him."

"Are you talking about the idiot who married your cousin? Please tell me you're not comparing me to him."

"Luke, I've been around men all my life. Brothers, relatives, coworkers—I'm surrounded by them all the time. I know what they want and I know how to read them."

"Well, you read me all wrong then, sweetheart. Because I want *you*. Not your reproductive organs or what you can provide me, but you. Just you."

He brushed a kiss along her lips, and Carmen wanted to open back up to him again. Then she remembered something.

"What about Samantha?"

"What about her?"

"You aren't still carrying a torch for her?"

Luke sighed. "I can't change the fact that I once loved her. But I was also a very different man when I was married to her." He paused, looking away for a moment, then went on, "I thought marriage and having children would ground me, settle me down. This may be hard for you to believe, but I'd always been the wild twin, the reckless one who got into trouble every time I turned around. Drew was the calm one, always thinking things through, and even though it was more fun to be naughty, I envied that. Getting married and doing the responsible thing made me feel more like him. I loved that feeling. But when she died, I no longer felt grounded. I don't know if that's because I'd lost that sense of security or because I'd lost her. Honestly, we never spent enough time together to give our relationship a chance."

"But the twins were three when she died. That's longer than you've known me."

"True, but I was away on deployments a lot of the time. We met at a bar one night, through mutual friends. I'm not proud of this, but what I thought was a one-night stand ended up as a pregnancy and a quickie wedding in Vegas in between duty assignments. We got along well enough and she handled everything when it came to the twins. Looking back on it, she probably took on all the responsibility of raising them because she felt insecure in our relationship. And I allowed her to because I was busy running off to save the world and didn't have to worry about it."

"Was that why you asked about protection earlier?" Carmen bit her bottom lip, not sure she wanted to know the answer. "Because of what happened the last time you had a one-night stand?"

"First of all, in case I haven't made it clear, this thing between you and me is *not* a one-night stand." Carmen's tummy did a little flip. "Second of all, I asked about protection because my commanding officer once read us the riot act about the possibility of diseases. I'm clean, just for the record."

"That's good to know," Carmen said, thinking that was really the least of her worries. "I am, too. Just for the record."

He smiled, and pulled her leg up and over him. "So now that you know about all my failings, I'll try not to stop you if you want to leave."

"I think your grip on my thigh says otherwise. But what failings would those be?"

"I don't always trust my judgment when it comes to knowing what a woman wants. I wasn't the man Samantha wanted me to be and I carried around a lot of guilt about her death. It still resurfaces from time to time."

"But why was it your fault?"

"I wasn't around a lot during my marriage. And Samantha was under a lot of stress with the twins and my deployments and handling everything on her own. It wasn't until I mentioned something to my brother about it the other day that I started to rethink things."

"Didn't she have anyone to help her? I know the military has programs in place to assist dependents."

"That's what Drew had pointed out, too. But then I added to that by volunteering for every dangerous mission under the sun. I felt like I'd failed as a husband, and therefore, I would eventually fail as a father."

"But, Luke, you're a great father."

He shook his head. "I try. I'm still getting my bearings, but I'm scared to death that I'm going to do something to mess it all up. I changed assignments last summer so that I can be around all the time now, but it's been a learning curve. My family has helped me so much, but when you took on the twins for that mentorship program…" He swiped his hand over his eyes, then cleared his throat. "Well, you'll never know how much I appreciate you being there for them."

"Are you kidding? I feel like *I'm* the one who benefited. I left my family and moved here knowing I would be all alone, with no hope of ever having children of my own. I was scared to death that people would think it was desperate or pitiful to see me spending so much time with them."

"I don't know about desperate or pitiful." Luke flashed that dimple again. "But they might think you need to be committed for a psych eval."

"No way. Anyone who spends more than five minutes with the boys sees that they're smart and talented and have so much love to give. I adore them, Luke."

"That's a relief. I'm not the best communicator, but you need to know up front that the boys and I are a package deal. I come with a lot of baggage, which is why I haven't even attempted to pursue a relationship before. I haven't felt like I deserved one and I didn't want to jeopardize the bond you share with them. But now that I've spent time with you, I don't think I could stand it if you walked out that door."

She took his face in her hands and kissed him lightly. "I love you, Luke Gregson," she said around the lump of emotion in her throat. "And I love your package deal. I'd been trying to protect myself, trying to avoid getting hurt. But it was a losing battle. I'd already surrendered my heart."

And with that admission, Carmen forced him to his back and rocked her body into place above his. Her long hair formed an intimate curtain around them as she kissed him with all the emotion she'd been holding inside.

His pulse seemed to be throbbing everywhere she touched him—against his temple, against his stomach, against the rigid hardness of his manhood. She tore at the Velcro cover of his board shorts and lifted her hips to allow him to pull her bikini bottoms off her.

She balanced on one knee to get the material past her ankle and he took advantage of her precarious position by rolling her underneath him.

He was hard and swift when he entered her, only pausing long enough to fuse his lips to hers and for her to get acclimated to his thickness. She felt him slide out of her and locked her legs around his waist, preventing him from withdrawing too much.

"I'm not going anywhere, sweetheart," he whispered in her hair, and Carmen realized he didn't just mean tonight. "And I'm not letting you run off again, either."

But Carmen no longer wanted to leave. She wanted to stay right where she was. She moaned as he sank deeper inside her. Actually, she *didn't* want to stay right here. She wanted to move with him. She wanted to move *for* him.

When his body lifted slightly, she rotated her hips and arched her spine, forcing him to lean back onto his haunches. But he took her with him, wrapping his arms around her waist as she sat up, bringing her breast to his mouth.

She moved quicker, rising higher and sinking deeper with each stroke of his tongue until he pulled his mouth away and said, "Not yet. We have to slow down or I'll…"

He didn't say what would happen, he simply hiked her up, his hands supporting her bottom as he repositioned her on the bed.

They fought for control, shifting their bodies so each one took turns being on top. His slow pace was no match for her frantic need and when she rose above him for the last time, she couldn't wait any longer.

"Now, Carmen," Luke whispered, reaching up to rub the sensitive spot directly above where their bodies met. And, like a good soldier, she followed his orders, calling out his name until every breath had left her lungs.

She tried to remain upright afterward, the conquering victor, but she was emotionally and physically spent and it was time for her to stop trying to control the situation and to just feel.

Before, making love had been sobering, but with Luke, it was intoxicating. And right now, she was drunk on pleasure.

Luke slowly stroked Carmen's naked back as she slept soundly beside him. They had made love a second time and he was hoping for a third round before it got too late in the morning.

"Carmen," he whispered, not wanting to wake her but not knowing when they'd get another opportunity to be alone. "The boys are going to be back soon."

"How soon?" Her voice sounded groggy—due to his keeping her up most of the night—and a little hoarse—due to all the cheering she'd done at the baseball field yesterday.

"Maybe an hour or so, depending on whether or not they have Honey Smacks at the free breakfast buffet. Yesterday, they stayed there eating until the cereal dispenser was empty."

"What are we going to tell them?" she asked.

"That they can have a bagel if their favorite cereal is already gone."

"Not about breakfast." She playfully pushed at his chest. "About us."

He laughed and intertwined his fingers with hers. "I'm going to tell them that you tried to go AWOL last night, but that I went rogue and retrieved you before you could cross enemy lines."

"Enemy lines? Really?"

"No?" He smiled mischievously, the way his twins often did when they wanted to charm her.

"There goes that dimple, again." But this time, she smiled back at him. "Maybe we should meet the kids at breakfast and tell them then?"

"I figure after the way you threw yourself at me in front of Elaine Marconi, we probably won't have to tell the twins anything. The whole town is going to know that we are officially a couple."

Carmen squeezed her eyes closed. "Don't remind me about that woman." When Luke laughed again, Carmen reached up her hand and used her thumb to trace around his lips.

"If you keep touching me like that, I'm going to remind you about a lot more that happened last night."

Yet, before Luke could demonstrate, he heard a steady stream of voices from the hallway outside.

"It's the boys," Carmen said, panic taking over the desire in her eyes. "I don't want them to know I spent the night here. But they'll see me if I try to go out to my room now."

Luke stacked his hands behind his head and stretched out, as if he didn't have a care in the world. "You know, my nana always said, 'Step onto the dance floor with both feet.'"

She jumped out of bed, pulling the sheet with her and wrapping it around her body. "Well, my abuela always said, '*El que no transa, no avanza.*'"

"What does that mean?"

"It means he who does not yield, does not advance."

"That actually explains a lot about you," Luke said, then dodged the pillow she threw at his head.

Rap, rap, rap, rap. Bang, bang. Tap, tap, tap, tap.

Both Carmen and Luke pivoted toward the door. "Dad, it's time for breakfast. Are you in there, Dad?"

"How am I going to get back to my room now?" she whispered.

Luke looked at the adjoining door between their rooms and his brain clicked on something he would have done back when he was nine. He pointed. "Just go through there."

"Luke, don't be absurd. Hotels usually have locks on both sides of the doors."

"Have you met my children?" he asked. "They've never met a lock that could keep them out of trouble."

She gave him a doubtful look before pushing on the door. When it sprang open, the empty toilet paper roll that the twins must have wedged into the latch fell to the ground.

Just as the secret knock sounded on Carmen's hotel door.

Rap, rap, rap, rap. Bang, bang. Tap, tap, tap, tap.

"Hey, Officer Carmen. If our dad's still in there with you, tell him they're out of Honey Smacks so we're going to walk to the doughnut store down the street with Choogie."

She looked back at Luke, and he lifted his arms and shrugged his shoulders. "What can I say? They'll always be one step ahead of us." He pulled on his shorts and tossed her the discarded cotton dress she'd been wearing over her bathing suit last night. "Besides, Officer Carmen, I'm done with hiding and pretending I can control myself around you. No more guilt, no more regrets, right?"

She nodded. "The Marine Corps taught me to never leave a man behind. But since you're the higher ranking officer, I'll let you do the explaining."

She slipped on her dress, then followed Luke through the adjoining room.

"Okay, you monkeys," he said when he opened her hotel room door. "You're going to wake the entire floor."

The twins rushed inside. "Hey, are you guys coming down for breakfast or what?" Aiden asked.

"And if you're in Officer Carmen's room already, does this mean she's your girlfriend now?" Caden wanted to know.

Luke covered his mouth to smother the chuckling sound he'd just made. Then he raised an eyebrow at Carmen, but she clearly wasn't going to get him out of this mess. Maybe he should've let her sneak back into her room when they'd had the chance.

"Well, I haven't quite asked Carmen if she was willing to become my girlfriend, yet," he said.

"You want us to help you ask her?" Aiden was

rocking on the balls of his feet, his bright smile turned her way.

"I think she'll say yes, Dad." Caden's grin was equally bright.

Carmen was smiling along with them. "And why would you think that?" she asked.

"Because then you'd get to see us all the time and not just on Tuesdays or when we get into trouble."

"Hmmm…" She pretended to ponder the decision. "I don't suppose I could resist an offer like that."

"So then I guess my work here is done," Luke said, wrapping an arm around her and pulling her in close. "Let's go get some breakfast with my new girlfriend."

The twins each grabbed one of her hands and pulled her toward the door.

"Wait," Carmen squeaked. "I need to get ready first."

"Ready for what? You're already dressed." Aiden continued to tug on her arm. "Grammie and Pop Pop are waiting for us. Besides, we need to get downstairs and tell Choogie our plan worked."

"Why don't you boys go down now," Luke suggested. "We'll get ready and meet everyone there in a few minutes."

The boys gave one last whoop, high-fived each other and ran off toward the elevators.

"What plan do you think they were talking about?" she asked when they were alone in the room again.

"I have absolutely no idea," he admitted. "But I have a feeling Choogie isn't the only one they're going to tell the good news to."

"That reminds me. We should probably talk to the person who runs the announcement booth at the baseball field and advise them not to let any nine-year-old twins near the loudspeaker today."

Luke laughed. "You sound like you know what you're getting into with us."

"I certainly like challenging jobs."

"You made them very happy, you know." Luke traced a finger under the shoulder strap of her dress. "And now it would make me very happy to help you take this thing off and get ready."

When Luke's lips touched her cheek, Carmen said, "I feel like the happiest one of all."

Epilogue

Carmen threw away a handful of napkins after cleaning up the spilled punch on the floor next to Caden, who wasn't technically her date for tonight's Mother-Son Dancing Safari. Walking back to where a group of third-grade boys were finishing off the last batch of cookies donated by the Sugar Falls Cookie Company, she tried not to scratch at the homemade pine-cone corsage on her wrist.

The DJ had announced the last song, and while Aiden danced with his aunt Kylie, several of the teachers and parents were already cleaning up, trying to turn the decorated room back into the school cafeteria.

She felt Luke's hands around her waist before she heard his voice. "Remember the last time we were in this room together?" he asked.

"I remember being a little higher off the ground,"

she said, placing her hands on his and leaning her head back into his shoulder.

He nodded his head toward the safari-themed wall hanging being taken down. "Yeah, and our monkeys were the only wildlife in here at the time."

Our monkeys. Carmen felt a rush of warm, tingly happiness and looked at Caden and Aiden, who'd finished dancing and joined his brother and their friends.

"My feet are killing me," Kylie Gregson said as she teetered in their direction wearing a five-inch pair of stilettos. "I haven't danced this much since the Boise State Spirit Squad Reunion."

Carmen had to admit the former cheerleader had a great sense of style and had outlasted all the other moms on the dance floor.

"Drew's waiting in the car," Luke told his sister-in-law.

"We could have driven ourselves," Carmen said, used to being independent and talking care of herself.

"No way." Luke smiled at her, then looked up to see the twins walking up. "The boys wanted this to be a full-service event."

"We tried to order a limo," Caden said. "But Dad said he had more expensive things to buy."

She turned to Luke, but not before the corner of her eye caught Aiden shooting an elbow to his brother's ribs.

"Hey, look," Luke said, reaching behind him for a chocolate pudding cup that Carmen could have sworn hadn't been on that table just a minute ago. "Remember the last time we shared one of these?"

Carmen raised her eyebrow. What was up with Luke's little trip down memory lane? "Yep. I thought Scooter and Jonesy had finished off the last of them."

"Apparently not all of them." Luke held the plastic container under her nose. "Here. You should have the last one."

"Oh, no thanks." Carmen wrinkled her nose. "I already had a ton of cookies from Maxine's bakery, and the only drink they offered tonight was that neon-red punch. I'm all sugared out."

"Just open the pudding cup, Carmen." She noticed the perspiration on Luke's brow and wondered if he was getting impatient because the boys were giggling and jumping around like a couple of caged hyenas.

"Come on, boys," Kylie said, waving her wrist with the matching pinecone corsage in the air. "Let's go wait out in the car with Uncle Drew."

"No way. We want to stay for this. Me and Caden worked way too hard on this project for the past few months. We're not gonna miss out on the bestest part of the night."

Carmen looked at the matching set of nine-year-old grins and could only imagine what kind of project they'd organized this time. But when she turned back to their dad, her breath caught in her chest and she had to blink several times to clear her eyes.

Luke was down on one knee, the foil wrapper of his pudding cup peeled back to reveal a diamond solitaire halfway buried in chocolate. "I love you, Maria Carmen Delgado."

"*We* love you," Caden corrected his father.

Luke nodded. "We love you, Maria Carmen Delgado. Will you marry me?"

"Marry *us*, Dad." Aiden got down next to his father. "You were supposed to ask if she'd marry *us*."

Caden joined the other two Gregsons on their knees

and Carmen, who always knew how to handle men, suddenly didn't know how she would handle being this happy.

"Of course, I will marry all of you!"

The boys jumped up, shouting and high-fiving, leaving their father still kneeling and holding the ring, which was now sinking down lower into the pudding. Carmen knelt beside him, and he dug the diamond out, then licked it off before putting it on her finger.

She laughed and kissed him, his mouth tasting like chocolate.

"I love you, too," she said, but Luke's attention was already on his celebrating sons, a look of suspicion on his face.

"Wait a minute. You guys said you'd worked too hard on this project for the past few months. But we only went to the jewelry store in Boise last weekend."

Kylie, who'd just snapped a picture of the pudding proposal, tossed her cell phone into her beaded designer clutch.

"I better go check on Drew," she said, leaving in an obvious hurry. His sister-in-law's abrupt departure must've put Luke on even higher alert, because he hadn't looked away from the smiling twins long enough to say goodbye.

"You boys have something you want to explain?" he asked when his sons both took a sudden interest in the design of the ceiling.

Aiden nudged Caden, who shot a frown at his brother before finally speaking. "We heard you tell the other dads at poker night that you wanted Officer Carmen to like you. And since we knew she liked us, we decided to get her to like you, too."

"But that was months ago." Luke, still looking perplexed, remained on his knees. "How did you come up with…?"

Carmen saw the realization hit his face seconds after it hit hers. "Did you guys plan this all on your own?"

"Mostly. But we had to get a whole bunch of help from everyone to make it work."

Like a movie reel playing in her mind, Carmen flashed back to the tipped canoe, the last-minute trip for party supplies, the hotel room next to theirs suddenly becoming available. All along, she'd been outsmarted and outplayed by a couple of nine-year-old twins. Then she started laughing, realizing that it probably wouldn't be the last time.

"You two little matchmakers are lucky this harebrained scheme of yours worked out and that Carmen and I ended up falling in love." Luke pulled both of his sons in for a tight hug.

The boys giggled again and Caden said, "Uncle Kane told us there was no such thing as luck."

"Oh, really," Luke said, standing and pulling Carmen into his arms. "You tell Uncle Kane that he just needs the right good luck charm."

* * * * *

LET'S TALK
Romance

For exclusive extracts, competitions
and special offers, find us online:

f facebook.com/millsandboon

🐦 @MillsandBoon

📷 @MillsandBoonUK

Get in touch on 01413 063232

For all the latest titles coming soon, visit
millsandboon.co.uk/nextmonth

JOIN US ON SOCIAL MEDIA!

Stay up to date with our latest releases, author news and gossip, special offers and discounts, and all the behind-the-scenes action from Mills & Boon…

 millsandboon

 millsandboonuk

 millsandboon

It might just be true love…

MILLS & BOON
True Love

Romance from the Heart

Celebrate true love with tender stories of heartfelt romance, from the rush of falling in love to the joy a new baby can bring, and a focus on the emotional heart of a relationship.

MILLS & BOON
MODERN
Power and Passion

Prepare to be swept off your feet by sophisticated, sexy and seductive heroes, in some of the world's most glamourous and romantic locations, where power and passion collide.